D1738790

Other Books by David H. Brandin

The Horns of Moses, A Novel
iUniverse, Lincoln, 2007
The Miracle of Alvito (And Other Stories)
xLibris, Bloomington, 2008
The Technology War **(co-authored)**
J. Wiley & Sons, NY, 1987
Japanese Edition, TBS Britannica, Tokyo, 1989

The Lodge

A Tale of Corruption

To Eric
Warm Regards

DAVID H. BRANDIN

Dave Brandin

iUniverse, Inc.
New York   Bloomington

The Lodge
A Tale of Corruption

Copyright © 2009 David H. Brandin

iUniverse books may be ordered through booksellers or by contacting:

iUniverse
1663 Liberty Drive
Bloomington, IN 47403
www.iuniverse.com
1-800-Authors (1-800-288-4677)

ISBN: 978-1-4401-7210-6 (pbk)
ISBN: 978-1-4401-7208-3 (cloth)
ISBN: 978-1-4401-7209-0 (ebk)

Printed in the United States of America

iUniverse rev. date: 10/6/2009

To
Sweet Charity
Purest, Truest, and Noblest of all the Graces

"It was beautiful and simple as all truly great swindles are."
−O. Henry (1862-1910)

*"It was without a compeer among swindles. It was perfect;
it was rounded, symmetrical, complete, colossal."*
−Mark Twain (1835-1910)

FOREWORD

This book is a work of fiction. A murder investigation uncovers a tale of massive corruption and leads to more violence—over a land deal worth millions of dollars. The land, acquired decades ago, is owned by a charitable fraternal order.

Fiction is often based on events that transpire in the author's life. I've been a member and/or an officer of not-for-profit organizations such as the Benevolent and Protective Order of the Elks of the USA, the Fraternal Order of Eagles, and several professional societies, including the Association for Computing Machinery (ACM).

The fraternal orders are similar in operations to the Loyal Order of the Moose and all are modeled, to some extent, after the Masons. Secrecy is paramount. The orders conduct elaborate rituals for their new members and meetings are rigidly controlled in their meeting rooms with altars, flags, and other accoutrements. For example, an Elks Lodge room contains a King James Bible, an American flag, and a large set of elk's antlers; all play major roles in every ritual.

Fraternal orders work to satisfy charitable objectives. The Elks charities, for example, are legendary; since World War I the Elks have contributed billions to help this country and the veterans of its wars. The Elks make substantial contributions to charities for children; they support the Boy Scouts; they finance scholarships for needy students; and their patriotism is unassailable. Professional societies work in the public interest to develop and disseminate information about their interests.

Both types of organizations depend on volunteers and paid staff to manage their operations. Generally, the volunteers are older people. In the orders, membership has aged and may, indeed, be dying out. In professional societies, it takes years to develop the credentials that enable one to reach a leadership position. In both cases, the volunteers become ingrained. Sometimes, the volunteers are weak, inept, and tired. In older societies and orders, volunteers must cope with archaic rules and government structures—not unlike the U.S. Congress—and some volunteers become partisan, or dogmatic. And, like all not-for-profits in the country, there is intense competition for competent volunteers. Sadly, there are not enough to satisfy the demand.

I've never witnessed the greed, avarice, and corruption which serve as the backbone of this novel. Most of the volunteers I've worked with were straightforward and honest. The events in this book did not happen. Still, volunteers are human and make mistakes. Could these events happen in an order? Perhaps they could. The thematic statement that most describes this book is *Charity is Helpless in the Presence of Corruption.*

Here's the recipe for this book: Take plausible events in an imaginary order—the Fraternal Order of Stags. Place them in a realistic environment; drop in greedy and inept volunteers—some with money problems. Add corrupt builders and agents and stir the pot with mob connections. Throw in a beachfront property worth millions and a town hungry for new housing. Mix until volatile and serve up a bonfire of corruption.

This book is dedicated to the goddess *Sweet Charity*, who represents Charity—one of the four tenets of 'Elk-dom' in a crucial Elks parable and ritual. The others are Justice, Brotherly Love, and Fidelity.

David H. Brandin
Los Altos, California
2009

(Readers' Note: A fraternal order is often referred to as a *Lodge*, e.g. the Los Osos Stags Lodge. The order usually owns a building which also is called a *lodge*. Throughout this novel, Lodge—with a capital 'L'—refers to the fraternal order or organization, and lodge—with a lower case 'l'— denotes the building owned by the order.)

CAST OF CHARACTERS

Harry Warrener, Retired Professor and ex-Navy SEAL
Janet Zimmer, Harry's Girlfriend
Thor, Harry's German Shepherd
Los Osos Stags Lodge
Jimmy Bateman, Trustee Candidate
Ted Granger, Hummer Dealer and Exalted Ruler (ER)
Carole Greene, Fitness Instructor and Trustee
Randy Lismore, Murdered Trustee
John Potempa, Pharmacist and Trustee
Mitch Mason, Consultant to Monterey Construction Company
Jerry Sloane, Chairman of Stags Board of Trustees
Jim Thatcher, Stags District Deputy Grand Exalted Ruler (DDGER)
Larry Yates, Trustee
The Mob and Developer/Builders
Salvatore Buck Califano, Chicago Hit Man
Don Alessandro Cicerone, Godfather of San Francisco Mob
Dominic Franchescini, Don Cicerone's Consigliore
Joey Gee Giannotti, Chicago Mobster
Ron Kelly, Don Cicerone's Nephew and Land Agent
Morty Greenspan, President of Monterey Construction Company
Leonard Hansen, Land Developer
San Luis Obispo Sheriff's Office
Deputy Luis Mendoza, SLO Sheriff Investigator
Sheriff John Ortega
The FBI
Sam Bernini, San Francisco Supervising Agent
Fred Harris, Special Agent
John Lewiston, Agent
Other
Billy Lawson, High School Student
Mamoru 'Zero' Matsuda, Proprietor, Big Bear Pipe and Tobacco Shop
Pamela McCracken, Clerk in SLO County Clerk's Office
Alessandra Cicerone Kelly, Ron Kelly's Mother and Don's Sister

TABLE OF CONTENTS

Foreword   vii

Cast of Characters   ix

One—Fiji   1

Two—Cayucos   3

Three—Vietnam   6

Four—Purple Heart   9

Five—SLO   11

Six—Inquest   13

Seven—Big Bear   20

Eight—Thor   27

Nine—Hummers   29

Ten—Big Bubba   31

Eleven—Rocky Point   33

Twelve—Reporter   38

Thirteen—Cessna   42

Fourteen—Stags   44

Fifteen—Pacific Heights   47

Sixteen—Investigation   52

Seventeen—Mendoza   56

Eighteen—Trustees   60

Nineteen—Janet   69

Twenty—Kelly   73

Twenty-one—Narrow Creek   75

Twenty-two—Morty 78

Twenty-three—Chicago 81

Twenty-four—Email 84

Twenty-five—Phone Calls 87

Twenty-six—Beach 90

Twenty-seven—Black Bag 92

Twenty-eight—Indoctrination 94

Twenty-nine—Informer 100

Thirty—Canvas Bags 102

Thirty-one—U.S. 101 105

Thirty-two—Recordings 107

Thirty-three—Black Ball 111

Thirty-four—Due Diligence 114

Thirty-five—Yates 116

Thirty-six—Starbucks 118

Thirty-seven—Asian Art 121

Thirty-eight—Union Square 125

Thirty-nine—C-4 127

Forty—Sole-Source 129

Forty-one—Buck 132

Forty-two—Diary 134

Forty-three—Letter 138

Forty-four—Pillbox 142

Forty-five—Santana Row 145

Forty-six—Buena Vista 147

Forty-seven—Pebble Beach   149

Forty-eight—City Hall   152

Forty-nine—Caught   154

Fifty—Tickets   155

Fifty-one—Sam's Grill   157

Fifty-two—Pamela   159

Fifty-three—SFO   162

Fifty-four—LAX   163

Fifty-five—Randy   164

Fifty-six—Initiation   168

Fifty-seven—Confession   172

Fifty-eight—Bateman   176

Fifty-nine—CO   179

Sixty—Max   181

Sixty-one—Civic Center   184

Sixty-two—Fisherman's Wharf   187

Sixty-three—Stow Lake   191

Sixty-four—Vacancies   195

Sixty-five—Election   198

Sixty-six—Opposed   201

Sixty-seven—Monterey   206

Sixty-eight—Poco-Poco   210

Sixty-nine—Good Catholics   214

Seventy—Apollo   216

Seventy-one—Attack   218

Seventy-two—Arrest   220

Seventy-three—New Balance   222

Seventy-four—Granger   224

Seventy-five—Interrogation   227

Seventy-six—Message   232

Seventy-seven—Macaroni   234

Seventy-eight—Warehouse   236

Seventy-nine—Caymans   240

Eighty—Fish   242

Eighty-one—Hansen   245

Eighty-two—Lone Cypress   247

Eighty-three—*Mano a Mano*   249

Eighty-four—Chairman   251

Eighty-five—Lower Level   253

Eighty-six—Mississippi   257

Eighty-seven—Home   259

Eighty-eight—Kiss   260

Eighty-nine—Son   265

Ninety—Land   267

Epilogue   269

Afterword   271

ONE—FIJI

Wednesday, December 12, 2007

The tiger charged! Harry Warrener's first instinct was to shout and his regulator popped out of his mouth; water flooded in. He wanted to race for the surface forty-five feet above his head. He turned right looking for his dive buddy and the regulator whipped behind him, trailing bubbles as it rotated and free-flowed. No buddy! Turn more, he thought, present the tank to the shark—but air, he needed air. His left hand instinctively located his backup regulator and he jammed it into his mouth. As he turned farther, he purged the mouthpiece and sucked in air. Unable to decide to flee or fight, Harry prepared to die. His mind raced; thirty years after Vietnam and he was still a coward!

He clenched his jaw and hunched over. Suddenly, he sensed a black shape shoot by his left shoulder. He turned left and saw Randy Lismore, his dive buddy, jam a knife into the tiger's snout. The shark jerked, ripping Randy's knife from his hand. Randy slammed his underwater light into the shark's eye. Unaccustomed to aggressive prey, the tiger turned and raced away. Tiger sharks move in bursts of twenty miles per hour, and it quickly receded.

Randy reached behind Harry's head and retrieved his regulator. He placed his thumb and forefinger together in a circle and waved the "okay?" diver's sign in Harry's face. Harry nodded. He spat out the backup and Randy pushed his regulator into his mouth. Harry purged again and took a breath, then another, and another. Bubbles flooded his field of view as he looked toward the surface. Randy grabbed his shoulder, and made the sign again. "Okay? Okay?" Harry nodded, checked his air supply on his dive computer, and took a slow, deep breath. As the bubbles cleared around his mask and his breathing stabilized, he repeated the "okay" sign. He pointed up and the men ascended to a depth of fifteen feet, where they hovered, arm in arm, in a decompression safety stop for five minutes. Fish, which had deserted the waters when the tiger appeared, began to re-populate the sea around the men. Schools of blue and yellow fusiliers and yellow long nose butterfly fish hovered nearby.

As they maintained buoyancy Harry scanned the sea for more predators. A few non-threatening white-tip sharks swam by. Visibility was good in Fijian waters, perhaps one hundred fifty feet. Harry could see a leatherback turtle some distance off. The waters were warm but Harry shivered. Damn, he thought, that was one big shark—at least fourteen feet; it was probably an adolescent, with its pronounced stripes.

On the surface, they pushed their masks down. Randy barked, "Jeez, Harry, what were you thinking? An ex-Navy SEAL doesn't panic in front of sharks."

"I lost my reg and locked up. I couldn't decide what to do, run or breathe. Thanks."

Randy touched Harry's cheek, smiled, and turned away. "Aw, c'mon, Harry. Forget it. You owe me for the knife."

The men swam to their dive boat, *Fiji Dream Dives*. The other divers had already returned and the boat's dive master waved them over. On deck, Harry stripped off his gear, leaned over the railing and threw up—a long stream of yellow bile. Retching, he stared at the sandy beaches that lined Beqa Lagoon. They reminded him of North Vietnam—dense tropical jungle, a jumble of tall palm trees, and random coconuts scattered across a wide expanse of golden sand; inviting yet barren and ominous. Harry hated the memory. That was the second time Randy had saved his life. Thank God, he'd never learned what had happened on that North Vietnamese beach. How would Harry ever repay Randy?

TWO—CAYUCOS

Sunday, February 10th, 2008, 4:30 PM

Tears streaked Harry Warrener's handsome face. His nose, which Harry always thought was too small, was running. His shoulders drooped, and his stomach was in knots. He clenched his fists as he stared down at the fresh grave. Randy Lismore was dead! They'd been on Fiji only eight weeks ago, in December. Now, his friend was dead and Harry hadn't been there when Randy needed him. He'd even missed Randy's funeral services and military burial.

Fifty-six, trim but with large shoulders, a full head of sandy curly hair framing large brown watery eyes, Harry wondered how he'd get by without Randy. He felt alone despite the dog at his side. He bent his five foot eleven inch frame to hug his eight month old pup. He'd just retrieved Thor, a German shepherd, from the kennel. The dog looked mournful, but Harry knew the dog couldn't help. Harry felt worse than after his parents had died. Randy Lismore had been Harry's best friend since Vietnam. Harry had been assigned to Randy's SEALS unit in Vietnam; the men had experienced combat together—they'd forged an unbreakable bond and now it was broken.

The wind off the ocean swept through the stark, treeless Cayucos-Morro Bay Cemetery, northwest of San Luis Obispo, scattering the flowers placed at some graves. Most of the markers were flat but a cluster of vertical stones stood like watchmen on the northwest corner of the cemetery. Some of the graves had plastic flowers but Harry had no flowers—natural or plastic; from the airport, he'd picked up Thor, made a brief stop at home to rummage in his desk, and then he'd driven directly to the cemetery. Harry scrounged around and assembled a bouquet of random flowers, placed it on the grave, and resolved to bring real flowers routinely to the grave. Thor mimicked him playfully and grabbed a flower with his mouth. Harry shook his head. "Thanks, but this won't do, buddy. Randy deserves better."

"Excuse me," said a voice behind Harry. "Are you a Stag?"

Harry stumbled to his feet. "Say again? Who are you?"

"Oh, hey, I've seen you with Randy Lismore, at the pipe shop. You're Harry, right? I didn't mean to startle you. I'm Larry Yates and the Stags are having a graveside ceremony for Randy in ten minutes."

Yates was a short, bald man with large, muscular arms. He had a sad smile and seemed friendly. Harry guessed he was in his fifties. Harry also knew that Randy had been a Stag; in fact, Randy had been a member of the

Los Osos Stags Lodge Board of Trustees and used to bug Harry to join. But Harry, until recently a professor of economics and computer science at Cal Poly, the state university in San Luis Obispo, had always pleaded he was too busy. His excuse when Randy, after the shark dive, had made his latest suggestion that he join the charitable order was that training his dog took all his time.

"I was his best friend," he said. "I just learned about it; I've been traveling. What happened?"

"It was an accident. He slipped and fell backwards. He broke his neck. At least that's what the cops said. There's an inquest tomorrow at City Hall, if you want more detail."

Slipped? No way, thought Harry. Randy was not the kind of guy who lost his balance. He'd been trained by the SEALS and had maintained his conditioning.

"Slipped how?" asked Harry.

"It happened in the Madonna Inn restroom."

"The Madonna Inn?" Harry knew the motel. It had over one hundred rooms decorated in unique themes, with quaint names such as *Buffalo, Caveman* and *Fabulous Fifties*. Because of the decor, it had a bar that rocked—with locals, and tourists attracted to the outlandish rooms. The men's room was outfitted like a cave, with rough brown granite slabs on the walls and floor. The sinks were carved out of white granite and looked like giant clams. Harry took a deep breath. He'd visited the toilet on more than one occasion; it was difficult to imagine how one could slip. Despite the cave decor, the room was narrow and not conducive to quick movements.

"They say he slipped on the wet floor, fell backwards, and must've smashed his neck on the urinal."

Harry's eyes narrowed. It didn't sound plausible. Bullshit, he thought. He turned back to the grave.

"His neck broke?" said Harry. "You must be kidding. I've been in there. How the hell can you hit your neck—the cave wall comes down to your waist in there. The water flushes below that."

"I also thought it was weird," said Yates. "But that's what they told us."

Harry pursed his lips and nodded. "Is it okay if I stick around for your ceremony? I know you guys are secretive."

"Sure. No problem." Larry extended his hand and Harry shook it. "I'm sorry we have to meet under these—well, you know what I mean. I'm a trustee, like Randy was. I miss him."

Yates looked at the dog and raised his eyebrows.

"This is Thor, just a pup."

The dog made a slight growl and looked at the road. Several cars had pulled up on the gravel access road. A tall, thin, gray-haired man climbed out of a blue Hummer. A sporty red Mazda Miata delivered a surprisingly large, husky man.

"That's Ted Granger, our Exalted Ruler, and the big guy is Jerry Sloane, the chairman of the board of trustees," said Yates.

Granger's eyes were narrow across a hooked pointy nose—more like a beak. He made a gray picture with an off-the-rack gray suit, no tie, gray thinning hair, a pale complexion; he struck Harry as nondescript. Harry watched as Granger rubbed his eyes and turned to say something to Sloane. Sloane wore beige trousers and a black windbreaker that sported the logo of a Las Vegas casino. Sloane was handsome and more interesting; he had the body of a professional athlete, like a football or hockey player.

Larry Yates continued. "They say they're heartbroken over Randy's loss but—"

The men turned as five more cars arrived kicking up gray dust. A flurry of doors slammed and ten more people walked up to the grave.

"You were saying?" prodded Harry.

"There was bad blood between those guys and Randy."

"About what?"

"I can't talk about matters confidential to the Stags. Let's just say Randy disagreed with them over a deal. Sorry, they're getting ready." Yates smiled and walked over to the Stags.

Harry nodded. He moved to the side as the Stags lined up along the grave. He tensed as he studied the features of Granger and Sloane.

Sloane leaned over to listen as Yates joined the group of men. Granger pointed at Harry and Yates said something. The men turned to look at Harry; he figured they were talking about him.

Granger nodded and frowned. Then Harry watched Sloane make eye contact with Granger. They looked concerned. That, thought Harry, was interesting. Why would guys running a fraternal order and charitable organization give a damn about him?

Granger stepped forward to the grave. He said, "We're gathered here to honor Randy Lismore. We mourn his loss. Once more we are reminded that life and death are inseparable and that our destinies lay under His care. We hope we shall once again be united in the great beyond." Granger stepped back. "And now, I've asked the chaplain to lead us in prayer."

Another man in the group stepped to the end of the grave. He opened a small pamphlet and began to read, "Almighty God, unto thy love and mercy we commend the soul of our member …"

Harry tuned out. His thoughts flashed back to Vietnam. It had been dark that morning. His mind reeled.

THREE—VIETNAM

Harry Warrener slid down a ladder on the port side of a *NASTY* class PT boat and joined three other U.S. Navy SEALS in the sea. He was laden with weapons bags, explosives, eight pounds of weights and his diving gear. As he floated near the boat, a seaman passed a fifty pound underwater propulsion vehicle (UPV) to him.

Harry was operating on adrenaline—this was his first combat operation. It was an auspicious date—just nine years earlier, to the day, the 173rd Airborne Brigade Combat Team, the first of U.S. armed forces rushed to Vietnam, had engaged North Vietnamese forces in South Vietnam. Operation Hump, a search and destroy mission, as it was known, had been a bloody battle—forty-eight U.S. paratroopers had died in vicious hand-to-hand combat. Harry knew the history and apprehension flowed through his veins. Still, he noticed, his training had kicked in—his breathing was more or less normal and, as the team swam below the surface, he had no buoyancy problems.

Harry followed the team as they propelled at a depth of twenty feet, one nautical mile westerly, towards a small lagoon along the eastern shore of North Vietnam. The UPVs pulled them along at one knot, timed for arrival at daybreak. When a bale of sea turtles signaled their arrival at the outer reaches of a reef which protected the target lagoon, Harry felt his stomach cramp in anticipation. The waters were shallow on the inside of the reef, and the team stashed its vehicles and dive gear on the ocean floor. The waters around the reef teemed with fish and more sea turtles and long tailed tuna roamed around the UPVs.

The team surfaced with their weapon bags and slithered onto the eastern shore. The sun peeked out of the sea behind them. As the men unzipped their weapons bags, Randy Lismore, the chief petty officer and team leader, checked their arms. On his signal, the SEALS team rose and headed for a North Vietnamese communications tower an eighth-of-a-mile inland. Halfway across the beach gunfire exploded—an NVA patrol had stumbled upon the men. Randy put down covering fire and the team crawled into the jungle. Bullets kicked up spurts of sand around them.

Randy loaded another clip in his MAC10 submachine gun. "We're only two hundred meters from the target. We need a distraction. Harry," he commanded, "you hold this position, lay down some harassing fire—and make them keep their heads down. While they're preoccupied, we'll set the explosives."

Harry nodded, but gritted his teeth to stifle a groan. His buddies' lives depended on him. He needed to cover the rear and he'd be alone. He felt bile rising and sweat, aggravated by the Vietnamese heat and humidity, drenched his face. He gagged on the sweet, cloying scent of rotting vegetation. His wet suit felt like an oven, yet he shivered. He tensed as the team slipped away.

The NVA patrol took up skirmishing positions. Birds fluttered out of the canopy as the soldiers moved through the jungle. Harry hugged the ground. He fired a magazine of rounds into the air, reloaded and fired again, several times. It was mostly to discourage movement towards him and to distract the NVA from his team. But he knew that it was only a matter of time before the enemy outflanked him. When he heard a rustle in the bush nearby, he lost control of his bladder. The smell of his urine added to his fear; he wondered if the enemy could smell it.

He heard the NVA searching on all sides. As they closed in, he ground his face into the dirt. Insects crawled over his face and hands and into his ears. Harry lay motionless, eyes closed, fighting a growing panic. Something was crawling in his hair. If it was a snake, he figured the hell with everything; he was headed back to the sea. He could hear the soldiers probing cautiously through the bush and shooting randomly. Suddenly, all thoughts of insects and snakes vanished and an intense pain in his right leg flooded his consciousness. An NVA soldier had plunged his bayonet into the lush jungle and slashed him. Frozen with fear, Harry held his breath and prayed he hadn't been discovered. But, when the explosives detonated, he gasped. The bayonet plunged again, into the bush beside his nose. The soldier had heard him breathe! Again the bayonet plunged. Then, he heard *crack*!—a gunshot—and Harry was flattened as the dead NVA soldier fell onto him.

Harry rolled the body off. He brushed the insects off and scratched furiously at his hair and one ear. As he tried to rise, his right leg collapsed. Then he saw Randy ten feet away, his weapon at the ready. Harry fell back and reached for his leg; his hand came back crimson and sticky.

"The other NVA must have taken off when they heard the explosion, Harry. We heard your fire. Good job. You okay?"

The rest of the team arrived and Randy examined Harry's wound. His leg had been ripped open. The wound pumped a torrent of his blood out that mixed in the sandy soil with the dead NVA soldier's blood. Harry gasped and stifled a moan when Randy applied a tourniquet and a field dressing.

"Sorry, Harry," he said. "We have to stop the bleeding before we put you in the water. I can't give you any morphine; we need you alert."

Harry nodded. His leg screamed at him but he resolved to remain silent; he'd already been too weak.

No one questioned Harry. His weapon had been fired and the SEALS saw empty magazines and cartridge shells on the ground. Harry didn't tell the guys how he'd been wounded. He knew he'd been a coward when he'd failed to follow up his earlier fire, when he'd been ready to bolt, and when he'd lain there, helpless, waiting for the slaughter. It was a secret, he decided, he'd carry to his grave.

The men dragged Harry to the beach. The bleeding had stopped but Randy continued to withhold painkillers until they made it back to the boat. The men swam out to the reef pulling Harry, and then dived to retrieve their gear. Someone slapped Harry's weight belt on him and stuffed his regulator in his mouth. The men powered up their UPVs. The scooters were most efficient underwater and a quick recovery by the boat was the main objective. As they headed east, submerged and pushing the UPVs to their limits, Randy lagged behind, grimly watching Harry's leg for any signs of additional bleeding. When the UPVs batteries began to fail they surfaced. Twenty minutes later the PT boat recovered them. Harry was administered his painkiller and whisked into the U.S. Navy medical system.

Later, while he recuperated from his wound, he shared quarters at a Naval Combat Base located at Chau Doc on the Bassac River, with a Marine K-9 reconnaissance team. Harry watched the marines training with their animals. The Viet Cong hated the dogs which served on sentry duty and as combat trackers, sniffed out booby-traps, and patrolled the perimeters of their bases. Some dogs were trained to detect trip wires, mines, and snipers in trees. When you had a dog, you were not alone, he thought. He resolved to get a dog if he survived the war. It would be comforting, he thought, to have a loyal partner. Perhaps he could fill the gap left by a disloyal wife.

Flying home Harry re-lived his cowardice over and over. The attack on the tower had been his only combat experience; he never had the chance to test himself again. He'd never know if he had the balls to face enemy fire again. He fingered his Purple Heart repeatedly. He wished they hadn't given him the medal—in that award the SEALS had honored his valor; in his heart he knew he didn't deserve it.

FOUR—PURPLE HEART

"… and may God's peace remain with us forever. Amen." The chaplain stepped back from the grave.

Harry listened as Ted Granger concluded. "May the memories of Randy and his love for his brothers comfort us in our bereavement and remind us always of our charitable mission."

The Stags left in small groups. Jerry Sloane looked over his shoulder at Harry once more. Then Sloane and Granger climbed into their cars and departed in clouds of pebbles and dust.

Harry sat on the grass next to the grave and mourned for his friend. Memories of their times together flashed through his mind: long camping trips in the Los Padres National Forest, deep sea fishing off of San Diego, chasing women, river rafting trips, and helping each other move. After Vietnam, they'd both avoided drugs but their Friday night beer sessions, accompanied by roaring laughter as they reminisced, were some of Harry's favorite memories—when he'd felt loved and secure.

Several times Randy had accompanied Harry when he'd attended international computer conferences around the world; Harry would present a paper and Randy would dive and scout out locations for more joint dives after the conferences. They'd dived the Red Sea, the Mediterranean Côte d'Azur off Cap Ferret, and the Great Barrier Reef in Australian waters. There'd been raucous parties with former Australian troops they'd met diving who'd served in the 1st Armored Division in Vietnam. The combat tales the Aussies related had made Harry uncomfortable but the men had been friendly and good natured.

Thor lay beside Harry and whimpered. Harry rubbed behind the dog's ears as he sat, tears turning dry. There was still one task. He reached into his pocket and retrieved his Purple Heart. Randy, he thought, deserved it more than he. He placed it on the grave.

Harry stared for some time at the medal on the fresh dirt. Then, he turned and walked towards his SUV. As he held the door open for Thor, he noticed a small airplane that circled over the cemetery. He realized that it had circled during the ceremony as well; he'd just been tuned out. There was a pilot training school next to the airport control tower in San Luis Obispo and Harry figured the plane was on a training exercise. He climbed into the car, turned on the engine, and drove off towards the gate. As he turned out of the cemetery, Harry saw Jerry Sloane's red Miata parked on the side.

Harry drove towards Highway U.S. 101. In his rear view mirror he noticed the Miata followed. A few miles later, he lost track of the sports car. Harry pulled over and looked over his shoulder. A few moments later the Miata roared past him. Puzzled, Harry waited to see if Sloane would pull over. Then he noticed the small airplane again. Harry, trained to be sensitive to hostile aircraft, smiled. Was the airplane following him or Sloane? One could make a great conspiracy theory out of that.

Randy's accident smelled and Harry didn't like the interest those Stags had displayed in him. He resolved to attend the inquest the next day.

FIVE—SLO

San Luis Obispo (SLO) was a nice town. Nestled in a bucolic county with the same name, livestock cluttered the golden fields and horses grazed along the sides of the roads. The Santa Lucia Mountain Range dominated the eastern horizon, the ocean hovered just over the western hills. Harry had migrated there after he graduated from the U.S. Naval Postgraduate School in Monterey with a Master's degree in electrical engineering. A quarter-million people lived in the county which included a dozen delightful towns and cities, such as SLO, Avila Beach, Atascadero and others. In Harry's opinion, SLO had the best weather in California. The town had a well-educated, and an above-average-income, population of forty thousand. Cal Polytechnic State University added twenty thousand students. Harry thought the small town had a lot of class; it was an oasis on the coast dominated by San Francisco in the north, and Los Angeles in the south.

Still, Harry was angry and restless when he arrived near SLO's City Hall. Early for the inquest, he stopped for a coffee in the Starbucks at the intersection of Osos and Palm Streets. He found a seat at a table with a discarded *Los Angeles Times* scattered on the surface. Harry picked up the headlines section. As he turned a page he heard the word 'inquest' behind him. He turned and noticed two men in San Luis Obispo county sheriff's uniforms at a table behind him. One sported a sheriff's badge, the other was a deputy sheriff.

The sheriff was considerably overweight; his stomach hung over his belt, and his face and hands were covered with freckles. He wore dark-framed glasses with clip-on sunglasses. He looked to Harry like the caricature of a man anticipating retirement. The deputy was stocky with large weight-lifter shoulders, jet black hair and a dark complexion. His hands were large and weathered. He wore pointed cowboy boots. Harry thought the picture would be complete with spurs. The deputy's eyes were active, darting everywhere. They lingered and seemed to record everything out of place; disorderly chairs, spilled coffee, an umbrella on the floor and an impatient customer—to Harry the deputy was the real cop on the beat.

"Damn it, Luis," said the sheriff, "just tell them the evidence. Don't invent anything in your mind. The security cameras may have nothing to do with this. It probably was an accident."

"I'm not inventing evidence," snarled the deputy, "and I don't like the FBI poking around in our business. That asshole Harris, from the San Francisco office, and his birddog Lewiston are messing with this investigation. There's a mob connection. We know that from the hot plates and these guys have their own agenda. I think—"

The deputy lifted his head and saw Harry, leaned over in his direction, no longer reading the paper.

"All right, keep it down," said the sheriff who'd turned and also saw Harry. "We'll see how it goes at the hearing."

Harry's vision blurred for a moment. He willed his heart to slow down. Were they talking about Randy? Why would the FBI be involved? What's going on? He watched as the two men carried their paper coffee cups to the trash, waved at the clerks behind the counter, and departed.

Harry walked out of Starbucks and around the small city block to kill ten minutes. He paused at the site of the new Court Street Center. It had been erected on the site of some building that had replaced the Obispo Theater, which had burned down in a spectacular fire in 1975. Funny, he couldn't remember what had occupied the site for thirty years. Jittery, he lusted for something to do with his hands. Maybe a cigar. Later, he'd hit the Big Bear Pipe and Tobacco Shop, it was only a few blocks from City Hall. If they were talking about Randy he wondered what he'd do. What could he do? Suddenly the air seemed to smell like rotted vegetation—the jungle. He breathed through his mouth as he entered City Hall with a minute to spare.

SIX—INQUEST

"This is a coroner's inquest," intoned Sid Salas, the bailiff. "Please take your seats."

The courtroom in the county courthouse used for the inquest was sparsely populated. The room was paneled in wood with a County of San Luis Obispo seal on the wall. American and State of California flags flanked the judge's chair, which was unoccupied. A man who was apparently the coroner sat on the jury side of a table, the two men Harry had listened to in Starbucks sat on the opposite side of the table. They were introduced as Sheriff John Ortega and Deputy Luis Mendoza. Six men and women sat in the booth which was normally occupied by a jury during an ordinary trial.

Harry was stunned. The cops *had* been talking about Randy. What was Randy involved in? The guy was a high-school teacher in SLO. Everybody had loved him.

Behind the railing sat a small bald man with eyeglasses in wire frames that gave him a studious appearance. He sat in the front row of the gallery, behind the sheriff, and jotted furiously in a small notebook. Harry concluded he was from the press. Another man, in a blue suit, sat in the same row, behind Deputy Mendoza. A teenage boy was behind the man in blue, slumped on a bench, radiating nervous energy—crossing and uncrossing his legs, and chewing his nails. A few people were scattered among the other benches.

The coroner banged his gavel. "Thanks, Sid. Okay, let's get going. Is the panel comfortable?"

All six members of the Coroner's Panel nodded obediently. Several of the men on the panel looked bored, one appeared irritated. The two women seemed attentive.

"For the benefit of our panelists and the audience," said the coroner, "I wish to make some comments. A coroner's inquest is an inquiry into the manner and cause of an individual's death. In this case, the dead person is one Randy Lismore, male, fifty-eight years old, and a high school teacher in our fair city. Did anyone on the panel know Mr. Lismore?"

"No, Sir," said one of the panelists. "We've already determined that, and we'd like to get out of here as soon as possible."

Harry rolled his eyes. Would the inquest be a farce?

"Are you certain?" asked the coroner. "Mr. Lismore was a football coach at the high school for some time; he undoubtedly touched many lives in town. He was also a member of the Los Osos Stags Lodge, are any of the panelists, or your family members, Stags?"

The panelists looked at each other and shook their heads.

"Thank you," said the coroner. "If I may continue, perhaps we can get everyone out by lunchtime. We're here to receive evidence and determine the cause of Mr. Lismore's death. These are non-trivial proceedings, so please—pay attention! Is Deputy Mendoza prepared to testify as to the evidence he collected at the scene?"

"Sir," said Mendoza, "I am."

"Sid, swear the witness."

Deputy Mendoza stood, took the oath, and seated himself back at the table.

"Please tell us your evidence, Deputy."

"Mr. Lismore was found dead in the men's room of the Madonna Inn, at the intersection of Highway U.S. 101 and Los Osos Valley Road, by his student, Billy Lawson, at 12:13 PM on Saturday, January 19th. He'd suffered a broken neck. It appeared, from the position and condition of the body, that he'd been urinating at the time."

"What was that condition, Deputy Mendoza?"

"Well … he was at the urinal and his penis was out of his pants."

Larry Yates hadn't said anything about how they'd found Randy. It was such an embarrassing position. Harry began to sweat and climb out of his seat.

The coroner looked up and frowned. "No disturbances, please! Take your seat, sir, or leave the room."

Harry nodded. "Sorry," he said and fumbled with his fold-down seat. As he sat he noticed Mendoza studying him.

"All right, as the deputy was saying he was found—"

"Excuse me, Mr. Coroner," said a woman panelist. "Is it possible that Mr. Lismore was a homosexual? I mean, most men … well, that is, most, you know … most men, don't they put it back before they turn away from a urinal?" She blushed as she looked at the man next to her on the panel.

"Deputy?" asked the coroner. "Is it possible?"

Mendoza shook his head. "I considered it and rejected the idea. We found no semen of any kind. Your staff examined the body. There's no evidence of homosexuality in his background—the man was an ex-Navy SEAL—or at the crime scene. In fact, there's evidence that Mr. Lismore had a spirited sex life with the pool ladies in his organization, as well as with some of the female teachers at SLO High School." The deputy stared at Harry as he concluded his answer.

Harry didn't want to attract any attention. He adopted a neutral mien as his eyes went blank and he stared at the flags. The deputy turned back to the coroner.

"I see. What else did you ascertain?"

"Well, from the position of the body, we considered the possibility that he had turned away from the urinal, slipped, and fell backwards. Personally, I think that's bull."

"You're saying it might have been an accident but you don't believe it?"

"There was other evidence at the scene. Mr. Lismore's glasses were crushed yet there were no glass shards in the soles of his shoes, and, there was a footprint—twelve and three-quarters inches by four and a half—a size ten and a half, in Mr. Lismore's urine on the floor. I'm talking about the floor paving stones, not the bottom of the urinal. I believe someone else stood next to him. Perhaps there was a tussle, I don't know. But that footprint did not match Mr. Lismore's size nine shoes. Someone else stepped on those glasses."

Fists clenched, Harry sat still. His pulse raced. Randy was murdered! He wanted to find the killer, and strangle him. He leaned forward and riveted his attention on the coroner.

"Thank you, Deputy."

The coroner turned to the panel. "My office examined the body and our findings confirm the deputy's testimony. Mr. Lismore's third cervical vertebra was broken and the damage to the spinal cord caused him to die of asphyxiation. I also ran a toxicology screen and found no traces of any drugs. Are there any more questions?"

The panelists shook their heads.

Mendoza raised his hand. "Please, if it is permitted, I have additional evidence … that is, well, additional information. It might be evidence."

Harry watched the sheriff give Mendoza an angry look and shake his head. Mendoza stared back. He seemed determined to speak.

The coroner turned back to Mendoza. "Yes?"

"Security cameras maintained by the Madonna Inn recorded a man entering the motel, and then departing, at 12:10 PM and 12:18 PM, respectively. He arrived, and departed, in a black Ford Explorer, with California license plates 3-L-K-J-4-6-7."

"Surely, Deputy Mendoza," said the coroner, "many people arrive and depart the Madonna Inn during the lunch hour. True?"

"Of course, and we ran the plates on all the cars in the video. However, the plates on this particular vehicle were registered to a Mercedes Benz 580SL in Atherton, California. It had been reported stolen three days before Mr. Lismore's death—January 16th. That stolen car, absent its plates, was found a week ago, on February 4th in a chop shop in Daly City, on the San Francisco peninsula."

A panelist raised his hand. "What's a chop shop?"

Mendoza looked to the coroner for permission to answer the question. He nodded. "Chop shops," volunteered Mendoza, "are garages where stolen cars are disassembled and sold, piece-by-piece, to disreputable auto repair and body shops. Once separated from the chassis, many vehicle parts don't carry identification numbers and can't be identified or traced. In some cases the chop shop will repackage the cars and sell them without disclosing their maintenance histories."

"Does that answer your question?" asked the coroner.

When the panelist nodded, Mendoza continued. "The shop in this case was owned by an alleged San Francisco mobster. This was confirmed by the FBI, who'd conducted the raid on the shop. The plates on the Ford Explorer at the Madonna Inn were obviously supplied by that chop shop. When combined with the other evidence, I believe it's plausible to conclude that Mr. Lismore was murdered."

"Thank you, Deputy. The panel should consider this evidence. It's our responsibility to determine whether this death is accidental or a homicide. While some may be quick to conclude there was foul play, it's still incumbent upon us to give this matter due consideration."

The panelists nodded in unison. Two of them looked at their watches.

"Let's hear from Billy Lawson now," said the coroner.

Harry watched the restless teenager two rows behind Mendoza stand and amble awkwardly to the seat next to the deputy.

Billy testified that Mr. Lismore had taken him to lunch as a reward for winning a calculus contest—he'd proven the Mean Value Theorem—quite an accomplishment for a junior math student in high school. Billy had neither heard, nor seen, anything suspicious.

"Mr. Lismore left for the restroom," he said, "and told me to order lunch for both of us—chicken fried steak and fries. I asked for a milk shake and—" Billy's arms were wrapped securely around his chest and his complexion was pale. "I ordered him—"

"We don't need to know what you ate, Billy," said the coroner. "Did you see anything after that?"

"Well, when he didn't come back, I went downstairs to the restroom and found his body. It was horrible, him lying there like that. I called the cops right away."

"Thank you, Billy. Is there anything else?"

"I just want to say Mr. Lismore was a good teacher and a nice guy."

"You didn't see a man go into the restroom with Mr. Lismore?" asked the coroner.

"No sir. As I told the deputy, I was ordering at the time."

"Thank you, Billy. You're excused. At this point I—"

The man in the blue suit stood. "Sir, I do not wish to introduce evidence, but may I speak? I'm Agent John Lewiston of the FBI. I work in the San Francisco office."

Mendoza's lips curled, his eyes narrowed, and his frown turned into a sneer. It was the same look Harry had seen on Deputy Mendoza's face in Starbucks, when the deputy had complained to the sheriff about the FBI. Harry thought Mendoza was going to snarl, but instead, he leaned over and whispered something to the sheriff. Then he said to the coroner, in a loud voice, "Don't listen to him."

The coroner sighed. "What is the nature of your comments, Agent Lewiston?"

"A federal task force is presently investigating an organization with loose ties to Mr. Lismore. I'd rather not disclose those ties now, but we'd appreciate a ruling of death by undetermined cause. This would ... it would facilitate our investigation. I understand that if additional evidence is presented later, this body may change its finding. We're working with Deputy Mendoza on this matter and such evidence, if relevant, will be made available to him."

A murmur ran through the courtroom and the coroner banged a gavel on the table. Harry saw Deputy Mendoza mouth the word "bullshit" to the sheriff. His mind reeled. San Francisco mobsters and a federal task force meant organized crime! Was a simple high school teacher caught up in something so large the government interfered with the inquest? He searched for possibilities as he excluded dope, larceny, gambling. What else was there? Randy was the straightest shooter he'd ever known. He looked back at Mendoza whose face was red.

Mendoza jabbed the sheriff's arm, raised his eyebrows, and stared into the sheriff's eyes.

"The Sheriff's Department," said the sheriff, with apparent reluctance, "does not agree with this request of the government. We believe we have a possible murder on our hands."

"Damn right!" exclaimed Mendoza in a voice heard throughout the room.

"Thank you, Sheriff Ortega and Agent Lewiston," said the coroner. "Deputy Mendoza, you're excused."

The coroner turned to face his panelists. "Members of the panel, the coroner is permitted to receive evidence from any persons that may have pertinent information about the incident. You therefore may consider the unsworn remarks of Agent Lewiston."

The coroner sipped at a glass of water. "If there is no further evidence, we'll move these proceedings to a conference room for private deliberation."

Harry stumbled out of the courtroom and down the hall. He found the men's room and splashed water on his face. He felt anger replace bewilderment. As he grabbed a paper towel from a dispenser, the door flew open. Mendoza stormed in.

"Who the hell are you?" he demanded. "What's your relationship with Lismore?" He grabbed Harry's windbreaker and lifted and pushed him up against a sink. Harry's butt jammed up against the cold water button; water spurted from the faucet.

Harry grabbed the deputy's hand and pulled it off his shoulder. "Let go, Deputy. I don't want to fight with you. I was his friend and I want to know everything you know—the truth, not some police bullshit."

Mendoza backed off. "Sorry. I've been stonewalled by everyone I talk to. What's your name?"

Harry glared at Mendoza. The faucet had an automatic turn-off but it had splashed water on the back of his trousers. He dabbed at the wet spot with a paper towel. "The name's Warrener. Harry Warrener."

The deputy studied Harry. "The truth, huh? Which version? You sure don't want to listen to that snake from the FBI. How'd you know Lismore?"

"Randy and I were SEALS together; we've been buddies since '74. I just found out about it. What's this crap about him being a homosexual? We shared lots of adventures and good times. I knew him like a brother; there was never a trace of it."

"I thought it was crap as well. Look, we can't talk now. I know this coroner; he'll be back in the courtroom in ten minutes. Maybe we can meet for a beer soon."

"What about after court? Lunch, maybe?"

Mendoza shook his head. "There's a big accident on Highway U.S. 101 that I need to check out. Give me a phone number and I'll call you."

Harry scribbled his phone number on a paper towel and the men returned to the courtroom.

Harry watched the deputy and the sheriff glare angrily at each other. After a moment, the sheriff seemed to relent and nodded.

Seven minutes later the coroner and the panelists returned to the courtroom. Harry heard other people walk into the courtroom but his attention was on the coroner.

The coroner smiled grimly at Mendoza and said, "It's the finding of this inquest that Mr. Lismore's death was due to undetermined cause. Should additional evidence be presented by the sheriff's office, or the FBI, we will reconvene the panel. The panelists are excused. I believe that we beat lunch by fifteen minutes. Thank you. This inquest is adjourned."

Harry shook his head in frustration. As he rose, the studious man with the notebook who'd sat behind the sheriff, approached him.

"Pardon me. My name's Max Cotton. I'm a reporter with the *Paso Robles Weekly Reporter*. Can I ask some questions?"

"Okay," said Harry with some reticence, "but I don't know anything."

"Thanks. Anything would help. What's your name? Did you know Mr. Lismore?"

"Harry Warrener. Yes." Harry was uncomfortable with the press and decided to respond only to the questions asked.

"Er, how did you know him?"

"I was in the Navy with him. We were friends."

Cotton wrote some notes. "Are you familiar with the Los Osos Stags' land deal?"

"I knew he was in the Stags. What land deal?"

"Did you see my article in the January 21st *Weekly Reporter*?"

"What did it say?"

"I think you ought to read it. I'll send you a copy but you can also find it the library. What's your address?"

Harry mumbled his address and turned to leave.

"Hey, Mr. Warrener, maybe after you read the article we can have a cup of coffee. Here's my card. Call me."

Harry grabbed the card and shoved it in his pocket. When he turned to leave he caught sight of a tall, large-shouldered man leaving the courtroom. Was that Jerry Sloane? He hurried up to the door but the corridor was empty.

He'd traveled to Oklahoma for his uncle's funeral and probate business. Randy had been murdered. The FBI was covering it up. The press was snooping around. Mendoza had said he was stonewalled by the people whom he'd interviewed about Randy. Maybe the Stags were involved. Harry craved a meal and a smoke.

SEVEN—BIG BEAR

Monday, February 11th, 2008, 2:00 PM

After lunch, Harry Warrener and Thor walked to the Big Bear Pipe and Tobacco Shop on Chorro Street in downtown SLO. Shops and cafes spread in all directions. Other cafes also fronted the creek that ran parallel to Marsh Street. They offered *al fresco* drinks and dining in a rustic environment. But Harry was more comfortable with the men in the Big Bear.

The inquest weighed heavily. Harry's head was bowed, and deep in thought, he frowned. But even so, Harry and Thor made a handsome couple and the pup caught the attention of many people.

A very pretty girl walked by but Harry ignored her smile. Harry had never had problems attracting women. Marriage had come easy; his only wife had latched onto him at the University of Oklahoma in Norman, but they'd divorced when she'd proved unfaithful. Adrift, and searching for comradeship, he'd joined the SEALS. He'd loved the diving—when you were below the surface there was no combat and it didn't matter what the weather was like. In fact, Harry hated storms. Anticipation of them made him uncomfortable; he'd feel his shoulders tense and his mouth become dry. He'd avoid outdoor activity. It was probably latent fear, he thought; his parents had died in a terrible storm when he was three years old. But Harry knew Vietnam had left its mark; during storms he'd think he smelled the jungle. He knew fear spawned the recurring smells; it was frustrating that internalizing that fact had not mitigated the symptom.

He'd promised himself to get a dog after Vietnam but graduate school had interfered. Then he'd begun teaching. He'd moved to SLO after Vietnam because Randy lived there and the town offered teaching opportunities. Cal Poly, an excellent architecture, agriculture, and engineering university, had been demanding. What with research, his students, diving trips with Randy, the occasional girl, summer travel, and the daily problems of life, Harry had never had, until retirement, the opportunity to get a dog.

His bank loomed on his right, next to a U.S. Armed Forces Recruiting Station. The juxtaposition of money and the military focused him again on Randy. Money, he wondered, was that the reason for Randy's death? He stopped and looked in the window of the bank. In the reflection, Thor's tongue hung out and his breath clouded the glass. Thank God he had the dog to occupy his time.

Harry had made a bundle on start-ups including CyberCash and

Ball Valve
Full Port • Solder

Válvula Esfera
Pas Completo-Soldar
Valve á Bille
Pleine Ouverture-Soudure

irst act, upon retirement, had been to locate a German
:r that specialized in purebred dogs. He'd found a black and
1 Indiana, flown there, and returned with ten-week old Bessel
nhaus—"Bessel," a famous German mathematician whose
vith B, so the second letter for the second litter; "Thor" for
name; "Stein" was the name of the breeder; and *haus*, the
for house. The pup's paws had seemed bigger than his body
iped into Harry's arms.

: months old now and still with enormous paws, was the light
. Only Randy had been closer. Heeling on a leash next to
g uttered a small growl as they approached the intersection
reet.

smell of cigar smoke had mingled with the scent of aromatic
and English pipe tobaccos and drifted into the doorway of Kuo's Chinese
Laundry, situated next to the Big Bear. A skinny old Chinese woman, Mrs.
Kuo, stood at the door. She sneered at the dog, mumbled something in
Chinese, waved her arms at the smoke, and harangued a Big Bear customer
as he left the shop. Harry shushed Thor and tied his leash to a parking
meter. Despite Harry's frustration over the inquest, he smiled affably at
the woman and entered the Big Bear.

The shop hummed with the usual crowd of lunch-break smokers—
several police, a teacher, city hall employees, two information technology
consultants, an UPS driver, a lawyer, some other men at the back counter,
and the shop proprietor, Mamoru "Zero" Matsuda. Zero was nicknamed
after his uncle Kozo, who only fifteen years old as a naval air cadet,
had flown a Japanese Zero during the war. Kozo had been the kamikaze
pilot who had slammed his plane into the *USS Missouri* in the battle for
Okinawa, causing a spectacular explosion, but only superficial damage.

A crowd sat around a long table. Two laptop computers; three ashtrays
filled to overflowing with butts, ashes, smoking cigars; and a couple of
Cokes cluttered the table under a haze of blue smoke. Most of the men
smoked expensive Dominican Republic cigars—women were welcome,
but they were repelled by the smoke and harsh repartee. Zero poured a
cappuccino while his wife, Hiroko, the only woman in the shop, rang up
several twenty dollar cigars for a customer.

Harry cruised by the table, headed for a large humidor.

Zero stopped him. "Harry-san, I'm sorry about Randy. I know you
friends." Zero bowed and added, "*Dame, Dame,* no good."

"Thanks. Did you hear anything about it?"

"There was deputy in here when happen. He heard on radio. I shocked."
Zero's bags sagged under narrowed, slanted eyes. "He said think accident

but cop at Madonna Inn say maybe crime scene. We see coroner's wagon go fast."

It was murder, damn it, thought Harry but he didn't want anyone to know he had given thought to conducting his own investigation. "Thanks, Zero. They said at the inquest that it was death by undetermined cause."

Zero waved his hand, palm out, fingers straight across his nose. Harry knew, from stops in Japan during the Vietnam War, that Zero's gesture reiterated his "no good" comment. "Harry-san has more friends? Welcome here anytime."

Harry muttered some thanks and turned away. He didn't have any other friends like Randy, and he was lonely. Further, he was bored in retirement. Randy often had suggested he join the Stags, but he'd been reluctant to join a fraternal order. He'd thought the Stags were like the Shriners, or Moose, with all that flag-waving stuff. But now he wanted to join, snoop around, and perhaps find out if Randy's membership in the Stags had had anything to do with his death. Perhaps Harry could volunteer for some activity. He recalled his service as an officer in a professional computing society. The work had been fun and had offered camaraderie and social contact. There'd been many women who'd gravitated to the power in the society. Unfortunately, the most interesting women were already taken. Maybe it was time to get serious about a woman.

"Harry," boomed Gary Walsh, one of the investors in the shop. "Sit down. We're smoking and joking. Have you met Larry Yates?"

Harry took a cigar from the shop humidor. "We've met," he said, and smiled at Yates.

Yates wore safety glasses and had a sweater draped over his shoulders. He was hunched over a buffing wheel, polishing a Savory Argyll pipe that had been made in England.

Yates nodded. "Terrible, wasn't it? Randy was such a neat guy. And honest. He was so concerned with due diligence on our land deal—"

"Is that what you meant yesterday—when you said there was bad blood?"

Yates scrutinized the room. He motioned to Harry to walk away from Gary. "Gary's a nice guy, but he likes to gossip too much. Yes, Randy was upset that we hadn't received an appraisal before we sold the Stags' land in Los Osos. He'd also wanted to get competition for the design and construction of the new lodge."

"That had to involve a lot of money, huh?"

Yates shrugged. "More than a lot."

Harry nodded. As they drifted back to the counter near Gary, he sliced off the end of a La Gloria Cubana Series R Belicoso cigar.

Yates stuffed tobacco in another pipe, a Peterson of rather large proportion, lit a match, tamped down the tobacco, and fired up a second match. He puffed a few times. "My wife hates these things; she won't let me smoke anywhere in the house. I'm exiled to here or the deck at my house. I have some heart problems and that gives her more ammo and she insists I reduce my activities."

"I might be interested in joining the Stags," said Harry, as he lit his cigar. "Can you tell me something about them?"

"Sure. We're going to construct a brand new lodge building with state-of-the-art fitness and gym facilities and we can always use some new blood—especially smart blood. We never have enough bright volunteers."

Harry could imagine inept volunteers. He remembered a hilarious Jacky Gleason spoof on another fraternal order, the Elks—Gleason's group had been called the Raccoons and it had had silly rituals. The Raccoons waved their coonskin caps in a salute and had an elaborate handshake. Even *The Flintstones* had poked fun at the Elks. Fred and Barney's group had called itself the Loyal Order of the Water Buffalo.

"What's the story with the Stags?" asked Harry. "What do they do? Randy rarely talked about internal stuff. He'd hit me up for an occasional contribution but that was it."

Gary smirked. "Do? You mean besides drink and roll dice for drinks?"

Harry nodded. "I heard it was an all-white men's club. I know they do some charitable work but I don't know what."

"The Fraternal Order of the Stags," said Yates, "was founded in 1903, in Chicago, by a bunch of singers and actors with ... large appetites for whiskey." Yates smiled. "They wanted a club to play cards in and to drink in, in private."

"That's it, Harry," said Gary. "They drink. And they have a big parcel of land at the beach, where you can smoke all the cigars you want."

"It's more than that," said Yates, giving Gary a frustrated look. "The Stags are similar to the Moose. We have almost a thousand Lodges and about a hundred twenty thousand members; most of the Lodges are in the western half of the country. We gave fifteen million dollars last year to charity—support of the veterans is one of our larger programs—"

"Last month," said Gary proudly, "the Los Osos Lodge sent ten boxes of cigars from the Big Bear to the troops in Iraq."

"That's neat, Gary," said Harry. "During Vietnam the nation wasn't so grateful."

"We sent books and CDs, too," said Yates, "and we do a lot of work at the VA Hospital. But, Gary, let me finish my spiel. We donate a lot to handicapped children; we run Easter egg hunts; we fight drug abuse; and we sponsor scholarships. Our non-cash contributions—hours, miles driven, books and the like, would total two or three million bucks. And the Stags are also very patriotic."

Harry remembered talking to Randy about the Order. Harry had asked if the Stags were like the Masons. Randy had explained that the Stags, like the Shriners, the Moose, Eagles, and the Odd Fellows, to name a few, had all borrowed practices from the Masons. All of the orders were charitable. Many of the Stags' rituals mimicked Elks' rituals and the Stags had used the same titles as the Elks for their officers. Randy had said that he thought the Eagles were too laid back, the Red Fez (Masons who were Shriners) were the group with which to drink, and the Elks were a little too old, formal, and ritualistic for his taste—but he liked the Stags Lodge in Los Osos. The memory prompted Harry to concentrate on the task at hand.

"Tell me more about the new lodge building."

"We just learned about it. We have a buyer; we voted last month to sell most of our land, twenty-seven acres, preserving two acres for our use. We'll net twenty-six million dollars and most of it, twenty million or so, will go towards the new building. We'll have a great aquatic facility with two pools, athletic machines, handball and racquetball courts, a Jacuzzi, steam room and sauna for both men and women, an enormous billiards room, and, of course, a spectacular bar and dining room—and drinks will still be four bucks."

"Any social programs?"

"We have several large events: an annual dance, picnic, Fourth of July barbecue, a Christmas party for children, New Year's dinner, and so forth. The bar's open all year and we serve dinner three nights a week. At the bar we roll dice for drinks. We don't call it gambling, just deciding who'll host the next round." He added conspiratorially, "There are regular gin-rummy games and the poker gang runs tournaments twice a year—Jerry Sloane always wins them. In the good old days we even had one-armed bandits—they made a small fortune."

"He's a poker player?" asked Harry, interested in Sloane's habits.

"Big time. He definitely fancies himself a semi-pro."

It was time to discover more information about the board of trustees. "Yesterday you said you were a trustee?"

"We have five trustees; every year we elect a new one for a five year term. Besides filling Randy's empty seat, the next vacancy will be mine. I'm not running for re-election because of my ticker."

"I'm sorry to hear that." Harry wondered if Randy had supported the sale. "Randy wanted an appraisal. Did he vote to sell?"

"It's pretty hard to turn down twenty-six million dollars," said Yates. "I think the Stags bought the land for about five thousand in 1946. Randy complained, but he went along after some arm-twisting by Granger and Sloane."

"Then what happened?"

"Randy brought up the issue of due diligence in future transactions. I'm concerned myself, and I have some problems with the leadership. We're arguing over the design job for the new lodge."

"What's involved?"

"Oh, it's a competition issue, but it's confidential to the trustees. If you're really interested, I can refer you to a past issue of the *Reporter,* an article by some guy named Cotton."

Harry knew that had to be Max Cotton and *competition* confirmed that money was involved. Harry's interest soared. "How does one join?"

"You fill out an application. You have just enough time to make the investigation on the nineteenth. But, seriously, with your background, you'd make a good candidate for trustee."

"I think trustee is a little premature, Larry, but I'm flattered. Is it expensive?"

"It's cheap. And seriously, the Stags can always use more members. We lost about two thousand members nationwide last year. Because we target for membership among young families with children we do better than the Elks; they lost about twenty thousand members—even their Lodges in California lost over one thousand."

"So how much?" Harry wondered if the losses in the orders were due to deaths or just a change in societal acceptance of archaic rules. Those rules had to date back to the nineteenth century, perhaps medieval times.

"The dues are three hundred a year but they'll drop during construction. The application fee is a hundred dollars, fifty for people under forty-two. But that's not you, is it? If you were in Vietnam you must be at least in your fifties."

Harry grinned.

"Uh-huh," said Yates. "You don't look it. Okay, first there's an investigation which is strictly pro forma, then indoctrination, and finally an initiation." Yates smiled. "I can't tell you what happens in the initiation, but the Stags are big on ritual. It's kind of quaint in a way; they honor flag and country and they're pretty strict on following their rules."

Harry smiled inwardly. It did sound like the orders were dying out. Still, he needed to join if he was going to ferret out any information about

Randy. "Are there any restrictions? I heard they don't take women or minorities."

"That stuff went out a long time ago. We have thirty new women who just joined; I'm sure it's because of the planned new pool and facilities where they can take their kids. But, as I said, we're after new blood, a younger culture—we even have a child care center in the plans."

"What's this investigation?"

"Do you believe in God? Were you ever a Communist? Are you an American citizen?" Yates grinned.

Harry gagged on his cigar. "They still ask questions about Communists? That's nuts? I thought the Supreme Court ruled those questions unconstitutional in the '50s or '60s."

"I think the court was concerned with the Attorney General's list of subversive organizations, as it was applied to federal applications. I agree it's a little archaic but that's it. Those are the three main questions. They'll even tell you what the correct answers are in the investigation. They don't come to your door anymore to check out your wife, like they did in the past." Yates raised an eyebrow and shrugged.

Getting the meaning, Harry asked, "Do you have any African-American members?"

"If you know any African-Americans who want to join the Los Osos Lodge, I'll sponsor them. Other Lodges have black members and there are no racial, religious or gender restrictions."

"Can I get an application?" Harry figured he'd see how it went. He wasn't sure how he felt about God, but he was willing to admit he believed. The Commie stuff was easy.

"You bet. I'll sponsor you and collect another endorsement from Jimmy Belgado. He hangs out here in the late afternoons."

Harry signed an application and gave Yates a check for one hundred dollars. He walked out of the Big Bear and untied Thor. "It's time to practice heeling, buddy. We just started an investigation and you go to school tonight." Thor wagged his tail and the two walked along Higuera Street.

EIGHT—THOR

Four black Dobermans, a dachshund, and two German shepherds, including Thor, lay in a prone position. Viewed from the side, the pack looked like an attack fleet in the ocean, except for a large, brown, Rhodesian ridgeback, which stood, waving his tail, with a blank look.

"What's the matter, Ed?" asked the trainer. "Does Ruger have a headache?"

Harry winced. Ed was Ruger's master and the dog had a problem with commands. Ruger was an enormous, though friendly, oaf, but his master was a pushover. Harry knew that you couldn't combine relaxed training with a slow dog. He knew what came next. Jamie, who ran SLO Guard Dog Training and Pet Grooming, Inc., was a tough taskmaster. She'd trained bomb-sniffing dogs for the SLO Police Department. She was headed for Ruger.

"Damn it, Ed! I've told you to only give the command once. You don't repeat 'Down!' If he doesn't obey, you have to correct him immediately."

Jamie pushed the ridgeback down, put her foot on Ruger's throat, and yanked the leash, choking him. "Down!" she commanded, and pulled on the leash until the dog drooled. Ruger's legs twitched and he emitted a high pitched whine. Two of the Dobermans rolled over on their side and the dachshund bolted for the trees at the edge of the training grounds, her owner in pursuit. Ruger's eyes began to roll, but Jamie pushed harder. Thor looked at Harry with large fearful eyes. Finally, Ruger puked.

"There," said Jamie, "he should be okay now." She handed the leash to Ed and walked away. Ruger gulped for air.

Thor whimpered as Jamie walked past him. Harry wanted a well-trained, sociable animal, which he could take anywhere, but Jamie's methods were cruel. Harry was grateful Thor was a bright animal and learned his commands quickly. Harry resolved he wouldn't let Jamie punish Thor like that. He looked up when she told the class to give the command, "Up sit." All the dogs responded immediately.

After class, Harry asked Jamie how he could train Thor to snarl and bark upon command.

"You should pick an unusual word," she said, "for a command. Use another language—like German—so the command won't be given accidentally, or by a stranger. How about *waffen*? It means 'weapon.'

When he starts to bark at you in play, you should say: 'Thor, *waffen*!' and encourage it. Then reward him with a rub or a milk bone. He'll get the idea. A barking dog is pretty good protection."

"He'll be a hundred ten pounds at maturity."

Jamie nodded. "Harry, do you ever wonder why dogs always bark at the mailman? They bark—the mailman leaves. Every time! It's called positive reinforcement."

Harry smiled. A dog that barked on command was just the thing. Should a real threat materialize he knew Thor would follow the basic instincts of German shepherds—it wouldn't be just noise. Harry would have the ally he'd lusted for since Vietnam. He suspected that if he ever found the guy that killed Randy he'd need assistance.

NINE—HUMMERS

Sunlight bounced off the hood of a competition yellow Hummer on the showroom floor and flashed into Ted Granger's office. Granger, exalted ruler (ER) of the Los Osos Stags Lodge, strummed his fingers on his desk wondering if he'd see a customer. 'SALE' and 'CASH BACK' signs flooded the lot and the showroom but customers were an endangered species.

A buzzer rang and he looked out onto the lot. His hopes rose. A candy apple red Hummer backed slowly into a parking spot. The driver, Ben Milton, the police chief in Arroyo Grande, walked into Granger's office as mechanics swarmed over the car.

"How'd you like the car, Ben?" asked Ted Granger. "Are you ready to swap it for a new one?"

"It's a neat car, all right, but Betty complains about the ride and the thing blows money out the exhaust pipe. This time I'm going to lease a hybrid from Foremost Motors."

"Damn it, Ben. You know I need the business." Granger's auto agency in Paso Robles was almost belly-up. Four dollars a gallon gasoline had rendered Hummers *persona non grata* on the roads. His wife, Marietta, was already complaining that they'd had to cancel trips to Europe and Asia, along with a cruise on the Caribbean; if she knew how close they were to bankruptcy, she'd file for divorce. In California, that meant she'd get half of anything left over, including the house. That would break Granger's back. It was one secret he had to keep.

"Sorry," said Milton, "but I'm looking at an extra two, maybe three hundred bucks a month, in gas. And that's when I stay within the twelve thousand miles a year limit on the lease."

Granger sighed. He wouldn't even collect for extra mileage. When his mechanic gave him an all-clear wave, he completed the paperwork on the car.

Milton stood to leave. "How about a lift to Foremost Motors?"

"Sure, check with Mike outside."

This was it, thought Granger. Next quarter the accountants would nail his hide to the door. His first kickback on the sale of the Stags' property was due after the Grand Lodge approved the transaction and the Lodge officers signed the sales transaction. But that money was already committed—a drop in the bucket. And more ominously, it in fact was an advance contingent upon award of the design and construction jobs for the replacement lodge building. That would also lead to a larger kickback but if those jobs didn't materialize he was in trouble. He picked up the phone. It was time for a little coordination with the chairman of the Stags' board of trustees, Jerry Sloane. Granger hoped Sloane wasn't in Arroyo Grande playing poker—his usual pastime. Getting him out of a poker game in the Narrow Creek Indian Casino was a pain in the ass.

TEN—BIG BUBBA

Tuesday, February 12th, 2008, 11:45 AM

Jerry Sloane, chairman of the Los Osos Stags Lodge board of trustees, sat in his Miata at the stop light at the intersection of Spring and 12th Streets in Paso Robles. En route to a meeting with Ted Granger, the ER, Sloane was upset. Sloane owed the Indians sixty grand; he'd been getting some decent cards and was angry he'd had to leave the casino early. When you were hot, you had to keep going.

Sloane stared angrily at the red light, convinced it was the longest red light in central California. Fucking traffic engineers, he thought, what do they need lights for in these rinky-dink towns? An impatient man, he willed himself to be patient. Ha, he thought, that's what his mother would have said about his father's gambling. *No*, he remembered, that's precisely what she had said. "Be patient, Jerry, and he'll lose it all." Sloane shivered. Like an oracle, his mother had been right. The old man had lost his hardware store, the home in Lafayette, Indiana, the car, and the twenty grand he'd borrowed from Uncle Tim in Yellow Springs, Ohio. They'd ended up trailer trash in Vandalia, ten miles north of Dayton, and Wright-Patterson Air Force Base, where those goddamn B-52s woke him up every morning as they soared into the sky. Sloane checked the stoplight.

Damn, it was still red. He wished he could slaughter a traffic engineer once a month—a public, ceremonial beheading, or a hanging would be good, just to set an example.

To distract himself, Sloane studied a sign that advertised the new Arroyo Robles Winery on 12th Street. A glass of wine would be nice—better, make it a bottle. Finally, the light changed and he roared north towards 24th Street. He ignored a large empty parking lot and parked next to a fireplug.

Ted Granger already sat at a table in Big Bubba's Bad BBQ Restaurant. Sloane grabbed a yellowed edition of the *Paso Robles Weekly Reporter* off a counter at the window and sat down. The old headline, on an article above the fold, rekindled his rage:

𝔓𝔞𝔰𝔬 𝔕𝔬𝔟𝔩𝔢𝔰 𝔚𝔢𝔢𝔨𝔩𝔶 𝔕𝔢𝔭𝔬𝔯𝔱𝔢𝔯
Monday, January 21, 2008

LOS OSOS STAGS SELLING
BEACHFRONT PROPERTY
Mob Connections Alleged
Reporting by Max Cotton

Sloane pointed at the article. "What are we going to do about this? Lismore's gone, but this article ain't."

"I know," said Granger. "I'm stonewalling Cotton's calls. But there's another problem—we have to fill the vacancy in the trustees."

"Goddamn it, Ted! The first kickback's one hundred grand and I need it now!"

"I'm also in a hurry," said Granger. "But if we want to keep it and get the bigger bucks, you know we need the trustees to recommend the Lodge award the design job to Monterey Construction as soon as possible. That's more critical."

"That son-of-a-bitch Kelly. I know he's on the take. We get a lousy hundred grand each and he's pocketing millions. You know he's getting more than the fee he charged the Lodge."

"Keep your voice down. The hundred is just the beginning and we don't know if he's getting more. Besides, we agreed to this scam. Remember?"

Sloane wondered how he could forget. He stared through the window at the gas stations across the street, lost in thought. The meeting with Ron Kelly had been in late December, at Rocky Point Restaurant near Carmel, about ten miles below the state marine preserve at Point Lobos. Jim Thatcher, the Stags' District Deputy Grand Exalted Ruler (DDGER) for the central coast Lodges, also had been there. Sloane had been looking out the window when Kelly made the offer. His eyes clouded as he remembered the meeting. Kelly had played them like a master …

ELEVEN—ROCKY POINT

Friday, December 28th, 2007 6:30 PM

It had taken over two hours to drive from SLO to Carmel and another ten minutes down Highway California 1 to the Rocky Point Restaurant. The road had been dark and twisty. Jerry Sloane followed a steep road down to the restaurant and parked under the sole mercury vapor light that illuminated the dirt lot. A few minutes later Ted Granger arrived in his Hummer from Paso Robles and they waited in the lot until Jim Thatcher, the Stags' District Deputy Grand Exalted Ruler (DDGER) arrived from Salinas. The men shook hands and walked into Rocky Point.

Surf crashed just below the windows behind the bar; sporadic plumes of spray soared to Sloane's eye level. The tide was at flood stage and the ocean surged and boiled as waves thundered onto the rocks.

Ron Kelly, a real estate agent, forty-six years old, and dressed in black chinos and a cashmere sweater, had been waiting for the Stags in the restaurant. Kelly was stocky; he had a Mediterranean complexion and a thick head of hair with light traces of gray that he pulled out every morning. A black ski parka was draped over the back of his chair.

Ted Granger had told Sloane that Kelly represented a buyer interested in the Stags' land in Los Osos. Sloane had wanted to sell off some of the land; the Lodge was broke and needed the money to refurbish or rebuild—he'd hoped he could feed in the food chain, somehow. The Stags' leadership was so inept, and the operating procedures in the Lodge so weak and archaic, that there had to be a way to ferret some money out of the deal. But he was nervous; Sloane knew Kelly had disturbing connections to an organized crime family in San Francisco. In fact, Kelly was the nephew of the alleged don of the Cicerone family. Sloane shook hands and hoped Kelly didn't notice his hands were damp.

After some small talk and the usual inane jokes about women and the government, the men ordered their dinners and settled down to business.

"Ron, thanks for coming," said Granger. "We're interested in your proposal to buy some of our land."

"Actually, Ted," replied Kelly, with a smile, "my proposal is for most of your land—but don't worry, if we do the deal there'll be plenty left over for your Stags' needs."

"What do you have in mind?" said Thatcher.

"It's quite simple. I have a well-qualified buyer, who wants to purchase twenty-seven acres. He intends to develop single-family homes and condos on the property."

"Can he get the financing for this deal?" asked Thatcher.

"I don't think that's a problem, Jim," said Kelly. "This is a cash deal, at least the first half, and the rest is conditional upon approval of the construction permits."

Sloane leaned forward. "Just how much are we talking?"

Kelly offered a purchase price that ranged from a minimum of thirteen and a half-million to twenty-seven million dollars. The ultimate price would depend upon the number of units the buyer built—one hundred eight units were targeted. But that number depended on approval from the local governments and the Coastal Commission. The minimum would constitute a non-refundable initial payment.

"I don't understand," said Granger. "What happens if he can't build all the units?"

"We should get approval for all one hundred eight," said Kelly. "This year, in about thirty decisions, the commission was fifty-six percent in favor of development. More than half the commissioners are likely to support the deal. And it's common knowledge that the county and the city are desperate for new housing. Still, the high end is a crap shoot."

"Who's the buyer?" asked Sloane.

Kelly refused to name the buyer. He suggested that the Stags had a reputation for leaking more than the Pentagon Papers. "Regardless of who the buyer is, the money will come from my agency's escrow account through Coastal Title and Trust Company."

"So Coastal holds the title 'til we get the money?" asked Thatcher.

"That's correct," said Kelly. "No one wants to steal your land."

Then he demanded a million dollar fee. "Look," he said, "this is a reasonable fee. I'm not collecting anything from the buyer—after all, you guys are a charity and do good work—it'd be improper to collect at both ends."

Jerry Sloane gagged on a piece of bread but he noted that Thatcher and Granger just nodded in agreement. They were gullible fools, he thought, but elected to keep his cynicism to himself.

Jim Thatcher smiled and said that if the Los Osos Lodge voted to accept the deal, he'd facilitate the Stags Grand Lodge's approval to sell the land to Kelly's buyer. The Grand Lodge, based on the west side of Chicago near the University of Illinois, he reminded everyone, was the ultimate authority; any transaction over twenty-five thousand dollars required its approval.

Sloane did some calculations. They'd been offered two hundred fifty thousand dollars for each unit built. With no capital gains taxes—after all, the Stags were a not-for-profit charitable association—they'd net twenty-six million dollars after Kelly's fee. But then Thatcher, who spoke with the authority of the Grand Lodge, insisted that a four million dollar preservation fund be set aside to guarantee the payment of future property taxes—they would soar when the Stags constructed a new lodge building.

Still, Sloane thought, twenty-two million dollars could be available. That should be enough to stifle any resistance to the sale and to build a new lodge that would pander to all the members. And, in a project of that size, there must be ways to siphon off another few percent. Perhaps one million dollars could find its way into his and Granger's pockets. That kind of money would solve all their problems; he knew Granger's agency was in trouble and he needed money.

Sloane was convinced Kelly was getting something from both sides and probably a hunk from the middle. That didn't bother him. Sloane reasoned that the sooner Kelly received his, the sooner he and Granger could. Everyone fed at the trough. Why not them?

The three Stags debated how to pay Kelly's fee. It needed to be approved by the membership of the Lodge. After some discussion, Thatcher proposed that Kelly receive half his fee when the Stags entered the design phase, and half when they broke ground—in that manner the fee could be characterized as related to the new lodge, rather than as a commission for the sale. Sloane argued with a glint in his eye, as Kelly had said, the Stags were a charitable organization; charities didn't like to pay commissions.

But Kelly wasn't happy with delay. "There's a limit to my patience," he said. "That could take six months. You guys need to act as soon you receive the first half of the proceeds from the buyer. Call the payment a preliminary design fee, or something. And I hope you understand the delay on the second half would be a philanthropic contribution!"

The Stags nodded and Thatcher said, "Thanks for the concession, Ron. We appreciate your help. I don't need to know any of the other details now." He looked at Granger. "As long as you set aside the preservation funds, I'll get the Grand Lodge permit approved. Just fill out an application and get your members to approve it."

"Right away," said Granger. "Right, Jerry?"

Sloane nodded in agreement.

"Great," said Thatcher. "Congratulations to the Lodge. I'm sure the new building will be wonderful. I have to leave now; I'm flying to Chicago tomorrow so just fax the application there."

After Thatcher departed, Ted Granger stared at his plate and rubbed his eyes. After clearing his throat, and another rub, he leaned forward and whispered, "Uh ... Ron, I was wondering if there was any opportunity for—well, you know—will this cake have any crumbs left over?"

Sloane smiled, pleased and a little surprised at Granger's initiative.

Kelly smirked. "Gee, Ted, I thought you Stags did this for love of country and flag."

"We do," Sloane interjected, "but if there's going to be any breakage; why leave it on the floor?"

Kelly nodded. "Let me ask a question. Do we need to cut Thatcher in?"

"No way," Granger said, "A new lodge in his district will earn him kudos in Chicago; it's the first new building in years. But he's an honest man."

"I thought you all were," said Kelly. After a pause, he added, "Are you sure? I need to know who my partners are."

Granger and Sloane reassured Kelly about Thatcher. Kelly sipped some wine and stared into his glass for a moment. Then, he offered to give them each a kickback of one hundred thousand dollars.

Granger smiled but Sloane thought they could do better. He was about to ask for more when Kelly raised a finger, dropped his voice and said, "Do you guys understand that once you're committed, there's no room for a change of heart? My partners—perhaps I should say your partners—don't like that. *Capice?*"

Granger, eyes downcast, mumbled, "I do."

"Jerry? Do *you* understand?"

Sloane felt a chill. His right leg twitched. He didn't like being reminded who Kelly's partners were—that *capice* unnerved him. He and Granger were dancing with the devil. He looked down at his meal. The sweet smell of caramelized onions on his plate fouled his appetite. A deal with the mob offered great reward but the risk was unnerving. Sloane hoped he wasn't jumping into a frying pan but he nodded.

Kelly went to the men's room. Granger worked on his food while Sloane stared at a sea otter that floated on the waves outside the window. The otter pounded a rock against an abalone shell but Sloane ignored it, lost in thought.

"Okay," Kelly said when he returned, "I want this deal to happen. I'll take a chance with you guys. You'll each get the hundred thousand when the land deal is signed. Understand, this'll be an *advance* against my fee!" Kelly pointed his finger at both of them as he emphasized the word 'advance.'

Sloane studied Kelly. A hundred long was such a pittance. Despite his unrest about the mob connection he wanted more money. "Can't we get more?"

"Maybe—that depends on you." Kelly leaned back in his chair. He reached into his parka, retrieved a cigar, mouthed it, and twirled it first clockwise, and then counterclockwise. The label seemed to bother him and he picked at it with a fingernail. He pulled his lighter out of a pocket with the other hand—Sloane wondered what the proprietor would do if Kelly lit up. His mind pictured the police arresting all of them, disgrace, and prison—all over a lousy cigar. This was California after all, crawling with tobacco Nazis.

"What would we have to do?" asked Granger, while he rubbed his eyes.

To Sloane's relief, Kelly placed the cigar and lighter on the table. "If you want more, you need to grant sole-source, fixed-price, design and construction contracts to Monterey Construction Company for your new building."

"But approval for that means we'd have to involve more people," said Granger. "The trustees—"

Kelly said, "I don't give a shit how you handle it. That would be your problem."

Sloane knew the Stags' statutes demanded trustee approval of any contract before it went to the membership for ratification. A sole-source not-to-exceed contract which meant no competition, should garner a unanimous vote on the board—to avoid internal political controversy and to minimize the likelihood of detection of the kickbacks. It wasn't absolutely necessary but any resistance would raise dangerous flags. Getting unanimous trustee approval introduced uncertainty, and possible delay, on the final construction deal. Since Kelly's fee depended on the timing, that meant the hundred thousand dollars for both Granger and Sloane would be at risk. Kelly might demand the money back if the Stags didn't build a new lodge or delayed it indefinitely. And, given the rotten interest rates available, every delay would cost Sloane money.

"If we do the sole-source," asked Sloane, "what's in it for us?"

"A half a million more, each. That'll eat up a million so we'll have to tell Thatcher I forgot one acre had to go to infrastructure, or fire lanes, or some similar bullshit, and the deal is only for one hundred four units or twenty-six million bucks. Which means the minimum the Stags will get is thirteen million. Then we'll—"

TWELVE—REPORTER

Jerry Sloane's eyes refocused on the sign on Big Bubba's plate glass window. It vibrated in response to a large truck that thundered past the restaurant. Sloane swallowed some coffee and nibbled at the sourdough. The bread was stale, nowhere in quality like the bread in Carmel. That night in Carmel had been a heady moment, all his money problems solved. But Kelly had warned them that once committed there was no way out of the deal. And the first hundred grand kickbacks in the deal were conditional, linked precariously to the subsequent award of the design job to Monterey Construction Company.

Unsettled, he asked Ted Granger, "Do you know anything more about that guy at the cemetery?"

"I ran his credit at my agency. Harry Warrener. He's fifty-six, a retired professor, has a rating of seven-fifty-three which means he has beaucoup bucks, and he had charges in Fiji a couple of months ago. Wasn't Lismore there?"

"He took a diving trip. So they were buddies?"

"They were SEALS together. Warrener was an underwater demolitions specialist and awarded a Purple Heart. He's pretty much a loner—no wife, children but he lives in SLO."

"We don't need anyone interested in Lismore."

"What do you care?" asked Granger.

"I followed the guy for a while from the cemetery. I took off when he pulled over."

Granger's face paled. He smeared a hunk of butter on his bread and chewed slowly. "Followed? Why?"

"I'm interested in anyone connected to Lismore." Sloane knew Granger had a cholesterol problem; the butter meant he was nervous.

"There's nothing to worry about," said Granger. "The coroner ruled it death by undetermined cause."

"I know! I was there and so was Warrener," snapped Sloane. "There's plenty to worry about. Remember that deputy who came sniffing around after Lismore died? I know he thought it was murder. Maybe he'll make the connection. Lismore was into that due diligence crap. We might have the same problem with Yates. I tested the waters with him and he's inclined to compete the design. We don't need anyone poking around."

"I know Randy frustrated you and made you angry. But, it was an accident, right? You didn't have anything to do with it, did you?"

"Tell me Ted, do you remember your argument with Randy when he told you the Stags weren't getting enough money? And all that crap about Kelly's fee and the design contract? Were you hoping it would just blow over?'

"Well, did you do anything?"

Sloane stared, unblinking, into Granger's eyes.

"I'll take that as a 'no.'" Granger rubbed his eyes. "We still don't know who leaked the article to the newspaper."

Sloane mumbled to himself and re-read the first lines in the article:

> *(Los Osos) The Los Osos Stags Lodge, subject to approval from their Grand Lodge in Chicago, intends to sell twenty-seven acres of prime beachfront property in Los Osos. The purchase price is $26 million. Ron Kelly, the agent representing the unnamed buyer, is related to the San Francisco Cicerone family—rumored to be the leaders of organized crime in San Francisco. Kelly refused to comment on pending deals but a reliable source told this reporter that a housing development is planned for over one hundred new single-family dwellings ...*

"I'm sure the source was Lismore," said Sloane. "He pissed in the soup from the beginning."

"I don't want to talk about it. You know I hate violence."

Sloane sneered. His lips curled. "You asshole, you mean it's okay when someone else facilitates it."

"It was an accident, right? Right?"

Sloane threw the newspaper on the next table. He smirked. Both men glared at each other for a while.

"Besides, anyone could have leaked the information," said Granger. "It was no secret. Your trustees passed the resolution to sell and notice went to all the members. Good heavens, we have four hundred members, including thirty new women. It could be anyone."

"My money's on Lismore," said Sloane. "He was probably trying to sabotage our plans for a sole-source deal with Monterey Construction by getting public attention. He wouldn't shut up about competition. We should never have mentioned Monterey Construction that soon."

"You're glad he's dead, aren't you? How fortunate for you."

"You mean for us, don't you? Don't forget we're in this deal together. Let's concentrate on awarding the design job to Monterey."

"The ER," said Granger, "gets to make all committee appointments. I'll appoint Mitch Mason, a Stag, as the head of a new construction committee. He knows Morty Greenspan at Monterey Construction. If you can't get the trustees to agree to the deal, maybe you can get them to delegate the authority to Mason's committee."

"What's his cut?" Sloane was concerned; more hands in the pie.

"No problem. He'll get his from Monterey and, meanwhile, he can control the info that gets given to the trustees—a single focal point."

"That's a damn good idea, Ted. Maybe we can hit him up—"

"C'mon, Jerry. Don't get greedy. Kelly will understand why Mitch has to get something from Monterey. But he's advancing us money, remember?"

Sloane nodded. He thought Kelly wouldn't give a damn and that Granger was a pussy. He wondered if he could squeeze Mason. That would be a coup, to get it from two directions. Still, Granger, to whom violence was anathema, could be a weak link. "Yeah, okay."

"According to the statutes," said Granger, "we need to replace Lismore within two meetings. He had a little more than a year to go on his term. I'm going to put up a used red Hummer for a raffle the night of that election. All the proceeds will go to the veterans. That ought to earn some good will for our nominee."

Sloane looked out the window and noticed traffic was stalled. It was just what he needed, a traffic jam on his way back to the casino in Arroyo Grande. He'd barely have time to play before he had to come back for the Lodge meeting. Too bad he didn't have a Hummer; he could just roll over the cars. "That's great, Ted," he said. "Stags are real men, and Hummers shout it to the world. Screw the price of gas. Now do us both a favor and think about the replacement. Who should we nominate?"

"Jimmy, what's his last name? Oh yes, Bateman. He's been a trustee before and he never argues with anything. He'll be a stand-up guy on this."

Sloane shook his head. "Are you certain? The man's eighty-seven. He can't find his front door anymore. Are you sure we can count on him?"

"We'll drive him to the meetings," said Granger. "He's our man. To ensure his election, I'll also get an email out to all the members telling them we need their vote, that if they want that new pool and health facilities, they must show up for the election, and support him."

Sloane grinned. More manipulation! The rules demanded that the ER preside with impartiality. He also knew that the Stags' statutes dictated that only the secretary could dispatch messages to the membership lists. "You shouldn't send that message yourself. It's a violation of the statutes."

"I'll find someone," said Granger. "He can tell them that we need Bateman because he's had great experience as a trustee. I think he built a pool once. He can be our pool expert. And we'll put up posters in the lodge and campaign in the lounge before the vote."

Sloane smiled sarcastically. "Get a pool lady to send the email. We all know why they joined the Lodge."

"Yates's term expires in another month," said Granger. "We'll have another vacancy in the trustees."

"That's good," said Sloane. "Yates is not as insistent as Randy was, but he's also being difficult about competition."

"Should we wait to approve the design job until he's replaced?" asked Granger. "I need the money—now."

"I'll give it a shot at the next trustee meeting, but, damn it, if we can't pull it off, we'll have to table it until after the general election—and that means you better be re-elected."

The men dug into their meals in silence. Sloane thought if it wasn't for a recording he'd made of that dinner with Kelly, he'd have zero leverage on the fool opposite him, or the mob. Maybe, he mused, it was time to call Kelly again.

THIRTEEN—CESSNA

Tuesday, February 12th, 2008, 4:00 PM

The Cessna 350 Corvalis flew at two thousand feet, east of San Luis Obispo. As the pilot pulled the yoke back to rise over the Los Padres National Forest, he turned to the man in the co-pilot seat. Occasional traffic flowed west below them on Highway California 58.

"Tell me more about these guys. Who's the target in the Miata?"

FBI Special Agent Fred Harris put his Nikon D100 camera in his lap. "That's Jerry Sloane. We've been tracking him since we saw him meet with Ron Kelly, Don Cicerone's nephew, and some other guys in Carmel. We're after the uncle. The old man's been in organized crime since Prohibition. His grandfather actually ran Canadian whiskey into the states in the good old days. Today it's heroin, marijuana, crack, ecstasy, and extortion, plus the traditional stuff, like linen services, girls, and gambling"

"What's your interest out here in the boonies?"

"We think a land scam is going down. We'd already seen Kelly meet with a land developer in Los Osos, and Sloane and some other guys in Carmel. In fact we have a shot of Sloane with a recorder after the meeting—we think he might have bugged the meeting."

"What's on the recording?"

"You don't need to know." Harris was being disingenuous. He also wondered what was on that recording. Harris thought Sloane had had a lot of balls if he'd recorded a Cicerone family member. If the FBI had that recording perhaps they'd have enough leverage to make Kelly give up the don.

He studied his camera and blinked several times as he flashed through the series of twenty photographs he'd taken at Carmel. The Nikon was fast—it shot three frames a second at high resolution. Harris studied the pictures on the camera's 1.8 inch LCD display. His long lens and zoom had captured Sloane, rummaging in the trunk of his Miata, as he handled a digital recording device and what looked like a microphone. They'd been lucky Sloane had parked under a high-intensity light.

Harris had a black bag operation planned to discover the contents of the recording; his boss Sam Bernini, the special agent in charge of the FBI office in San Francisco, wouldn't go for a warrant—Bernini didn't want to risk alerting the Cicerones that a task force was investigating them. But Bernini also had lusted for the information on the recording, if it existed.

He'd authorized a sneak and peek—well, Harris admitted, Bernini had said he didn't want to know, and that was authorization, sort of.

"We might also have a murder involved," said Harris to the pilot.

"You have any evidence?"

"Not really, just opportunity—and coincidence—so far. The SLO sheriff's deputies are running this down; they're pissed at us—we interfered at the inquest to cover up a determination of murder."

Harris smiled as he remembered the dance between Bernini and Deputy Mendoza, the San Luis Obispo County sheriff's deputy. Mendoza had tracked the Fibbies down by calling an organized crime task force in Los Angeles. He'd discovered the license plates on a Ford Explorer at his crime scene had come from a chop shop associated with organized crime. On a speaker phone with Bernini, Mendoza had reported that he had a possible murder and a video of a possible perpetrator. He'd said, "There were hot license plates on the guy's car, connected to the San Francisco mob. This was information circulated by you guys."

Bernini had asked Mendoza to fax a copy of the perp's picture and agreed to put it on the FBI wire. Then, after a promise of further cooperation, he'd promptly told Agent John Lewiston to go to SLO and shut down the cops' investigation. Shut down, my foot, thought Harris. It was a matter of Mendoza's honor now, according to Lewiston.

"So, who's the perp?" asked the pilot.

"The SLO cops have a security camera video of a driver who they think is the killer. We put his photo on the wire. Hopefully some local cops somewhere will recognize the guy." It was one week since Mendoza had put out the alert; Harris wondered how long it would take to get an ID.

"Where to?" asked the pilot, interrupting his thoughts.

"Put me down in Redwood City. I'll catch a cab to San Francisco." Fred took off his headset, turned off the camera and enjoyed the view.

The pilot pulled the yoke and put the aircraft in a 1200-feet-per-minute climb as they flew over the Santa Margarita Recreation Area. The hills were still green from winter rains. It was an exhilarating ride.

FOURTEEN—STAGS

Thursday, February 14th, 2008, 7:30 PM

At the bi-monthly meeting of the Stags Lodge in Los Osos, Jerry Sloane was bored. Loud rock-and-roll music, barely muffled by walls, poured out of an old jukebox in the bar and irritated him. The Stags were supposed to close the bar during Lodge meetings but no one followed that rule anymore. Sloane remembered with a smile how the Stags, who'd numbered in the hundreds in the good old days when they *did* follow the rules, would empty out of the lodge bar, hit a bar down the road, and then return for more drinks after the meetings had concluded.

To top it off, Ted Granger ran a slow meeting; most of the items were pro forma and trivial. But excitement came when Granger reported that the Grand Lodge had approved the application for a permit to sell the land and build a new lodge. There was a loud cheer. Sloane beamed as he and Granger were congratulated with applause from the floor.

Granger then moved to Sickness and Distress on the agenda. "It's my sad task," he said, "to report the death, on January 19th, 2008, of our brother, Randy Lismore. As a trustee, Randy helped close the land deal and we'll all miss him. We'll make an official record in the minutes and the chaplain will offer a prayer." He banged three times with his gavel and the audience rose.

As the chaplain spoke, Sloane's attention roamed around the meeting room. The Lodge's set of stag's antlers was parked in front of the esteemed lecturing knight. It was huge and served as an important accoutrement in every Stags' ritual. In initiation ceremonies, new members were welcomed 'under the stag's antlers of brotherly love.' What a joke, he thought, and closed his eyes while he considered his problem with Yates. Damn, he needed the man's support on the contract to Monterey Construction Company. But Yates had become aloof since Lismore had died. Sloane wanted to ram the antlers up Yates's ass.

Granger signaled the Lodge secretary to turn on the chimes. The audience remained standing for eleven tolls of an electronic clock, a standard item in most Stags Lodges which switched the backlighting on the hours of the clock on each stroke, and counted from one to midnight. The old air conditioner kicked in on the second chime and the roar of the fans, plus the rattles from the vibration of the ceiling panels, drowned out the sounds of the remaining chimes.

"In vain," said Granger, "we look for our brother. He has gone beyond the valley of the shadow of death. The light at the end of the tunnel has failed. We know him no more; but his memory shall remain forever in our thoughts."

As the meeting continued, Sloane thought back to his teenage days in Dayton, Ohio. He'd learned how to hustle craps in the alley behind Betty Greenwood's Cascade Lounge on Main Street. It was so easy when you knew the odds. He repeated them in his mind: Two to one; three to two; six to five—the odds against making the numbers were his personal mantra. Sloane still was zoned out when Granger asked if there were any candidates for new membership. This procedure was an initial screening and they wouldn't be voted on until they'd passed an investigation, but everyone knew the investigation was a sham. He'd almost nodded off again when the secretary announced, "Harry Warrener nominated by Larry Yates, Joe Becker nominated by …"

Harry Warrener? Sloane twitched. He could object or wait to see what Granger would do.

Granger thanked the secretary. He looked pointedly at Sloane. "Does anyone have any comments? Remember," he said, pointing his finger in the air, "that the oath we all took dictates that we propose for membership only those who share our values."

Yates sat opposite Sloane, watching him, so Sloane saved his objections. Hell, Sloane remembered, blackballs were rare—the last time a candidate had ever been blackballed in a Lodge vote was three years before, when the man had lied about his American citizenship.

After the treasurer's report, one member offered a resolution to donate fifty Webster's dictionaries to the fifth grade students in Los Osos Parochial School. The secretary objected on the grounds it had not been submitted to the charity committee; loud boos and hoot calls returned him to his seat. The treasurer said, "What the hell. Thirteen million dollars are coming. What's a couple of bucks?" Granger put the resolution to the floor and it was approved with one nay.

After the meeting, Sloane took Granger aside. "Shit. If we'd spoken against Warrener, it would've just raised a red flag."

"I wasn't sure either," said Granger. "But I remembered what you'd said about not needing anyone snooping around so I reminded them of their oath. You know, if you had anything to do with—"

"Will you stop dwelling on that crap?"

Granger nodded and rubbed his eyes. "We can always vote against him after the investigation."

"If we'd known he was on the list, we could've squeezed the secretary to leave him off."

"Maybe Warrener is just interested in the Stags," said Granger.

Sloane rocked on his heels. "You're a fool, Ted. It's a complication we don't need. And Yates, he's a pain in the ass." Sloane turned away in frustration. He felt a headache forming behind his right eye.

FIFTEEN—PACIFIC HEIGHTS

Ron Kelly smiled at his uncle, Don Alessandro Cicerone. He watched the don heft a large black leather satchel containing one million dollars. The men were in the don's house in San Francisco, on Jackson Street, a palatial home in Pacific Heights, just down the hill from the French and German Consulates. A Bosendorfer grand piano, sixteen feet long, sat off the entryway. A tenth century carving of *Ganesha*, the Hindu Elephant god, welcomed visitors at the bottom of a curved stairwell to the upper stories, bringing good luck to those who passed. Eleventh century wood and stone Buddha statues, from Tibet and Cambodia, flanked a roaring fireplace in the living room. Cicerone was an avid collector of Asian artifacts and a generous benefactor and contributor to the San Francisco Asian Art Museum.

The don smiled. "You're telling me the developer is paying over forty million dollars and we're only giving the Stags twenty-six million?"

Kelly nodded. "I also get a fee—one million dollars."

The don looked up. "Tell me how this deal works."

"It depends on the number of units. If it goes all the way to the construction of one hundred eight units, Hansen Property Development pays us $400,000 per unit. We pay the Stags $250,000 per unit."

"Ah, yes, I believe we've worked with Leonard Hansen before. Nice. They're privately held, with no required SEC reports."

"Hansen pays a non-refundable minimum of $21.6 million at this stage—about four million in cash; the rest in a check to my agency's escrow account. This million's sincere money. Thirteen million will go to the Stags—we finesse seven million then—eight plus, counting the sincere money."

The don smiled. "Hansen has big plans for the property?"

"I'd guess about one hundred fifty millions worth," replied Kelly.

Don Cicerone looked thoughtful and waved his hand to continue.

"These guys, Granger and Sloane—the Stags' leaders—didn't even quibble. Maybe they were afraid to negotiate over their cut, but they should have at least haggled over the price for the land. I offered the Stags a quarter million per unit and they didn't blink. They're officers, they had a fiduciary responsibility to maximize the return on their Lodge's assets."

"What did you use for bait?"

"We pay them a hundred K each, upon the sale. Hansen pays us half then and I'll transfer thirteen million dollars to the title company. Then, another half a million each is kicked back, after Hansen pays the balance. In other words, I found a way to cover the money; the kickbacks come out of the sincere money and the land deal, we don't have to front anything."

"That's almost incredible—really, very clever."

"In fact, I could probably have squeezed a little more out of the deal."

"Let's not be greedy, Ron. After all, they're a fraternal order."

Kelly nodded. The deal sounded too good to be true and Kelly hoped it would go through to completion. But there was risk; the Stags might uncover the last stage of the scam. Still, that was Granger's and Sloane's problem.

"This deal is quite impressive," said the don. "I always knew you were a producer—but I never dreamed you were so prodigious. I must admit my sister did an excellent job. After all, she married an Irishman and we haven't worked well with them since Prohibition. I wish that my children had your initiative. Congratulations. You'll be well rewarded."

"Thank you. There's been progress. The Stags' trustees have approved the request for permission to sell the land, which makes it possible to plan the replacement of the existing structure. The membership also endorsed the plan. A permit to execute the sale, and construct their new lodge, has been approved by the Grand Lodge in Chicago. This man, Thatcher, whom I met in Carmel, shepherded the proposal through the parent organization in record time."

The don stood, stoked the fire, and poured himself a cup of coffee. "Would you like something, Ron?"

"Just water, thank you." Kelly knew that Don Cicerone disapproved of alcohol or dependence on drugs. Cicerone's role model was Gaius Julius Caesar; he also had considered spirits a weakness. The don poured mineral water into a Waterford tumbler and passed it to Kelly who placed it on the coffee table.

"Ron, please use a coaster. Thatcher, is he in on the deal?"

Kelly shook his head. "No, Granger, the guy they call the exalted ruler or ER—what a goofy title, eh?—Granger was emphatic that Thatcher was an honest man."

The don raised a questioning eyebrow.

"I understand," said Ron, "that he has ambitions inside the Stags' national organization. This deal will be a feather in his cap."

"I see. It's comforting to know everyone gets something."

"Besides," said Kelly, "I figure Granger and Sloane thought they'd get more this way." He sipped his water, eyeing the don's reaction.

"Honest men are hard to find. Charities need them or we'd bleed them dry. Let's try to keep him out of this."

"I did have to apply some, er … well, I brought the consigliore into it. We had a problem. Someone spoke to the press. I asked Dominic to apply some pressure. I'm afraid his man got carried away."

"I heard about that, of course. Dominic came directly to me for my concurrence. That newspaper article was very unfortunate."

"I didn't want it to go that far."

"Ron, you see the statues of Buddha? Buddha, of course, would never have approved of actions that are sometimes necessary to bring a deal together. And, while it would be ludicrous to suggest we seek Nirvana, still—we must control our impulses. As you have just learned, unintended consequences can confound the best of intentions. I do expect you to manage the situation so that the … pressure is not necessary again."

Kelly gulped his water. How could he manage the situation? He was dealing with loose cannons. He'd told the Stags to take care of business and they couldn't handle a lousy trustee. What did the don expect? He'd brought him a multi-million-dollar windfall—these things didn't happen by accident—they often required a push. He leaned back in his chair and remembered how Dominic Franchescini had chastened him for mentioning anything related to violence in the don's home. The consigliore had said, "We don't talk about those things in this house." Apparently a million dollars in cash changed things.

"Er, yes, of course," said Kelly, eager to move on. He placed the tumbler carefully on the coaster. Too bad it wasn't vodka. "Regarding the deal, now that the Stags have permission from the Grand Lodge, they'll execute the sale. That locks up the first half of the deal and the first funds should arrive soon. We'll see a little more when I collect part of my fee from them. It's a rubber stamp."

"I take it the paperwork is under control?" asked the don.

"I believe so. There are grant deeds, preliminary title reports, and the chain of ownership to deal with, which includes the U.S. Army—they occupied the land back in the early '40s. However, the land is deserted so there's little concern about some of the inspections."

"What about environmental issues?"

"Those, if any, will be Hansen's problem. There are no gas stations or schools in the vicinity so I expect it'll be fairly simple." Kelly knew that the paperwork would be more involved—there had to be purchase orders, disclaimers, a title company report, natural hazard reports, and the like, that would pass legal tests. Some of the drawings had to mask the site development plans and hide the true value of the transaction, but he decided not to raise that issue with the don.

"What happens if Hansen receives fewer permits?"

Kelly shrugged. "Well, we do share the risk with him on the second part of the deal. But the original payment is non-refundable. If Hansen were to receive no permits, even if the deal fell apart, we'd still have our eight million and the Stags would have their thirteen million minus my fee, of course."

"Did they ask whether you receive a fee from Hansen?"

"I told them no, that I was only demanding a small fee, less than four percent, from the Stags, since they were a charitable organization."

"When do we receive the balance of the money?" To Kelly's eye, the don tried to hide a sarcastic smile.

"As I said, that's a little out in time. We'll see it when Hansen breaks ground. I've already lined up the preliminary permits for the units—I arranged a fifty grand payoff to a dyke, in the county clerk's office."

"Well done, Ron. But I'd appreciate it if you would not use those kinds of words in this home. The word is déclassé. I'm quite confident God will give those people their just reward."

That million dollar benefit had a short life, thought Kelly and he still couldn't ask for a drink. "Of course. Sorry. The only fly in the ointment is the Stags' trustees and members haven't yet approved the design or construction job for the new building, since they didn't know the price. That means another vote later."

"When do you collect your fee?"

"Well, half a million, is paid as soon as they authorize the design phase. The other half comes when they start construction of their new lodge."

"Ron, half a million dollars is a considerable sum. You wouldn't want to lose your action. I'm sure you'll work to confirm all the elements of the deal."

"Yes, of course. I'm also working to guarantee the entire job—design and construction phases—to our friends at Monterey Construction Company."

"That's quite important, Ron," said Don Cicerone. "Morty Greenspan may be a Jew, but he's proved a faithful partner in past deals. I'd hate to disappoint him or his friends in Chicago. Needless to say, we also wouldn't want to lose the grease from the deal with him."

"If all goes as planned, that, ah, grease will be another million." Kelly wondered why he was giving the don so much information. But, he was committed now. "I still have to work that part of the deal. I need to get the

Stags to approve a sole-source fixed-price contract to Monterey. To that end, Granger and Sloane have identified a pawn, a guy named Mitch Mason, who'll serve as the consultant to the Lodge and work with Greenspan. Mason is in the construction business and already knows him."

"Yes," said the don as he rose and walked to the wooden Buddha. "The Buddhists, of course, would frown upon our interest in wealth. But we mimic here, in a small way, the Holy Mother Church. This deal sounds good. You should concentrate now on the construction job. I'm relying on you. And please give my regards to your mother. Please tell her we're expecting both of you for dinner next month. It's not necessary for your father to come. The last time he was here, your Aunt Doris reported that three linen napkins were missing."

"I'll need two hundred fifty thousand dollars for the payoffs when the sale is signed. That includes the fifty for the ... ah, clerk."

"See Dominic."

Kelly nodded.

Don Cicerone reached for a *San Francisco Chronicle* on his desk. Kelly, obviously dismissed, mumbled a thank you and turned away from the desk. He rubbed the *Ganesha* on his way out of the house. He hoped he'd done the right thing, bringing the deal to his uncle. If not, he'd need all the luck he could get from *Ganesha*. He headed to Van Ness Avenue for the first bar he could find.

SIXTEEN—INVESTIGATION

The investigation meeting at the Los Osos Stags Lodge began at 5:30 PM and Harry arrived early. It was his first visit to the lodge and he wanted a feel for the property. Morro Rock, an extinct volcano dominated the entrance to Morro Bay and cast an enormous shadow across a causeway. Light from the late afternoon sun over Morro Bay flowed across deserted sand dunes and a patch of grasslands to the south. After he parked, he circled the building to enter the back door of the lodge. The siding of the building was constructed of clapboard; the paint had faded to a dirty gray. Sunlight had decomposed the boards. A plywood door with no window, faced west. A cheap cardboard sign, with red margins sporting the word 'OPEN,' was mounted with masking tape on the outside of the door.

Two men drank beer and smoked cigarettes outside the door. Harry nodded at them and pulled it open. It swung outward with a tortured groan. Absent a window, he thought it likely it had broken a few noses in its day. The inside of the door had a sign that read,

> **EXIT**
> What you do here,
> What you see here,
> What you hear here,
> Let it stay here,
> When you leave here.

The sunlight illuminated a handful of bar stools and a Route 66-era mahogany bar. Colored lights flashed on an old jukebox in one corner. *California Dreamin'*, a 1968 hit by The Mamas and The Papas, poured out of corner speakers. The backrests of the stools cast shadows on some empty beer steins and a handful of cardboard coasters were strewn across the bar. Two enormous models of football helmets with Budweiser and Bud-Light markings hovered over the bar. Several men played pool in one corner, next to a rack of warped cue sticks, and a popcorn machine bubbled with activity. One of its glass doors was open and occasional kernels flew out of the machine onto the floor. A dart board was mounted on the wall under a stag's head with a large set of antlers. The bartender, talking to two men at the right hand end of the bar, looked up and squinted in the light. "Can I help you?"

"I'm looking for the investigation meeting."

"Sure. Down to your right and keep moving."

Harry walked past a large projection TV system. A noisy air conditioning system blasted lukewarm air into the building. Harry almost tripped on worn carpeting as he entered a long musty hallway. One side of the wall displayed dusty trophies in glass cages and pictures of previous exalted rulers covered the other. Fluorescent lights with mismatched bulbs hissed and flickered while he wandered past a set of meeting rooms and offices. He stopped in the men's room for a moment and was dismayed at the condition of the fixtures—dark brown water splattered out of a broken faucet and swirled down a stained drain. No wonder they wanted to replace the building. It might not survive the next storm.

He joined four men and two women who sat at a large conference table. Later he'd learn he'd been in the Los Osos Stags Lodge card room, a site of spirited and high-stakes gin-rummy and poker games. Harry recognized two associate professors from Cal Poly and the barber, from the shop on the other side of Kuo's Chinese Laundry. He didn't know the women. A Stag, Mike Fuller, began the investigation by introducing everyone. Harry felt an immediate attraction to Janet Zimmer, a brunette, with high cheekbones, and dark, curious eyes with long lashes. She wore little make-up. He heard her tell the other woman, who seemed to have permanent frown marks etched on her face, that she worked at City Hall, in the records department. Janet wore Nike running shoes and, despite her blue running pants, he could tell she had long shapely legs. She wore a black running jacket and her hair in a pony tail. Harry thought she had a nice smile and he planned to invite her for a drink after the meeting.

The session began and Fuller reviewed their applications. The investigation consisted of going through some new questions as well as revisiting the old ones on the application form.

"The form," said Fuller, "in front of you will be compared to your application form so let's begin. First, let me thank all of you for your interest in our fraternal order. The Stags are excited to have you join and, assuming we have no problems tonight, you'll be invited to the indoctrination and initiation ceremonies over the next few weeks. Here's the first question."

Harry raised his head. Was this all there was to it? In his professional society at least there had been an educational requirement. But in the professional society, there had been no initiation. He wondered what the Stags' would be like. Harry hated initiations. When he'd gone to Boy Scout camp as a twelve year old, the older Explorer scouts, who'd managed the younger scouts from his troop, had tied him to a tree and whipped him ten times with a sheath. He wasn't going to put up with such humiliation again.

"Do you believe in God? The correct answer is 'yes.'" Fuller smiled at the group as the candidates dutifully wrote down 'yes.'

"Have you ever been a Communist? The correct answer is 'no.'"

"Have you ever been convicted of a felony? The correct answer is—"

Harry shook his head in amazement—this was an investigation?

"Are you an American citizen? The correct answer is 'yes.'"

"Excuse me," said the woman sitting next to Janet Zimmer. "Can our children bring their friends to the pool?"

Harry smiled. They were joining a charitable organization but some peoples' motives were less than altruistic. He raised an eyebrow and looked at Zimmer, who had a frown on her face, but who smiled when he made eye contact.

"The pool is reserved for members and their families," said Fuller, "but let's save those questions for the indoctrination session next week." He smiled and the woman shrugged and sank into her chair.

The group reviewed a few more questions and completed their questionnaires. Mike Fuller collected the forms and thanked everyone for coming. "We'll double check these forms and you should receive a call inviting you to the indoctrination a week from today."

After the meeting broke up, Harry snatched a peek at Zimmer's application and discovered she was forty-six years old and lived in Los Osos. That was convenient—even though she looked too young for him, she wasn't. He went out of the lodge and spotted her at the water's edge. She was in a post-stretch position, working her calves, when he caught up with her. The setting sun, just at the horizon, cast an intense red-yellow image across the water. It flashed and sparkled in the waves and ended in the surf. Gulls wheeled, squabbled, and soared over the Morro Dunes Natural Preserve.

"Excuse me, I saw you in the meeting. I'm Harry Warrener."

"I'm Janet. That silly woman—"

Harry nodded. "I wanted to ask if you'd like to have a drink some time."

She smiled and bent down to re-tie the laces on her New Balance running shoes. She looked up. "Not tonight. I have to get my run in. But maybe we could have a cup of coffee later this week."

Harry extended a hand to help her rise. "That'd be great." A firm, confident hand grabbed his and he pulled her up. She was almost his height and he liked her eyes, which sparkled mischievously.

Janet laughed. "Did you notice? The questions were so inane. And the men in the bar—they're so old. These guys are desperate for new members."

Harry grinned. "Maybe we'll bring down the average."

They picked a time for coffee in a few days and she gave Harry her address and phone number, which Harry didn't admit he'd already filched.

Harry watched her take off. She had a nice rear-end, he thought.

He went back to the car and let Thor run the beach. Behind the building, the Stags had prime beach property, marred only by a fleet of picnic tables and benches, a dirty Weber broiler, and an old red Coke machine with a lid that lifted. Harry hadn't seen one of those in thirty years. The building had a *Stags* sign, hanging crookedly from a rafter. Shells and a few dead fish and jellyfish were scattered along the shore. As he trudged around he noticed the top edge of an old concrete structure. It was near a sole grove of trees that sat high on the property and looked like an old pillbox from a World War II movie. It was a strange place for a pillbox but the overall property had to be worth a bundle in development.

He could still see Janet as she loped along the distant water's edge. He smiled. So far he'd found a promising motive for Randy's death and a woman—interesting possibilities. The sun dipped below the horizon with a spectacular blue-green flash. Harry knew it was an unusual phenomenon; he took it as a good omen. Pleased with himself, he called Thor back to the car. It was time to meet with Deputy Mendoza.

SEVENTEEN—MENDOZA

The crowd in the Black Sheep Bar and Grill, a beer and burger joint on Chorro Street in SLO, roared as Detroit scored its third goal against Colorado in a hockey game. Deputy Mendoza sat at a table on the rear patio, next to a deck heater, with a Chain Jumper Honey Blonde Ale. He waved Harry over and yelled for another. The beer tasted good but Harry nursed the drink, intent upon pumping Mendoza for information.

"Thanks for coming." Mendoza eyed Harry.

"I thought we were going to meet a week ago. It's been seven days, damn it!" Harry banged his beer stein on the table and stared at Mendoza. "My buddy's been murdered and you're dragging your feet."

"Look Warrener, we can only move so fast. So far the coroner has not called it murder. The Feds are a big problem, we're shorthanded in the sheriff's office, and we had to provide some security to the Diablo Canyon Power Plant after a terrorist threat. Take it easy."

"Randy was my friend and I want to know what happened to him."

"Well, I sure want to know. I promise we won't let up."

"We?" blurted Harry. "I could tell the sheriff wasn't on-board. You're doing this yourself, aren't you?"

"We're still tracking the guy in the car. The Feds did put his picture on the wire."

"Who owned the chop-shop—where'd the plates come from?"

"Stay out of this, Harry. We don't need civilians getting in the way."

"Whose shop is it?"

Mendoza sighed. He lifted his stein and drops of condensation dribbled across the table and onto his lap. "Ah, if you must know ...." He eyed Harry. "You sure you don't want to think about curiosity and the cat?" Mendoza raised an eyebrow.

"Tell me!"

"Okay, it's your funeral. The shop's connected indirectly to Dominic Franchescini. He's the consigliore to Don Alessandro Cicerone, in San Francisco."

Harry's eyes narrowed. "I read an old issue of the *Paso Robles Weekly Reporter* yesterday. Isn't Cicerone related to a guy named Ron Kelly?"

"You've made the connection to the land deal, have you?"

"It wasn't difficult. I can't believe Randy was involved in anything shady."

"You were SEALS together, eh? See any combat?"

Harry twirled his coaster, and then flipped it over to Mendoza. He was uncomfortable talking about Vietnam. "A little. Randy saved my life."

Mendoza turned to catch the coaster and saw a pretty girl in a miniskirt with ugly black gym shoes. "Amazing, ain't it," he said, "how they can ruin a perfect picture?"

"You weren't happy with the inquest results, were you? Is there anything that can be done to change it?"

Mendoza squinted. "The fucking Feds. They want to push the whole thing under the table to protect their own investigation. I should go to the press but the sheriff would shoot me."

"What do you know about how Randy died?"

"You want me to reconstruct the scene—as I see it in my mind?"

Harry nodded.

"You sure? It can be pretty graphic."

"I owe him. Maybe I can help."

"Okay. Randy invited Billy to lunch—you saw him at the inquest."

"Billy Lawson," said Harry.

"He told Billy to place an order and left to take a leak probably leading or following the guy from the Ford Explorer."

"I assumed that at the inquest."

That's right, but there's more. Did Randy have any trouble urinating?"

"He told me his prostate was giving him problems. The docs had said it was benign prostate hyperplasia, BPH, he was going a lot. Why?"

"Remember the footprint in the urine? I figure he was splattering. His urine was on his shoes, and on the floor next to where we found him. He might have pissed on the guy's shoes."

"Do you think it was an accident?" said Harry. "I saw that happen once during an *Oktoberfest* in Munich. An old German was clobbered by a skinhead with a one-liter beer stein for the same thing. Maybe the guy got mad and pushed Randy?"

"I suppose it's possible but, the way I see it, it was an arranged hit. I figure the guy grabbed him—"

"No way," protested Harry. "He was a trained SEAL, he'd had plenty of hand-to-hand combat training."

"Maybe so. But look at it this way. His dick was hanging out, he'd just pissed on the guy's shoes, he was embarrassed, not expecting an attack, and his hands were preoccupied."

Harry pictured the scene. Randy must have been apologizing at the same time he was putting it back in his pants. "Okay, go on."

"The killer spun him around. Randy was short, what, five foot seven? He grabbed Randy's chin, pushed him down, and broke his neck on the leading edge of the urinal wall. Lismore's glasses popped off, and he dropped to the floor with his head in the flushing water."

"My God, you didn't say that in the inquest." Harry felt a pain in his left eye. He rubbed it and quickly wiped away tears that formed in both eyes.

"His glasses were crushed. I don't see that from a man lying on the floor. I figure the other guy must have stepped on them. And then there were the shards—"

"Yes, I heard."

Mendoza nodded. "When I arrived on the scene, Lismore was dead. Billy was a mess; he could barely talk. I saw a small stain on his pants, he might have wet himself, but I didn't press the boy. I called in a 10-100 and a 10-79."

Harry raised his eyebrows.

"Those are the corpse and possible crime scene call signs."

"You figured it was a crime scene right away?"

"Have you been in that toilet? To break your neck in a fall on that wall, you'd have to be more acrobatic than Richard Nixon's secretary. It would've taken longer than the eighteen minutes it took her to erase the Watergate tapes. I was suspicious right away."

"Okay, so tell me something about Cicerone."

"He's the boss of the San Francisco mob. They're into everything from numbers, their own illegal lotteries, to drugs. They run the biggest linen and garbage collection services in town. Extortion is one of their specialties. Cicerone is also an avid Asian art collector, and gives big bucks to the Asian Art Museum in San Francisco."

"So Cicerone's connection to Randy is through the agent in the land deal?" asked Harry. "The paper said it was a twenty-six million dollar deal."

"There could be a hundred fifty million on the back side with the new housing. Did Randy ever say anything about the Stags?"

The Stags were the key, thought Harry. The Feds, the mob, the Stags, and Randy; they were all tied together in a Gordian knot.

"Not much," said Harry, "but Larry Yates, a Stags trustee—he told me that Randy had disagreed with the deal and that there was bad blood with the Stags' leaders, Ted Granger and Jerry Sloane."

"Is that so? I spoke to them in my investigation, of course, but they told me nothing except that the Stags had agreed to sell their land."

"It was over some due diligence thing related to that land deal. That ought to give you a motive and some more suspects."

"Do you know them?" asked Mendoza.

"I only saw them at the cemetery. I might have seen Sloane at the inquest. Did you notice him?" asked Harry.

"I didn't think anything of it," said Mendoza. "I assumed he was there representing the Stags."

Harry nodded. "I learned about the land deal from Yates and picked up some more details when I read the *Paso Robles Weekly Reporter*. That was yesterday at the library. What do you know about Granger?"

"He's their exalted ruler, owns a Hummer agency in Paso Robles."

"And Sloane, he's the chair of the board of trustees, right?"

The deputy said, "There's a little more than that. I understand Sloane's a big poker player. Rumor has it he's in hock to the Indians in Arroyo Grande."

"I heard he played poker at the lodge. What about Granger? Does he have money problems?"

"I don't know, but I'm sure that sales stink these days."

Harry settled back in his seat and looked around the grill. It was half-time and the crowd was quiet, into their cups.

"Tell me more about Lismore," said Mendoza. "Was he dating anyone at the time? Did he have money problems?"

Harry shook his head and reached for the beer. It was cold and condensation ran down the sides of the stein like tears, forming puddles under the glass. "Randy was not a big spender. He lived a quiet life and, while he saw a few women now and then, there were no serious relationships. As Billy said at the inquest, everyone liked Randy."

The deputy nodded and picked up a menu. "Want to join me for dinner?"

Harry, still upset, shook his head. "No, I have plans." He threw ten dollars on the table and walked out, turning right towards Marsh Street. He was convinced he had to learn more about Granger and Sloane—he decided he also had to pay more attention to Don Alessandro Cicerone.

EIGHTEEN—TRUSTEES

Thursday, February 21st, 2008, 5:30 PM

Jerry Sloane had arranged a closed meeting of the Stags' trustees. He'd booked a meeting room in the Kon Tiki Inn, on the Pacific Coast Highway (California 1), in Pismo Beach. The room was at the end of a long narrow hallway on the ground floor, cramped with a conference table flanked by a whiteboard and easel on one side, and a catering cart with ice; soft drinks; cups and glasses; and a coffee pot on the other. A window opposite the door faced the ocean to the west, which was several hundred feet down a steep stairwell from the hotel pool.

Sloane had chosen the Kon Tiki Inn for privacy. He didn't want any distraction from Stags who might otherwise sit in the trustee meeting when it met in the usual conference room at the lodge. He had one objective—to get the trustees to agree, with a unanimous vote, to bring a resolution to the floor of the Los Osos Lodge to grant a sole-source design contract to Monterey Construction Company.

He'd invited one guest to the meeting, Mitch Mason, the Stag who'd been appointed by Ted Granger, to represent the Lodge in its dealings with Morty Greenspan, the owner of Monterey Construction.

Sloane knew a unanimous vote of the trustees would be like a gut-shot draw in poker—a lousy chance to pull it off but the reward was worth the chance. Those were good pot odds. And, if he couldn't get unanimity, he'd go to a back-up plan. It was a pain but Sloane dreaded any attention dissent might generate. His plan, if necessary, was to ask the trustees to delegate the responsibility for recommending a builder to a new construction committee. Since the Stags' statutes dictated that the exalted ruler controlled all committee appointments, he and Granger could control the committee membership and pick the contractor.

Larry Yates was seated at the window end of the room, talking to Ted Granger when Sloane arrived. The ER was ex-officio; he could attend trustee meetings but not vote. Granger, Sloane assumed, was working on Yates. Thank God, Sloane thought, Randy Lismore was gone. He'd always insisted upon accurate minutes, multiple signatures on checking accounts, detailed accounting, and he'd been a stickler for following *Robert's Rules of Order.*

The remaining two trustees and Mitch Mason walked into the meeting room. Mason was sandy-haired, which matched his ruddy complexion, and was pushing middle-age. He had large shoulders from years in the construction business; his specialty was swimming pools and retaining walls. He was known among the Stags as a hothead; this opinion was reinforced by his facial expressions. He'd given up racquetball recently, due to bad knees, and his girth had grown. He reminded Sloane of a small tank and his face was flushed more than usual. Carole Greene was a fitness instructor with a slender, attractive figure; John Potempa served as the only pharmacist in Los Osos. He carried some motel brochures and mumbled a hello.

Sloane thought Greene was a lightweight but he admitted he'd like to sleep with her. She was a good looking woman with great curves and every Stag had coveted thoughts about her. He smiled when he remembered what the bartender in the Los Osos Stags Lodge had said when they talked about her. 'Every good looking woman, Jerry, is some guy's pain in the ass. Don't forget it.' He hadn't forgotten but he still looked longingly as she fetched a Diet Coke. Well, in any event, he thought, she'd support him on the vote.

Potempa was a go-along kind of guy, usually bored, and easy to manipulate. Sloane suspected Potempa had a problem with nose candy. Surrounded by drugs and compounds every day, Sloane was convinced Potempa had developed drug habits years ago. And the junkie had symptoms—his nose ran, he was a thin, skinny guy who ate sporadically, but binged on those meals; his eyes teared and he hated bright lights. Sloane had promised himself he'd never fill a prescription in Los Osos. He watched as Potempa turned the dimmer switch down and pulled the shades on the window. Still, Sloane reasoned, unless Potempa was stoned out of his mind at the moment, he could rely on his vote.

Sloane worried most about Yates, who'd been a builder, and who was familiar with construction costs. Yates had already expressed resistance to a sole-source contract and wanted some competition. Yates, like Lismore, also had complained about the lack of an appraisal when the Stags sold their property.

Sloane called the meeting to order. He waved an agreement in the air. "I have good news. Given the Grand Lodge permission, Ted and I have signed this sales agreement. We'll collect the rest of your signatures now. Coastal Title and Trust said they've received our money from the agent's escrow account. The money will be wired to us as soon as we turn over the document. We'll have thirteen million dollars in our Wells Fargo account any day now."

"That's great," said Carole. "We owe this to the hard work that you and Ted put in. The Lodge owes you its thanks." She took the document and signed it, then passed it to the others.

"Carole, no thanks are necessary. It's what we Stags do and we couldn't do it without your support."

"Don't forget Randy," said Yates, signing the agreement. "Maybe we should nominate him for Stag of the Month—it would be a fitting gesture."

"That's a nice thought," said Carole.

"It is," said Sloane. "Ted and I will make the recommendation to the committee. But, can we get down to business? I have one item. I want to get approval for a design contract with Monterey Construction Company. We need to pay the agent the first half of his fee and get moving on our new lodge building. I've asked Mitch Mason, our Stag consultant, to describe the proposal we've received."

Mason stood and dragged his hand through his hair. He looked nervous and Sloane thought Mason probably was worried about getting his kickback.

"Thanks Jerry," said Mason. "I'm excited about this proposal." He passed out copies of a two page document. "The sooner we get our lodge built, the sooner we can replace the old building and invite the scouts to meet there, and have parties for handicapped kids—my favorite charity."

"Wait a second, Mitch." said Potempa as he blew his nose. "I'm sorry to interrupt but don't we need to change the signature authorities on the bank accounts? We've never had thirteen million dollars before—I think we should increase the number of signatures required on checks. Right now we only need the treasurer and any one trustee, right?"

Sloane was startled. Potempa, the guy who couldn't count his fingers sometimes, was correct. In the past they'd never had more than a couple of hundred thousand dollars in reserve accounts and a small monthly operational account—and that was easily covered by the Directors and Officers Liability Insurance. But he didn't want to be distracted. Besides he needed to consider whose signatures he'd want when withdrawals were made. Perhaps there might be additional *opportunities.*

"You're right, John," he said, "We do need to think about that as well as how much income there is."

"Well, where's the money going?" asked Larry Yates. "We should do better than the lousy rates in money markets at Wells Fargo."

"How much interest will we make?" asked Carole.

"We need to discuss this in executive session," said Sloane. "Let's have Mitch finish his presentation and then we can close the session." He retrieved the sales document from Potempa; his signature was barely legible.

Mason's complexion deepened. He didn't look happy being cut out of the meeting. "I've been working," he said, "with Morty Greenspan on our requirements. He's prepared a proposal for a fixed price, one hundred thousand dollar study, to lay out a preliminary design for the new lodge building. His company, Monterey Construction Company, built the Monterey Aquarium, the YMCA in Watsonville, and the UC Santa Cruz stadium so we know they're qualified."

The trustees leafed through the proposal.

"Any questions?" asked Mason.

"I heard a rumor," said Potempa, "that there are cracks in the foundation of the UC stadium which appeared after that earthquake last October. Is there any truth to that rumor, Mitch?"

Mitch's face turned red. His eyes danced around the room and settled on Granger. Sloane saw Granger shake his head.

"Not that I know of," said Mason. "This is a very qualified contractor and they use only the finest materials. Further, Greenspan keeps his subcontractors very busy so he always gets good prices from them. He told me he'd treat our lodge like his own building."

"Is that why you want to go sole-source, Jerry?" asked Yates.

Mason answered first. "Look, Larry, we considered other builders and architects but Monterey is the best choice. Besides, Greenspan always gets competitive bids for the work among his subcontractors—that ought to be enough competition! He said we'd never see a change order!"

"Monterey," added Granger, "has offered to take care of us and ensure we get the best prices possible because we're a charity. They said they would build us a free parking lot and basketball court, if they get the construction contract later. And we know they can get the best prices for construction materials."

Sloane didn't like Yates's question and wanted to get to the vote. "Ted's right. The longer we delay, the greater will be the costs of materials. Thanks, Mitch. We'll take the vote in closed session. We'll give you a call after the meeting."

Mason looked quizzically at Granger, who tilted his head in agreement. Mason frowned. "Okay," he said "please support this proposal. Greenspan's waiting for a call so let me know ASAP."

Mason gathered his things and walked out quickly. Sloane didn't know the deal Mason had cut with Morty Greenspan, but he knew Mason was upset that he wouldn't hear or participate in the debate. Sloane ginned inwardly—Mason would be downright furious when he was squeezed for some money.

After Mason closed the door, Sloane introduced a resolution to give the design contract to Monterey.

"Thirteen million dollars is a lot of money," said Greene, as she waved the proposal in the air. "This proposal is only for a hundred thousand and it seems to me to be a good investment."

"Yes, it is," said Granger. "If we move fast enough, we could be in our new lodge in twelve to eighteen months."

"I have lots of questions," said Yates. "Should we start this job before we complete the land deal? How did we make the first contact with Monterey Construction? I heard what Ted said, but Mitch never answered the question. Did they put that offer for a free parking lot in writing? It sounds like bullshit to me. Shouldn't we get competition for this project even if it's small? You know Randy would've insisted on competition!"

Sloane's right leg twitched. He thought it moved faster than usual. He knew Morty Greenspan hadn't offered anything about the parking lot in writing—just platitudes to Mason and a measly two-page proposal for the design job. The terms and conditions were vanilla—they offered Monterey all the protection and the Stags little, in the form of guarantees. The Stags wouldn't even own the work product. He crossed his ankles under the table. "There's nothing in the statutes that requires us to wait until the sale closes or to go to competition or spend a lot of time qualifying companies. We have a good company here, and I want to go with them."

John Potempa surprised Sloane. He threw a Kon Tiki Inn brochure in a wastepaper basket and sat upright, with an uncharacteristic alertness. "What about our requirements? Did anyone do a marketing study?"

"We selected Monterey because—"

"Don't we need to talk about signature authorities?" asked Greene. "And will the money be insured by the government?"

"Wait a minute, Carole," said Yates. "How many members do we have anyway and how many do we want?"

"Larry," said Potempa, "what kind of members do we want? Seriously, do we want a family-oriented Lodge with kids? I'm not sure."

Sloane made eye contact with Granger. They'd lost control of the meeting and watched helplessly as the three trustees exchanged comments.

Ted Granger stood and slammed a glass pitcher of water on the table. When the trustees became quiet, he said, "Look, I know this is Jerry's meeting but please, let me speak. I'll appoint a finance committee to recommend where we place the money—T-Bills, CDs, or Ginnie Maes, and worry about the signatures. We'll even consider a temporary increase in our Directors and Officers Liability Insurance policy. And we'll set up a marketing committee to work with the house committee to study the membership question—although I thought that was settled when we brought in the thirty new members with young families. But please, let's concentrate now on the proposal that Mitch brought to us. I think it's excellent and timely."

"Well," said Potempa, wiping his nose on his sleeve, "if the ER wants it, I suppose I could go along. But Ted, you should do the market study soon."

"You should look into FDIC insurance on the money, now, Ted," said Yates. "Randy would've had a list of one hundred banks by now in which to place insured CDs. He'd have shouted capital preservation, not growth, in today's markets."

"I'll check with the treasurer and our CPAs next week," said Granger.

"Okay, John agrees," said Sloane. "How about the rest of you?"

"I'll vote yes," said Greene. She looked at her watch, frowned, and reached for her purse.

"Can't you guys wait a couple of weeks?" asked Yates. "Look Jerry, I don't want to be a spoiler, but I can't support this. My lawyer sent me an article about the responsibilities of directors of charitable not-for-profits. It said directors are obliged to exercise due diligence, make informed decisions, and to use prudent skepticism. As far as I'm concerned we've done none of that. My term expires in a month. If you want a unanimous decision, get it from the next set of trustees. I'm going to put this in writing, to the trustees in an email."

Granger blanched. "We don't need—"

"Hey," said Potempa, "write away, Larry. That'll give us time to do the marketing study and help Mitch with the requirements. We really need one. Maybe we can get some grad students from Cal Poly to help us."

"Jerry," said Yates, nodding his head, "the idea of a single focal point for questions about the design phase is good. I'm sure Mitch is qualified. But I know the business. We've talked about this before. Competition for the job will make Monterey Construction sharpen its pencil. Regarding Mitch's earlier point, I would expect competition among the subcontractors, but that's not in any sense equivalent to competition for the prime contractor. I hope the future trustees agree and I hope you'll forward my email to them."

Granger retreated into his chair. Sloane feared the trustees might simply vote no at this point in the meeting. His face flushed and his shoulders tensed. He grabbed a bottle of water, knocking down two adjoining bottles.

"All right, goddamn it. We'll wait 'till after the election."

John Potempa looked bewildered. "Jerry, please watch your language. Stags don't swear in meetings. What's the big hurry?"

Sloane flushed and felt a flurry of missed heart beats—premature ventricular contractions (PVCs). He wondered why the cokehead gave a damn what he said. Granger, whom he could see in the mirror behind the table, must have noticed his anger. Granger shook his head slightly. Sloane swallowed and forced himself to remain calm. He turned around. "Oh, of course, you're right, John. Excuse me. We'll table this until after the elections." He dropped into a seat and watched the other trustees leave the room as his pulse slowly returned to normal.

After the meeting Granger and Sloane descended a seemingly endless wooden stairway behind the motel's pool and crossed the sand to the ocean. Sloane kicked at the rocks and threw stones at the sandpipers along the shore. The sales contract was rolled up and sticking out of his back pocket.

"Take it easy, Jerry. We just have to wait a few more weeks."

"The fucking Indians don't want to wait. I owe them a bundle."

"My Hummer agency's also in trouble," said Granger. "But what can we do? We have to wait. If you'd have pushed, we'd never have gotten the unanimity we need. We might even have lost—on the record."

"What happened to the plan for the construction committee? We need to get control."

"I'll establish the committee and appoint Mitch the chairman. But the trustees tonight would have insisted the construction committee be just advisory; delay actually helps us."

"Keep Yates off that committee. Keep him off of all the committees you just promised. Email? Who needs this in writing? Son-of-a-bitch, this also means we can't pay half of Kelly's fee." Despite the cool air after sunset, Sloan's armpits were drenched in sweat. "He said he'd advance us our hundred grand when we signed the sale, but we both know that he expected Monterey to get the design job fast. Where do you think that advance is coming from?"

"He said it would come out of his own funds." Ted rubbed his eyes. "I don't know, Jerry, it's probably coming from—"

"I know where it's coming from!" yelled Sloane. He twirled around like a dog chasing his tail, grabbed the contract out of his pocket, and sat down on the sand, silent, lost in thought.

Gulls wheeled and a pelican dove into the water. A small aircraft cruised north over the beach and then turned eastward. The moon was high and clouds cast shadows on the men. A cold mist formed on the water and waves lapped at the shore. Sloane's sweat had turned into a chill and he wanted a drink.

"Okay," said Sloane, "here's what we'll do. We get Mitch to call Kelly and Morty Greenspan and tell them we're ready to deposit these papers with the title company."

"Mitch was upset when we threw him out of the meeting," said Granger. "He's going to be more than angry."

"Fuck Mitch! You call Kelly and tell him we want our money."

"What about his fee and the design job?"

"Say it anyway you like. After all, it's just a matter of weeks, like you said." Sloane stood and jammed his face close to Granger's face. "Right?"

"We're in serious trouble," said Granger, "if Monterey doesn't get the job."

Sloane sneered and barked, "Duh?" He pulled his head back. "It was Yates. Maybe he should have a heart attack before he sends the email." Sloane could imagine what would happen if the design job went elsewhere. Kelly would be out the two hundred thousand he was supposed to pay them and he might want the money back, with interest. Or, they might not see the first kickbacks until they broke ground and they'd never see the big bucks.

"Are you suggesting—?"

"I ain't suggesting anything. Just thinking out loud. We have a problem we can't talk away and a month is a long time."

"My God, Jerry, you're talking about murder. Did you have something to do with Randy's death? Forget that idea. Let's concentrate on getting Jimmy Bateman elected." Granger rubbed his eyes. "I don't want to hear that kind of talk. We wait."

Sloane shook his head. Granger had his hopes on Bateman, a guy with one foot in the grave. He fumed for a while. Defeated for the moment, he said, "Okay, we'll wait. Meanwhile, appoint me to that finance committee. Now, let's go up those damn stairs. I need a drink." Sloane was frustrated. Granger was a wuss. Half a million—no, six hundred thousand bucks—were at stake and the clown wanted to wait. The mob wouldn't wait. Sloane's recording was his only leverage. The problem was how to use it and not get killed. Still, there had to be a lot more being skimmed and he wanted some. He needed it—he now owed the casino seventy thousand. The monthly vig—the interest on the money—was ten grand alone. He'd owe them double in less than a year.

At the top of the stairs, the men paused, breathing hard. The water in the pool looked black and colder than the sea. Despite the climb Sloane was still chilled.

Granger asked, "Where you going to get a drink?"

"I'll head over to the Mission Inn; it's too cold near the ocean. You go home, Ted. I ain't in the mood for company."

"You going to take the papers to Coastal Title?"

"I'll call and make an appointment."

Granger nodded. "I'll go with you. Meanwhile, we wait for the election, Jerry!"

"That better not be a mistake—and screw that marketing committee. We'll work that later."

Sloane climbed into his Miata and threw the sales contract on the floor. Damn, he really needed to win in the poker game the next day.

NINETEEN—JANET

Harry Warrener collected two cups of coffee from the bartender at the Madonna Inn bar. He carried them to a booth in the corner, near the rear entrance to the coffee shop. He passed a deep stairwell that led to the men's room, the room where Randy had been murdered. Janet Zimmer smiled at him as he slid into the booth balancing both coffees. He shook his head clear of thoughts about Randy. "What did you think of the Stags' investigation?"

She smirked. "Investigation? I thought it was silly. The Stags seem trapped in the past. I'm surprised they accept women."

"Why'd you join?" Harry was curious. He wondered whether Janet's expectations merged with his. "I mean, I know the Stags do a lot of charitable work, but that seems the province of older folks."

"Do you want the truth or polite conversation?" she replied.

Harry smiled. "The Stags, I understand, are big on the truth. We can switch to polite later."

"Okay, I had two reasons. The planned health club facilities are very nice. I live nearby and I could walk or run to the lodge. And secondly, I'm divorced. I'm looking for a safe place to meet people, and have an occasional drink."

"You know that every Stag is going to hit on you, don't you?" Harry raised his hands in a what-the-heck gesture.

"Oh, they'll try, I guess. But I'm not a naïve little girl anymore. I can handle it and, over a little time, I'll just be one of the boys."

Harry didn't think Janet would ever be 'one of the boys,' but he kept his thought to himself. Janet asked Harry why he was joining the Stags. It was an awkward question for him. He liked the woman and didn't want to start a relationship with a lie. Plus, he'd already demanded the truth from her. To gain some time to think, he returned to the catering station and retrieved some artificial sweeteners. On his return, the stairs reminded him once more of Randy, and, as he stirred his coffee, he decided to tell a partial truth.

"One of the Stags' trustees just died, Randy Lismore. He was an old friend from the Navy—actually he was my best friend—and he'd always asked me to join."

Harry paused, swept with memories. Harry and Randy had travelled together often and visited remote Stags lodges; he smiled when he remembered visiting the Juneau, Alaska lodge with Randy and two women they'd met on a chairlift in town and getting smashed. Randy had always kidded about taking Harry to a Stags convention. He'd say "We'll hit the hospitality suites; you can have the good looking ones, if there are any." Janet was definitely one of the good looking ones.

"I guess I'm doing it, in a sense, for him."

"That's nice," said Janet, "I'm sure he would have appreciated it."

Harry nodded glumly. "What do you do in the city? I know you're in the Records Department."

"I work on building applications, permits, and recordings with the city and coordinating projects with the county. I must admit that my computer skills are not up to snuff but I'm improving. It's mostly boring work, and the money is poor, but it beats staying home and feeling sorry for myself."

"What does the city think about this new lodge building?"

"They haven't seen the plans for the Stags lodge but I know they're desperate for the new housing planned by the developer. Cal Poly places demands on the entire community and housing for the students, faculty, and staff, is always in short supply. Those new homes are needed."

"So you think the developer will have no problem getting permits?"

"I think the provisional permits have been issued for the new homes, but there still are environmental issues, construction permits and the like to get, plus at least one sensitive issue that I can think of—beachfront access. Someone's bound to complain—there's always a fight over public access."

Harry nodded. The battles over beachfront rights were legendary across southern and central California. Celebrities with beachfront homes in Malibu always had access problems with the public. He wondered if the Stags had received enough money for the land and how the new homes would be priced. Perhaps he'd buy one—he'd always wanted to live close to the water. He could throw on his dive gear and walk into the ocean. Randy, of course, would've chided him for diving alone but Randy wasn't around anymore.

He was mulling whether the tiger shark attack had been a wake-up call when Janet interrupted his thoughts. "Where are you from, Harry? Do you have any siblings?"

"I was born in Norman, Oklahoma. My parents died in a tornado when I was three. My uncle, on my mom's side, was an old Navy hand and he raised me. He made me take ROTC in school. That led to Vietnam after I graduated from the University of Oklahoma."

"I'm so sorry. It must have been sad, raised without a mother."

"I guess so. There weren't many women in my life. Uncle Red was—well let's just say he liked his beer. It didn't help my one and only marriage. Virginia divorced me when I joined the SEALS and went to Vietnam."

"I'm sorry. What was Vietnam like?"

"It was nasty. That's where I met Randy. I was wounded—I took a bayonet in my leg, but the wound healed all right. It left a hell of a scar."

"You were that close to the action?"

Harry was not happy talking about his experiences in the war. He regretted the mention of the wound. This was the second time he was evasive. He shifted in his chair and hid his mouth behind the coffee cup. "It happened on a beach."

Janet looked at Harry with what seemed like admiration.

He decided he wouldn't mention his medal. "How about you? Are you a native Californian?"

"Born and bred in Santa Barbara. I went to school there and studied Asian Art and History."

Asian art? Harry sat back abruptly.

"What?"

"Oh, I just thought Asian art's interesting, that's all."

Janet smiled. "I love it. I worked in a small museum on Carrillo Street, just downtown, and met my husband there. He was a lawyer, an assistant district attorney, in Los Angeles."

"Any children?"

Janet shook her head. "We had a son, but he died in Iraq three years ago on his second tour as a Ranger. It was such a terrible, senseless death. I wish we'd never gone into that country."

Harry didn't know what to say. He'd decided to ignore politics after he retired; he thought all politicians lied incessantly. And he was largely ambivalent over Iraq sensing that Saddam had talked himself into a war. 'I'm sorry' seemed so meaningless, but he blurted it out anyway.

"It ruined the marriage," she said. "We both blamed the other and divorced two years ago. That's when I moved to SLO. But there were some other reasons." Janet's eyes dipped, as though she were reminded of a troubling memory.

Harry decided to distract her. "My marriage was in trouble from the start," said Harry.

"What was Virginia like?"

"Beautiful. Smart. She was an engineering student, like me. She was from Phoenix, very sheltered, and she loved to party."

"And you, Harry?"

"I was serous and hated parties. I thought they were stupid—in those days everyone was on the make, before AIDS."

"Why'd you join the SEALS?"

"As I said, she liked to party—a little too much. I came home early one night." Harry smiled sadly. "Let's change the subject. I'm glad you're here. If I can ask, you look like you're in good shape. How do you keep it up?"

"I run. Four miles a day, every day. Pretty fast for an old gal, less than nine-minute miles."

Harry was impressed.

"So what do you do now?" asked Janet.

"I retired a few months ago …."

Later, Harry drove her home and asked her for a dinner date. "We could go to the Gardens of Avila on Avila Beach Drive. It's near Pismo Beach."

"I know the restaurant. It's a very romantic place. Are you hitting on me already, Harry?"

"Er. Well, I just thought—"

"I'd like to go to dinner with you, Harry. How about next week, after the Stags' indoctrination session?"

Harry felt a rush of pleasure. Janet was nothing like the women he'd met before. There'd been a girl or two on a few trips with Randy that had proved interesting but the flames had always sputtered and died out.

"I'll look forward to it," he said.

They walked through the coffee shop and out into the parking lot. Harry wondered if the motel's video cameras were recording him as he escorted Janet to her car. He wanted to kiss her and had an awkward moment when she extended her hand. But he recovered quickly and shook her hand. He opened her door, and watched as she drove out of the lot, onto Madonna Road and turned towards Los Osos Valley Road.

On the way home Harry considered the ways Janet might help him with his own inquiry into Randy's death. Cicerone was big on Asian art. Maybe they could visit the Asian Art Museum in San Francisco. Janet could give him some insights, they could check out Cicerone's contributions. Perhaps they could talk to the curator. He had a warm and comfortable feeling and he wished he could bottle it along with the air; the late breeze carried a light touch of spring. It was still winter yet Harry felt like a teenager looking forward to his first date.

TWENTY—KELLY

Friday, February 22nd, 2008, 9:30 PM

Carmel Valley, nestled between the Monterey Peninsula and the Sierra de Salinas, bristled with multi-million dollars homes. Ron Kelly's three-bedroom home on Valley Green Drive had a Jacuzzi and he'd soaked in the tub for over an hour. Now, water poured down his back under the shower from a two hundred dollar showerhead. He'd soaked in the shower for an additional twenty minutes but his back still was tense. The Stags' deal was expected to go through any day and over seven million dollars were on the line. The don would expect the money and the waiting was almost unbearable. His cell phone rang. He turned off the water, pulled a towel off the rack, and grabbed the handset from the counter.

"Kelly."

"Sloane."

"How come you're calling instead of Granger?" Ron fumbled with the towel and it dropped in a puddle on the tile floor.

"He'll call you. He gets the privilege of telling you we signed the sales doc. I want to give you a heads-up. We have a problem. There's a trustee running around complaining about our fiduciary responsibilities."

"I thought that problem went away."

"It did. But this is someone else. And he's going to put it in writing."

"So how do you get *we* have a problem?" Kelly dragged the towel across the floor with his foot.

"He says we need to get competitive bids for the design phase. It could screw up the entire deal with Monterey."

"So fix it. Cut him in. I can probably find another twenty-five K."

"This guy is not fixable," said Sloane.

"Maybe I could do fifty."

"He's not interested in money."

"Are you calling me because of the reason I think you're calling me?" Kelly felt a twinge, a premonition the deal was headed south.

"A little pressure's all that's needed."

"Why do I think I've heard this bullshit before?"

"Look Ron, it would be more useful if it came from … let's say, other people. Not as extreme as last time. Like in the movie, you know, stick a dead horse's head in his bed, or something, after a casual chat."

Kelly snorted. "You're a crazy fucker. How can you be so stupid to say something like that on the phone?"

"I'm sorry—"

"Forget this phone number in the future. I'll think about what you said."

"Thanks,"

"Yeah, fuck you."

Kelly picked up the soggy towel and threw it in the tub. He grabbed another towel from his linen closet and dried himself. The don had said to control the violence. Why couldn't these guys manage their own problems? No way would he call the consigliore again. If necessary, he'd bring it up when he delivered the money from Hansen. He looked back at the shower. Maybe another five minutes? But he'd used his last clean towel. Screw it. He needed time to think about the call and the don's admonition. He called and made an after-hours appointment with his masseuse in Carmel, just a few miles away. The massage parlor offered whole body therapy with skilled-sensitive-deep caring. It promised each client would regain comfort and ease, mobility, balance and inner calm, enhanced by the healing properties of lavender. It sounded nuts but it was consistent with the artsy-cutesy shops in town and it was just what he needed.

TWENTY-ONE—NARROW CREEK

Jerry Sloane looked at his cards. He'd played all day and it was the first decent hand he'd been dealt since he'd called Ron Kelly—a pocket pair of sevens. The game was five and ten dollars high-stakes Texas Hold'em and he was fifth after the big blind. The guy on his right had brought in the betting with a hundred dollar bet. Ten times the big blind was considered a large bet pre-flop but Sloane figured it was positional; the bettor had sensed weakness in the earlier players at the table. Sloane just called and the rest of the players dropped. There were two hundred fifteen dollars in the pot when the flop came down seven-five-five. He'd flopped a full house of sevens over fives!

Sloane felt his leg twitch. It took superhuman effort to control it. It could be a costly tell in poker; he'd struggled with the nervous habit before. Today it could cost thousands if he didn't suppress it.

The first bettor pushed out two hundred fifty dollars, Sloane raised the bet to one thousand and the player called. Sloane reasoned the other guy also had a pocket pair, which gave him two pairs. The sevens were gone so there were only two cards in the deck that could help the guy. There were over two thousand dollars in the pot. He smiled when the turn card produced a deuce. It was a rag and couldn't help the other guy, even if he had pocket deuces. When the guy checked, Sloane pushed his chips in. "All-in," he pronounced. It was three thousand dollars. The pot contained over five thousand dollars. Some bystanders drifted over to watch. The other player dithered with his cards and called, "Time."

Sloane wanted his bet called but didn't want to make eye contact, so he glanced around the Narrow Creek Indian Casino. There were three cash tables in play and the evening tournament was down to its final table; Sloane's table had the only high-stakes cash game. His hand was a lock, he thought, and he turned back to study his cards.

A loud gasp from the bystanders caused him to jerk his eyes up. The other player had pushed all his chips in. The dealer counted the stack of chips; the other player had two thousand seven hundred dollars. The dealer threw three hundred dollars in chips back to Sloane and piled all the bets in the center of the table. The pot was almost nine thousand dollars.

The players were expected to turn their cards up when it was head-to-head and there were no further bets but Sloane refused. "Just deal it out," he said.

The dealer turned the river card. It was the five of diamonds. There were now three fives on the table. Sloane smiled, the other player would have turned his two pairs in a full house of fives. They were both all in so there were no more bets. He slammed his cards face up on the table. "I win!"

The dealer reached over and turned up the other player's cards. He had an ace-five. "Four fives win," intoned the dealer. He pushed all the chips to the other player. Sloane had lost almost four thousand dollars.

He stood to leave when Red Hawk, the casino manger put his hand on Sloane's shoulder. "That's a marker for another five thousand, Jerry. You're down for seventy-five long. When do we see the money?"

"I have a hundred K line," said Sloane. "What's the problem? I've always made good before."

Red Hawk shook his head. "This is getting to be an embarrassment. It's been two months. We think you're on tilt. I need you to settle up soon. Don't take too long." Red Hawk, a large man, ground his thumb into Sloane's shoulder.

Pain flooded Sloane's mind. He twisted his shoulder and reached for Red Hawk's hand but the Indian just squeezed harder. "Okay, okay, I get the message," he mumbled.

Red Hawk turned and walked away in silence.

Sloane stumbled into the men's room and splashed cold water on his face. His shoulder still hurt. Son-of-a-bitch, he'd forgotten the fucking five. No wonder the guy had called his raise to a thousand. He'd had five's full from the get-go and probably made the same assumption Sloane had made about two pair. The poker gods had simply stuck it to Sloane.

He stared in the mirror and wondered what else he'd forgotten. The Indians weren't forgetting, that was certain.

His mind wandered back to the conversation with Kelly. He'd been right; the phone could have been tapped. Maybe he should dump that recording. He still hadn't figured out how to use it without incurring the wrath of the mob. His mind swirled between lust for more money, and fear, as he drove home.

Later, in his home office, he connected a USB cable to his digital recorder and downloaded the recording of the Rocky Point meeting onto his IBM ThinkPad T40 laptop. Then he erased the recorder. He stared at the icon of the recording on his computer's desktop. Sloane grabbed a Steuben glass paperweight, an award for a past service to the Stags; played with it, tossed it in the air, and watched it shatter on the hearth of the fireplace.

He fetched a tumbler and poured a stiff double Cardhu single malt Scotch whisky, neat, and swallowed. He couldn't stop equivocating—keep the recording and squeeze Kelly—there was no risk in squeezing Granger—or dump it? Then he remembered the five of diamonds. He grabbed the mouse, highlighted the icon, and dragged it all over the screen. Then he double-clicked and listened to the recording with Windows Media Player. The quality of the recording was good and he smiled at Granger's awkward introduction of the topic of kickbacks; he paled when he heard Kelly say "*capice*" once more. He downed another double Scotch and dragged the recording into the computer's recycle bin on the screen. That, he thought, was it—no more recording, and no more risk or foolish notions about putting pressure on Kelly. He'd just have to live with the six hundred thousand. When was the damn money going to arrive?

TWENTY-TWO—MORTY

Saturday, February 23rd, 2008, 9:30 AM

Morty Greenspan, president of Monterey Construction Company, a fifty-three-year-old ex-Chicagoan, had migrated to California when the University of Illinois tore down all the buildings in his family's neighborhood for its Chicago campus. He was reading the *San Francisco Chronicle* when his receptionist, Alice, buzzed him.

"Yo, Alice. *Qu'est que-c'est?*" Greenspan knew Alice thought that French was a flirtatious language.

"Sorry to disturb you, Mort," she said, "but that sleazy little man, Kelly, is on his way to the warehouse. He was quite rude on the phone when I told him you didn't wish to be disturbed."

Greenspan smiled. Alice was a cute, saucy, attractive twenty-year-old with a lovely figure, who was man-crazy. But, despite her attraction to men, she'd disliked Ron Kelly from the moment she'd met him.

"He should be here in ten minutes or so," she said.

"Okay, Alice, screw it. The man's a shmuck, but you have to be careful with him."

"I know. He's involved with those gangsters in San Francisco, isn't he?"

"Got to go, sweetie. Wave him in when he arrives." Greenspan smiled, hung up and threw the newspaper in the can. Rag! There wasn't a decent paper on the entire west coast. He looked out the window at the docks. Monterey Construction Company was in an old building, originally constructed to service the sardine fishing fleet, with a corrugated sheet metal roof on the edge of Monterey Harbor. It sat at the end of the longest pier in the harbor, visible from the Fisherman's and Municipal Wharves. Elephant seals romped on one of the parallel docks. Greenspan could have afforded more elegant offices in Monterey but he enjoyed the sights. There was nothing like it in the yellowed brick tenement building, with a view of the alley, that he'd grown up in on Taylor Street in Chicago. He was reflecting on his conservative politics when Ron Kelly barged in.

"Good morning," said Greenspan. "What brings you down to paradise on the Sabbath?"

Kelly dropped into a chair and reached for a cigar. "You're quite the Jew, Morty, working on Saturdays. Mind if I smoke, and fuck you, if you do." He lit the cigar. "You know that Stags job I talked to you about? There's some delay but you'll still get it."

"That's nice. How much more will it cost me?"

"Don't get smart, Morty. I know the don likes you but that could change. You wouldn't want that, would you?"

"Okay, what kind of delay?" Greenspan remembered guys like Kelly from Chicago. Greenspan had been the Jewish kid growing up in an Italian neighborhood—guineas everywhere. The Italian kids beat him up all the time, until he showed them how to boost TV sets from the rear of Apt Appliances on Roosevelt Road. After that, they'd become friendly and he still numbered among his close friends Joey "Gee" Giannotti, and some other connected guys, high up in the Chicago establishment.

"The Stags are getting half their money, thirteen million, soon."

"Mitch Mason told me. Wasn't he supposed to grease the skids—to make the design job happen?"

"The plan hasn't changed. It's still a hundred long for the design and twenty mil for the construction."

"So what's the problem?" Greenspan frowned. He wanted the job. He'd figured it would probably cost twelve million to build and three million to equip—leaving almost four million for him after he kicked a million back to Cicerone and a couple of hundred to the moron, Mason. It had sounded good. "What do we need to do to start?"

"They signed the sales contract and have your proposal to do the design and specification. But it'll take a month for them to approve the proposal. They need to swap out a trustee."

Greenspan watched a bull elephant seal mount a female. He figured it was about sixteen hundred pounds of sex. Rain began to fall but it didn't seem to daunt the animals.

"Can we do anything to make it happen?"

"No. And by the way, the deal's changed. I want one hundred thou just for me, besides, of course, the don's cut—for that I'll get you the construction permit for the new lodge building. But that stays between me and you."

Greenspan smiled to himself. Kelly was just like the kids on Taylor Street. "I can go fifty K."

"Seventy-five!"

"Sixty—but it comes out of the construction contract, not the design."

"Okay," replied Kelly. "One month. We need to pretend here, and let the trustees resolve their differences. After that, you'll have another month to do the design, and then Mason can work with them for another month so they think they're actually involved in the design. The final payment on the land deal that pays for the construction closes about then."

"We'll get started on the drawings anyway."

Kelly stood up. He left his cigar on the edge of Greenspan's desk, ashes scattered over the desk and floor. "Don't forget, that sixty K deal is between us."

"Hey, take your goddamn cigar with you. And give my regards to your uncle. Tell him thanks."

Greenspan knew the don would never hear his thanks. Not that it mattered; he knew Cicerone hated Jews in general. If it wasn't for Joey Gee and the gang in Chicago, the don wouldn't give him the time of day. He smiled when he remembered that Joey Gee had told him the don had once said the "Antichrist would come from the circumcised race." The don had read it in an Umberto Eco book and loved the expression.

Turning his thoughts back to Kelly, he muttered to himself "asshole." Greenspan was opposed to bringing family into the business; it was always a problem when you had to get rid of them. He wondered how long the don would put up with the putz.

He picked up the weekend edition of the *Wall Street Journal* and turned to the editorial pages. At least these writers knew how to think. Too bad he was a voice in the wilderness in liberal California. While he read, he reached into his desk drawer and switched off his recording devices. They fed his Dell Latitude 810 laptop and he backed them up on an external hard drive. Special recordings, such as conversations with Joey Gee or Don Cicerone, he copied onto CDs. Those were his disaster-recovery plan. Every night he encrypted the day's recordings with his private key.

He thought to himself; three, maybe four million—that'll be nice if the Stags don't screw it up. Damn charities—can't they get people who know what they're doing? Maybe he'd get an Audi S5 as a little reward, when the dust settles. After all, Joey Gee owned European Auto Works, on the north side of Chicago, and could get him a price.

TWENTY-THREE—CHICAGO

Harry Warrener eyed the blue Hummer. It sat in the parking lot of Granger's Hummer agency near the intersection of Niblick Road and Highway U.S. 101. A Ford Lincoln Mercury agency sat next door. Harry could see Ted Granger on the phone in his office, which fronted Niblick. He'd been staking out Granger for several hours. Thor, in the back seat, drooled on his shoulder; he reached for a tissue to wipe it off.

He bent down and was startled when the passenger door of his Hyundai SUV flew open. Deputy Mendoza said, "What the hell are you doing here? I told you to stay out of this."

Thor growled. Harry smiled. "Oh, it's you. I'll get out of the car, otherwise he'll bite you, or worse, drool on you." Harry stepped out of the car and walked to the curb.

"So what're you doing?" asked Mendoza.

"I just figured I'd check Granger out, see where he goes, who he meets with, you know, the usual stuff."

"I don't know! What's the usual stuff? Since when did you become a detective?"

Ever since his friend had died, thought Harry. "Look, this is personal. All I'm doing is watching, is there a law against that?"

Mendoza looked at the agency. Granger had left his office. "Get in the cruiser—I don't want him to see us talking if he comes outside. He can think someone's getting a ticket."

Harry climbed into the front seat of the deputy's rig. A shotgun, barrel up, sat in the middle of the dash. A thick wire mesh separated the front seat from the rear. He noticed the rear doors had no inside handles. On the dash was a photo of a gruff looking man wearing a baseball cap and a black windbreaker, climbing out of a vehicle that looked like a Ford Explorer. His interest piqued, Harry waved the photo at Mendoza when he jumped into the driver's seat. "Who's this?"

"Gimme that," snarled Mendoza. He reached for the picture.

"Is this the guy?"

Deputy Mendoza sighed. "That's him. We don't know who was driving the car. But this guy ain't local. His picture's been on the wire ten days or so but no one's ID'ed him.

"I'm joining the Stags." Harry pointed at Granger, who'd stepped outside, and unlocked his Hummer. "I intend to find out what Randy was doing with him and Jerry Sloane."

The two men were silent as Granger started up his engine, and pulled out of the driveway in front of Harry's car. A car passing by blasted its horn and Granger slammed on his brakes.

"Damn," said Mendoza, "he looks distracted. I should give him a ticket."

Granger's eyes flashed on the deputy's cruiser. With a sheepish grin, he completed a turn to the left and departed.

"Did he see you?" asked Mendoza.

"I don't think so. I bent down when he stopped."

"Look Warrener, you can't get involved. Even the Feds, those jerks, will get pissed off at you. Something big is cooking—otherwise they couldn't care less about this murder."

Harry's jaw clenched. He felt like arguing but knew it would accomplish little. "Can you at least tell me what else you've learned? No one knows the guy? Why are you here?"

"If I promise to give you updates occasionally, will you stay out of it and let me do my job?"

Harry knew it would be a promise he couldn't keep but he waited for a few seconds. This was it, he decided, despite the return of that old familiar smell of the jungle. The smell was just his imagination and he pushed it out of his head. He was going to find the guy if it killed him, courage or not. He knew he had to lie to make it look like he was serious. "Okay, I promise, but if you—"

"Yeah, sure" said Mendoza. "All right. It ain't a lot. The guy is likely out-of-town muscle."

Harry raised his eyebrows. "Why?"

"They went to a lot of trouble, whoever they are. Stolen plates. Probably a stolen car."

"You haven't found the car?"

"No and even if we do, I don't expect to find anything."

"So where'd the guy come from?"

"I'd think they imported someone from Chicago or New York, or maybe Kansas City. But if I had to pick, I'd say Chicago."

"That seems," said Harry, "like a lot of trouble. It sounds like they meant to kill him."

"I don't know. Getting caught on a security camera was careless. Maybe they only meant to rough him up and the guy lost control when your friend pissed on his shoes."

"And you think Chicago because—"

"Cicerone knows the guys that run the mob there. Joey Gee Giannotti is one of his oldest acquaintances. They were in federal prison together back in the '70s."

"So sooner or later, you expect to ID the guy?"

"What? You think I'll give him up to you? Revenge, Warrener—leave it to us."

Harry wondered if he had the nerve to go after the guy. It was going to take a lot, he decided, remembering Vietnam and the cloying scent of jungle vegetation that plagued him. After a pause of reflection he said, "What else?"

"Granger's agency is in serious trouble. No one wants to buy a Hummer these days. Hell, even the Arroyo Grande police chief dumped his."

"It's all tied together, isn't it?" asked Harry. "Money, the land, the mob, and these guys in the Stags."

Mendoza reached over and opened Harry's door. "Go home now, take your dog for a walk, do something, anything, but stay out of this."

"Okay, thanks."

"Watch out! Don't be a fool. You don't want to attract the attention of Cicerone's people."

Harry nodded and walked back to his car. He waved as Mendoza drove away and stood at the door lost in thought. It was time, he decided, to find out more about Jerry Sloane. If the man was involved, he'd have to confront him. That'll be the moment he knows for sure. He felt a chill in the back of his knees. Harry shook his head clear. He wanted to avenge Randy; but if he froze in a confrontation again, he'd probably die. His shirt felt clammy but this time he was going to come through. Randy, he thought, had deserved a stronger friend.

TWENTY-FOUR—EMAIL

Saturday, February 23rd, 2008, 2:30 PM

Larry Yates's email message arrived in Mitch Mason's email box at 11:00 AM. It was mid-afternoon when he turned on his computer and connected to the Internet. The message infuriated him:

> *From: Larry [LYates365@yahoo.com]*
> *Sent: Sat 02/23/08 11:00 AM*
> *To: Trustees [TR@osostags.org]*
> *Cc: mmason238@comcast.net*
> *Subject: Due Diligence*
>
> ... We are officers and any decision to give the design contract, given its magnitude to a single vendor without some form of due diligence and price validation, is unthinkable; it would be irresponsible and fails even the weakest tests of informed consent and prudent skepticism which are demanded of any director or officer. Nor has the land deal closed yet. This award would simply grease the skids for a no-compete construction job which would be an even greater insult to good business practices ...

The prick was screwing up Mason's deal with Monterey Construction. Yates wanted competitive bids for everything. Mason knew that any other firm would come in cheaper—probably half on the preliminary design and two or three million cheaper on the construction job. The Stags would have to award it to someone else and Mason's piece, which he'd negotiated with Morty Greenspan, would be in the toilet. That was two hundred thousand dollars!

Yates's email also complained about long-standing material business relationships between Kelly and Monterey, and Mason and Monterey. This, thought Mason, was exactly the kind of crap that made for lawsuits. He slammed a marble paperweight into his desk, gouging the wood. Then he slammed it again.

He picked up his phone and dialed Morty Greenspan. When Alice, Morty's secretary, answered the phone, he could hear rain thundering on the sheet metal roof of Greenspan's building.

"*Bonjour,*" said Alice, "Monterey Construction. How can I help you?"

"Alice, lose the French, it's Mitch. I need to talk to Morty."

"You know he doesn't like to take calls on Saturday."

"Alice!"

"He's busy right now."

"C'mon, Alice. I need to talk to him now! I'll take you to lunch—"

"Make it the Sardine Factory in Cannery Row."

Mason paused. Was Alice hitting on him? He had to admit she was a hot little number. He felt a stirring in his loins which almost overpowered his anger at Yates.

"Okay, the Sardine Factory. But I'm busy right now, how about in a couple of weeks?"

"That's a date," said Alice.

Despite his anxiety, Mitch grinned. "Great, put him on."

"He isn't going to be happy. He's with—"

"Alice, please; unless he's on the crapper, put him on the phone."

"Okay, but I'm not responsible."

"Just think about the lunch." Mason waited while she transferred the call.

"Jesus, Mitch," said Greenspan. "You're worse than Kelly. I have a girl up here."

"Stick it back in your pants. I need to talk to you about one of the trustees. He's messing with the deal."

"Okay, make it fast."

Mason described Yates's email. "This could cost us both a bundle. Sloane said a month. If you believe that—"

Greenspan paused for a moment. "Is this the same guy you told me about last week or have these jerks started reproducing faster?"

"Same guy, but the email is new."

"So what do you expect me to do?" asked Greenspan.

"Maybe you apply some heat. Bring in Kelly."

"Me? Not my style. I'm just a businessman. Did you talk to Granger about this guy?"

"Just about the design contract. But it wouldn't do any good; Granger may be a thief—but he's a wimp."

"All right. Let me think about it. I don't want to bring Kelly into it unless it's necessary."

Mason clicked off and walked to the window. He pictured the rain washing away his two hundred grand and that brand new Jaguar convertible over at Central Coast Motors.

He decided to call Sloane; maybe he would put a fire under Greenspan. If not, Mason might call Kelly himself.

TWENTY-FIVE—PHONE CALLS

Cold rain intensified as Ron Kelly locked the front door of his home in Carmel Valley. Rivulets of water ran down his driveway and the rain gutters roared. Despite the weather he intended to get a coffee at the Carmel Valley Roasting Company in the Crossroads Shopping Center. He'd been drinking too much, he felt, and the coffee shop served a certified organic cappuccino with coconut; maybe the organic stuff would compensate for all the booze. His home phone rang and he swore, unlocked the door, and ran back inside.

"Kelly"

"It's Mitch. Granger called me. He and Sloane collected the trustees' signatures on the sale. They delivered the sales documents in person to Coastal Title and Trust today. The officer bitched about working on Saturday but he said he'd wire thirteen million dollars to the Stags' account at Wells Fargo on Monday morning."

"It's about time. I moved those funds from my escrow account to Coastal days ago."

"What do you mean?" asked Mason. "They had to wait for the Grand Lodge and the trustees are squirrely. I just told Morty there'd be a delay on the design job."

Kelly frowned. It was time to set up the transfer to the don; four million more in cash was due the family. He'd score big points with his uncle. Still, Kelly already knew there was a problem with another trustee, from the call he'd received from Sloane, so he feigned ignorance to increase the pressure on the Stags. "What's the hold-up with the design?"

"Like I said, there's a problem on the board of trustees."

"I thought that was solved."

"It's just a matter of time until they hold a new round of elections."

"My partners don't like delays."

"Look Ron, I have my own interest in this."

"Whatever."

"Granger told me he's going to call you soon."

"I guess he wants to thank me."

Kelly heard a sarcastic snort on the phone.

"I think he wants more than that, Ron."

"Good-bye, Mitch."

Kelly set the phone down and wondered if those jerks could solve the problem. They'd been unable to convince that trustee Lismore to go along. Kelly had gone to Dominic and the consigliore had brought in a man from out-of-town. Then he'd gotten carried away. The man was only supposed to apply some muscle to Lismore. Who knew Lismore would piss on the guy's shoes? Maybe if Lismore had been taller he'd only have been roughed up when his head banged the wall. Damn! Now Kelly had a murder on his hands and the don didn't want any more. If they'd only just apply a little heat, he was sure the other trustee would back off his resistance. But the money was coming. Admonishment or not, that ought to make a difference. He called the don's home.

"This is Dominic."

"It's me, Ron."

"Yes?"

"There's a bundle of money coming, four million plus and there's three in the escrow account already."

"Your uncle will be pleased. We'll transfer those funds from the escrow account immediately."

"I may need help with another problem."

"Hang on. I'll be back in five."

Kelly waited impatiently. The urge for coffee faded. Damn, that request for assistance looked weak. He'd been rash. He'd decided to wait and then had blurted it out. A few minutes later, Dominic returned. "Okay, call when you have the money."

"Was the don upset?" asked Kelly.

"Which day will you be here?"

"I got to talk to the buyer first, call you back."

Rats, he thought. He'd be driving for two days in lousy weather. First he had to pick up the goods and deliver them to his uncle, then he'd have to drive to San Luis Obispo to *shmear* Granger and Sloane. Despite the fear that he'd irritated the don, Kelly smiled at the word; his uncle hated Yiddish expressions. First, though, Kelly had to arrange a meeting with Leonard Hansen.

On the phone, Hansen agreed to meet him the following Wednesday, the 27th, in an underground parking lot at Ghirardelli Square, on the San Francisco waterfront. After calling back Dominic and setting up the delivery date for the evening of the 27th, Kelly reached for a bottle of Irish whiskey. One drink. He deserved it; seven mil, and he was worried?

The phone rang again.

"Kelly."

"It's Ted Granger. When do we get—"

Kelly saw red. He was becoming a switchboard. He began to fear there were too many people involved.

"When do I see that design contract?"

There was an awkward pause. He could hear Granger breathing. "I'm sorry Ron. I expected it by now. We have a recalcitrant trustee, but don't worry, it'll happen. Can we get those funds now? We really need them."

Kelly forced himself to calm down. He'd have the rest of the money in two days. These guys were inept but if he wanted the next tranche, he needed to give them their kickbacks. "Thursday, SLO, Embassy Suites, breakfast."

"Thanks, Ron. We appreciate this."

Kelly hung up. He wondered, if the whole deal unraveled, would he have to kill Granger and Sloane, notwithstanding the don's admonishment. Kelly had never murdered anyone but he was complicit in Lismore's death. It was murder two already, so what were a few more?

He gulped the whiskey. Then he poured another.

TWENTY-SIX—BEACH

Saturday, February 23rd, 2008, 4:55 PM

It was an unusual day along the central coast; a warm weather front from the southwest had followed the earlier cold storm from the north. It brought rain from the direction of the Hawaiian Islands. The forecasters called it a Pineapple Express. Rain fell in thick sheets, occasionally pushed horizontal by strong gusts of westerly winds. Jerry Sloane nosed his car too far in front of the lodge and his front wheels sank into the wet sand. He slammed the Miata into reverse and spun his rear wheels until they gained traction and the car jerked backwards. A flock of gulls swept away at the squeal of the tires and flew across the lodge building. Sloane saw Ted Granger's car and stormed into the bar. The jukebox roared with another selection from its collection of '58 oldies but goodies—Little Richard's *Good Golly, Miss Molly.* The beat to the music seemed to amplify the adrenaline rush in his body. Sloane walked up to Ted Granger's stool.

"We talk—now!" he demanded. "Meet me on the beach."

"It's raining like a—"

"So what?" Sloane turned and snarled at the bartender. "Gimme a beer."

The bartender raised an eyebrow after Sloane paid and walked away. "Asshole!"

Granger nodded. "I know." He gave the bartender free drink chits for the guys at the bar, chatted amiably about the upcoming raffle for a Hummer, borrowed an umbrella from the lodge's collection by the door, and strode through the back door onto the sand.

Sloane waited at water's edge. He was soaked. He had his bottle of beer and stared at the ocean; water lapped at his shoes. A small aircraft flew over the beach, its engine roaring in the downpour.

"It's about time. I've been waiting three minutes."

"Jerry, you're too impatient. It'll kill you someday."

Sloane grumbled to himself. "What are we going to do about Yates?"

"What do you mean? Kelly's bringing the money Thursday. After the election next week, we'll have Bateman, and after Yates is replaced a few weeks later, we'll have a unanimous vote. Who cares what Yates says?"

Sloane swept water off his brow. At least in this weather there were no other people on the beach. "You fool! You're still relying on Bateman? Yates's email is a fucking red flag. Sooner or later someone will actually ask about that fiduciary responsibility and competitive bids. So far Yates has only circulated his email to the trustees and Mitch. But the man's unpredictable. What if he goes public? Hell, he might have been the one that leaked that article in Paso Robles, not Lismore. Or what if there's another leak? This place is worse than the White House."

"All right, take it easy. Let me think."

Sloane chugged his beer and threw the bottle in the water. He watched it bob for a moment. "You know, Ted, we don't know who'll replace Yates either. It could be another wild card."

The wind whipped Granger's umbrella into an inverted position; he fumbled and forced it back into a normal shape. "Jerry, you're pushing us into something dangerous. Before I consider applying the kind of pressure you're talking about, I want to talk to Yates—in private. And I should have said something to you about Randy."

"Forget Lismore. What're you going to say?" Water dripped off Sloane's nose.

"I don't know. Maybe I'll ask him to simply withdraw the email. I don't have any good reason. Perhaps he'll read between the lines and back off. Christ, it's only a design contract that we want approved now. Do you really want to kill him?"

Sloane reached instinctively into his pocket and fumbled for his recorder. But, he remembered, he'd left it back in his office when he'd deleted the recording of the meeting with Ron Kelly at Rocky Point.

"I don't want to kill him. I just want to threaten him, make him see reason. What the hell? Why should Yates care who designs the building?"

"I don't want you to do anything before I talk to him," said Granger.

Sloane walked away, kicking at the sand. "Make it fast. If we can move before the election, it'll take Kelly off our back. I'll believe the money is coming when I see it."

TWENTY-SEVEN—BLACK BAG

Saturday, February 23rd, 2008, 5:00 PM

Fred Harris's van was parked around the corner from Jerry Sloane's home, in Pismo Beach. Water pounded on the roof of the vehicle. Harris nodded at his two men, wearing dark trousers and windbreakers, as they climbed out of the van. One carried a small toolbox, the other an orange cone marker. All the men wore wireless earpieces to communicate. Harris cracked the window and lit a cigar. He puffed nervously as they dropped the cone at the rear bumper, vaulted over the side fence, and made their way through Jerry Sloane's back yard.

"This yard is a mess, Fred," said one of the men. "It's overgrown, weeds everywhere. The yard furniture is falling apart. It's a swamp out here in the rain."

"Who cares about the yard? Just get on with it."

"We're at the back door."

The van filled with blue smoke. Harris turned on the ignition to engage a fan and rolled the window down a few inches.

"Everything cool in there?" asked Fred a few minutes later. "Our spy in the sky reports Sloane just left Los Osos and presumably is en route to the casino in Arroyo Grande—you have plenty of time unless, of course, he changes in mind. They say he's soaking wet—so hurry up."

"The door was a snap."

"Take your shoes off, don't leave tracks."

"We're in the kitchen now. The place is cluttered so we need to be careful; he might notice if we move stuff around. I'll zap you when we find the briefcase."

"Don't forget to plant that bug on the phone."

"We're on it."

Harris settled back. The van had Time Warner Telecom markings and the orange cone marker was on the street. Fred hoped there'd be no nosy neighbors out walking their dogs before dinner. It was unlikely in the rain but one never knew.

"Okay, we found his home office," said a voice in Harris's ear. "Poker magazines piled two feet high and Stags documents and folders strewn all over the place. Broken glass on the hearth in front of the fireplace. The desk isn't locked—we're looking."

"We saw him put the recorder in a briefcase in the trunk of his car," said Harris.

"Okay. Maybe we found it. There's a briefcase in the closet."

"Did you find the recorder?"

"Patience, Fred."

Harris strummed his fingers on the steering wheel. He ran the wipers once and looked for pedestrians. He saw a bicyclist in a poncho coming down the street and slid down in the seat.

"Got it," said the voice. "It's an RCA Thompson digital recorder with sixteen hours capacity but there's nothing on it. Sloane must have erased it. Do you want us to grab it; see if the lab can dump memory?"

Harris pondered the question. Sam Bernini had wanted a black bag operation. That meant no traces of the break-in could be allowed. He frowned and said, "No. Anything else?"

"We're booting up his laptop. The recorder's digital, maybe he downloaded the file onto his machine."

"Well, keep looking." Damn! He needed that recording.

A few minutes later, his earpiece blurted, "Fred?"

"I'm here."

"We looked in the computer. There's a filename in the machine's 'My Recent Documents' called Rocky Point—but the file wasn't on the screen or in any of the folders. You can relax, though. We found it in the recycle bin. We listened to two minutes; it sounds like what you want. We're copying it onto a CD. The bug on his office phone is in."

"Thanks. That's great work. I'll buy the beers."

"We'll be out in five minutes. We need to put our shoes on."

TWENTY-EIGHT—INDOCTRINATION

Harry picked up Janet at her home in Cuesta-by-the-Sea, a northwestern section of Los Osos. She was dressed casually in jeans, a red cashmere sweater, and her black windbreaker. Harry wore his old professor garb— beige corduroy trousers and a sport jacket. Thor was in the back seat and Harry introduced Janet to the dog.

"He's a handsome animal. How old is he?"

"He's almost ten months. Don't worry. He's in training; he won't jump on you." Thor licked Janet's hand.

"I love dogs. Let's take him for a walk after dinner."

En route to the Stags' indoctrination session, Janet was talkative. "They just appointed a new county clerk-recorder to oversee the county records. She came to see me to talk about the interface with the city and, damn, if *she* didn't hit on me."

"What?" Harry was amazed. He'd had one coffee date with Janet and she'd been ladylike, proper, and interested in his story. He thought it was a little early in the relationship to talk about sex but she'd opened the door. "Well, tell her to get in line."

Janet laughed. "Harry, not to worry. I'm not that way. Even if I was, I wouldn't like her. She's way too aggressive."

"So it's okay? I can hit on you?"

Janet smiled. "In due time, Harry. Keep a cool tool. What happens at this indoctrination?" She reached over and grabbed Harry's hand.

Harry liked that. "Larry Yates told me that they'll show us a fifteen minute video prepared by the Grand Lodge, walk us through some protocols specific to our Lodge, and prep us for the initiation ritual. It shouldn't take more than an hour."

Twenty cars were parked perpendicular to the sand dunes that ran along the road. The lodge lights were on and a bunch of Stags stood by the entrance smoking cigars and cigarettes, and drinking beer. As Harry and Janet strolled by they heard a Stag relating a story, "… And there they were, two deputies standing right next to the ER's personal crop of pot plants, on the edge of the pool. I thought he'd shit a brick …"

Janet grinned and Harry tried to keep a smirk off his face. They entered the lodge and looked for the meeting room.

All Stags Lodge's meeting rooms were organized in a rectangular manner. Large stags' heads with impressive sets of antlers were mounted on two walls and an altar stood in the middle of the room. When the meeting opened, a large King James Bible rested on it. A star-shaped symbol hung from a cord above the altar and represented fidelity. Three sides of the room were lined with fold-down upholstered chairs.

Janet giggled when they walked in. "Gee, Harry, it looks like grown men playing at little boy's games."

Harry frowned. "Don't let them hear you say that."

After the other initiates were seated, the same as those at the investigation session, the secretary stood and welcomed them. He asked the tiler to dim the lights and began to play a videotape.

The room was hot and the air conditioner roared and drowned out the TV. Harry's chair was torn and he shifted uncomfortably. He tried to stay focused on the TV despite the presence of Janet. She wore perfume, with a light scent on her wrists that stirred his imagination.

Still, Harry was impressed by the video. The Stags had spread across the nation in a matter of a few years. Founded by a group of entertainers who called themselves *The Water Tower Boys*, the first Lodge had been established in Chicago. The San Francisco Lodge was third; the one in Los Osos was founded in 1945. The Stags raised huge amounts of money for the American veterans and pumped donations into multiple charities for children. They were extremely patriotic and dedicated to the support of their members and communities. They conducted veterans' dinners, widows' luncheons, and they provided funds to schools for supplies and books. Harry heard "Stags Care, Stags Share" several times. He liked the comment, "A Stag is never forgotten, never forsaken." The national organization maintained a magnificent and stately retirement home, in the northwest, for retired Stags.

Over the years, the Stags had established a code of law that governed their order. At the initiation, the candidates would be required to take an oath to be governed by the Stags' statutes. The initiates were assured it would not conflict with their religious or political views.

The statutes book was an inch thick and contained the constitution, by-laws, decisions, and opinions for regulating Lodge business, as well as formal methods for bringing charges against members. An entire section was devoted to the judiciary procedures, available to all members. This surprised Harry since, in his professional society—although its governing board had passed resolutions—there'd been no compilation of the decisions. Constitution and bylaws existed, of course, but the probability of bringing ethical charges against a member had been vanishingly small—in all the time Harry had been involved he could think of only one member who had been pressured to resign—over a criminal conviction. In most cases, *Robert's Rules of Order* had controlled the society's business. In the Stags' case, *Robert's* prevailed only when the statutes were silent. Harry anticipated the rules were important in the Stags and resolved to master them.

Janet asked the hours of the lodge. One person asked whether the annual dues would be reduced during the construction phase. The secretary replied that the fees would be reduced considerably, and that further arrangements had been negotiated with the local YMCA for the use of its health facilities, at a modest fee. The Embassy Suites, on the other side of Highway U.S. 101, would offer food and beverages, at discounted prices to Stags. Further, members could visit other Stags lodges such as the one in Santa Maria. The secretary waxed about other benefits when the other woman who had been at the investigation interrupted him.

"Can I bring my children's friends to the pool?" she asked.

The secretary grimaced. "We try to discourage that be—"

"Why not? I also asked last week and was told 'no.' My friends, who are new members, told me that's why they joined."

"The answer hasn't changed but I'll be happy to discuss this with you off-line." The secretary looked around. "Any other issues?"

The man from the barber shop wanted to know when the Lodge would close the building for demolition. "Will it be soon? I know the Lodge has sold most of the land."

"The complete land deal hasn't closed yet, we're still in the permit process stage," said the secretary. "We've received half the funds so I don't anticipate demolition for at least several months."

Janet leaned over and whispered, "I guess the rest of the money doesn't get paid until the environmental impact report (EIR) is completed and the builder gets his final permits."

"Maybe you'll have a chance to see the county clerk again," said Harry grimly. "You might be the first to know when the lodge comes down."

"Why don't we adjourn?" said the secretary. "Don't forget that the initiation is next week. The ceremony takes about forty minutes so please wear comfortable shoes. Gentlemen will wear jackets and ties and the ladies, please, wear business attire. Thank you."

Harry took Janet's arm and ushered her to the bar. "They said we could drink here, after we passed the investigation. Well drinks cost four bucks, let's have one."

"That woman, Harry—the one who asked about the pool. Where do people like that come from?"

"They're in the air; they're everywhere," said Harry. He quoted, he remembered, from a '60s *John Birch Society Coloring Book*. It was a caption he'd read on a blank page: 'How Many Communists Do You See?'

"I hope we're not making a mistake joining the Stags." Janet leaned over and kissed Harry quickly on the cheek.

"It sure doesn't feel like a mistake to me. That's how I met you."

"That's sweet." Janet ran her hand over the bar and noticed dozens of tiles embedded on the surface—small brass plaques that contained the names of deceased members. "Look, Harry," she said, "they've already mounted a plaque for Randy."

The bartender noticed Janet pointing at the tile. He said, "I liked Randy. I was in 'Nam too so I put the plaque right there, in the center of the bar. Jerry Sloane gave me static for displaying it in such a prominent position but I told him Randy was a war hero."

"From what I heard, Randy was a good Stag, too," said Janet. "Is Jerry?"

The bartender shook his head in disgust and walked away.

After the drink, Harry and Janet went to dinner in Avila Beach. The Gardens of Avila served in an elegant dining room. They both ordered Coriander Crusted Ahi Tuna with a bottle of 2003 Grgich Chardonnay from Napa.

It was an enchanted evening. A warm storm front had passed through and the air sparkled. The moon shone brightly through the restaurant's windows. Harry smiled and reached for Janet's hand; she responded by wrapping her hands around his. "I'm having a good time," she said. "Can we take a walk along the water?"

Harry's mouth went dry and he swallowed some wine. "The main body of the storm is due but … sure, okay, it's clear now. We'll take the dog." The inbound storm was predicted to be a strong one and Harry felt somewhat unsettled. The old, familiar scent of Vietnamese vegetation toyed with him. But he didn't want to disappoint Janet and the smell dissipated.

She grinned. "Thor is a nice dog, Harry. Does he like the water?"

"He'll splash in the surf but he's not a water hound, like a lab. Let's go." After settling the bill, he helped her with her chair and she kissed him as she rose.

Harry let the dog roam free as he and Janet walked hand in hand along the ocean. A good-looking woman, who liked his dog, was just about all a man could want. He decided the hell with the storm. Harry laughed as Thor bounded into the water, chasing a stick thrown by Janet.

Thor retrieved the stick and dropped it at Janet's feet. She snatched it and began running down the beach, Thor loped along and jumped at the stick. "Come on Harry, catch us if you can."

Harry knew he was outclassed. He watched two graceful creatures charging down the beach. He wondered what Randy would have thought of Janet. Randy would have been enchanted, but the thought of his death spoiled the moment. Then the storm began to splatter them with large raindrops and they all ran back to the car.

They drove back to Harry's house on Pastiempo Drive. He put Thor on the back deck. Harry lit a wood fire and poured some wine. He made eye contact with Janet. She smiled, placed her glass down. Suddenly, she was in Harry's arms. The contrast from that morning when he'd been alone and felt restless and melancholy was startling. This was love and he reveled in it.

To Harry's mind, time stood still, and raced, simultaneously. When he opened his eyes, he saw Thor was restless. The dog whined and ran back and forth, under the awning outside Harry's screen door. Despite the storm which had intensified, Harry smiled to himself. The dog was getting quite a show. Harry and Janet lay on a rug in front of his fireplace. They were locked in a passionate kiss, arms wrapped about each other's body, stroking, wandering, petting, exploring. The fireplace roared in defiance of the deluge outside.

"Harry, this is getting pretty serious." Janet took a deep breath.

"I know. What do you think? Should we spare the dog and move to the bedroom?"

Janet laughed and rolled on top of Harry. She pulled off her sweater, exposing still-firm breasts and an incredibly flat stomach. Harry surged with desire.

"Let's do it right here, Harry. Do you have protection?"

Blood pounding in his ears, Harry stood reluctantly to walk to the bathroom for a condom. His pants bulged and Janet put her hand there.

"I'm pretty hot. Janet. Give me a chance to cool down a little. I'll be right back."

Harry splashed cold water on his face and studied his smile in the mirror. He'd looked forward to making love to this woman since he'd first seen her. This time, though, it was different than with other women—there was more than lust involved. He marveled at the feeling. He grabbed a condom and walked slowly back to the living room, relishing his thoughts.

Janet had let her pony tail down and her hair flowed down and around her shoulders. She reached for Harry's belt as he knelt beside her.

Thor became agitated and began to whimper.

"Poor Thor," muttered Janet.

"He's going to learn something tonight," said Harry. His breath caught and he groaned with anticipation as Janet pulled off his trousers.

Later, they let the dog in the house. Thor ran around the living room, shaking water off his fur and nuzzling both of them. When Thor's nose became too inquisitive, they ran into the shower, giggling like adolescents.

TWENTY-NINE—INFORMER

Wednesday, February 27th, 2008, 9:30 AM

Don Cicerone kicked his wife's cat, Livia, out of the room. The cat was named after Caesar Augustus' wife—the woman who'd spawned generations of emperors—but fools—in the don's mind—and sat down at his desk. It had served in the stateroom of the *USS Susquehanna,* the side-wheeler flagship of Commodore Perry, when the Americans sailed their 'black ships' into Tokyo Bay in 1853. The don fancied the combination of big gun ships and Asian artifacts. He looked at his consigliore, Dominic Franchescini, who nursed a cigar and a glass of white wine. The men were discussing the don's nephew.

"How did he sound when he called?" asked the don.

"He was nervous. I believe he expected you to be thrilled about the money. But then, he said again, that we may need to apply some more heat. He didn't say to who, and I cut him off."

"To *whom*, Dominic."

"Of course, Don Cicerone. I apologize for my poor grammar."

The don nodded. "That was quite careless of Ron."

Dominic shifted in his chair. "I also thought so. But he's young and has more to learn."

"What else have we heard about the federal task force in Los Angeles?"

"Last week our informer told me they're concentrating on our family. Agents in San Francisco have the lead right now. He said there may be a recording of the Stags' land deal."

"What information do you have on this informer? What's in it for him?"

"I never met him; one of Joey Gee's men referred him. He's an FBI agent," said Dominic. "He was reassigned to San Francisco from Chicago some months ago, and had to leave an ill child behind."

"You never met him? Isn't that a little careless?"

"The child died—some blood disease. He'd requested permission to stay on the assignment but Washington refused. He wants payback, and I offered to give him several thousand dollars a month. I send the cash to a post office box in Redwood City."

"Are you certain you vetted him?" asked the don.

"He first called me after they stung the chop shop on the peninsula. I had the story checked out with Joey Gee's consigliore; so far his information has been first class."

The don drained his cup and reached for his desktop humidor. He offered a cigar to Dominic. "I believe I'll join you in a cigar. I'm touched by the story. Please send him another box of these cigars."

As he snipped the end of the Bolivar Belicoso, Cicerone reflected. The family was in a federal spotlight and his nephew had become flakey. Violence was so *passé* these days; it attracted attention and he didn't want it—especially with the task force investigation underway. But, Kelly *was* bringing in another seven million dollars.

"Do we know who they recorded?" he asked.

"As I said, they weren't sure a recording existed. But it's probably Ron—at his first meeting in Carmel with the Stags. The informer said the FBI was trying to get a copy of the recording. They think one of the Stags made it."

Smoke rings blew out of the don's mouth. He leaned back, perturbed, in his chair.

"We may have to do something about that. I know my sister and you are friends and Ron is your godson. Can I count on you, if need be, to ask him to take a trip? Perhaps it might be something more permanent."

"I'm quite fond of the boy, you know, and your sister would be—"

"Yes, Dominic, I know you've sheltered her, even before Ron was born. I appreciate that but the family must come first."

"I'm your man, Don Cicerone. However, if it were necessary, perhaps you'd permit me to ask for help from our friends in Chicago again. I've always looked after the boy, and, it would be, well … it would be complicated."

"Dominic," said the don, "the federal authorities always hassle us. This will probably blow over, especially if they don't have that recording. The amount of money the boy has brought in is quite staggering so … I'm prepared to cut him some slack—for the time being. However, to express my displeasure at this request for muscle, only you shall receive him tonight."

Dominic nodded.

"I think a small bonus in addition to the cigars to our informer would be appropriate. Please arrange it. That will be all. Thank you for your loyalty and fidelity."

Dominic nodded and the don stood and walked to his library wall filled with books about Asian art and small Han and Tang Dynasty artifacts. He reached for a copy of *Pure Land Buddhist Paintings.* The book was just the thing to relieve his anxiety about the task force.

THIRTY—CANVAS BAGS

The City was cold, damp, and a thick foggy mist penetrated to the bone when Ron Kelly drove two blocks up the Jackson Street hill from Franklin Street. Earlier he'd met Leonard Hansen in the Ghirardelli Square parking lot on Beach Street. A bunch of revelers had been shouting in front of the Buena Vista Café at the corner of Hyde Street, and Ron had wished he could stop for an Irish coffee. But he was late for his meeting. Hansen had $4.4 million in cash—the balance of the non-refundable initial payment to Don Cicerone—and it hadn't seemed prudent to stop. Indeed, Hansen had been relieved to see Kelly and to transfer the cash. He'd already sent a check for $16.2 million to Kelly's escrow account. They'd transferred the money in the lowest level of the lot. Kelly had the cash in three canvas bags stuffed with one-hundred-dollar bills in the trunk of his BMW 540i. Each bag weighed almost thirty pounds.

Funny, Kelly thought, it was cold and miserable. Why was he sweating? Was it his concern about the need for action against a trustee? He regretted his new request to Dominic for action, but his piece of the pie depended on the design contract. He'd told Morty Greenspan it could take a month to get the contract, but Kelly didn't want to wait.

The gates opened when he tapped his horn three times and flashed his headlights. He coasted down the driveway and into the garage. He parked next to a Range Rover and climbed out of the car, popped the trunk, closed the garage door, and pulled out the three bags. After counting out the cash he needed for the payoffs and placing the money back in the trunk, he left the bags on the garage floor. At the entryway to the lower floor of the mansion, he took the mansion's small elevator. It ascended slowly to the second floor.

Dominic waited and pulled open the elevator door. He escorted Kelly into the don's study. Eucalyptus logs burned in the fireplace and scented the air.

"Drink?" asked Dominic.

"No thanks. Where's my uncle?"

"He asked me to take care of any business you might have. Is the money downstairs?"

"I pulled two hundred and fifty grand out of the cash for the payoffs to the clerk in the county office and the two Stags. Otherwise it's all there."

"Good. We've already transferred the funds from the agency's escrow account."

"What about the cash?"

It's not a good idea," said Dominic, "to leave that amount of cash in the house. The first million has moved already and I'll take the rest tonight. Perhaps you can bring me up to date, in your uncle's absence."

Kelly summarized the state of the deal. "We're halfway home. The most pressing item is my fee from the Stags." Kelly swallowed, his eyes darted around the room. Then, with compressed lips and a mixed sense of reticence, hope and fear, he added, "And, uh … we have another problem, like the last one."

Dominic sat stone-faced and Kelly fiddled with a cigar during a long uncomfortable moment.

"Don Cicerone," said Dominic, "disapproves. He feels that … more unfortunate acts will call too much attention to the deal. After all, the Stags are a charity and there's already been an unpleasant newspaper article. These kinds of things are not good for business. We're fortunate that the story hasn't been picked up by the major dailies."

"Can I talk to him?"

"I'm sorry but he's not available."

"Dominic, look, I don't want to kill this guy. Maybe someone can talk some reason into him. I'm sure that if I can talk to the don everything—"

"Who said anything about kill? Must I remind you again not to discuss those things in this home? I thought you knew better."

"Sorry. Will you talk to the don?"

"I don't think that's necessary, Ron. Can I give you some advice?"

Kelly looked up. Dominic had spread his hands, palms facing in a you-need-to-hear-this gesture. He nodded.

"Ron, after your mother married that drunken Irishman, it was clear to me she'd need help with her brother. I took it upon myself to provide that assistance. Then you came along and I watched over you. You know I've always had your best interests at heart, don't you?"

"Dominic, look, I—"

"I think you might want to plan a trip to Japan. Somewhere far away, and soon. Perhaps you could take your mother. The Imperial is a wonderful hotel, near the Ginza in Tokyo, and I know a lovely *ryokan* in Kyoto; she'd love it. You could hunt for antiques, a gift for your uncle. That would be nice."

"But I just gave him over eight million dollars. And I hate the Japs."

"The Japanese are hard-working people. You give yourself too much importance. Remember, false pride or hubris, is one of the seven sins. You should know that. Even the Irish are Catholic."

Kelly leaned back in his chair. "Do I need to worry about this?"

"Not at all," said the consigliore. "It would be a good idea to let things calm down a little. Just plan to leave soon and concentrate on closing the rest of the deal without ... assistance."

Kelly nodded. "I need to get south tonight. I should leave."

"I'll walk you."

The men descended to the garage. Kelly helped Dominic move the three canvas bags into the back of his Range Rover. Then Kelly opened the garage door and climbed into his car.

"Please give my best to your mother," said Dominic. "Have a good evening."

Kelly backed up the driveway and watched the garage door drop automatically, closing off the view of the Range Rover.

As he drove east down the Jackson Street hill, he thought about why his uncle chose not to speak with him. It was a troubling sign, a lack of confidence. Dominic's recommendation to run confirmed it. He should have taken the bags with the four million dollars and run. Now he had to think about getting out of town without the money. Kelly looked in the rear view mirror but the fog obscured everything. He turned down Gough, and headed south for the freeways. Lafayette Park was a black hole on his right; it seemed to swallow him up. The fog amplified the outside sounds and Kelly heard a pack of dogs barking in the park. The dogs unnerved him. He knew the fog enveloped everything and he was invisible—it should have been a comforting feeling. Why did he feel threatened?

THIRTY-ONE—U.S. 101

Wednesday, February 27th, 2008, Midnight

Traffic was light on Highway U.S. 101 but Kelly was exhausted. He'd driven all afternoon and evening. He was angry, scared, and confused. Every now and then some northbound driver wouldn't dim his bright lights and Kelly, irritated, would shout, "Fucking asshole." He fumed. Ted Granger and Jerry Sloane had done squat about the design job and now they expected their payoffs at breakfast. He had two hundred thousand dollars, in two paper shopping bags in the trunk. The fifty thousand dollars for the clerk had been shifted to a briefcase that he'd stashed under the passenger seat.

Working south, he stopped in a rest area to take a leak. This was the way that jerk Lismore got it, he remembered. He looked around the men's room; to ensure that he was alone. He jumped when a man emerged from a stall. The man washed his hands and complained about the lack of paper towels. Kelly smiled weakly. The toilet was hot, stank of piss and other stuff, and hadn't been cleaned. The mirror was cracked and rusted. The man left as Kelly washed his hands. He looked in the mirror. The fear and tension on his face was palpable. If he wasn't overwhelmed by the stench he could have smelled it. He wondered if he'd sleep when he reached home.

Kelly began to get furious. Screw these guys, he decided. He would only give them fifty K each; they'd get the rest when he got the design contract. Maybe that would jolt them and speed up the award of the design job.

He walked back to the car with wet hands. He scanned the area for loiterers and drunks, or kids getting it on, but there was just one semi, parked a few hundred feet away. Kelly heard its engine start. Traffic whizzed by on the freeway; the headlights made tunnels that morphed into gray walls in the fog and rain. He hit the remote trunk button on his key and rummaged around in the trunk. He emptied one shopping bag and stowed the money under his spare tire. He split the remaining money into the two bags, fifty K each. He climbed back in the car and pushed it up to ninety. Usually the cops left his BMW alone at eighty. Kelly figured the hell with it. What's a ticket?

When he arrived at 2:30 AM a Miata was parked in front of his house and a blue Hummer sat in front of his driveway. The big vehicle looked black in his headlights. The car was so long it blocked access to his garage. Fuming, he stormed out and bumped into Ted Granger and Jerry Sloane.

"What the hell are you guys doing here? I thought we were meeting in SLO for breakfast."

"We want our money, Ron," said Sloane. "Time is money, they say."

It drizzled and drops of rain splattered all of them.

Kelly noticed Sloane's left leg was twitching. It made, he thought, for a nervous man. He looked at Granger.

"It's not that we don't trust you, Ron," said Granger, "but a hundred grand's a lot of money. We'd like to get it into the bank tomorrow."

"The bank?" asked Kelly. "Are you crazy? You're going to deposit it all in one swoop?"

"Well," said Granger, obviously in distress, "I thought that—"

"Keep your crap explanation. I got the money but it's only fifty K each."

"What's that? Bullshit," exploded Sloane. He advanced in a menacing fashion.

"Back off, Jerry," said Granger, rubbing his eyes. "What do you mean, it's only fifty K?"

"That's all I could get today. It's an advance, remember? I can get the other fifty when you guys sign the design deal—that shouldn't take long. Right?"

Granger rubbed his eyes again and Sloane made a fist with his right hand.

Kelly reached inside his pocket and wrapped his fingers around his car keys. "Sloane," he sneered, "if you come forward another inch, I'll shoot you."

Sloane froze. "All right, calm down. What the hell, Ron. You'd be pissed too. It's a hell of a time to tell us this."

"Sorry." Kelly turned around and opened the BMW trunk with his remote key. Relieved his bluff hadn't been called—Sloane, he knew, could beat the shit out of him—he grabbed the two paper bags and gave them to the men.

"Listen carefully. You do not deposit this all at once. Keep each deposit under ten K and spread it around. Otherwise, the Feds will spot the transactions. *Capice?*"

Both men nodded and took the bags.

Granger said, "We'll work on the design contract."

"You do that," mumbled Kelly as he slammed the trunk lid.

Kelly watched them drive away. Amateurs, goddamn amateurs. Maybe he should go to Japan. He retrieved the briefcase and took it into the house. He left the extra hundred thousand under the spare tire. If he had to run, he at least had that money—it was the first comforting thought of the night.

THIRTY-TWO—RECORDINGS

Thursday, February 28th, 2008, 12:00 PM

The weather in San Francisco had cleared. It was a bright, sunny day in the City when Fred Harris placed a CD player on Sam Bernini's desk and hit the power switch. He twirled an unlit cigar while the machine sat idle. "Sam," he said, "we copied this off of Sloane's computer Saturday. He'd dumped it in the recycle bin on his laptop computer, but the idiot forgot to empty it."

"You could have found it anyway."

"Maybe, but we would've had to dump memory and that's more involved—you wanted a black bag ops. Remember? We were moving fast and got lucky."

Harris inserted a CD containing the recording that Sloane had made at the Rocky Point Restaurant.

"So it's a land scam," said Bernini, after listening to twenty minutes of excerpts.

"This baby could make Kelly give up the don," said Harris.

"You have anything else?"

Harris dug into his briefcase. "Here's a recording we just made from the bug on Jerry Sloane's phone. It's a conversation with Mitch Mason, a Stag."

"Sloane was talking to an animal?" Sam Bernini had a smile on his face.

"Wiseass. They're both Stags—you know, like the Moose or the Eagles?"

Sam Bernini had his hands wrapped around a Quiznos sandwich. "Okay, play it."

Harris replaced the CD in the machine and pushed the key to play the recording. "The first voice is Mason's."

"We got to do something about Yates. The deal—"

"I know, I saw the email."

"That's Sloane's voice," mouthed Harris.

"I talked to Morty. I wanted him to sic Kelly on Yates."

"That," said Harris, as he hit the pause button, "would be Morty Greenspan, over at Monterey Construction."

Bernini nodded. "He's connected to Joey Gee in Chicago."

"Well, so is Cicerone," said Harris.

"I know. Who's Yates?"

"He's a trustee in the Stags."

"Have we seen this email?"

"No."

"Let's try to get it. Keep going."

Harris hit the play button and Bernini recognized Sloane's voice.

"What did he say?"

"He said he'd think about it. I called Kelly too, to report the sale was signed, like I was supposed to."

"Did you complain about Yates?"

"What do you think?"

"I think you better consider cutting me into a piece of your action if you want me to get more involved."

"What? Fuck—"

"You don't want to say that!"

Bernini took a bite of his sandwich and reached over and paused the CD player. "My, my, such language. And these guys are in a charity?"

"I believe," said Harris, with a wicked grin, "that Oscar Wilde once said 'Charity creates a multitude of sins.'" Harris pushed the play button.

Bernini smiled as the playback resumed.

"How much?" asked Mason on the recording.

Sloane's voice came through. *"Ten per cent."*

"What? That's five thousand bucks."

"I'll take it."

"So," said Bernini, "there're kickbacks on top of kickbacks?"

"Apparently," said Harris. "My bet? Mason is getting more than fifty K." He pushed the play button.

"What else did Kelly say?" asked Sloane.

"His partners didn't like delay."

"Who does? I got to talk to Granger."

"Who's Granger?" Sam munched on his sandwich.

"Ted Granger is the guy they call the exalted ruler in the Los Osos Stags Lodge. He also owns a Hummer dealership in Paso Robles; the accountants say it's in the shitter, about to close."

Bernini nodded. "That's interesting. A man without money involved with the Cicerones. Turn it on again."

"You guys have to do more than talk." Mason sounded irritated.

"Granger doesn't want to have anything to do with that kind of stuff."

"Listen here, Jerry," said Mason. *"The train has left the station. Either*

Yates gets out of the way or he gets run down. I suspect he won't be the first trustee, either."

"There's a long pause in the conversation here," said Harris. "Sam, do you remember when that sheriff's deputy, Mendoza called? The guy he was talking about was Randy Lismore, another trustee. He's dead. Mendoza thought it was a murder. Even Lewiston thought so. Now these guys are talking about pushing another trustee—Yates."

"Let's hear more," said Bernini. "What's Sloane say?"

Harris hit the play button.

"All right, I'll think about talking to Kelly."

"That's just what I want. Morty wants us to solve the problem ourselves. For five grand, I expect some progress." Mitch Mason hung up.

Harris switched off the recorder.

Bernini threw the remains of his sandwich in the wastepaper basket. "Fred, we're talking murder, tax evasion, extortion, conspiracy, bribery, and violation of the Racketeer Influenced and Corrupt Organizations Act (RICO). Can we prove any of it?"

"Mendoza's working on the murder. Right now, we have Sloane, maybe Granger, Mason, Cicerone, Kelly, Franchescini, and a guy who we think hit Lismore, in our sights. The recordings could nail some of them right away. We also put the hitter's photo on the wire."

"We following the money?"

"Trying to," said Harris. "The Stags have sold the land and received thirteen million. Who knows how much money Leonard Hansen, the developer, actually paid?"

"Anything on him?"

"We made an informal call," said Harris, "to an IRS investigator. They suspect Hansen's dirty but don't have a case. I checked our files, there's nothing on him. Still, a land deal is cooking and Kelly ain't doing this for nothing. We know, from Sloane's recording of the meeting with Kelly that his fee from the Stags is a million dollars—I'm sure there's more, somewhere."

"Is that it?"

"You have to admit—nailing Cicerone for murder would get you a promotion."

Bernini smiled and then frowned. "It would, indeed, but let's make sure it ain't two murders."

"You want me to talk to the U.S. Attorney about picking up Kelly?"

"I'll do that next week but we better get a warrant for a bug on Kelly. In fact, let's bug Granger and Greenspan. I assume you have enough to get a warrant for the tap you already placed on Sloane."

Harris smiled. "I'll need more resources."

"Call L.A."

Fred nodded and looked out the window. It faced north and he could see Pacific Heights. Beyond the wealthy neighborhood's hills were the Golden Gate Bridge and Alcatraz. To the northwest was Don Cicerone's home. He wished he had a bug in that house. Too bad those Buddha statues the don owned were priceless. Otherwise, they'd be a perfect place to drill a hole and plant a mike.

"Okay," he said. We keep the point on this investigation? What about L.A.?"

"Screw L.A.!" exclaimed Bernini. "These guys are in our territory. This'll be a good excuse to get more of that task force money."

Fred grinned. "I'll get the guys on it right away."

"Lock those CDs in the safe. We don't want to lose them."

THIRTY-THREE—BLACK BALL

The Los Osos Stags Lodge meeting was underway when the exalted ruler called upon the esteemed leading knight to report on community activities. The knight read from an endless list of DDGER visitations at ten Lodges scheduled over the next three months, ranging from Santa Maria in the south to Gilroy in the north. Ted Granger listened with glazed eyes to his knight with little enthusiasm; as ER he was required to attend every Stags district meeting he could. Some were mandatory. Most were tedious and it was a demanding load. The knight completed his recitation with an announcement that the initiation of new members was scheduled for the following meeting. Granger thanked the leading knight and banged his gavel. There were no committee reports so he moved on to balloting for candidates for new membership. Sloane had insisted they follow the statutes and vote for each candidate separately rather than in the relaxed custom that they'd developed in Los Osos, in which they voted *en masse* for all the candidates.

"Jerry Sloane," said Granger, "has asked for separate ballots for each candidate." He directed the esquire to ready the wooden ballot box used for elections.

The first candidate was Harry Warrener. Granger dropped a black ball in the hole. He heard it plop onto the floor of the box. He watched as other Stags lined up behind him to cast their vote for the new candidate. Most grabbed white balls. Granger turned away as Yates, looking strained, followed Sloane, to cast his vote.

Granger frowned. The earlier conversation with Yates about his attitude had not gone well. He'd asked, "Larry, why do we need to put the design job out to competition?"

"C'mon, Ted," Yates had replied. "You were at the meeting. I explained everything again in my email. Have you been talking to Jerry? I could tell he was pissed at my position."

"Damn it, Larry!" Granger's eyes had flashed with fury. "It's a lousy contract for a hundred thousand. Can't you just go along with us sometime?"

Yates had been startled. "Take it easy, Ted," he'd said. "What's the big deal? What's the hurry? You can always have a majority vote; elect Jimmy

Bateman and it'll be four to one. Heck, you could have had a three to one vote at the last meeting."

"I want a unanimous vote and you know it. Your email has caused all kinds of problems. Dangerous people! Don't you realize that—" Granger had stopped and rubbed his eyes.

Yates had shaken his head and walked away, looking troubled. Granger had regretted his last remark; it had been threatening. He'd sensed that he was making thoughtless remarks with increasing frequency. He'd doubted if Yates would come around. His remaining fifty thousand dollars kickback was still over the horizon.

At the ER's lectern, Granger returned his attention to the balloting. He instructed the esquire and the leading knight to inspect the ballot box and count the votes.

"Exalted ruler," said the knight, "Harry Warrener has passed with twenty-eight white balls and two black balls." Granger saw deep furls form between Sloane's eyes.

Members were asked if they wished to examine the ballot box. Hearing no requests, Granger instructed the knight to "break the ballot" and to prepare the box for the next vote. In this manner, the Lodge continued balloting on the other candidates in random order. Since each vote required resetting the ballot box, it seemed interminable to Granger, whose mind kept returning to his earlier conversation with Yates. Every few minutes the knight would announce another result: "Joseph Argento, thirty white balls …" pulling Granger back temporarily to the present and his repetitious commands to "break the ballot." Finally, the knight announced the balloting on the last candidate, "Janet Zimmer, thirty white balls, passed."

Granger struggled to focus. He rubbed his eyes and announced that he'd conduct the election for a trustee to replace Randy Lismore at the next Lodge meeting and asked for nominations. Sloane nominated Jimmy Bateman and several other members made nominations. Seconds were not required.

After congratulating the nominees and adding an extra "Well done, Jimmy," Granger told the floor he intended to donate a used red Hummer for a raffle the evening of the election. Scattered applause and cat-calls drifted through the room. "Just trying to get a good turnout," he said. "These trustee positions are important! Anyone who comes to the meeting is eligible to win the Hummer."

After another thirty minutes, in which the secretary read some thank you letters to the Lodge for charitable contributions and the treasurer asked for, and received, permission to pay a list of bills, Granger brought the meeting to an end. As he closed the meeting, Granger reminded the members of their obligation not to disclose anything of a confidential nature that had happened at the meeting. They were admonished that only Stags in good standing could receive that information.

Granger was removing his officer's regalia, a large chain similar to the chains worn by sixteenth century British chamberlains, when Sloane approached. "Did you talk to Yates?"

Granger had dreaded the question. He nodded sadly. "It didn't go well, I'm afraid."

Sloane snorted. "I told you we were wasting our time."

"Let it be, Jerry. Please. Bateman will win and we'll get the vote next month for Monterey Construction."

"We should give Yates a plastectomy!"

"What's that?"

"We insert a Plexiglas sheet in his stomach so he'll see where he's going after I shove his head up his ass."

Granger rubbed his eyes as Jerry stormed away. Sloane didn't have a sense of humor and Granger suspected Jerry really wished he could do it.

THIRTY-FOUR—DUE DILIGENCE

Thursday, February 28th, 2008, 10:30 PM

Harry and Thor returned from the latest obedience training class. The evening lesson had worked their skills as a team, jumping and weaving through an obstacle course. Some of the barriers and surfaces included tunnels, jumps and contacts which the dog had to leap, or stop on the surface. They'd practiced moving in unison and Harry was pleased with the dog's progress.

The phone rang while Harry made an omelet. "This is Harry."

"Hey, it's Larry Yates. Got a minute?"

"What's up?"

"I don't know, Harry. I think I was just threatened by Granger. I have a bad feeling—"

Harry laid the frying pan in the sink. "Say that again?"

"Granger," said Yates, "asked me to change my position on the design job. He didn't like some email I sent, and he said some, quote, dangerous people, unquote, were involved, well, I don't know, he sort of trailed off. I just didn't like it. And I wouldn't be surprised if Sloane was behind it, either—those two are joined at the hip."

"What else did he say? Anything specific?"

"No—maybe I'm being an alarmist but my heart started thumping. I thought of Randy, and decided to call you."

"All right, Larry. Take it easy. They're just anxious to get going on the new lodge building."

"I hope so. What with what happened to Randy, I thought, you know, maybe I should just go along."

Harry lost his appetite. He stood at the sink, turned on the hot water, and watched it splash on his eggs. Bits and pieces flowed over the edge of the pan and swirled down into the disposal. Randy again!

"Maybe you should agree," said Harry. "You need a design, don't you, and it's not a lot of money, right? What did your email say?"

Yates described his email to the trustees. "Due diligence, Harry—that's the point. Randy would've told them to fuck off. Maybe he did."

"Can you send me a copy of the email?"

"I'll send it tonight. I'm going to take an Ambien, maybe a double Scotch."

"Lay off the booze, Larry, and get a good night's sleep."

"Hey, wait a sec, Harry. They elected you to the Stags tonight. You received two black balls but passed anyway. Should we guess who cast the black balls?"

"Go to bed, Larry. Thanks."

As he cut the connection, Harry knew he wouldn't sleep well.

THIRTY-FIVE—YATES

Saturday, March 1st, 2008, 1:30 PM

Thor plopped on the sidewalk and Harry tied his leash to a parking meter. It wasn't necessary; the dog obeyed long stay commands. But a loose dog might intimidate some pedestrians.

Zero Matsuda stopped Harry when he walked into the Big Bear Pipe and Tobacco Shop.

"Harry-san, did you hear news?" Zero looked dismayed.

"What happened?"

"Yates-san had heart attack yesterday in shop. He's in Rossi Cardiac Center at French Hospital, on Johnson Avenue. This very bad. First Randy, then him. I concerned."

"I'm sure they're not connected, Zero." Harry wondered if that were true. Granger had placed considerable pressure on Yates at the meeting Thursday night. Harry imagined Sloane—he was the bully with the menacing bearing—contributing to the pressure. Larry had sounded terrible when he'd called.

Harry looked around the shop and walked up to Gary Walsh whom he knew loved to gossip. "Gary, were you here?"

"It was weird. A fight broke out and Larry tried to break it up."

"A fight? In here?"

"One of the guys, Matt, the religious nut—remember him? He kept yelling Jesus saved him. The other guy told him to keep his evangelist crap to himself and the next thing we knew they were going at each other." Gary pointed at a display counter. "That's how this glass display cage got kicked in."

Harry looked at the counter.

"And Larry?"

"He got in the middle of it and then grabbed his chest."

Harry turned back to Zero. "How bad is it?" he asked.

"We call paramedics and they come fast. He in much pain."

"Do you have the telephone number of the hospital?"

Harry called the nurse on duty in the intensive care unit. She said that Yates was resting comfortably, and his wife was present. But the nurse could only give medical information to family members.

Harry digested the information. Damn, those guys had pushed Yates even though they knew he had a heart condition. He shouldn't have meddled in the fight but maybe Granger and Sloane had wanted the heart attack.

Harry turned back to Zero. "*Dōmo arigatō*, Zero. I'm sure he'll be okay."

Harry forced himself to walk slowly out of the shop. These guys, he thought, were rough. He might be in combat sooner than he thought. Could he handle it? Would that yellow streak that only he knew about, make him freeze again? Thor wagged his tail as Harry untied him. No way, that wasn't going to happen—not this time. They ran the two blocks to his car on Palm Street, and roared off for the hospital. Maybe he could get a status report from Larry's wife.

THIRTY-SIX—STARBUCKS

Saturday, March 1st, 2008, 4:00 PM

The Starbucks at Mill and Toro Streets had tables scattered around an outdoor plaza. Harry and Janet, carrying coffees and a brioche, grabbed a table under a large umbrella. Thor lay in the shade cast by the umbrella—the afternoon sun was warm for early March.

"What's up, Harry? You sounded upset on the phone. Is there a problem?"

"Larry Yates had a heart attack yesterday."

"Is he okay?"

"I went to the hospital but they wouldn't let me see him. He's in intensive care. His wife said the docs called it a moderate attack and that it probably started earlier than yesterday."

Janet nodded with sad eyes.

"He called me two nights ago and told me he was under pressure from Granger over some email he'd sent to the trustees. He wasn't cooperating on the new lodge building project, just like Randy." Harry paused and stared at Janet. He was reluctant to drag her into the mess.

"What is it?"

"I'm also convinced Randy was murdered. I understand this is sudden, but I might need some help. It could be dangerous."

Janet recoiled and put her paper cup down. "Murder? My God—in SLO? Are you serious?"

Harry started with a description of his meeting with Yates three weeks earlier at the cemetery. He told her what he'd learned about Randy's death at the inquest. "There also were lots of suspicious circumstances."

"Like what, Harry?"

"Larry told me Randy was upset about the land deal. He thought the Stags were getting screwed and that there might be some sticky fingers. Larry said he also was concerned about due diligence and that he'd sent out an email to the trustees about it."

"What's it say?"

"He sent me a copy. It was fairly explicit about the fiduciary responsibilities of trustees. It's strange but the land deal was never mentioned during the inquest; I only learned about it from Larry and Max Cotton, the reporter."

"What else did you learn at the inquest?"

Janet's eyes widened as Harry described the meddling by the Feds. He went on to relate Mendoza's information about Granger and Sloane, the Cotton newspaper article, and Yates's mention of the two black balls on Harry's candidacy. "Randy's death just doesn't add up. It was no accident. And I'm pretty sure who cast those blackballs."

"My God, Harry, that's terrible. Do you think—was Yates deliberately threatened?"

He shook his head. "I don't know. But the pressure couldn't have helped. Maybe it was premeditated."

"Are you sure you're not overreacting, or jumping to conclusions?"

Harry mulled the question. It was reasonable to ask. After all, Janet hadn't known Randy; she couldn't fathom his character. Perhaps he was paranoid about the 'no' votes.

"Of course, it's possible I'm wrong," he said. "But look, Randy was a school teacher. His students considered him their friend. He wasn't entangled in any sordid affairs or an unhappy marriage. Take out love and that leaves money. The only thing I can think of that involved money was the Stags' land deal."

"I hate corruption, Harry. I didn't tell you but the event that finally triggered my divorce was when I found a large stash of cash in the house. My husband denied he was on the take, of course, but I knew he'd recently dropped some charges in a big investigation into a procurement scandal in Los Angeles."

Harry smiled grimly. The man had been a fool to throw this woman away. "I guess we've both been disappointed."

Janet smiled sadly. "On the other hand, maybe Randy's death was an accident."

"I think Granger and Sloane are in it, up to their ears. I think it involves the land—someone's skimming money off the top. Hell, for all I know, they're skimming off the sides. Will you help me?"

"What can I do?"

Harry told Thor to 'up-sit' and rubbed the dog's back. He dug a biscuit out of his pocket and let Janet give it to the dog. "I need to get into the land records. I want to see the title, the deeds, the contracts, charts, maps, anything on file in the city. And the permits, like we discussed during the indoctrination session."

Janet stared at the dog. She gave him her hand and he licked it. As she rubbed behind his ears, she said, "I want to help. That kind of corruption is unthinkable. My God, Harry, charity's the cornerstone of the Stags. But, you said it might be dangerous?"

He nodded. "There's more I didn't tell you. The mob is involved, too—the Cicerones from San Francisco."

"Cicerone? He's a big donator to the Asian Art Museum. There's a special Hiroshige and Hokusai exhibit of eighteenth century Ukiyo-e prints there, right now, that he sponsored. You say he's in the mob?"

Harry nodded and fed Thor another biscuit. "Could we go to it? I'd like to learn more about the man."

"Sure. There's a reception tomorrow night. I'll get us tickets. Now I know why you said you were interested in Asian Art. I thought you were just being nice."

Harry smiled sheepishly. "Do you think we can get into the county records?"

"I can. I may have to butter up my new so-called friend in the county clerk's office, but that ought to be easy." She frowned and paused. "Well, perhaps not so easy, but I'll see what I can do."

Harry nodded but he was worried. Snooping around could put Janet in jeopardy as well as increase his risk. If Granger or Sloane, or worse, the mob, found out he was interested in their business, they might come after both of them.

"Thanks, but you need to be careful. I'm not sure about that clerk. She might be gay but keep in mind that she could be in on it, too."

Janet nodded. She gave the untouched brioche to Thor.

Harry hoped he wasn't making a mistake. If anything happened to Janet he'd be devastated. He'd discovered that he wanted to be with her all the time; Thor helped, but in her absence Harry was lonely beyond imagination.

THIRTY-SEVEN—ASIAN ART

Sunday, March 2nd, 2008, 7:00 PM

The Asian Art Museum was situated near the San Francisco Civic Center, on Larkin Street. Recently relocated from Golden Gate Park, where it had shared quarters with the M. H. de Young Museum, the Asian's seventeen thousand pieces resided in the City's old public library building, refurbished and re-designed by Gee Aulenti, who'd also designed the *Musée D'Orsay* in Paris.

Harry admired the bright open space as he and Janet took an escalator to the third floor. Janet was eager to demonstrate her knowledge of Asian art and she'd promised a personal tour.

"We'll do a quick tour," she said, "and I'll highlight some pieces before the reception gets underway. We start here in India. The first piece is a *Ganesha*, the Hindu god with the head of an elephant and the body of a man. He's supposed to bring good luck."

"How did he get the head of an elephant?"

"His father, Shiva, cut his head off accidentally. Shiva grabbed the first head he could find, from an elephant."

Harry admired the statute. "What's that around his belly?"

"You've never heard of *Ganesha*? His mother was Pavarotti, the consort of Shiva—he was the Hindu god of creation and destruction. *Ganesha* loved sweets so much his belly burst and he wrapped a snake about it to hold it closed."

"What's he doing with his trunk?"

"Those are sweets in his hand, of course. He's grabbing them with his trunk. You know, *Ganesha*'s also known as the remover of obstacles."

That, Harry thought, was just what he needed. And the good luck, too.

The next piece was a *Linga*, a penis carved out of stone about three feet high.

"This," said Janet "is the representation of Shiva's procreation powers. It's usually the focal point in a Hindu temple; people come to worship and place flowers on it."

"I can see how men would worship it," said Harry. "Does it come in any size besides huge?"

Janet laughed. She grabbed his arm and dragged him to a Buddha with

121

Greco-Roman features. "This piece is from Pakistan, or Afghanistan, and reflects the influence of Alexander the Great."

Harry was impressed. His wonder increased as Janet pointed out elegant pieces from fourteenth century Cambodia and Thailand. When they entered the Jade Gallery she showed him some donut-shaped pieces of jade. "Three thousand and more years ago, they placed these donuts on the bodies of royalty because they thought it would preserve their bodies."

"You know your Chinese history, don't you?"

Janet beamed and dragged him into the Bronze Gallery. "The Chinese," she said, "believed that the soul went to heaven and needed money when it arrived, so they buried their princes with trees of money." She showed him an artifact which looked like a tree with leaves made out of bronze coins.

"Money, huh?" said Harry. "I suppose they murdered for money as well."

"Harry, every time a Chinese dynasty changed hands, millions of peasants died. Let's look at some Qin pieces. The Qin, or the Ch'in, were the first to unify China into an empire. They created the first dynasty."

"How many dynasties were there?"

"Many. Some of the famous are the Han, Ming, and Ching. And the empire lasted until 1912—over two thousand years. The only empire that's lasted longer is Japan's."

Janet showed him a life-size figure of a Ch'in underground army soldier that had been found in a tomb near Xian. "There were thousands of these statues in that tomb."

"Thousands?"

"Harry, during a ten year period around 220 BCE, the great emperor, Ch'in Shih-huang-ti consolidated over six different kingdoms into China. These statues were found in his tomb—they're all different and they're believed to represent the actual men in his army. Even terracotta horses were found in the tomb."

They moved through the other Chinese sections into the Korean and Japanese sections and stopped in front of some nineteenth century woodblock prints. "These are by Hiroshige," she said. "The Cicerone exhibit downstairs is filled with work by him, and Hokusai. Had enough?"

Harry smiled. His legs were tired; he was ready for a drink and to snoop around. They descended to the first floor and wandered into the Hambrecht Gallery, one of two galleries used for visiting exhibits. The walls were covered with Japanese woodblock prints.

"This," said Janet, pointing at a print about ten by fifteen inches, "is very famous. It's called *Under the Wave at Kanagawa* by Hokusai.*"

"What's that mountain?" An enormous blue wave in the picture wrapped around a distant mountain, much like one might wrap around a surfer.

"That's—"

"That is Mount Fuji, or Fuji-san, or sometimes, Fuji-yama," said a tall, distinguished man behind Janet. He was dressed in a blue Wilkes-Bashford Suit with an Hermès tie that sported small elephants and tigers.

Harry turned around. "I thought 'san' meant a person. I know 'yama' means mountain."

"Yes," the man said, "'san' means—"

"In this case the word means spirit, Harry," said Janet. "The Japanese Shinto practitioners believed local gods or spirits presided over mountains, trees, streams, and villages."

The gray-haired man smiled. "Yes, there were thousands—perhaps tens of thousands of them. I see you know your Asian art, young lady. I'm glad you had a chance to see this print—it took quite an effort to loan it to the Asian."

"Oh," said Janet, "you must be Mr. Cicerone. Harry, this is the gentleman who contributed the pieces in this exhibit."

Harry felt his body tense, but he smiled and extended a hand. "Hi. Pleased to meet you. My name's Harry Warrener."

Cicerone shook Harry's hand. "And the lady with the unusual knowledge?"

"I'm Janet, Janet Zimmer."

Cicerone grabbed two glasses of wine from a passing waiter and handed them to Harry and Janet. "Here, please. I'd join you but I only drink water." He turned to a man behind him and said, "Dominic, would you please fetch me a Pellegrino, no ice?"

Harry gulped. Both men responsible for Randy's death were there, right in front of him. He wanted to shout "These are the killers." Janet clenched his hand and squeezed hard, twice. She flashed her eyes at him, cautioning him, and he willed himself to relax.

"May I ask what you do, Mr. Cicerone?" asked Janet.

"Please, call me Alessandro—I'm named after Alexander the Great, you know."

"Thank you, Alessandro," said Janet. "I know these gifts to the museum are quite expensive. What is it you do?"

"They are, indeed, but it's my joy to donate most of them. I'm in several businesses: linen services and garbage collection."

Harry stifled a chuckle. "Sort of like Tony Soprano, is it?"

"Did you like that TV series, Mr. Warrener?" Cicerone smiled but Harry sensed tension behind his question.

"Well, I guess—"

Cicerone turned to Janet. "So, Ms. Zimmer, you seem to know your art. Where, might I ask, did you learn?"

"In Santa Barbara, at UC. I love it."

"Perhaps you and er ... Mr. Warrener would like to visit my home sometime, on Jackson Street. I have some extraordinary Buddhas there."

"I've heard, Mr. Cicerone. Your generosity, and your interest in Asian art, is very well known."

"You might be surprised to learn that I have a recent addition, an astonishing Tang camel, in the sansei multi-colors—it's quite large."

"Oh, I'd love to see it," said Janet. "Yes, we'd like to visit, wouldn't we, Harry?"

Harry forced out a smile.

Cicerone presented Janet a card. "Please call. My aide, Mr. Franchescini, would be delighted to set a time." Cicerone took his glass of Pellegrino from Franchescini. "Nice meeting you, please enjoy the exhibit."

Harry nodded as Janet smiled sweetly. As Cicerone left Harry grabbed her arm and pulled her over to a water fountain. "You want to go to his house?"

"Don't you?"

Harry thought for a moment. "Yeah, I guess I do."

"You know what Harry? This is exciting and a turn-on. Let's hurry through the rest of the exhibit and check into the hotel."

Later, they walked out of the museum, crossed Larkin, and descended into the Civic Center underground parking lot. Thor greeted them as they opened the door. "Let's take a walk first," said Harry. "He needs a break and I need to think."

THIRTY-EIGHT—UNION SQUARE

After the walk Harry drove to San Francisco's Union Square. He parked on the roof of the lot at Sutter and Stockton streets. He and Janet let Thor out of the car, fetched two small bags, and walked to the elevator. The foyer and the elevator stank of piss and beer. As the door opened at ground level, a drunken panhandler blocked their exit. Harry moved to sidestep him but the man spit in Harry's ear. Thor, who'd had a controlled growl in his throat, erupted in a roar and lunged at the drunk's throat. Harry pulled the dog back and stared at the man, lying on the floor in a fresh pool of urine.

"Should I report this?" asked Harry.

"Fuck ya," mumbled the panhandler and curled up in a ball in the corner.

"Let it be," said Janet. "There's no harm and the man's humiliated himself."

"It's disgusting," said Harry. "They pee in the bus stops, defecate on the sidewalks, and all the City cares about is providing a sanctuary to illegal aliens. It's a terrible thing to show tourists."

"C'mon Harry," she said. "And hold onto Thor. He looks ready to go for the man's jugular."

Harry studied Thor. The dog was poised ready to launch himself. Thor's attention was riveted on a perceived threat. At last, Harry thought, he had the ally he'd lusted for in Vietnam. But, he realized, he needed more work with the dog to manage his instincts. He nodded and led Thor out of the lot with Janet following. They crossed Sutter Street and walked to the Campton Place, a luxury hotel on Stockton Street, opposite the Hyatt Union Square.

A doorman in fine livery opened the door for them and they strolled though a narrow foyer, flanked by a boutique bar on their right and the check-in counters on their left. A receptionist stared at Thor. Harry walked directly up to her.

"Reservations for Warrener," said Harry, "for two and ... I booked for the dog."

"Yes, Mr. Warrener. However, there's a non-refundable fee of one hundred dollars for your dog."

Harry nodded and the bellman escorted them to a room on the fourteenth floor. It was a deluxe king with a western view. The Hyatt, across Stockton Street, dominated the sights but Harry could see the northeast corner of Union Square, with its sparkling nighttime lights.

Janet walked up behind Harry and wrapped her arms around him. "Make love to me, Harry," she whispered as she nibbled at his right ear.

He turned and kissed her. His hands slipped through her blouse and explored her back and then slid down to her hips. She could feel the urgency in his touch as she pressed into him.

"Let's put the dog in the bathroom this time," she said.

Janet stripped off her clothes as Harry locked up Thor. She threw herself on an enormous California king-sized bed and opened her arms to Harry, who fell into the bed as his pants dropped. Laughing, she nuzzled his chest and began sliding down his body.

"Slowly, Janet. I want to do this slowly. I think I'm in love with you."

"It's special for me, too, Harry." She rubbed the scar on his leg, then kissed it and ran her tongue over it."

Harry, fully erect, felt a pang of guilt. "There's something I have to tell you, now."

Janet raised her head with a curious look.

"I was a coward in Vietnam and I let down my buddies. That's how I earned the scar. I always wanted to tell Randy the truth but I was afraid he'd hate me."

"You're no coward, Harry. I could tell the way you talked to Mr. Cicerone. Somehow I suspect Randy knew what happened and he loved you anyway. I think I love you."

Janet moved forward and her mouth sought his, as their bodies coupled hungrily.

THIRTY-NINE—C-4

The Marina Green sits at the northern edge of the San Francisco waterfront. Harry parked facing the water. The fog was worst in San Francisco in the summer but no traces lingered this winter morning. It was clear, the sky blue, few clouds, and the air had a freshness that came from an earlier mist. To his right in the bay was the former prison island of Alcatraz. In front of Harry, a small flotilla of sailboats from the Saint Francis Yacht Club tacked in the bay. The Golden Gate Bridge dominated Harry's view to the left.

"I'm going to run Thor to the bridge," said Janet. "It's about four miles round trip; that's a little over a half an hour. Do you want to wait and grab a coffee at the kiosk?"

"You guys go ahead. I'm going to take a quick ride over to Pacific Heights. I want to check out Cicerone's house on Jackson."

"Harry, don't—"

"Not to worry. I just want to get the lay of the land."

He watched them run west until they disappeared in a sea of walkers and joggers. Thor ran at Janet's side and ignored the other dogs that roamed the trails and the beach.

Harry drove over to Gough Street and took it south to Jackson Street. He turned right and worked his way up Cathedral Hill, which peaked to his left. He paused in front of Cicerone's home; parking on the street was permitted most of the time. He saw a Range Rover, parked at a steep angle in the driveway. The car, he thought, belonged to Cicerone's consigliore, Franchescini. Cicerone, Harry reasoned, would have a Rolls or a Bentley. He studied the gate and the side yard. There was a path to a small house in the rear. Two men smoked in the yard. They wore zipped-up windbreakers and were likely Cicerone's bodyguards. Harry hadn't noticed them at the museum.

He fantasized that he had a pound of C-4 explosives; he'd just slip it in the rear right wheel well of the Range Rover and wire it up to the brakes. Maybe he'd get the don. His musings were interrupted when the garage doors began to rise and he saw the consigliore exit the building and walk to the car. Harry pulled away. Damn, he thought, he hoped he hadn't been seen. He pulled over and watched as the Range Rover turned right and headed west, past him, on Jackson Street. Apparently the car did belong to Franchescini.

Janet and Thor waited at the Marina Green when he returned. Janet pulled a towel out of the car and wiped herself down while Thor lapped at some water from a bottle in Harry's hand.

"What'd you find?" asked Janet.

"The place is enormous. I saw some bodyguards."

Janet's lips pouted. "This is getting scary, Harry. Are you sure you want to pursue this investigation?"

Harry wiped his hands on the towel. "I don't have a choice. If I let it drop, I'll never forgive myself. I've been miserable for over thirty years and I have to prove I can do it." He wondered if he really meant it.

"Okay," said Janet. "I'm committed. I'll help in any way I can." She pulled a clean T-shirt and some jeans out of her bag and changed quickly in the car.

Harry put Thor in the car and they drove down Bay Street, towards downtown. They stopped at Yank Sing, a Chinese restaurant on Stevenson Street, for dim sum and then drove to the Junipero Serra Freeway— Interstate 280. I 280 ran down the center of the San Andreas earthquake fault line, through a magnificent set of hills on the San Francisco peninsula. The Stanford linear accelerator ran crosswise across the freeway; wags joked that it would hold the state together during the next great earthquake. But all thoughts of earthquakes and Cicerone evaporated as they enjoyed the scenery. When they reached Highway U.S. 101 they turned south and began to plan Janet's break-in into the county records.

FORTY—SOLE-SOURCE

Thursday, March 6th, 2008, 6:30 PM

Music poured into the Los Osos Stags lodge card room from the bar but Jerry Sloane's leg had stopped twitching. Finally! Yates was still in the hospital. It was the opportunity to finesse the troublemaker and award the design contract to Monterey Construction without dissent. He'd called another trustee meeting and looked about the room, as he closed the door to muffle the music. Carole Greene had her ubiquitous health magazine and John Potempa, nose running more than usual—he'd brought a box of Kleenex with him—talked with nominee Jimmy Bateman, a guest for the trustee meeting. Ted Granger sat alone, at one end of the table. Granger looked like he was trying to distance himself from the meeting.

"Thanks for inviting me, Jerry," said Bateman. "I'm looking forward to joining the board."

"Uh-huh," mumbled Sloane while he wondered about Granger. "How do you feel, Jimmy? You look a little under the weather."

"I'm getting over a bout of pneumonia. I'm better but it's a good thing Ted picked me up. Donna was quite upset with me for going out— she insisted someone else drive and made me take my meds earlier than usual."

"Well, enjoy the meeting. We have a short agenda tonight, primarily the award of a design contract for the new lodge."

"What about the other candidates for the board?" said Carole. "Did you invite them?"

Sloane shook his head. "I didn't think it was necessary. They don't have the support of the ER and they told me they were too busy anyway."

Bateman coughed and settled down in his seat. To Sloane's eye it was more a slouch—he wouldn't have been surprised if the guy fell out of his chair.

"Okay," he asked, "who wants to approve the minutes of the last meeting?"

The minutes approved, Sloane moved into his agenda. They discussed rates for advertisements in the *Los Osos Stags Bulletin*, Granger's plan to appoint a finance committee to manage the signature authorities on the Wells Fargo bank account, and the misbehavior of a few Stags at the Embassy Suites bar the previous week.

"We'll need the deal with the Embassy Suites," said Potempa, while he blew his nose. "When the lodge comes down, it's one of the few places we'll get reduced rates on drinks and meals."

"I know," said Sloane. "We should ask the house committee to punish those guys for conduct unbecoming a Stag. We need some discipline, damn it."

"We don't need a confrontation now, Jerry," said Granger. "I'll talk to them. Let's move on."

Sloane studied the other trustees, who looked uninterested. "Okay," he said reluctantly, "but make sure you deliver the message. Let's move into the financials."

After an analysis of the pro forma monthly financial statements—the balance sheet reflected the thirteen million dollars in the bank that had transferred from Coastal Title—Sloane asked for approval of the Monterey Construction Company design proposal.

"Shouldn't we wait for Larry Yates?" asked Carole.

Sloane looked for support to Granger but he seemed preoccupied with the financial statement. "Why bother? You've already expressed support and this allows us to take a unanimous decision to the floor of the Lodge, right John?" He looked at Potempa who blinked a few times, and nodded. Sloane noticed Potempa's eyes were bloodshot. Stoned again!

"Okay. Is that it?" asked Carole. "There's a show tonight on the Discovery Channel I want to see."

"Let's vote," said Sloane. He recorded a 3-0 vote in favor of the design contract with Monterey. "Thanks. Is there any New Business? Otherwise we can let Carole get to her show."

"Er ... when does that contract start?" asked Bateman.

"As soon as the Lodge approves it. Hopefully, that will be at next week's meeting. Why?" Sloane's leg twitched—this guy was supposed to be in their back pocket. He looked at Granger but he stared at the ceiling.

"I don't ... well, I was just wondering." Bateman coughed up some phlegm and borrowed a tissue from Potempa. "Did anyone analyze the costs? What if we never see the other thirteen million dollars? Shouldn't we hold off a major design effort until it's settled? I haven't seen the bid but—"

"Don't worry about it Jimmy," said Granger. "Mitch Mason, our Stag consultant, took care of that. Mitch said the agent is confident the developer will get the one hundred four units authorized. They already received the preliminary permits. Jerry, why don't you adjourn the meeting, and I'll take Jimmy home."

"A motion to adjourn is always in order," said Potempa, who gathered up his copies of the financial statements and stood and looked expectantly at Sloane.

Sloane adjourned the meeting, still aggravated over Granger's interference in the matter of the misbehaving Stags.

In the parking lot, Sloane watched Granger help Jimmy Bateman into his Hummer. When Granger came around to the driver's side, Sloane whispered. "What the hell, Ted. Is he going to be a problem? Is he going to stay alive long enough to do the construction contract?"

"I'll talk to him on the way home," said Granger as he rubbed his eyes.

"You looked preoccupied today, Ted. I don't like that. I sense some distance. Are you getting cold feet?"

"Not at all."

"That's good because distraction," said Sloane, in a menacing voice, "would not be healthy!"

"It's okay, Jerry. I'm just worried about the money."

"Well, Kelly owes us another fifty thousand each. Now that we have trustee approval we're almost there."

"Why don't you call him?" asked Granger. "I need to get Jimmy home now."

"I hate to wait," said Sloane reluctantly, "but let's get the floor approval from the Lodge first."

Granger nodded and opened the driver's door. "It should be automatic."

Sloane watched Granger's tail lights disappear. Damn, he thought, now he had to worry about Granger. If he became flakey, or developed a conscience, Sloane would be out on a limb.

He drove over to Highway U.S. 101 and turned south for Arroyo Grande. Maybe the cards would be better tonight.

FORTY-ONE—BUCK

Deputy Luis Mendoza spotted FBI Agent John Lewiston looking through the window of the 2 Dogs Coffee Company and Internet Café on Monterey Street in SLO. Mendoza was online, exploring the Stags' Grand Lodge's website. He'd been searching for statutes concerning the responsibilities of trustees but he'd been stymied by the log-in requirement for a Stags' ID number. Randy Lismore's number no longer worked. He quickly closed the browser window and turned to Lewiston as he came in.

"How'd you find me?" asked Mendoza.

"They told me where you were in the sheriff's office. We're supposed to be working together, aren't we?" Lewiston grinned.

Mendoza stifled a snort. "What, are you trying to be funny? So far all the help you've given me is squat."

"Well, I have something for you. Harris told me to tell you that we've identified the possible perp. A cop in Chicago recognized the photo."

"What's it going to cost me? You ain't giving me this information for the hell of it."

"C'mon, Mendoza. I'm only following orders."

"Sure, and now you're pounding sand. What's the guy's name?"

"Salvatore 'Buck' Califano—'Buck' because he always carries a buck knife."

He handed Mendoza a Chicago Police Department mug shot. Mendoza studied the photo. "If they had a mug shot, how come it took so long?"

"They sent a fax but it was lost in the office mail."

"Are you kidding? Is he connected?"

"He hangs out in Schiller Park—that's near Chicago's O'Hare. He works for Joey Gee Giannotti."

"Is he still in California?"

"We don't know. We asked the Chicago cops to locate him. You have anything for me?"

"Why would you be interested?" Mendoza grinned. "This is just a small town murder. I'm looking at a couple of guys—Stags. There was some difference of opinion between them and Lismore—nothing that would be of interest to your office."

"Would one of them be Jerry Sloane?"

Mendoza jumped out of his chair. "Now that's an interesting question, Lewiston. You have something on him?"

"He met with someone from Cicerone's family in Carmel."

"So you have the link," said Mendoza, "Lismore to Sloane to Cicerone to Joey Gee to this guy, Califano. When are you going to pick him up? I need to see if his shoes match the print in the Madonna Inn and whether there are any glass shards embedded in the soles."

"As I said, we've asked Chicago to find him."

"You have any other connections between Califano and the Stags' deal?"

"Not yet."

Mendoza figured that Lewiston was lying. There had to be some links to the big money, Sloane and Granger were small town thieves, the big bucks were on the development side of the deal.

"I guess we both have to wait for you to find Califano." Mendoza sat down again and turned back to the keyboard.

"I just gave you something, Mendoza. Stay in touch. See ya."

After Lewiston left, the deputy drove back to headquarters and walked into the sheriff's office.

"What's up, Luis?" Sheriff Ortega dismissed another deputy and waved Mendoza to a chair.

"We have a name—a mobbed-up killer in Chicago. I want to go there and snoop around."

Sheriff Ortega shook his head. "There's no money for a fool's errand to the Midwest. Let the FBI handle it."

"Goddamn it—"

"Look Luis, you pushed me at the inquest. Why mess around with the Feds? It will only get them pissed off. Don't you have enough to do?"

"You didn't see Lismore lying in the toilet, John. No one deserves to die like that."

"The coroner made his determination. No money, no travel. Let it be."

Mendoza stormed out of Ortega's office and ordered a search on Salvatore Buck Califano and Joey Gee Giannotti. "Check out their backgrounds and known associates," he demanded of an assistant deputy, "as well as their federal prison records, if any. I want to know who these guys are and any connections they have to California."

FORTY-TWO—DIARY

A few hours later, the phone rang in the San Luis Obispo county sheriff's office. The call was directed to Deputy Mendoza.

"Mendoza."

"Deputy Mendoza?" said a lady's voice. "This is Sarah Lowe. Do you remember me? I was Mr. Lismore's landlady?"

"Sure. How can I be of assistance?"

Mendoza remembered the lady. She'd let him wander through Randy's duplex the day he'd died and search for information. Mendoza had scoured Lismore's desk. There'd been little in it except Lismore's financial files, some old school documents including a college degree from George Washington University in St. Louis, his Navy discharge papers, and miscellaneous items such as a social security card, and student grades.

"I was cleaning out the garage," said Ms. Lowe, "that I'd shared with him and I saw a box stashed in the rafters—it must have belonged to him. My nephew used a ladder to bring it down. It has photos, some files, a sealed envelope addressed to a Harry Warrener—that was his friend, I believe—and an old diary. There's also a big gun in there and a box of— they call it ammunition, right? I wasn't sure what to do so I called you."

"That's the proper thing to do, Ms. Lowe. I'll come by and pick up the box, if you don't mind. We'll make sure the weapon and the ammunition are disposed of properly."

"I'll be home another hour."

Damn, thought Mendoza, how could he have missed stuff in the garage? He smiled. "Any idiot," his training supervisor would have said, "looks up as well as down." Mendoza jumped into his cruiser and drove to Ms. Lowe's duplex.

It sat on Couper Drive just west of North Santa Rosa Street, about two miles from central San Luis Obispo. The duplex was a low, California ranch-type stucco structure with a two-car garage in the front. Randy had occupied the front unit; he'd shared the common garage with Ms. Lowe.

Ms. Lowe invited Mendoza into her living room. It was small, with a picture window that faced her landscaped back yard. A magnolia tree cast shadows into the room from the overhead sun. Mendoza, ensconced in an old fashioned but recently re-upholstered sofa, stifled his impatience and drank the requisite cup of coffee served up by Ms. Lowe. His boots sank into a thick, solid beige carpet which looked new and made the room look larger.

"I miss Randy," said Ms. Lowe, as she pushed a tray of chocolate chip cookies under Mendoza's nose.

"Everyone seemed to like him, Ms. Lowe." Mendoza took a cookie off the platter. "Thanks for the cookies."

"Yes, I only heard him angry once, in all the years he lived here."

Mendoza looked up. Ms. Lowe had not mentioned anger before. "When was that?"

"Oh, it was around New Year's Eve. I heard him shouting, quite loudly, at someone right out in front of the garage."

"But your unit's in the rear. How could you have heard him?"

"I wanted to park in the garage. They stopped arguing when I asked the tall man to move a very big car out of the driveway."

"Was it a Hummer? Blue?" asked Mendoza.

"I'm sorry but I don't know anything about cars. It was night and all I noticed was a dark color."

"Did you know the man? Ever seen him before?"

Ms. Lowe shook her head.

"That's okay. What did Mr. Lismore say?"

"He was standing there yelling 'It's not enough money.' His hands were clenched in fists and he looked furious. The other man just shook his head and drove away."

"Do you think you could recognize him again?"

"Well, he was tall and I remember, he looked gray in the light from the garage—everything about him seemed gray ... and I think he had trouble with his eyes. He kept rubbing them."

"Did you talk to Mr. Lismore about the argument?"

"Randy was in his unit by the time I came out of the garage."

"Well, thanks Ms. Lowe. I might come by with some pictures sometime." Mendoza collected the box and carried it back to his cruiser. He'd climbed into the vehicle and started the engine when he noticed Ms. Lowe running toward his car carrying a package. He lowered the passenger window.

"Deputy, I forgot to give you this. I think Mr. Lismore's friend would want it." Ms. Lowe stuck a Safeway's shopping bag through the window and dropped it on the seat.

"What is it?"

"It's an American flag," she said. "It was used at his funeral—you know, they draped his coffin with it. He didn't have any relatives so the Navy officer presented it to me at the funeral."

"Okay, Ms. Lowe, thanks. I'll see his friend gets it. Thanks."

Mendoza drove to the sheriff's office. On the way he concluded the man Lismore had argued with had to be Ted Granger. There was too much circumstantial evidence. The men must've argued about the Stags' land deal.

In the office, he began an inventory of the contents of the box. The gun—a 1911 nickel-plated model A1 Colt .45, with a box of 225 gram Super-X Silvertip hollow point cartridges, lay on top. He examined the gun; it was loaded and clean—well maintained. A standard issue seven-round magazine was in the weapon. He unloaded the magazine and found the first round was a .45 (ACP) shot shell that contained buckshot, used mostly for scaring intruders or shooting snakes. The next six were hollow points. Lismore, decided Mendoza, had been a very careful man—he'd made certain that if it were necessary to fire the weapon indoors, the first round would not penetrate the walls of the duplex.

Mendoza copied the serial number of the weapon and logged onto the National Crime Information Center computers. A search for the serial number resulted in no hits. The gun wasn't on a want-list or registered to a previous owner.

Mendoza set the weapon aside and opened one of the files. It contained a variety of Los Osos Stags Lodge documents; invitations to visits of deputy directors, minutes of trustee meetings, old Lodge bulletins, financial statements of the Lodge, and a copy of the sales agreement in which the trustees transferred twenty-seven acres of land in exchange for a minimum thirteen million dollars—with an additional payment, based on the number of units that were developed on the property. The maximum number of units was one hundred four, the minimum was one unit. The maximum was highlighted with a yellow marker and several large yellow question marks.

He looked over the diary. It was beat up and stained. Some of the pages were loose. It looked like some of the stains might be blood. Some pages were torn out. The entries dated from 1964, and went forward to 1976—with one additional entry for December, 2007.

He set aside the diary and turned over a large, sealed manila envelope. A bold black marker had been used to write 'Personal and Confidential—For the Eyes of Harry Warrener' across the seal.

He sat down and pondered his options. Warrener didn't know he had the diary or the envelope; he might never know. On the other hand, Mendoza had promised to keep him informed and he felt honor bound to deliver the flag. The son-of-a-bitch probably never meant it when he'd said he'd stay out of the investigation. But Mendoza wanted to know what was in the sealed envelope. Sorely tempted to break open the seal, he made a copy of the other documents and then reluctantly threw the originals back into the box, filed the copies and the inventory in his desk, and carried the box back to his cruiser. He decided to drive by Warrener's house on Pastiempo Drive after lunch. Maybe he'd trade Salvatore Califano's name for some information.

FORTY-THREE—LETTER

Thor lay next to Harry's front stoop when Deputy Mendoza climbed out of his car with a shopping bag and a box. He gave the animal a wary eye; the dog ignored him. He walked up to the door and knocked, but the animal stayed prone. When Harry answered the dog looked up.

"Thor! Stay!" said Harry and shook Mendoza's hand. "He's on long stays now. Did he react to you?"

Mendoza shook his head. "I have something for you."

Mendoza carried the box and shopping bag into Harry's kitchen. "Nice digs. You did this all on a professor's salary?"

Harry grinned. "I had some luck in the market. What's in the box?"

Mendoza pulled a .45 out of the box. "Ever seen this before?"

"The last time I saw that gun—it was Randy's right?—was in Vietnam. Where'd you get it?"

"There's more." Mendoza handed Harry the sealed envelope. "This was addressed to you."

Harry looked quizzically at Mendoza and sat down. He reached for the envelope and then stopped. "Where's my manners? You want a beer or something?"

Mendoza was anxious. "Let's open the envelope. Maybe it'll help my investigation."

"What's in the shopping bag?" asked Harry.

Mendoza pulled out the flag. It was tightly folded in the regulation triangular shape.

Harry stared at it and grimaced. He placed it on the kitchen counter. "I need some water." He drew a glass and gulped it down, nervous and regretting his absence at the funeral.

"Okay. Let's open the envelope," said Mendoza.

It produced a letter. Harry read it out loud:

> *Dear Harry, if you're reading this—well, I guess I'm dead. I hope it was an accident but I've made enemies and there's a lot of money involved.*

There's a diary and a Colt .45 in this box. I want you to have them. Take good care of the weapon; it was my father's. You can burn everything else, including the Stags documents, if you want. There're a bunch of assholes in the local Stags but the documents could bring disrepute on the order. I don't want that. I collected this stuff just in case I wanted to make a stink. But now, writing this letter, I realize I can't do it; the Stags do good things. Do me a favor and join. Maybe you can help. Most of the guys are good people.

I always wanted to show you the diary. I'm sure you remember what happened when we raided that beach communications tower in North Vietnam. I want you to know that I knew you were scared and that you'd locked up. I knew that you'd considered yourself a coward. I regret the war ended so soon after that— ain't that stupid?—and you never had a chance to prove yourself in combat. I know you would have. No doubt. You had plenty of guts—I knew it when you stared down the CO when he wanted to re-assign me for smoking dope. I should have told you this sooner, but I didn't want to remind you. You earned that Purple Heart!

Harry looked up at Mendoza, who shrugged.
"What happened in Vietnam?"
"I already told you we were in combat together."
Mendoza nodded.

"He assigned me to protect the rear and I locked up. I was bayoneted in the process. I didn't know Randy had known I'd frozen in combat."

"Is there more in the letter?"

Harry nodded. "Just a little."

The diary covers our dive trip
to Fuji. Read it! Take care of that
dog and don't dive alone!

Your best friend, Randy

"I made copies of those documents," said Mendoza. "Some of them are highlighted."

"What? You can't do that! I want them back. Randy thought I should burn them."

"He might have died over those documents."

Harry looked at the box. "I need to think about it."

"Don't think too long. I'll trade you some info."

"Trade? Bullshit. You're supposed to keep me informed."

"I have a name."

Harry jumped up. "Who is he? Can you prove he did it? Where is he?"

"Califano, Salvatore Buck. He's from Chicago."

"Are you sure it's him?"

"All we know is he was in the Madonna Inn at the time and that he climbed out of the Explorer with the hot plates."

Harry looked at the gun.

"Be careful," said Mendoza, "the magazine is loaded."

"Where is this guy—Califano, was it—now?"

"The Feds say the Chicago cops are looking for him. They're probably lying but who knows. Don't do anything stupid."

Mendoza decided not to say anything about Lismore's presumed argument with Granger. He stood and walked toward the front door.

"Deputy Mendoza—thanks," said Harry.

Mendoza turned. "It took a lot of guts to read that letter out loud."

"You need to know this. I met Cicerone." Harry shrugged.

Mendoza turned a chair around and leaned both hands on the back. "Are you crazy? How? Does he know your name? Who you are?"

"I and a lady friend met him at the Asian, in San Francisco—at a reception, Sunday night."

"What'd he say?"

Harry grinned. "He said he was in the garbage business."

"And?"

"I asked if that was like Tony Soprano's business."

Mendoza sat down. "Jesus, Warrener, you're nuts."

Harry nodded. "He invited me to his house to see his Buddhas."

Mendoza stood, pushed his chair around and laughed. "Well, you may have shit for brains, but maybe your friend was right—you're braver than you think."

"Thanks for the gun."

"I hope you don't need it," said Mendoza. "I assume you know how to use it. To keep it legal you better go to a federal firearms licensed dealer and take a copy of Lismore's death certificate."

Harry acknowledged him and escorted Mendoza to the door.

FORTY-FOUR—PILLBOX

After Mendoza departed Harry stared at the flag and gun. Randy's words burned into him. Thirty years—more—Randy had known and thought nothing of it. Harry felt his back stiffen. Maybe, just maybe, he could find out what happened to Randy. He removed the snake shot cartridge and reloaded another hollow-point round in the magazine. Then he pulled the slide back, chambered a round, popped the magazine out of the weapon, and added another cartridge. He smiled. Eight rounds for whom? The killer—or killers? Maybe Califano, Cicerone and Franchescini. More? No way was he going to register the weapon. If Randy had inherited it, then it probably had never been registered—back in those days anyone could own a gun. He released the hammer slowly and stowed the weapon in a cabinet.

He carried the flag into his small living room and placed it on the narrow mantel over the fireplace. Returning to the kitchen, he looked at the diary. Perhaps later, he thought; he'd read it later. He felt good and liked the feeling. Harry went outside to fetch Thor and rewarded the long stay with a tummy rub and a fistful of biscuits. He decided to take the dog for a walk along the beach near the Los Osos Stags Lodge and then visit Randy's grave.

A half-hour later, after a stop at the florist, Harry trudged up the sand towards the old concrete structure on the Stags' property. Thor ran ahead, investigating dead fish and clumps of seaweed. The wind had whipped the sand off part of the ruins and Harry saw the corner of a window at the northwest edge of the concrete. Thor stuck his nose in the window, tail wagging. Harry dropped to his knees and scooped out a few handfuls of sand.

"Say, young feller, I wouldn't go poking around in there."

Harry turned and saw an old man, skinny as a rail, pointing a walking stick at him. The man looked in his eighties with yellowed eyes, and a mottled, freckled face and hands. He wore a large straw hat.

"Just curious," said Harry. "It looks like a pillbox."

"They built it in '42."

"What for? The Japanese were nowhere near California."

"That's true," said the man with a smile. "But a Jap sub had shelled a refinery near Santa Barbara, and a couple of torpedoes exploded along the coast, just north of here around Cayucos. Those idiots up at the Presidio in Frisco went nuts. They must have shit themselves thinking it was an invasion."

Harry was skeptical; he thought the old man was a little senile. "So they built one pillbox? Here?"

The old man nodded. "Yup, they ordered a company of troops from Fort Ord down here on the double with a couple of 90 mm guns and planted the battery right here under the trees. Came in with a 'dozer and mixer and built it."

Harry turned towards the sea. It was difficult to imagine a Japanese fleet and troops attacking the central coast. It might have scared the locals but it would have had little strategic advantage. The Americans would have had air superiority and controlled the local waters. Any landing would have faced land attack from three directions.

"That's nuts," said Harry.

The old man grinned. "It was good duty."

"You were here?"

"Yup, 59th Coast Artillery Regiment; PFC. We was hauled out of bed and hustled down here in 2-1/2 tonners. We set up a couple of machine guns—Browning .50 cals—stocked up the pillbox, and spent four months here until the Nips lost the Battle of Midway. After that we was shipped up to the Aleutians."

Harry nodded and looked at the pillbox. "What's down there?"

"Who knows? We had diesel, kerosene, batteries, ammo, fuses, shells—the orders to pull out came in the middle of the night and the next morning the Lieutenant ordered us to just fill 'er up with sand."

"You're telling me there're shells down there?" Harry was incredulous.

"Might still be. I ain't seen anyone poking around in there since the Stags bought the land. There's asbestos all over the place, and lead—must be tons of it. We was still in training and had a lot of fun with those Brownings. In fact, the beach is probably littered with lead and brass casings."

"Does anyone know? Did you ever tell the cops? That stuff is dangerous."

The old man shook his head. "Nope, no one ever asked. In those days no one cared—the war was over and it was back to business as usual."

"Well, thanks," said Harry. "You have a good day."

The old man nodded. "You too." He walked back to the wet sand and turned south.

Harry, deep in thought, wandered back to the road in front of the lodge and climbed into his car. "Someone's in for a surprise," he told Thor who bounded into the back seat. "It's a good thing they have the thirteen million already—I wouldn't bet on the rest."

He headed for the cemetery with the bouquet of white roses and lilies.

FORTY-FIVE—SANTANA ROW

Saturday, March 8th, 2008, 6:45 PM

Traffic was heavy on Winchester Boulevard in San Jose when Dominic Franchescini pulled his Range Rover onto the surface parking lot at fashionable Santana Row. He parked next to Ron Kelly's BMW 540i and walked the two blocks north to Straits Café, a Southeast Asian restaurant and bar.

Buskers performed live music. The local intellectual crowd was planted on benches reading books, some cigar smokers hovered in a small park, and a gaggle of Japanese shoppers roamed the shops. A fleet of new Lexus automobiles, parked along one side of the street, flaunted its wares.

When Dominic arrived, Kelly was already in the restaurant, ensconced at the bar, talking to two attractive women.

Franchescini was polite but insistent that he and Kelly take a table without the women. He overcame Kelly's reluctance with a curt reference to his uncle. "I have a message from the man."

Kelly ordered a vodka Martini, steamed mussels and a Caesar salad while Franchescini asked for the daily catch, bread and a glass of red wine.

When the drinks arrived, Dominic adopted a stern face. "Ron, we have a problem."

Kelly, still staring at one of the women at the bar, turned his head slightly. "What's that? I heard from Mitch Mason that the trustees have approved the deal so it's just one more step to half my fee. It sounds good to me."

"Listen, you fool. A trustee had a heart attack. When your uncle hears about it he'll be more than disturbed."

"I had nothing to do—"

"It doesn't look good. The press might get interested. Have you given any further thought to going to Japan?"

"Aw, Dominic, I thought that was just your way of cautioning me—you know, like you used to do when I was just a kid, and I needed a midcourse correction."

"It's more serious than that. The don loves you but he's quite capable of cutting you loose. Do you realize that?"

"Let's eat," said Kelly. "Here comes the food."

Dominic sat back. He wondered if Kelly would ever get the message. He smiled at the waitress and watched as Kelly attacked his food.

Ron's fingers were dripping with sauce from the mussels. He sucked them dry, smiled at another passing waitress, and reached for a napkin.

"Did you hear me?" demanded Dominic.

Kelly nodded.

Dominic sighed. He knew what would come next if Kelly didn't get going. The don was on edge; one more problem would push him over. "Ron, it's time to get out of Dodge. I know it's an old cliché but this is good advice."

Kelly stopped eating and pushed his dishes away. "Am I in trouble? The money doesn't cut me any slack?"

"Let's just say that violence has been counterproductive and your uncle is considering his options. I think it best if you plan to be gone by next weekend."

Kelly waved down their waitress for another drink. When she left he said, "You still want me to go to Japan?"

Dominic pushed his plate aside and stood. "This message has been delivered. I hope it's been received. Let's keep this low-key; stay below the radar and out of trouble. Next Saturday, Ron—I want you airborne—no later, and no bullshit. I'll get the ticket."

Dominic stopped at the bar and whispered to the two women. Kelly saw him hand the bartender some money for their drinks. The women turned and looked at Kelly. He waved for them to join him but they gathered their bags and departed. Dominic watched them leave, turned to Ron, pointed his finger at him, and mouthed, "No trouble."

Kelly slouched in his chair. A waitress walked by and asked him if something was wrong. "No," he said, pointing at a lone woman at the bar. "Would you take a drink to that blonde—my treat?"

Dominic, watching from the window, shook his head in disgust. Kelly might get killed and Dominic wasn't certain he could avert it. And, if that happened, Ron's mother, Alessandra—she'd never forgive Dominic.

FORTY-SIX—BUENA VISTA

Sunday, March 9th, 2008, 9:30 AM

Ron Kelly drove to San Francisco to meet his mother for breakfast at the Buena Vista Café—BV to the locals—near Ghirardelli Square. He drove into the same parking lot he'd used two weeks earlier. That night he'd collected over four million dollars, now he was being ordered out of the country. He sat at the bar, considered the injustice of it all, and watched the crowds outside the windows.

Kelly ordered an Irish coffee. The BV, at one point in time, had been the single largest importer of Irish whiskey in the country. Its Irish coffees were a San Francisco tradition—like the green and brown Powell and Hyde Street cable-car which was being turned around by hand on a turntable, to the admiration of dozens of tourists who waited for a ride up the Hyde Street hill. Locals and foreign visitors sat at large round tables that faced the windows. The crowd generated a noisy background hum.

When Kelly's mother joined him at the bar, he smiled weakly. "How's my father?"

Alessandra was tall, like her brother, the don. At sixty-two, she still colored her hair dark black. Dressed in black slacks, a Ferragamo sweater, and sporting a Hermès scarf, she was a handsome woman, who'd aged well, despite her drinking. Kelly knew his father had dragged her into drink; he'd always thought of it as their version of *Days of Wine and Roses*. He knew she didn't like his question.

"I sent him to Ireland, back to Galway, to dry out," she said as she waved to the bartender.

"You sent him to Ireland for a drinking problem? Are you trying to kill him?"

"Never mind. Why'd you call me?"

Ron explained the Stags' deal he'd brought to Don Cicerone and why he needed to travel.

"So why'd you take the deal to him?" she asked with a frown.

"What do you mean?"

Alessandra gulped a vodka Martini and ordered another. "If you needed help, you should have just talked to Dominic. You know that if you'd asked, he'd have kept it between the two of you."

"But, my God, Mother, you're talking about stiffing the don. What is it with you and Dominic?"

"We grew up together. He was like an older brother that protected me from that sadistic asshole—my real brother. I have a special relationship with him and I know he's very fond of you."

"Uh-huh." Kelly had always wondered about that "special relationship." His father was light, thin, and fair and he'd lost his hair in his twenties. Kelly had a dark complexion, almost Mediterranean in coloring, and still had a thick head of hair. Even their noses were different—Kelly had a classic Roman nose, his father had a narrow pointy one that reminded him of a parrot. And, unlike his father, he didn't drink to excess every day. Maybe, he thought, it was his uncle's influence, but maybe …

"He's the consigliore," he said. "You think he'd double-cross the don? I had to go to Uncle Alessandro."

"You fool. You're just like the Irishman. He thought he could get along with my brother. The don is a killer; I've known it since I was seven years old when he tortured a cat. And all that money! Why didn't you just keep it for yourself? What do you need him for?"

"Greed, mother, is what gets people killed. The first eight million was easy and I'll get a big cut. Unfortunately I have problems with the rest of the deal."

Kelly's mother sipped at another Martini, shaking her head. He gulped his Irish coffee and considered another. Then he switched to a double espresso.

After the bartender turned away, she said, "I told you to stay away from your uncle."

Kelly munched on a piece of sourdough toast. "Please don't give me that 'I told you so' crap." Kelly was irritated. He had a feeling she was right. This was it, he thought. Now he had to run. "Dominic wants me to leave the country, to go to Japan. Come with me. I don't know anyone over there and I'll be more comfortable."

"I don't want to go," said his mother. "No fucking way. But it sounds like good advice. Good luck."

He asked for the check. At least, he thought, he hadn't given the rest of the money to Granger and Sloane, or the dyke—yet. As Kelly walked down Beach Street he wondered about his mother's relationship with Dominic.

FORTY-SEVEN—PEBBLE BEACH

The all-terrain blue Hummer entered the Carmel gate, climbed a steep hill, and sped west on the 17 Mile Drive. Several miles later it turned left into the driveway for The Lodge at Pebble Beach. As Ted Granger passed the seventeenth hole, he was troubled. Remorse and guilt nudged him towards the relief that comes from confession while the fear of punishment anchored him in place. Still, in a moment of weakness, he'd arranged a meeting with Jim Thatcher, the Los Osos Stags Lodge's DDGER.

Granger knew the walls were closing in on him. His wife had talked to his lead mechanic and he'd told her that the agency hadn't sold a car in three weeks. She'd become angry and upset and wanted to argue all the time about money. Granger, desperate for some peace, had used his standard excuse to get out of the house—he had a Stags meeting

Jim Thatcher was parked in the small circular driveway that fronted up-scale shops and a putting green. When Granger arrived Thatcher climbed out of an old Lincoln Continental. The car had a California vanity license plate with the words "NVER LSE." He wore a blue suit with a red tie emblazoned with the words 'STAGS USA.' Granger grimaced. He knew that Thatcher had never lost a case. He was a civil attorney and he frequently litigated contract disputes and liability cases. Thatcher had made a lot of money in his career and worked now for the fun of it. Granger expected Thatcher to go ballistic when he heard about the kickbacks and Granger's suspicions about Sloane's involvement in Lismore's death. Granger smiled grimly. It was more than a suspicion. If Thatcher decided to prosecute him, he was doomed.

Both men handed their keys to a parking valet and walked through the lobby into the Tap Room, a bar and restaurant populated by guests and golfers after their rounds. It was a high-class crowd and Granger felt out of place.

"What's this about, Ted?" asked Thatcher. "Are there problems with the deal?"

"We have thirteen million in the bank already. We're about to authorize a preliminary design for the new lodge building."

"That's good news. I wish all the Lodges were this wealthy."

Granger smiled bleakly. He'd asked for the meeting; he wanted to tell Thatcher, to confess, to clear his conscience. It wasn't just the money. He felt guilty about Yates' heart attack and Lismore—he didn't want to think about him.

Jim Thatcher smiled at the hostess who seated them near the front bay window. There was a soccer game on a large screen over the bar but it didn't distract Granger. He wanted to unload, but first, he sensed, he should loosen Thatcher up. Stags were notorious drinkers and he and Thatcher often had been in the bag together. Most recently, they'd flirted with some women at the Stags Grand Lodge sessions in Yuma, Arizona. More than flirt, he remembered. They'd met the women at a Cub Scout flag memorial outing and slipped off to a motel. Maybe, he hoped, that experience would grease the skids.

"How about a couple of Bloody Mary's?" asked Granger. "Remember Yuma last year?"

Thatcher's smile turned into a frown. "Ted, sometimes it's best not to remember something. Make mine a Screwdriver."

Granger, chastised, caught the attention of the waitress and ordered the drinks. The men made small talk while they waited. When the drinks arrived he gulped his and ordered another round.

Thatcher looked at him expectantly.

"I think we may have a problem with Jerry." Granger rubbed his eyes and stared at Thatcher.

"Sloane? What do you mean?"

"There've been some kickbacks on the land deal. It's clearly conduct unbecoming a Stag, a violation of section 4.05 of the statutes."

Thatcher put his drink down. "How much is involved?"

"So far, about fifty thousand dollars."

"What? Where's it coming from?"

"I also took some."

"I thought you said we had a problem with Jerry."

"Well, it was his idea." Granger regretted the remark. He wasn't sure whose idea it had been, it had just happened. He had a nagging thought he had been the first to ask Ron Kelly for money, that night at Rocky Point. Still, he thought, it was Sloane who was the violent one and he remembered how excited Sloane had become when he'd learned about Kelly's interest in the land.

Thatcher looked out the window and finished his first drink. He picked up the second drink. "You guys are jerks. What, is that why you brought up Yuma—you were looking for some leverage?"

"Gee, Jim, I was just—no, ah, screw it. I wasn't thinking."

"Are we still getting the rest of the twenty-six million?"

Granger remembered that Thatcher wasn't aware of the rest of the scam. "I think so. They're still working on the paperwork. It's a hundred thousand each for me and Jerry," he said, "but it doesn't come out of the Stags' money." He looked at Thatcher praying his comment would mitigate the crime.

Thatcher nodded and stared gloomily at the golfers at another table. "That money is coming from somewhere. You know this is contumacy, don't you? We could throw you both out of the Stags."

"I know." Contumacy was a catch-all phrase for just about any financial misbehavior in the Stags. Granger laughed inwardly. That was nothing. If Sloane had had something to do with Lismore's death, contumacy was the least of his problems.

"There might be other problems," said Granger.

"I don't want to know. Clean up your house. Look Ted, the new building must go forward. That must be on the front burner. But start no construction until you get the rest of the money and a signed contract is in place."

"You're giving me a pass?"

"I'll think about the charges after the building is finished. I don't need another troubled Lodge in my district. Meanwhile, I recommend you get Jerry to think about resigning and, good God, don't take anymore of the money. Will you do that?"

"But what if—"

"I don't want to hear it. Some questions shouldn't be asked."

"So you want me to keep going?"

Thatcher nodded. "Just get the damn lodge built. I think I'll skip lunch. Thanks for the drink. I better not see a bill for this on your expense report." He stood, dug in his pockets for the valet parking stub, and departed quickly.

Granger rubbed his eyes. He'd hoped to bare his soul and he was still lying. He didn't have the nerve to bring up Lismore's death. What was he going to do about Sloane? He knew Sloane would never resign before he collected the rest of the money—the fifty thousand dollars and the half million—and that was far out in time. What if Sloane killed someone else? Granger reached for the check. Frustrated and scared, he paid the tab with a one-hundred-dollar bill from his kickback. He suspected he would take the rest of the money, too.

FORTY-EIGHT—CITY HALL

Sunday, March 9th, 2008, 12:30 PM

Janet Zimmer sat at her desk on the second floor at City Hall and pondered her problem. She'd already fished all the city records on the Los Osos Stags' property out of the city files. She had a copy of a bill of sale for up to twenty-six million dollars, a copy of a cancelled check from Coastal Title and Trust endorsed by the Los Osos Stags Lodge for thirteen million dollars, and copies of the paperwork for the original deed to the property dated January, 1946—when the Stags had bought the property for five thousand dollars from the state of California. A memo stated that Hansen Property Development had bought the Stags' land with funds funneled through a Kelly Agency escrow account. The ultimate price depended on permits and Janet knew those permits would not be a matter of public record until they were finalized. She saw a note that documents had been submitted to the Coastal Commission's Architectural Review Board for approval but the application was not in the file. That was strange, she thought; both the city and the county also had to approve the general plans before any new construction could be authorized. She wondered if an Environmental Impact Report (EIR) had been completed. She reasoned there should be other documents in the files including soils and traffic analyses, and other potential hazard reports—although those reports might not be required until the application for a construction permit was filed.

The county offices were on the third floor on the other side of the building. The ladies' room was on that floor so she had a good excuse to be up there. But how would she get into the files in the county clerk's office?

Janet climbed the stairs to the third floor. She wandered around the floor and checked the hallways. They were deserted. She strolled over to the county clerk's office and tried the door. It was unlocked. She stuck her head through the door and asked, "Anyone home?"

No one answered. A bank of file cabinets was lined up on the opposite wall. She walked over and scanned the labels on the drawers. She found the drawer labeled "Development L—P" and was reaching for the handle when the door opened. Pamela McCracken, the new employee, walked in. She was dressed slovenly, not apparently concerned with her appearance.

"Janet, what a lovely surprise," said Pamela. "What are you doing in here on a Sunday?"

Janet turned around, flustered. Damn, the woman would think she's blushing. Might as well take advantage of it. "I was, well … I was looking for you."

"Really?" Pamela grinned and her nostrils flared. "Have you thought about what I said last time?"

"To be honest, well … I've never done anything like that before but I thought we could talk about it. Can we do that? Just talk?"

Pamela walked up, grabbed Janet and kissed her. Janet, stunned, told herself this was for Harry—don't do anything. When she felt Pamela's tongue searching, she willed herself to respond slightly. She almost recoiled when Pamela's hand stroked her breast.

"Isn't that better than talking?" asked Pamela.

Janet took a deep breath and a step backwards. "I need to talk about this."

"Are you seeing someone now?" Pamela's tongue was on her lower lip; she breathed hard, inhaling though her nose.

Janet nodded. "Harry Warrener, he's a retired professor."

"I'd prefer an exclusive relationship, Janet, but I'd understand … if it took some time to get there."

"Maybe we could have lunch tomorrow."

"I'd love it," said Pamela. "I'll fetch you at noon."

"Actually," said Janet, "I'll come to you. I have some questions about a land transaction I've been working on. I was in the building working on it today when I thought of you."

"What land deal?" Pamela's demeanor changed to one of suspicion. "Is that the reason you're here?"

"Of course not, silly." Janet realized she'd made an error bringing up the deal. She had to do something to distract Pamela. She walked up to Pamela and kissed her; this time Janet opened her mouth fully and Pamela moaned with pleasure. Janet clenched her fists and her fingernails dug into her hands.

"I'm looking forward to lunch tomorrow," she said. Janet turned and hurried out of the office. She went to the ladies' room and flushed her mouth with water, hoping she wouldn't retch.

FORTY-NINE—CAUGHT

Sunday, March 9th, 2008, 1:30 PM

The doorbell rang while Harry prepared a ham and cheese sandwich. When he opened the door Janet lunged in.

"Don't ask," she said. "I need a drink. Do you have any wine?"

Harry took her into the kitchen and opened a bottle of Kendall Jackson white wine. "What's wrong?"

"I was caught by that bitch—the one that propositioned me—in the county office this morning."

"No! What happened?"

"I was just getting ready to pull open a file when she walked in. She must have been in the toilet. That's why the door was unlocked. I'm such a fool. I checked the hallways but never thought to look in the ladies' room."

"Did you—"

"She didn't see anything. But damn it, I had to pretend I was interested in her. She kissed me."

Harry winced.

"And now I have to have lunch with her tomorrow."

"I'm sorry."

"I told her I'd meet her in her office, because I was working on a land deal. I'm pretty sure she's suspicious."

"Did you mention the Stags' land?"

Janet shook her head. "Just that I was working on a transaction. But I did mention your name, that I was seeing you. That was probably stupid."

Harry didn't know what to say. "Do you want a sandwich?"

"Just hold me, Harry."

Later they agreed that Janet would express mild interest in the Los Osos Stags' land deal and concentrate on the EIR at lunch with Pamela McCracken. Then Harry and Janet would see what the Coastal Title and Trust Company could tell them.

FIFTY—TICKETS

Monday, March 10th, 2008, 10:00 AM

Ron Kelly was surprised when someone banged on his door. He peeked out the window and saw a long black limousine with a driver parked on his driveway. Dominic Franchescini stood at the entrance. His hands were clenched in fists and he rocked back and forth on his heels.

"Open up, Ron."

"Jeez, Dominic, what are you doing here?"

"I'm accelerating your departure. You leave tomorrow at noon and I'm here to make sure you get on that plane. I have some tickets for you."

"What? Why so soon? I'll have half the fee any moment now."

"The Feds have identified Joey Gee's hit man and the don is going to hear about the trustee with the heart attack. He's already concerned about the exposure. You don't question—"

Kelly's phone rang. "Give me a minute."

"Yeah?" said Kelly.

A woman's voice answered. "Kelly? This is your friend down south—remember me?"

He recognized the county clerk, Pamela McCracken's voice. "Pam—what's up?"

"Well, first of all, you owe me fifty grand. Second of all, I suspect some people are interested in the deal."

"What people?" Ron looked over at Dominic who raised his eyebrows. Ron waved him over to a chair.

"Tell you what," she said. "You give me my money and I'll give you a name."

Kelly exploded. The tension, Dominic's presence, the link to the hit man, the orders to go to Japan, and the squeeze from Pamela all came together and he blew up at the easiest target. "Listen, you fucking dyke, I'll give you the money when I feel like it. Who's interested in the deal?"

"The money, sweetie. I want it today."

Ron was speechless. His mind reeled and he couldn't concentrate. "All right, let me think for a minute. Can you meet me at SFO tomorrow? I'm on my way out of town—"

Dominic grabbed the phone from Ron. "This is a friend of Ron's. How can I help you?" He glared at Kelly.

"He owes me some money," said Pamela, "and I believe I have information he'd find useful. I thought a trade would be appropriate."

"Does he know how to find you?"

"Tell him the Starbucks at Mill and Toro, in SLO."

"We'll be there in three hours."

Kelly watched Dominic hang up.

"What's this?" Dominic asked. "You're using your home phone for business?"

"I wasn't—"

"Not only that, you told her you were leaving town. From SFO? Goddamn it, you little turd. Haven't I taught you anything?"

"Ah, leave me alone, Dominic. Do I really have to leave town?"

"Not only that, you fool, we're going to find out what that woman knows and give her the money you owe her. How much is it?"

"Fifty long."

"You still owe her for the permits?"

Kelly nodded.

"Get packed. We're leaving in thirty minutes. Fuck, now we have to drive to SLO and back—because you didn't take care of business."

Kelly slithered back into his bedroom and began to pack. Then he ran back into the living room. "Hey, I get a half a million dollars this week. Can't we delay the trip until then? I still owe those Stags half of their kickbacks. If they don't get their money, it could become a problem."

"We'll talk about it in the car. Bring all the money. Hurry up!"

FIFTY-ONE—SAM'S GRILL

The waiter had left with the lunch orders when FBI Special Agent Fred Harris's cell phone rang. He looked at the LCD display and put the phone back on the white linen tablecloth.

"Aren't you going to answer?" asked Sam Bernini, Harris's boss. He sipped at his double extra-dry Absolut vodka Martini on the rocks.

Harris had ordered the crab au gratin. The men were in Sam's Grill at the intersection of Belden and Bush Streets in San Francisco. The crab was a house specialty along with the veal chop, a two-inch behemoth, which Bernini had ordered. The men were seated in one of several small paneled compartments that flanked a hallway which ran parallel to Belden Street. The compartments catered to the privacy demands of the regular clientele—San Francisco wheeler-dealers.

Harris examined the call-bell on the wall. "We don't get here too often. Let's enjoy the meal. The call was from Lewiston. If it's important he'll call back. He was down in San Luis Obispo checking on the Stags' deal with that local cop."

"Anything new?"

"There's a hit on the guy we think is the killer."

"So who is he?"

"The Chicago cops ID'ed him, Salvatore Califano—Buck, they call him. You know the name?"

Bernini shook his head.

The waiter brought the meals and another basket of sourdough bread. Fred grabbed a French fry off of Bernini's plate and munched on it. "He's one of Joey Giannotti's men."

"There's your connection to the Stags—through Don Cicerone and Morty Greenspan," said Bernini. "That's more than a coincidence."

Harris's phone rang again, displaying Lewiston's name. He decided to answer.

"What is it, John?"

"Kelly's on the run."

"Say that again?"

"We just had a call from the guys at the monitoring station. Kelly said he was leaving town, from SFO tomorrow. He's on his way to San Luis

Obispo right now, for a meeting with some woman. There's another guy with him; we think he's Franchescini."

"All right. Check the airlines. Find out which carrier and where he's going. I'll ask Sam to get a warrant." Harris clicked off. He looked at Bernini and pulled a cigar out of his pocket.

"You going to smoke that in here?" asked Bernini.

Harris shook his head reluctantly. "Kelly's going to ground tomorrow. We have a chance to get him. I need an arrest warrant." Harris laid the cigar down and dug into his crab. "Damn, this is good."

Bernini, struggling with his enormous veal chop, dropped the knife and fork. "I don't know if L.A. is ready to act."

"We can't let him run. We may never see him again."

"L.A. may not see it that way. Their main target is Cicerone."

"And I'm relying on him to give up the don."

"I know Fred, but I have to ask."

Harris nodded. He rang the service button. When the waiter stuck his head in the compartment Harris ordered a double Scotch and a glass of milk.

Bernini looked inquisitive.

"The Scotch is for me," said Harris. "The milk's for my ulcer. The cigar's for later."

FIFTY-TWO—PAMELA

"Do you see her?" asked Dominic.

Kelly nodded and pointed at Pamela McCracken sitting in a chair on the plaza in front of Starbucks in San Luis Obispo.

Pamela's white T-shirt bulged. She was plump, turning to fat, Dominic thought, and the jeans she wore did nothing to help. Her shoes were cheap, worn flip-flops.

"You stay here," said Dominic. "Don't move."

He grabbed the briefcase in Kelly's hand and started toward Pamela.

The sun was high and Pamela was moving her chair into the shade when Dominic slammed the briefcase on the table. His eyes narrowed. "I'm the friend. You have something for me?

Startled, she said, "Who are you? Where's Kelly?"

Dominic was in a hurry; it was five hours or more back to the San Francisco airport where he'd planned to park Ron overnight in the SFO Marriott Hotel. He stared at her.

"You can call me Joe."

Pamela looked at the briefcase. "Is that my money?"

"Maybe. You said someone was snooping around?"

"Give me the briefcase!" Pamela's face broke out in sweat.

"You want the money—I want the information."

"You guys owe me fifty grand—I issued the provisional permits, didn't I?"

Dominic put his hand on the briefcase. "Seems kind of stupid to do this in public, doesn't it?" He looked around the plaza. Several nearby tables were occupied with some college kids and a couple of dogs dueled over a beat up Frisbee. "You told Kelly someone's been interested in your files."

"Yes! That's new information and it'll cost you." She wiped her forehead.

"Not another fucking dime. Don't make me ask again!"

"Look ... Joe," said Pamela, "I did as asked. I arranged the permits for Hansen Property Development. Ron owes me."

"And you can have it—soon." He patted the briefcase. Dominic glared at Pamela, who stared back, uncowed. He reached into his pocket and toyed with his knife. The sun was warm and he noticed a sheen on her forehead. He sensed fear despite the set of her jaw.

"Listen, you stupid dyke, don't mess with me. This ain't my dick in my hand and I'll cut your heart out."

Pamela's eyes darted around and Dominic thought she might actually disobey him. Then, she said, in a defiant tone, "I don't know if this is something or not, but I found a woman in my office yesterday. Her name's Zimmer—Janet Zimmer. She had no business there."

"So what?" Dominic was disturbed. He recognized the name from the reception at the Asian Art Museum.

"Well, it's not that unusual—except it was Sunday. It's true she works on that kind of stuff. But she was snooping around the files and she had her hand on the drawer containing the Los Osos files when I caught her."

"That's it? What'd she do? Turn you down?"

"I admit I was interested in her but there was a complication—a boy friend. Then, after I talked to you and Ron earlier today, we had lunch. She asked me about an Environmental Impact Report for the Stags' deal."

"What'd you tell her? You lie to me and you're dead!"

Pamela nodded.

"So, is there one?"

"No. The permits are provisional, related to how Hansen intends to carve up the property. Hansen needs an EIR, as well as traffic, soil and other engineering analyses when he goes for his final construction permits."

"What's the boyfriend's name?"

"Warrener, Harry."

Dominic nodded. Warrener had been with the woman at the Asian. He grabbed Pamela's arm. "Let's take a walk."

Pamela was shocked at the strength of his grip. "Don't hurt me. You know I won't tell anyone—I can be trusted."

"Sure you can."

"Fuck you; Joe." The defiance had returned. "You guineas all think you're God. You won't like it if I blow the whistle on your little scam. What is it—a hundred fifty million? The fifty thousand you owe me is chump change."

"Are you crazy, talking to me like this? Where's your car? I ain't doing this in public."

"It's in the city lot, south of here, on Higuera."

"C'mon." Dominic snatched the briefcase off the table.

"Just give it to me here."

Dominic yanked her arm and started walking.

"Let go of me, you ape."

"Lady, people of your persuasion don't want to go calling other people names."

"Is it all there?"

Dominic ignored her and looked over his shoulder. Kelly, he thought, that idiot had put him in this ridiculous position. At least he wasn't following them.

They reached the parking lot and Pamela pointed at a black Toyota RAV4 with a large dent in the front right fender. "That's mine."

An ambulance raced by and Dominic wished he could stuff Kelly in the damn thing and ship him off to a mental institution. He hesitated. The Stags' deal was beginning to generate too much heat. The don already was concerned and he might order him to cap Kelly. He knew he couldn't do that and he had to get him out of town. Even Tokyo would be dangerous. He wondered if he should kill the dyke but the streets were crowded. He handed Pamela the briefcase and stormed away.

"Hey Joe," yelled Pamela, "You're welcome."

Dominic winced. He knew he was leaving a loose thread. He turned again, menacingly, and watched her throw the briefcase into the RAV4 and race away.

He walked back to Kelly and the limousine deep in thought. "Get in," he snarled. "Change of plan! We're going to Los Angeles. Now!"

FIFTY-THREE—SFO

The new international terminal at San Francisco International Airport (SFO) buzzed with activity. Passengers lined up for the Philippine Air flight to Manila and jammed the concourse. Fred Harris and Agent John Lewiston dodged around baggage carts that overflowed with large suitcases and enormous cardboard boxes tied with string.

"My God," said Lewiston. "Do you think there are chickens in there?"

Harris smiled. "Who knows?" He motioned to the Japan Airlines Counter, around the corner. "C'mon, we'll stake out over there."

"What time's he coming?"

"The flight leaves in an hour. He should be here already."

"What if he doesn't show up?"

"He'll show. They must want him out of town. And that's good. The more pressure the bet—"

Harris's phone buzzed and he fished it out of his pocket.

"Hello?"

"He ain't coming." Harris recognized the voice of an agent in the Los Angeles FBI office."

"He's going airborne, just boarded a JAL flight from LAX to Tokyo that leaves at 1:30 PM."

"You guys didn't issue the warrant, did you?"

"We didn't want to alert anyone. We suspect a leak somewhere in the system."

Harris shook his head. "He must have been given a heads-up. Now we have to figure out how and why." Harris clicked off.

Lewiston looked at Harris inquisitively. "What?"

"He's gone. Something's up. What's the latest on the land scam?"

"I don't know. I can't talk to Mendoza, he's pissed. All he told me was he had some suspects. Let's find out if any money has moved."

Harris and Lewiston circled around the baggage check lines and made their way to Harris's car on the parking lot roof.

FIFTY-FOUR—LAX

Tuesday, March 11th, 2008, 1:30 PM

Dominic Franchescini, parked on Manchester Boulevard, sighed with relief as he watched the JAL aircraft roar down the LAX 24R runway. He'd been uncomfortable ever since the conversation with Pamela McCracken on Kelly's telephone. After Pamela had driven away from him, he'd changed plans. He'd ordered the limousine driver to go straight to Los Angeles from San Luis Obispo. He and Kelly had spent the night at the Kyoto Grand Hotel in downtown Los Angeles. Kelly had been booked again, late that morning, on a different flight to Tokyo and the consigliore had taken possession of the remaining hundred thousand dollars to be split between Ted Granger and Jerry Sloane.

"I'll see that these guys get the money as soon as we see the Stags' check for a half-million made out to you," he'd told Kelly in the suite they'd shared at the Kyoto Grand.

Kelly had nodded glumly and stared out the window. He'd looked north at Parker Center, the decrepit headquarters of the Los Angeles Police Department.

"Can't I stay a little closer than Japan? How about Mexico?" he'd asked. "It's going to be difficult working this thing from Japan. Perhaps the don would consider a closer spot?"

"Look Ron," Dominic had said, "this is for your own good. Just go. I'll call you at the Imperial Hotel when you can come back."

Dominic watched as the plane disappeared over the large cylindrical fuel tanks to the west of LAX. He returned to the limo.

"Next stop is San Francisco."

The driver nodded. "We'll just take 405 north to the 101."

"Whatever. Take your time. I'm in no hurry." Dominic shivered when he thought about telling the don that Kelly had left the country, and why he'd expedited his departure. That would show weakness and was risky. He crawled into the corner of the back seat and tried to sleep.

FIFTY-FIVE—RANDY

Harry stared at Randy's diary. The notebook was old and ragged. The handwriting had changed over the years—Randy's early entries were scribbled and wandered over the pages; as he'd matured the writing had become smoother and more orderly. The first entries were about his experiences in high school, in St. Louis in the middle '60s. At sixteen, Randy, with a false ID, had been invited by the maître d' of a restaurant/bar in Gaslight Square to go drinking in some late-hours bars, after closing. He'd taken Randy to a strip joint in East St. Louis, on the Illinois side of the Mississippi River. Randy had slugged the man when he'd made a pass at him and then had to walk back—it had taken all night to get home. Randy had written,

> *"It was stupid; looking back it was obvious the guy was queer. I hope I didn't hurt him; but from now on I need to pay more attention to my surroundings."*

So much for Randy being gay, thought Harry. He smiled when Randy wrote about his first couple of experiences with girls and a trip to Biloxi where he'd learned how to dive and earned his Open Water Diver certificate. He'd written about his intentions to join the SEALS when he graduated from high school. The entries during SEALS training were graphic and reminded Harry of his experiences—the demanding physical conditioning, the training in depth, and the long sessions where he'd learned to tolerate, while he shivered mercilessly, extremely cold conditions.

Harry leafed through the pages to Vietnam. He found an entry for October, 1974 which referred to when he'd joined Randy's team.

> *"A new guy, Harry Warrener, joined today. He's an underwater demo expert and knows his stuff. He's a great diver and fills out the team. We'll probably go into combat soon."*

Harry skipped some pages and found the entry for his confrontation with the commanding officer.

> *"The CO was pissed today when he caught me with a reefer. Warrener heard him yelling at me and told him that he'd rather dive with me stoned, then go into the water with anyone else in the squad. He walked right up to him and got into his face. When the CO threatened to write us up, Harry said: 'Why would you want to do that? Your best diver and team leader? Let it be. He'll stop, won't you, Randy?' and damn, I am going to stop. It took real balls for him to do that."*

Two days later was the entry for the mission into North Vietnam. Harry was entranced as he read Randy's description of that day.

> *"Into the water at 0500. Target NV comm. tower, 1 nautical mi. to shore, with UPVs. Hit beach at sunrise. Bumped into NVA patrol – 5 or 6. Laid covering fire. Warrener to hold rear, about 1/8 mile to target. Heard Warrener firing … planted explosives, tower blown, shot NVA soldier, found Warrener with leg wound gushing blood, face covered with dirt, suit smelled of urine. Probably panicked, first time in combat. Reminds me of me, dressed wound. Not a sound or complaint when morphine refused. Back to UPVs, Tough. Next time he'll be a terror."*

He knew it all, thought Harry. He wondered if it would have changed his life, if Randy had simply told him that he'd known about his fear. He turned back to the diary. The last of the Vietnam entries concluded when the team had been returned to the states. Randy had written,

> *"Warrener and I have become good friends. I hope it continues after the war. It's too bad he never had another chance to test his mettle in combat."*

The entries trickled off in the late '70s. There was one entry added recently—the shark attack the previous December. Harry wondered how Randy would explain his behavior. He was torn between reading it and burning the diary. He dialed Janet's number.

"It's me. Harry."

"Hi. How are you?"

"I'm reading Randy's diary and I could use some company."

"I'll be there in an hour."

Harry took Thor for a walk while he waited. When Janet arrived, they went into the kitchen. The diary lay on the table.

Harry poured them both a cup of tea. "I never told you but Randy also left me a letter. I read it last week when the cop, Mendoza, delivered it to me with the diary and a gun."

Janet took Harry's hand, leaned over the table and kissed him. She picked up the diary. "There's an entry here for last December. What does it say?"

"Why don't you read it?"

"Is it about you?"

"Harry nodded grimly. "A shark attack. The second time I fell apart. Go on."

Janet examined the book. Randy had written with a fountain pen and the strokes were neat, pronounced, much like someone had used a calligraphy brush.

> *"Last week we dove Fiji. Harry was attacked by a Tiger; a big fish, about 12 feet, maybe longer. He lost his reg but did the right thing, turned, presented his tank, and bundled himself into a ball. I stabbed the shark and hit him with a night light and it turned and ran. Harry was hyperventilating,*

*probably thinking he'd failed
again—but I was the one with the
weapon. I should reassure him,
talk again about Vietnam—but
how do I bring it up? Maybe, I can
tell him about the time the punks
in St. Louis tortured my dog and
I did nothing. Damn."*

Janet laid the diary down.

"You didn't tell me about the shark. Why not?"

"I wanted to but—"

"Harry! You need to stop thinking you're not the man your friend was. You're all the man I need."

Harry wiped his eyes and stood. "I'm going to get them—all of them."

"You don't have to prove anything to me."

"It's not for you, it's for Randy."

"Are you sure it's not for you, Harry? You don't have to do this to prove you're not a coward."

Harry stood and walked to the kitchen sink. He rinsed his face with cold water and dried off with a dishtowel. "I'm not sure why I have to do this,' he said, "I'm confused, scared, angry—but this is certain, I know I need you."

Janet rose and hugged Harry fiercely.

FIFTY-SIX—INITIATION

Thursday, March 13th, 2008, 8:00 PM

The Los Osos Stags Lodge meeting had been underway for some time when Harry, Janet, and the other new candidates lined up outside the Lodge's meeting room for their initiation ceremony. The Lodge's esquire had arranged them according to height and had taken Janet's arm as the lead. He wore a red sport jacket, with his regalia and scepter he looked like a character in a Disney Christmas film. The group would follow the esquire and Janet through the entire ritual. Harry figured that they always selected the best looking woman for that part.

"While we wait," said the esquire, "I want to give you some more information. As new members you'll be immediately entitled to vote. We have an election tonight, to fill a trustee position vacated by a death. It's required by the statutes, even though we have a complete election cycle coming up in a few weeks. Ted Granger, our ER, has endorsed Jimmy Bateman who was nominated by the chairman of our board of trustees. Jimmy's done a great job before and we need him to get the new Lodge building completed. Ted put up a red Hummer that we'll raffle off this evening. That money goes to our charity account."

"Are there any other candidates? Who are they?" asked the man from the barber shop.

"There're two. They're both nice guys but they lack the knowledge necessary to run the Lodge and they were only nominated so there'd be an election, instead of a slam dunk. Some haven't been around long enough to know the history. Any other questions?"

Harry grinned to himself. He'd noticed posters plastered on the walls and doors endorsing Bateman. Just another democracy with rigged elections. Harry had no personal grudge against Bateman. He figured the other new members didn't know these people anyway. Like sheep, they'd take the name they'd been given. Randy, he knew, would have wanted a real contest and he'd have expressed outrage at the posters, especially those publicly and prominently displayed on the outside walls of the lodge.

The tiler opened the door and the esquire led them into the room. The audience stood in silence. As the candidates walked in a circle around the room and passed the various stations, the knights spoke their leading lines.

The esteemed loyal knight said, "Let your path be guided by justice."

The esteemed lecturing knight said, "Love your brother." The esteemed leading knight said, "Always be charitable." The group then assembled at the altar. Janet and the esquire stood directly behind the altar, an American flag to their right. Harry and the others were lined up in a row behind them.

The esquire presented the candidates to the exalted ruler.

Ted Granger looked down on the field of candidates. He banged his gavel once and the members in the audience took their seats. "Congratulations. You have been accepted ..."

The first item was the binding oath. The candidates were asked if they believed in God. Harry lost track of the words but he noticed they swore to support the Stags and the U.S. Constitutions, not permit any political or personal prejudice to influence their votes in the order, exhaust all Stags' remedies before appealing to a civil court, never use their membership in the Stags for any business or commercial purposes, and to never bring reproach upon the order.

Harry liked those rules. He thought it was déclassé to exploit a membership in a fraternal order. It reassured him to think that everyone had taken such a pledge. He thought, with sarcasm, that Granger and Sloane must had held a rock when they took their pledges—the ancient Romans had believed such contact with the earth rendered oaths non-binding.

Next was a non-sectarian prayer led by the chaplain, followed by a solemn ceremony in which the Lodge clock tolled eleven times. The esquire then said, "It is the hour of recollection."

Granger explained that Eleven O'clock in the evening, every day, was a solemn moment. "Wherever Stags roam," he said, "when the clock strikes this hour, we recall our members, those who have passed beyond the great river that separates the living and the dead."

As the ritual continued the group was escorted once more to each knight. The esteemed lecturing knight spoke about his station's devotion to brotherly love, symbolized by the set of stag's antlers positioned on his podium. The esteemed loyal knight lectured on the motto of his station, justice, symbolized by the bible.

Harry's legs began to ache when the esteemed leading knight lectured on the motto of his station, charity, and then launched into an old legend about a gathering of the gods on Mount Olympus. They'd assembled to select the noblest goddess. The tale told how the gods, dressed in gold and adorned with jewels, came paired: Hope with Fear, War and Peace, Wealth and Riches, and so forth. After the assembly was complete, an uninvited god, Sweet Charity arrived alone—dressed in a plain white gown and bearing a bouquet of flowers. The other gods were indignant; they protested that a poorly dressed god should not belong in the competition. Sweet

Charity acknowledged her simple clothing but pleaded for admission so that she could speak of those in need. As the gods heard her words they stilled their ambitions and offered the crown to her. But Sweet Charity said she sought no crown in fact but only in the hearts of mankind.

Harry loved the story. Janet, he thought, had a tear in the corner of one eye. Harry had thought earlier parts of the ceremony were hokey but, upon reflection, the pomp and ceremony warmed him. There was something wholesome about the whole process. He understood why Randy had enjoyed the Stags. Janet turned around to proceed to the final station and made eye contact with him. She smiled as though she were enjoying herself.

The last stop was the ER's station. After reiterating the obligations the candidates had pledged, Granger spoke of the motto of his station, fidelity; he stressed the need to adhere to the binding oath and to be faithful as members of a fraternal order.

Harry, reluctant to ruin his mood, stifled his cynicism.

There were three raps of the gavel and the entire audience rose. The ER said, "Please salute our flag."

Each new member was then presented with a small American flag and membership card.

The ER then asked, "How do Stags receive their new members?"

The audience responded, "Under the shadows of brotherly love cast by the Stag's antlers." The audience then raised their arms straight up, palms out, and fingers splayed, in the Stag's hailing sign.

There was a brief recess while the new members were welcomed by the old members.

Sloane shook Harry's hand. "I understand you were a friend of Randy Lismore. I saw you at the cemetery during his graveside ceremony. Maybe we could have a beer sometime."

"That would be nice, Jerry." As Harry turned, he rolled his eyes. Janet, watching him, said, "What?"

"He wants to talk. I just don't trust him."

They seated themselves and watched Granger conduct the rest of the meeting. Granger asked Sloane for a trustees' report.

Jerry smiled. "Welcome, again to the new members. I'm pleased to report that the trustees have recommended unanimously to the Lodge floor that we approve a hundred thousand dollar design contract with Monterey Construction Company for our new lodge. As you can imagine, we've done our homework, with the help of Mitch Mason, and spent some time considering the proposal—about a month. Monterey built the UC Santa Cruz stadium, just to name one of their prominent projects, so I'd like a motion from the floor to approve the contract."

"Where's Mitch?" yelled one of the members. "We should give him a 'well done.'"

"He had to work tonight," said Granger, "but I'm sure he appreciates the thought. Who'll offer Chairman Sloane's motion?" He looked around the room and spotted several arms in the air. "The secretary will record Anita Cochran's motion. Any seconds?" More arms flew in the air, including Harry's.

Janet leaned over. She whispered, "What are you doing?"

Harry muttered, out of the side of his mouth, "This is clearly a done deal. I'm just making my new friend, Jerry Sloane, a happy camper."

Granger accepted Harry's second and the motion cleared the floor by acclamation. "Thank you," said Granger. "This also means that we can pay half the agent's fee, subject to the terms of the sale of the land which was already approved by the floor and pursuant to our permit granted by the Grand Lodge." He looked at Sloane and smiled.

Under New Business, Jimmy Bateman was elected in a landslide. Then, a host of women, apparently the pool ladies that had been mentioned at the inquest, asked permission to leave *en masse*. "We were told in email we could leave after the elections and we have baby sitters," said one of them. Harry chuckled. They'd been told how to vote and had little interest in the real business of the Lodge. He nudged Janet when Granger granted permission for the group to depart.

The meeting droned on. At the treasurer's request for authorization to pay bills, a motion to pay Ron Kelly's bill of five hundred thousand dollars was approved. Harry thought he saw a fleeting smile of victory on Sloane's face. Granger rubbed his eyes once and looked relieved.

At the conclusion of the meeting, Granger asked Janet to pick the raffle winner for the used Hummer. The meeting ended amiably with Janet, Granger, and Sloane congratulating the winner. Granger passed out free drink tickets to the new members and the crowd adjourned to the bar.

At the bar Janet asked Harry what he'd thought of the initiation.

He reflected for a moment. "The principles remind me of the things we're taught in elementary school about truth and justice, you know, like George Washington and the cherry tree. If only the world behaved according to its principles, it would be a wonderful place." Then his voice turned conspiratorial. "Maybe, if Granger and Sloane had believed the words, Randy would still be alive."

"I would have liked to have met him, Harry."

Harry nodded. "Too bad Mason wasn't here. I'd like to know what he looks like." He toyed with his drink and decided to ask Deputy Mendoza what he knew about Monterey Construction Company.

FIFTY-SEVEN—CONFESSION

The limousine glided noiselessly to the curb on Jackson Street and Dominic Franchescini stepped out. He signed a voucher for the driver, threw five one-hundred-dollar bills on the front seat for a tip, and turned and stared at the mansion. A light shone in the southwest corner on the second floor; the don's private study. Dominic walked to a keypad at the main gate, entered the combination and followed the front walkway. He was tired, concerned about Kelly, and loathe to explain the reasons he'd spirited Kelly out of town.

Inside the mansion's foyer, he rubbed the *Ganesha* statue and started up the stairs. Don Cicerone's study door was open; he was ensconced in an Eames chair, reading a book entitled *The Quest for Eternity*. The book, Dominic had been told when he'd purchased it as a gift for the don, addressed Chinese beliefs in the afterworld.

"Dominic," said Cicerone, "thank you for this book. I've been reading how Confucius always concentrated on life on this earth while not denying the possibility of a hereafter. How different from the Holy Church, eh? Why are you so late?"

"I'm glad you like the book. But I'm afraid you may not be happy with me." Dominic stared sadly at the don.

"You've done something with Ron, haven't you?" asked the don. "I understand the federal authorities were stymied in an attempt to arrest him at SFO."

This amazed Dominic who realized the informer must have gone directly to Don Cicerone with information that Dominic didn't have yet. "Did you speak with the informer directly?"

"Yes, the servant thought I should get the call. It was directed to you and rang incessantly. Why didn't you tell me the man muffles his voice?"

"I didn't think it was necessary. I'd already cleared him through Chicago; I guess he thought it prudent to cover his tracks with us."

"And Ron?"

"I thought it best he leave the country so I put him on a plane in Los Angeles. We both knew the Chicago police had identified the suspect in the trustee death. There have, alas, been several missteps and unfortunate events—a second trustee is ill."

"How ill?" asked the don.

"A heart attack is all I know." Dominic looked around the room. The don had a small fire burning in the corner fireplace, and music from San Francisco's only classical station, *KDFC*, was playing a Mozart flute concerto. The don threw a wrap off his legs, stood, and walked to his couch. He gestured to Dominic to join him. "Was Ron involved?"

"I don't think so—but I don't know. Sometimes he does rash things. But after we last spoke, I knew you had thoughts about getting him out of town, so I jumped the gun."

"I must admit," said the don, "that I'm curious why you acted without my authorization. It is unlike you to act alone in family matters."

"Yes, of course. I was only trying to protect the family."

"You mean Ron, don't you?" asked the don.

"Well, naturally ... I thought—"

"Please, Dominic. Don't dissemble. Actually, your actions foiled the arrest. The police were laying in wait at San Francisco International. It's unclear why they were so eager to arrest him; perhaps it was because he was bolting from the country. I do know it involved recordings and wire taps. However, an arrest seems premature to me. Your decision to drive to Los Angeles was quite clever. Apparently they hadn't issued a federal warrant yet so he could depart via LAX."

The don pushed a button and a servant came to the door. "A brandy, please, for Dominic and a pot of coffee for me."

Dominic waited apprehensively while the don shuffled some papers on his desk and appeared lost in thought. He looked out the window and noticed that fog had moved in. It obscured the view; the streetlights were enveloped and emitted a hazy distant glow.

The don nodded to himself. "All right, Dominic, please let me have a status report on the land deal. Are the payoffs completed? What are these other missteps you mentioned?"

Dominic breathed a sigh of relief and nodded. "When I arrived at Ron's home, he received a call from the San Luis Obispo county clerk's employee—a Pamela McCracken. Ron owed the woman her kickback and she had some additional information she wanted to sell. We drove to SLO and I confronted her. She was pretty gutsy considering who she dealt with. I paid her off and she said that a Janet Zimmer was poking around her office—"

The don looked up. "Zimmer? Didn't we meet her at the Asian?"

"Yes, and McCracken mentioned her boyfriend—Harry Warrener, too. We met him."

"I remember," said Don Cicerone, frowning.

The servant returned with the brandy and coffee and Dominic sipped at his drink.

"What did Zimmer want?" Cicerone stirred his coffee.

"She was interested in the EIR for the Los Osos deal. That's just too many coincidences for me."

"Are there any other payoffs due?"

"Kelly had only given the two Stags—Sloane and Granger—half their money. I took the rest from Ron and said I'd arrange to get it to them. I told Ron to work the deal by phone, as necessary, from Japan. I was glad to see his flight leave."

"We may need to do more than that," said the don. "Ron is apparently on tapes offering kickbacks and loosely connected to discussions about intimidation. They have Morty Greenspan and some Stag, Mason, on tape as well. Tell me, does Morty make his own recordings?"

Dominic shook his head. "I don't know. I've never heard of it before. From his point of view, it wouldn't be a bad idea, though."

"Dominic, this is spiraling out of control. We better find out fast about Morty. This is clearly directed at us and we need to close down the transaction as soon as possible."

"But Hansen still owes us another eight million."

"Only if the deal goes through to completion and he gets all the permits. We've already made eight, and the risk-reward ratio has turned sour. Plan a program to shut down the county clerk's operation. If necessary, we'll pass on the second payment."

Dominic gulped. It was uncharacteristic of the don to walk away from eight million dollars. "I'll do that. The Stags will get the rest of their kickbacks this weekend and I'll start checking out Monterey Construction."

"Make sure Joey Gee doesn't learn about our suspicions. And, to distract him as well as prepare for the worst, ask him to send someone to Tokyo to, er, watch over Ron—just in case. You understand I'm honoring your request here?"

"But Don Cicerone, you can't mean extreme action. This is family and your sister—"

"My sister is a weak leg that would bring down the League of Nations for lack of guts. No, strike that. Make it the United Nations. They're no different."

Dominic, distraught, gulped the rest of his brandy and nodded.

"We're not done," said the don. "We have a potential threat in Ms. Zimmer and Mr. Warrener. What do we do about them?"

"At the moment, they are not in the Stags' decision-making chain. Maybe we should wait."

"Perhaps it's time to follow up on my invitation to have them visit the mansion. I'll think about that. Meanwhile, you find out precisely what the Feds know and what's on those recordings—all the recordings!"

"Yes sir."

"Get some sleep, Dominic. I need you alert."

Dominic walked to his room on the third floor and crawled into bed. He grabbed a prepaid cell phone from the nightstand and called Jerry Sloane. When Sloane answered, he said, "Sloane, I have some envelopes for you."

"What? Who's this?" asked Sloane.

"The agent works for me and he asked me to arrange a delivery. You can call me Joe."

"Where's the agent? You're talking about Kelly, right?"

Dominic shook his head in disgust. "At the moment the agent is elsewhere. If you guys want your envelopes, you need to come to San Francisco and don't forget a check for half the agent's fee."

"Okay, Joe, you're a pain in the ass," said Sloane, "but we'll come to the mountain. Where do you want to meet?"

"Be at the Civic Center in San Francisco at 12:15 PM Saturday. Bring your sidekick and don't be late. I'll call with instructions. And be careful what you say and where you say it."

Dominic clicked off.

FIFTY-EIGHT—BATEMAN

Friday, March 14th, 2008, 11:30 AM

Ted Granger turned his Hummer into the driveway of his agency and slammed on his brakes. Jerry Sloane's Miata was parked crossways in the main entrance. Sloane sat on the roof of the vehicle, legs over the windshield, swilling a beer. His leg twitched; his heel left scratches on the hood.

"My God, Jerry," said Granger, "it's 11:30 in the morning. People are trying to work here. Get the car out of the way—and you're drinking?"

"Better get used to it. We got problems." Sloane threw the empty beer bottle over his shoulder. It slammed into the windshield of a used BMW and bounced onto the ground.

"Damn it," said Granger, "it's a good thing you didn't crack the windshield."

"Screw it. When's the last time you had a buyer? For starters—Bateman's dead. The fucker drowned in his bathtub. Apparently he climbed into some really hot water. The paramedics said he looked like a roasted walnut; probably had a heart attack and was DOA. But we'll have to wait for the coroner—remember him?"

"Oh my God, Jerry, did you—"

"What are you talking about? He was our man, remember? It's too bad Yates didn't die. You want to worry? Worry about him!"

"This can't be good. They're dropping like flies. First Lismore, then Yates's heart attack, and now Bateman. What will Kelly think?" Granger rubbed his eyes and leaned back against Sloane's Miata.

"Kelly? He ain't even in this anymore. We've been promoted. We're dealing with some goombah named Joe, who's probably the consigliore. I ain't sure, but if he is, his real name is Dominic Franchescini."

"Consigliore? You mean the mafia?"

"What? You've been confused? Who the hell did you think Kelly worked for?"

"Where's Kelly?" asked Granger.

"I don't know and I don't give a shit. It sounds like he went to ground. But we need our money and we have to deliver half his fee tomorrow to that dago in San Francisco; he said he'd give us the rest of our payoffs then."

"I don't know, Jerry. They could kill us."

"You can be damn sure they'll kill us if we don't deliver the fucking money. But we're committed—all the way, so cut the bullshit and let's get down to business."

Granger trembled and rubbed his eyes. He felt a pain in his chest and thought it would be a good time to just drop on the spot. As the pain passed, he said, "How are we going to control the trustees? There are two vacancies now."

"Maybe," Sloane said, "we should call an emergency meeting right now and pass a sole-source contract for construction—the twenty million. After all, we control all three votes."

"But we only have twelve and half million after we pay the first half of Kelly's fee."

Sloane smiled grimly. "Maybe we should just rip off the money and run."

"We can't do that. I won't stand for it. We can't screw the Stags; the payoffs are bad enough." Granger's mind filled with the thought of his last conversation with Thatcher. He wondered if Sloane would kill him if he learned that Thatcher knew about the deal.

"Okay," said Granger, "we'll just have to tough our way through it. What's the status with the EIR?"

"I don't know. We need to find out. Meanwhile, you plan on meeting me here at 7:00 AM tomorrow and we'll drive to San Francisco. I'll get a check cut this afternoon. We can both sign it and deliver it to this guy, Joe, or Dominic—whomever."

"But what about the treasurer's signature?"

"Ain't necessary, Ted. With the new bank accounts, he hasn't turned in a signature card yet. Right now it's just you and me."

"But they could prosecute us for contumacy without his signature."

"Get real, Ted. Who cares?"

Granger was scared. Jim Thatcher might learn about the next payoff. He'd come down hard. And, if Yates died there was no way they could avoid a full scale investigation. There might be one anyway. "What do I tell the authorities? What if the press noses around again?"

"Hey Ted," barked Sloane, "You're a car salesman. You people lie better than congressmen. Do what comes natural. Spew a little bullshit." Sloane slid off the roof, hiccupped, and climbed into his car. He started the engine, stuck his head out the window, and snapped, "Get your act together. Be here tomorrow. I need that friggin' money!"

Granger watched Sloane peel out of the lot. He was swept with conflicting feelings; guilt over Lismore, fear that the whole deal would unravel, fear that Sloane would plan another murder when he learned he'd blown the whistle to Thatcher, and fear about taking more money—

Thatcher had told him to stop. Was he actually going to San Francisco tomorrow? Granger felt his heart skip a beat, then another and another spasm of pain in his chest. He knew the PVCs were associated with tension; he thought he'd welcome a heart attack—if it was fatal.

FIFTY-NINE—CO

Pamela McCracken smiled at Joann, a supple twenty-two year old college girl she'd picked up in the Black Sheep Bar and Grill earlier that evening. The women were in Pamela's studio apartment above her landlady's garage. A little earlier she'd heard the woman come home when the garage door rumbled shut. It was cold outside, all the windows were closed and the heater was blasting air into the room; it had been delicious to crawl into the arms of a young woman with a tight, lean body. They'd made love for hours and lay exhausted on Pamela's bed, sipping wine. The air was heavy; they were drowsy but Joann giggled as McCracken rubbed several one-hundred-dollar bills on her body, concentrating on her breasts.

"Where did you get the money?" asked Joann, in a sluggish voice.

"Shush. Just enjoy. If you're nice, I'll let you take a few with you." Pamela smiled. Earlier, she'd struggled with an approach-avoidance conflict. She'd reach for the money—five hundred one-hundred-dollar bills and the closer her hand had come to the money, the more reluctant she'd become to touch the money. Then as her hand receded, the greater the urge became to touch the money. She should never have done that deal, she thought—but then she couldn't play with Joann. Why was she so drowsy? She rubbed a bill across Joann's mouth and bent down to kiss her but the girl had drifted off to sleep. McCracken shook the girl but she seemed unconscious. She was so beautiful—especially when she slept. Pamela laid down next the girl. She could hear her landlady's car's engine running in the garage downstairs. Why was she so drowsy? She closed her eyes.

Both women were dead from carbon monoxide poisoning when a man slipped noiselessly into the apartment. He walked to the side window and released a hose which had been attached to the landlady's Lexus sports vehicle in the garage. He retrieved the white towel that he'd used to wedge the hose in the window and seal it, watched the end of the hose fall, and closed the window. He looked around the apartment and found a large brick of one-hundred-dollar bills under the bed. He grabbed the money, sprinkled a few more bills over the two dead women, and crept down the stairs. Downstairs, he fetched the hose which had fallen over the hood of Pamela's RAV4, coiled it, and threw it in the back of a Range Rover. He

179

reentered the garage through a side door and checked the fuel tank on the Lexus. It was almost empty; the fuel reserve warning light was on. He left the engine running and slipped outside, climbed into his car and departed.

SIXTY—MAX

Harry felt Thor stir. The dog slept at the end of his bed. Thor issued a faint growl and then someone banged on the front door. Harry grabbed a bathrobe and walked to the front door.

Max Cotton, the reporter for the *Paso Robles Weekly Reporter*, rocked on his heels. He stared at Thor with some apprehension and Harry grabbed the dog's collar to reassure him.

"What the hell, Warrener? I asked you to call me. Now there's another dead Trustee and a third one had a heart attack? What's going on?"

"Come on in," said Harry. "I didn't call you because I hate the press. But you're right, I'm worried about Yates and I heard about Jimmy Bateman. You want some coffee?"

Cotton nodded and the men went into the kitchen.

"Bateman died in his bathtub," said Harry, while he ground some coffee beans. "Do you think it was deliberate?"

"Well, what do you think? I keep trying to get information about the land deal and I get stonewalled by everyone. Granger hung up on me. That agent, Kelly—the mobbed-up guy? He's nowhere to be found now. I can't get squat from anyone."

"Christ, Max, I don't know anything."

"Bullshit. Lismore was your best friend. You guys were in combat together. And you just joined the Lodge in Los Osos."

Harry smiled. "You're accusing me of sniffing around?"

"Okay," said Cotton, "*mea culpa*. So what do you know?"

Harry poured coffee into two mugs and sat down. Thor sprawled under the table, his tail flopped on Cotton's shoes.

"Thor, cut that out!" commanded Harry. "Look, I think Randy was murdered. I joined the Stags to see if I could learn more about the land deal. I think that Granger and Sloane are involved but I have no real evidence. In fact, a lot of my suspicions were based on your article in January."

"There've been a lot of heart attacks."

"Yes," Harry admitted, "I think Larry Yates's attack might have been due to stress applied by Granger, but Bateman was an old man. Who knows?"

"Granger? Why would he apply stress?" Cotton sipped his coffee while Harry pondered what to tell him.

"Look. I don't know anything for sure. Maybe there are kickbacks but I'm in no position to make accusations."

"Can I quote you on any of this?" Cotton scribbled some words in his notebook.

"Absolutely not. I don't need any attention. It would mess up my own investigation—"

"You conducting an investigation?" asked Cotton.

"Maybe I misspoke. That's too strong a word. Let's just say I'm nosing around. Mentioning me would interfere and probably aggravate Mendoza, the cop—just let it be."

"You know," muttered Cotton, "Los Osos should have re-zoned that land years ago for recreation-use only. Now there are conditional permits issued already. When do you guys vacate the old building?"

"I'm not sure. I know there are plans for the members to use the Embassy Suites and YMCA facilities while the new lodge gets built."

"Did you guys get paid yet?"

"From what I understand, half's been received—thirteen million dollars. The rest depends on the number of permits."

Cotton frowned. "Those permits bug me. They were issued awfully fast. One hundred and eight units. That has to represent a lot of money!"

"I thought it was one hundred four units," said Harry. "At one hundred eight, they'd owe us another million dollars."

"Did you know that the clerk that issued the permits is dead?"

"How's that?" said Harry.

"McCracken—Pamela, her landlady yesterday called it in. The police found her dead—carbon monoxide poisoning."

"An accident? Another so-called accident?"

"There was another woman with her."

"That's not surprising," said Harry.

"What, you know something?" asked Cotton.

Harry shook his head. It didn't feel right giving personal information about the woman to the press. He decided to wait until he'd talked to Mendoza.

"Well," said Cotton, as he rose, "someone ought to check out the number of permits and whether they're related to McCracken's death. I won't quote you but I'm writing another story. It'll be out on Monday, day after tomorrow." Cotton turned to leave.

"Are you going to mention Pamela McCracken in an article?"

"I haven't decided. You have to admit I have a lot of fodder. I need to go."

"Wait a minute, Max. Do you have any info on Monterey Construction Company?"

"They built the UC Santa Cruz stadium. Why?"

"Do they do good work?"

Cotton laughed. "You know that earthquake last fall? Well, a bunch of deep cracks have appeared in the stadium foundation; the repairs are going to cost millions. Why do you ask?"

"Just wondering," said Harry. "The Stags gave the design job for the new lodge to Monterey."

"I'll look into it."

Harry shook Cotton's hand and walked him out. As he watched Cotton drive away, Harry thought it would be a good idea to check out Monterey Construction Company himself. Tomorrow he'd take a ride up to Monterey, and the next time he saw Mendoza, he'd ask some tough questions.

SIXTY-ONE—CIVIC CENTER

A light drizzle blanketed San Francisco and glazed the asphalt roads into a slick shiny surface. Jerry Sloane's wipers smeared his dirty windshield.

"Did I ever tell you," he said to Ted Granger, "about the night I was nailed for DUI?"

"Why am I not surprised?" asked Granger. "Have you been nipping at the bottle? I noticed a little indecision as we came up 101."

"Is the pope a Catholic?" said Sloane. "The only real question is why aren't you drinking? There's a bottle of Dewar's under the seat—want a hit?"

Granger slumped in his seat and wrapped his arms around his chest. "Tell me about the DUI."

"I was in Los Angeles, coming up from Commerce City, a poker game. I was headed for the bars in Manhattan Beach—lots of hot women in those days—and three sheets to the wind. I'd been winning and every big pot was rewarded with a giant Mojito. The LAPD nabbed me on the Imperial Highway, near Sepulveda,"

"This kind of stuff doesn't make me confident you can hold it together in this deal, Jerry."

"Better than you, my ER, better than you."

"So you were pissed at the police?"

"Ted, you have a sense of humor for a wimp. I was pissed—in the British sense. The whole episode cost me ten grand and a suspended license for six months. I had to play more poker to make up the fine."

Sloane sped up as they crossed San Francisco's Market Street. They were headed north on Van Ness Avenue. Panhandlers and homeless, camped in large cardboard boxes, cluttered the sidewalks.

Sloane's cell phone rang.

"Where are you jerks?" Sloane recognized 'Joe's' voice.

"Is that you Joe?" he asked. "What's your real name?"

"You don't need to know that. Where are you? You're supposed to be in the Civic Center right now. I don't see you or your car."

"We're just coming up on the Civic Center now. Traffic was a little heavy on 101."

"You have the check?"

"You got our money?" asked Sloane.

"I'll meet you on the stairs to the Asian Art Museum in five minutes. I'll find you."

Sloane roared around a Muni bus, turned right onto McAllister Street, crossed Polk Street and then drove down the ramp into the Civic Center parking lot. He and Granger rode the elevator up to the Civic Center Plaza and crossed Larkin Street. Traffic roared north on Larkin, behind them, as they mounted the steps to the Asian.

Halfway up the steps, a man grabbed Sloane's arm. "You Sloane?"

"Joe? Or is it Dominic?" asked Sloane. "This is Ted Granger."

"We don't need names. Give me the check."

"How about our money?"

The man handed Sloane a Gump's Department Store shopping bag. "It's all there, a hundred thousand, fifty each."

Sloane nodded and Granger passed an envelope to the man.

"Okay," said Joe, "this transaction is complete. Now go home and get that sole-source construction contract awarded to Monterey Construction."

"We haven't even seen the detailed design yet," said Granger.

"You want the rest of the money?" said the man. "You need to earn it. We expect construction to start soon! Remember—this is an advance against our million dollars fee."

Granger paled and grabbed his chest. Then he recovered and nodded weakly. "Yes, I know. We'll work on it."

"You do that. And Sloane," said the man with a menacing tone, "no more heart attacks. If there's another one, you can be damn sure there'll be more!"

The man stormed down the stairs and walked east on McAllister.

"C'mon, Ted," said Sloane.

"How are we going to get out of this, Jerry?"

"Relax. Take it easy. We have the money."

"But if we don't close the deal with Monterey, they're going to want the money back. He said *advance*, remember?"

"That's not news, Ted. Nothing's changed. Now let's work on the contract."

The men walked back to the Civic Center parking lot. Sloane inserted a five dollar bill in the pay machine. It charged him two dollars and fifty cents; he took his change in quarters, ignored the receipt option, and swore under his breath. At the car, Sloane stashed the shopping bag in the trunk. He reached under the front seat and pulled out the bottle of Dewar's Scotch. "Want some?"

Granger shook his head. "Maybe you should swill the whole bottle and get us killed on the way home."

"Just get in the car," mumbled Sloane. "I don't know what you're doing with the money but I'm taking mine to Arroyo Grande this afternoon."

"When do you think we'll see the big money?"

"This deal better close, and soon!" Sloane drove over to the exit gate. He fumbled with the exit ticket and swore again.

Back on Van Ness Avenue, Sloane swallowed a large gulp of the Scotch. "Let's see," he said, "if I do better this time than in LA. I got more money so I can drink more whisky." He sped up. "Ever notice," he asked, "how little cars always seem to be going faster than big cars?" They whizzed past traffic and Sloane ran a red light at Grove Street.

"My trouble, back in the dope days in the '70s," said Granger, who took the bottle and sipped, "was going too slow; I could never get the car to go over twenty miles per hour. I wish we were doing twenty now."

"Ted baby," said an astonished Sloane, "I never knew you smoked dope. When we get the rest of the money, we can have chauffeurs, eh? You can take your wife to the Caribbean and I'll play in the World Poker Tour. Gimme the bottle."

Granger rubbed his eyes and stared at his feet. Sloane wondered if Granger could keep it together long enough to get the large kickback, which was the real prize. He hoped this wasn't one of those cases where he'd see the Promised Land but never get there. He gulped down some Scotch and passed the bottle back to Granger. They careened onto the Central Skyway connector to Highway U.S. 101.

SIXTY-TWO—FISHERMAN'S WHARF

Monterey Bay sprawled to the west. Harry Warrener stood on the wharf leading to Monterey Construction Company. He leaned against the railing. His elbows were placed precariously between large piles of white droppings. He could see Fisherman's Wharf, loaded with tourists to the south. Crowds milled around t-shirt, toffee, and sweatshirt shops; they indulged in chocolate and clam chowder, and watched the sea lions rampage on an abandoned pier. Pelicans and sea gulls squabbled, perched on piers and railings, and left more droppings on posts. The gate to the construction company loomed on his right.

The company's large metal warehouse sat at the end of the wharf. The building was poorly maintained. It was painted in a classic industrial gray similar to a naval warship. Rust splattered the walls, and the corrugated sheet metal panels on the roof were loose in spots. 'No Trespassing. Violators will be prosecuted' signs were posted on the chain-link gate which was topped by three strands of barbed wire. An empty flag pole with a twisted halyard towered over the yard behind the fence. Harry saw multiple video cameras mounted below the roof, monitoring the yard area.

He wondered how he'd get past the gate and what excuse he could offer if challenged. Then the gate rumbled open and a couple walked out. The girl was young and pretty. She wore a tight short black skirt that highlighted sleek hips and long legs. A black ribbed woolen turtleneck sweater was topped by a perky blonde pony-tail that bounced with every stride. She had her hand linked over the man's arm. Harry sneaked a peek in the yard, before the gate closed again, but all he saw were piles of lumber, a bulldozer, and a forklift.

As the couple walked by he heard the girl say, "Mitch, I've been looking forward to this lunch for several weeks."

"I think about you a lot, Alice," said the man.

Mitch's hair was dirty and dish-water blondish with a few gray streaks. Harry noted some blemishes on a ruddy complexion. Sort of squat, with large shoulders, Mitch was pushing fifty, maybe, a little old for Alice. Could it be Mason? Harry decided to follow them as they walked down to the end of the wharf. They climbed into a beat-up blue pickup truck with a mismatched yellow camper shell. It had a sign on the door which read 'M&M Construction Company' and a pair of bumper stickers, "Be Kind to an Animal, Kiss a Stag" and "Support the NRA." Harry brightened—it was probably Mason.

Mason started the truck and began to back away.

Harry swore to himself. His car was parked several hundred yards away, in the Fisherman's Wharf lot. He couldn't possibly get to the car, pay the parking bill, and still manage to tail Mason. Pondering the problem, he noticed a taxi disgorge some people with a large cooler, day sailors or fishermen, in front of the Municipal Wharf. He ran over, jumped in the cab and blurted at the driver, "An extra twenty if you don't lose the pickup."

The cabbie threw the meter's flag down and followed Mason. The convoy turned south onto Del Monte Avenue, merged onto Lighthouse Avenue and drove towards Cannery Row. A few minutes later the truck pulled into the Cannery Row parking lot entrance on Foam Street. Harry rewarded the cab driver and walked over to the corner. A moment later, Mason and Alice walked out of the Prescott Street pedestrian entrance and walked south. He followed them to a popular restaurant, the Sardine Factory. He stood on the corner and watched them climb the stairs to the entrance. They passed an old wooden fishing boat perched next to the stairs—the restaurant's signature tourist attraction. Harry was surprised when they turned and walked down the stairs. He hoped he wasn't noticed. He hung back and followed again as they walked to Willy's Smokehouse BBQ and Grill which stood kitty-corner to the Sardine Factory. He gave them a few minutes to get settled and then climbed a few steps to the restaurant's entrance. He could see the old signs for the extinct Monterey Canning Company to his left.

Mason and Alice were in the lounge. An L-shaped bar separated two large dining rooms from a row of booths. Empty seats were on both sides of the couple at the corner of the bar. Harry sidled up to the empty seat directly next to Alice. He received a dirty look from Mason but ignored it. To appease Mason's testosterone, Harry turned his back to Alice and studied a menu.

Mason worked on a beer while the girl drank something that looked like a Strawberry Daiquiri. Harry ordered a cappuccino and tried to eavesdrop.

Mason smiled at Alice. "I'm glad we finally managed to get together."

"*Moi aussi,*" she said with a coquettish smile.

"I'm sorry the Sardine Factory was closed for lunch," said Mason.

"Oh, that's okay. I thought you were just stringing me along to talk to Morty."

"You like Morty?"

"He's a good boss but he's so secretive. He's obsessed with security."

Mason nodded. "He should be. It's a tough business and you can't be too careful."

"Do you like me, Mitch?" The girl leaned into Mason's arm suggestively. "Why'd it take you so long to hook up?"

"C'mon Alice, I've always thought you were special. And, you know, I'm a little older than you."

"I like older men." She ran her hand through Mason's hair. You want another drink?"

Harry worked through a second coffee as the lovers had two more drinks. Alice was excited. She'd let her hair down and her hands were all over Mason. She nuzzled his ear repeatedly.

"How come I had to pick you up at work on a Sunday?" asked Mason.

"Once a month, I have to recycle the video tapes on the cameras around the yard."

"You mean those cameras actually work?" asked Mason.

"Just a few … and, you know, there're more than videotapes," slurred Alice. "Ooops, that's supposed to be a secret. Forget I told you."

Harry's interest piqued, he stood and rummaged though his pockets as though he intended to pay his bill. He leaned towards the girl.

"What do you mean a secret?" said Mason. "What else is there?"

"I shouldn't say." She looked at Mason and smiled wickedly. "Oh, okay, *mon amour*, if I tell, can we go somewhere after this?"

"I'd like that," said Mason. "You sure like French, don't you?"

Alice nodded and dropped her voice. "Morty records everything, phone calls, office visitors, he's even recorded you—and that seedy agent, Kelly, who I just know is a mobster."

"Me? Son-of-a-bitch. Where does he do it?"

Alice became a little louder. "He's got all the recordings taped—is that what you say? They're on a hard disk in a computer inside his desk. He makes CDs of the recordings, too."

"How do you know Kelly's a mobster?" asked Mason.

Harry figured Alice was so tipsy she'd forgotten to whisper as she said, loud enough to catch the bartender's attention, "Morty recorded a conference call with some Italian—Cicero, I think was the name—and his friends in Chicago, and they were talking about Kelly."

"Alice," said Mitch, looking around. "You shouldn't say things like that out loud. Forget I asked. And forget that phone call, sweetie. Do you want to eat or go somewhere now?"

Harry decided he'd exhausted all his good luck. He placed a ten dollar bill on the bar and turned to leave. The last words he heard were Mason's, proposing to take Alice to the Portola Hotel in Monterey.

Harry exited the restaurant and wandered down Recreational Trail looking for a taxi. He was piling up information to trade with Deputy Mendoza. Morty Greenspan was meeting with mobsters—that was interesting. And that conference call between the don and Chicago that Alice had mentioned—it had to be Cicerone—was golden.

SIXTY-THREE—STOW LAKE

Dominic Franchescini watched the don frown. A copy of the *Paso Robles Weekly Reporter* lay on his desk. The don snarled "son-of-a-bitch" and plunged a letter opener through the newspaper and into the top of his cherished antique desk. Dominic shuddered. "Please, Don Cicerone," he said, "you'll mutilate the desk. I know how much you love it. This is a problem, I know, but I'll take care of it."

The don pulled the letter opener out and threw it aside. He re-read the article:

MYSTERIOUS HEART ATTACKS PLAGUE STAGS
Epidemic Sweeps Los Osos Lodge
Reporting by Max Cotton
(March 17, 2008)

(Los Osos) Several members of the Los Osos Stags Lodge have been struck with heart attacks, after the death of Trustee Randy Lismore in January. Trustee Jimmy Bateman was found dead in his bathtub days after Trustee Larry Yates, rumored to be suffering from emotional distress, suffered a heart attack at the Big Bear Pipe and Tobacco Shop in San Luis Obispo. The Stags' officers have refused to be interviewed about reports the illnesses are related to the sale of their land in Los Osos. However, unnamed sources confirm that the sale is progressing and the Stags have received half the purchase price, about $13 million.

Police are tight-lipped about the Lismore death, which the coroner ruled death due to undetermined cause. However, federal authorities suggested to the coroner that such a determination would facilitate their investigations of organized crime. The real estate agent who handled the sale of the Stags' land to Hansen Property Development, Ron Kelly, a nephew of Don Alessandro Cicerone—a reputed leader of the San Francisco mob—has not returned our calls.

> *Over 100 conditional permits have been issued for construction of new housing units, pending an Environmental Impact Report and other inspections, and the Stags plan a new lodge, financed by the proceeds for the land, on their remaining property. The Los Osos Lodge has awarded a design contract to Monterey Construction Company in Monterey County to design a new building. The old structure is expected to be razed upon completion of the reports and the land transaction closes …*

"Just how do you expect to resolve this?" asked the don.

"It could be worse," said Dominic, "much worse. Perhaps God is watching over us. There are other things which could have been reported." He chose not to mention the county clerk, Pamela McCracken. Perhaps the authorities really thought her death was an accident.

"If these are acts of God, I'm afraid God has been too active. This reporter has brought the entire family into the spotlight and associated it with violence. I think the time has come to disengage from the deal—close down all the links."

"I know we talked about this," said Dominic, "but Hansen still owes us a lot of money. So will Morty Greenspan. I collected half of Ron's fee two days ago."

"The money we've received is enough. After all it was a windfall; we never expected anything like this from Ron. What we should have expected was trouble—he's just too reckless. It's time to cut our losses and remove him from the equation."

"I don't know if I can do that." Dominic felt his heart thump in his chest. The don had never known how close Dominic was to Kelly or the don's sister. It had been folly, of course. He remembered the time he and Alessandra had made love in Golden Gate Park. He'd been twenty-one then, just a wannabe. She'd been eighteen when he'd driven her to the Japanese Tea Garden, in Golden Gate Park. Alessandra had said she'd changed her mind. Instead of wandering the garden and having tea, she'd wanted to go to Stow Lake a few blocks away. They'd parked just south of the lake and she'd leapt upon him. To a man of twenty-one—a boy truly—the girl with the woman's body was irresistible. And he'd wanted her a long time. They'd made love on the front seat of the car.

Dominic shook his head clear. There was no way he could tell the don he'd violated his trust, that Kelly was his son. Alessandra, who'd felt guilty herself, had quickly married the Irishman, Liam Kelly, who'd been dating her occasionally. A marriage Dominic had probably doomed, he thought ruefully.

"How can we do that to your sister?" he asked. "Ron is family."

"She'll get over it. She's a Cicerone and she's always known that the family business is more important than any member." The don paused. "Look, Dominic. Ron's in Tokyo. We've already placed someone there. Have it look like an accident."

Dominic wondered if he should admit the truth but the thought quickly left his mind. "This has to be done by Joey Gee's man," he said. "And Hansen and Morty Greenspan will not be happy losing Ron."

"You can tell Hansen that we're pulling out of the deal. He can keep the rest of the money. That ought to make him happy."

"What about Greenspan?"

"Have you learned anything about the recordings? I asked you to look into it five days ago."

"My best source for that would be our informer but he may not know. I could ask Ron if he'd noticed anything but …. We could stage a break-in but I haven't had a chance yet."

"Don't dally. Morty can take his chances with the Stags, but we stop all communications with them. Send him a 'Dear John' message. He can keep his kickback, if he ever gets the construction job."

"And the Stags?"

"We'll see how it goes and whether we need to take care of them."

"The newspaper mentioned Monterey Construction."

"I understand," said Cicerone. "It's very disturbing. Any attention from the press is a problem. I'm certain Joey Gee won't like it."

Dominic was troubled by his orders. He sensed it was visible on his face. He rose to leave.

"If it will make it easier for you, Dominic, I will ask Joey Gee to make the necessary arrangements in Tokyo."

"Yes, I'd appreciate that." Dominic could feel his body explode in sweat. The don must have noted his weakness. He thought this would be a kindness, but it was really a curse. How could Dominic permit his son to be murdered?

"We're closing it down, Dominic."

Dominic mumbled a good-bye and fled the room. The world had turned dark. He was going to be complicit in the murder of his son. How would he ever face Alessandra?

Thirty minutes later the don called him back to his study.

"I spoke with Joey Gee."

Dominic looked up. "Is he going—?"

"He told me some troubling news. He said Greenspan always had a fascination with tape recorders. He'd bought one of the first cheap tape recorders sold in the early '60s and taped the girls he slept with for the hell of it. Joey Gee wasn't sure, but he had the feeling Morty taped everything for insurance."

"So we break off contact."

"Immediately. See if you can get someone into Monterey. Put a priority on it."

Dominic felt an ache in his stomach and reached into the don's desk humidor and grabbed a cigar. "May I?"

"Of course. Enjoy it. And get to work."

He stood miserably, descended past the *Ganesha* he considered worthless, exited the mansion, and walked to Lafayette Park. It was a bit early for a cigar but Dominic needed it.

SIXTY-FOUR—VACANCIES

Tuesday, March 18th, 2008, 5:15 PM

Harry smiled when he saw Janet through the window walking towards Starbucks. He sat at the same table he'd occupied when he'd heard Deputy Mendoza talk to the sheriff about Randy's death. Janet, with a broad smile, made the Stags' hailing sign in the window.

She gave him a quick kiss, ordered a non-fat decaffeinated latte at the counter, and sat down. "What's happening, Harry?"

Harry grinned, "You're only supposed to make that sign in the lodge room. Don't you remember the initiation?"

"Oh, c'mon—that's that silly ritual stuff. Where's Thor?"

"I left him at home today. Listen, I've been thinking about this Lodge business and all the heart attacks. I talked to that reporter Max Cotton. Did you see his latest article, published yesterday?"

Janet shook her head. Harry explained the visit from the reporter. "On Sunday I drove up to Monterey Bay and looked around. The construction company sits at the end of the middle pier on Monterey Bay. You can see it from Fisherman's Wharf."

"You're not thinking about going in there, are you?"

Harry decided to keep his information about the Greenspan recordings to himself. "I hope it's not necessary. I'm thinking, though, that perhaps I should run for trustee. Yates suggested I would make a good one. There'll be two vacancies—his and Jimmy Bateman's. Randy always wanted me to be a Stag—in fact he used to kid around about how I should be a trustee."

"That'd be a wonderful way to honor Randy," she said. "I'll nominate you."

"If I win and fill Bateman's seat, I'd actually be in Randy's original slot. That'd be nice. It's an opportunity to find out what's going on in those trustee meetings. Further, it would get me closer to Sloane. He strikes me as the leader—Granger's too wimpy."

"There's a Lodge meeting on the twenty-seventh," said Janet. "If you win the election, you can get copies of the trustee minutes and the sales contract."

"We could see them as members anyway, but this avoids calling attention to my interest. I do want to see those minutes and see if the information matches what's in the city's files."

Janet's name was called and she fetched her latte at the counter.

Stirring some sugar into her cup, she said, "We still need to get into Pamela's and the title company's files."

Harry didn't say anything about Pamela. He looked out the window and saw Luis Mendoza park his cruiser at the curb. "Here comes Deputy Mendoza. Let's see what he has to say."

Mendoza acknowledged Harry with a wave and collected a black coffee. He walked over to Harry's table and gave Janet a friendly smile when they were introduced. "Warrener," he said, "I understand you're a Stag now. Just can't stay out of trouble, can you?"

"The lady is a Stag as well. She's been helping me collect some information."

Mendoza frowned. "Did you see that article by Cotton yesterday? He put the spotlight on the mob. Can't you see you're just asking for trouble?"

"I believe Randy was murdered, Deputy," said Janet. "Are you making any progress in your investigation?"

"I'm sure your friend has told you we identified the suspect." Mendoza turned to Harry. "What have you learned?"

"Cotton told me that he saw some document that said there were one hundred eight units being built. The deal we had with Hansen was for one hundred and four."

"Did you know," asked Mendoza, addressing his remark to Janet, "that the county clerk, Pamela McCracken, died four days ago?"

Janet gasped. "Pamela? That's terrible. What happened?"

"I should have told you," said Harry looking at Janet, "but I thought it would scare you. I found out from Max Cotton this weekend. That's one of the reasons I drove up to Monterey."

"What the heck, Harry—was it an accident?"

"Ask Deputy Mendoza."

Mendoza stirred some sugar in his coffee. "She died from CO poisoning. Apparently, the landlady left her engine running on her SUV, in the garage below McCracken's apartment."

"Just another accident, eh?" said Harry. "How convenient!"

"The landlady said she was certain she'd turned off her engine; the SLO police, not the sheriff, are investigating."

"Well, if Pamela was involved in this deal," said Harry, "and she messed with the permits, there could be another million bucks in play."

"I found out," said Mendoza, "from the Feds that the agent, Ron Kelly, flew to Japan a week ago. Has he received his fee from the Stags yet?"

"I think so," said Harry. "They said at the Stags meeting that they were going to pay half the bill."

"I wonder who they gave the payment to," said Mendoza. He looked thoughtful.

"What do you know about the Monterey Construction Company?" asked Harry,

Mendoza chugged his coffee and threw the cup at a wastepaper basket next to the counter. "Not much."

Harry decided to test one of the comments he'd heard in Cannery Row. "I understand the owner, Morty Greenspan, is a mobster. He has connections to Chicago and Don Cicerone. Did the Feds tell you that?"

"I've heard rumors. Some research turned up connections between them. Why do you ask?"

"I'd like to check them out. They have the design job for the lodge and, if extra money is floating around, maybe their hands are in the cookie jar."

Mendoza nodded. "Warrener, your nose is growing longer. I'd call it bullshit but we're in the presence of a lady. Who've you been talking to?"

"I just heard some small talk in the Big Bear," said Harry, evasively. He wasn't ready to disclose all the information he'd picked up in Willy's Smokehouse. "Can you look into that?"

Mendoza stared at Harry. "I'll turn up the heat a little. Other than Kelly's trip to Japan, I haven't heard squat from the Feds since they ID'ed Califano. I hope you're still alive when I find out something."

"I'll be careful."

Mendoza smiled at Janet, waved at the clerks behind the counter, and departed.

"What's that about Greenspan?" asked Janet.

"I'll tell you later. Right now it's safer if you don't know."

"Are you sure you want to be a trustee? It sounds terrible."

"So goes the politics of charities," he said. "I'm committed to discovering what happened to Randy. The best way is to follow the money. I'm nervous, of course, but sometimes—"

Janet nodded. "I know this is important, Harry, but it sounds dangerous. It's terrible what happened to Pamela. I didn't like her but no one deserves to die. Do you think it was an accident?"

"No, but it was probably painless, not like Randy's death."

Harry looked away. Damn right, it was dangerous. He hoped he wasn't dragging Janet deeper into the cesspool.

SIXTY-FIVE—ELECTION

Thursday, March 27th, 2008, 7:30 PM

The audience was restless. There were thirty or so members scattered about the Los Osos Stags Lodge's meeting room. Most members looked forward to a short meeting and a quick return to the bar. The '56 favorite, *Wake Up Little Susie,* by the Everly Brothers, roared out of the jukebox in the bar and pounded against the internal wall to the room. Ted Granger banged his gavel once. "I'm about to open the meeting of Lodge Number 218 of the Fraternal Order of Stags. Inform the tiler ..."

When Granger banged twice, the officers rose. Harry nudged Janet and pointed towards the empty chair where Randy Lismore would have sat. "Did you see the notice of the election to fill Bateman's vacancy?"

"In the hall," she said, "I heard they're going to nominate someone named Campbell."

He nodded. "I don't know the man. I wonder if I should run against him."

"I haven't changed my mind," said Janet. "It might be the right thing to do but it's still dangerous. I won't think less of you if you don't run."

Harry sniffed. The characteristic tropical jungle smell that haunted him frequently was back. He felt himself vacillate. Then he closed his eyes and told himself it was time to take the next step forward in the investigation. He hoped Mason wouldn't recognize him after his adventure in Monterey; at least Mason wasn't at this meeting.

"I guess I'm committed," he said with apprehension. "When we get to the election, nominate me. I think they're getting to the part about Randy now."

"… He has passed," said Granger, "into the light which is beyond the valley of the shadow of death ..."

The meeting continued. Later, when Granger reached new business on the agenda, he announced an election would be conducted to replace the departed trustee Bateman. He asked for nominations from the floor.

Janet rose. "I nominate Harry Warrener."

Jimmy Belgado, the Stag who frequented the Big Bear Pipe and Tobacco Shop, wanted to second the nomination but Granger told him seconds weren't required. Granger then nominated Lloyd Campbell. When there were no further nominations, Granger asked if any of the nominees wished to speak. "You each have three minutes," he said.

Lloyd Campbell said, "Thank you, Exalted Ruler. Most of you know me. I've been a Stag for thirty-seven years. Ted's asked me to fill Jimmy Bateman's slot and I'm pleased to do it. I'm eager to serve."

Harry took the floor. "Thanks. Many of you don't know me. I admit I'm a new Stag and have limited experience in the Lodge. But if it's okay, I'd like to summarize my background." Harry launched into a quick description of his education. He told them he'd been an underwater demolitions specialist in the SEALS but he didn't mention his Purple Heart. "After I received my Master's," he concluded, "I served as a professor of economics and computer science at Cal Poly. Randy Lismore was my friend and I want to honor him with my service. I'll do my best. Thanks."

Jerry Sloane raised his hand. "Ted, are we going to have any discussion on these candidates before the election?"

"What about Larry Yates's position, Ted?" asked a Stag. "His term expires soon and we need to elect a five year trustee. His wife told me she won't allow him to run again."

Granger rubbed his eyes. With all the stress he'd forgotten about Yates. He looked around the room. The faces of the Stags were in their usual bored and nondescript state. Most eyes that were open were glazed. A few members scowled and a few smiled eagerly but the electorate, in general, Granger knew, was anxious to vote. "Okay, does anyone want Yates's job?"

No one raised their arm.

Sloane jumped out of his seat. "Ted, we should table this. We're talking about a five year appointment. Think about the timing. You can appoint a temporary trustee next week to fill this vacancy when the term's up. If Campbell loses, you can appoint him and we can run an election for the permanent replacement at leisure, after more people have a chance to consider the job."

Harry smiled. He'd noticed that Sloane had not suggested that Granger appoint him if he lost the vote. These guys were relentless.

"Okay, Jerry," said Granger. "I hope we don't have a problem with the district. Let's vote. The members can write in Warrener's name on the ballot." He instructed the secretary and the esquire to pass out written ballots.

The room broke into conversation during the distribution of the ballots. Several Stags received multiple ballots. Janet ended up with three and one Stag handed six ballots back to the secretary. Pens and pencils were in short supply; Stags crisscrossed the floor borrowing pens, and looked over each other's shoulder to see the *secret* ballots. Five minutes later, the ballots were collected.

All the existing officers, save one, were re-elected by substantial majorities. That candidate had withdrawn in the race for leading lecturing knight and his opponent had run uncontested. Despite the flood of extra ballots, Harry was declared the winner in the election for trustee by three votes. He guessed that he'd scored some votes among the members who'd supported Randy. He smiled at Janet who offered her congratulations. When he turned toward the station of the exalted ruler he noticed Granger wasn't smiling and Sloane scowled. Well, thought Harry, he knew what that was about. His intentions were honorable, he mused, but he was going to be an enormous thorn in their side.

"I liked Jerry's recommendation," said Granger. "I appoint Lloyd Campbell as a temporary five-year trustee effective April 1st. We'll take additional nominations and run an election at the next meeting."

The meeting concluded with the usual ritual and proscription against divulging confidential information. Harry and Janet climbed into his car, told Thor the good news, and headed for the Big Sky Cafe in SLO to celebrate.

SIXTY-SIX—OPPOSED

Jerry Sloane pulled his Miata into the lot at the Kon Tiki Motel in Pismo Beach. High clouds led a storm front eastward off the ocean and the waves behind the motel were topped with whitecaps. He could feel the rain coming and the air had the characteristic smell of ozone.

The special trustees meeting began in thirty minutes and Sloane was firm in his decision to force the trustees to award the construction contract to Monterey. Morty Greenspan had submitted a flat fixed-price not-to-exceed twenty million dollar proposal and promised the Stags the 'Taj Mahal of Stag-dom.' The price was outrageous but they'd still be able to satisfy Jim Thatcher's reserve requirement of four million dollars and nothing was going to interfere with Sloane's kickbacks. It was fish-or-cut-bait time. He figured Harry Warrener would never be easier to handle than at his first meeting. He grabbed a folder of Stags documents out of his trunk and smiled at Mitch Mason who waited for him in the parking lot.

"We're doing it today," said Sloane, "the whole bloody contract. All twenty mil."

"That's my man," said Mason. "No more bullshit. Get it approved today and the whole Lodge can vote the deal at the next meeting."

"That's the plan. Maybe you could come to a fucking meeting sometime."

"I was busy—there's a new girlfriend and she's hot."

"Yeah, well, there's this new trustee; I'm not sure where he stands. But he did vote to approve the design job."

Sloane waved as Harry Warrener drove into the lot. He introduced Harry to Mason. They all shook hands and walked into the motel lobby.

"Do I know you?" asked Mason. "You look familiar."

"I don't think so," replied Warrener.

"You guys can kiss later. We have a meeting," said Sloane.

The other trustees, absent Yates who continued to convalesce at home, were already assembled in the conference room.

"Is Ted coming to the meeting?" asked John Potempa. His eyes were tearing.

"I sent him notice," said Sloane. "He said he'd be late."

Sloane distributed copies of Monterey Construction Company's design and new construction proposal. "You probably have some questions about some of the design features," he said, "but the overall plan is pretty good. I'm sure that Mitch can work with Monterey on any minor adjustments—"

"The drawings are nice but I have one issue," said Carole Greene. "The deep end of the adult pool needs to be deeper if we want to avoid liability from people jumping in. Otherwise, I like the plan."

"Those are the kind of minor items I'm referring to, Carole," said Sloane. "We'll appoint a committee to work out the fine details later. Let's vote to approve the contract now so it can go to the Lodge floor at the first meeting in April."

Lloyd Campbell, in the meeting as an observer, raised his hand. "I know I can't vote, Jerry, but I'd be in favor."

"I agree with Carole and Lloyd that the drawings are nice," said Potempa. "But the cost summary is a little thin; there're just lump sums for some pretty large categories. I don't know much about construction but couldn't we get more detail?"

Sloane wondered at Potempa's ability to ask a coherent question, especially a question Sloane didn't want. "John, it's a not-to-exceed price. We don't need detail. We just concentrate on the total."

Harry Warrener shook his head. "I don't understand, Jerry. We just looked at this proposal. From what I understand we haven't completed the sale or received all the money. Even if we liked the total cost, which I don't, how can we approve this contract without all the money in the bank?"

"Let me answer that," said Mason. "I've been working with Morty Greenspan at Monterey and he understands we still need to close the rest of the deal. By authorizing this contract now, he'll start on the construction permits, and razing, but he won't start construction yet."

"Can we only approve part of the proposal?" asked Carole Greene. She looked at Potempa who had his hand raised.

"I don't think we can do that Carole," said Potempa. "What's the status of the land deal, Jerry?"

"We're waiting for the Environmental Impact Report. It's required to close the deal," said Sloane.

"Do you know there's a pillbox on the property?" asked Warrener.

"A pillbox? What's that got to do with the lodge building?" asked Mason.

Sloane didn't like the direction the conversation was taking. He knew there'd been a pillbox on the property; he'd seen parts of the structure sticking out of the sand from time to time. But he'd never thought anything of it. "Forget the pillbox issue. It's been there over sixty years and never made a difference to anyone. Are we going to give the contract to Monterey or not? Every day of delay on this side is another day we're not in the new building on the back side."

"But, Jerry," said Warrener, "I did a little homework and Monterey's record is not unblemished. Also we should get an independent validation of the quote and we need to clean up—"

"Look Harry, let it be. You don't know the history here. We don't want to queer this deal. We can't afford to let that happen. You know the Lodge needs the new building and the rest of the money. We give the job to Monterey and it's business as usual. They know we're a charity and promised to take care of us. If there's an environmental problem, they'll fix it."

"Can we negotiate payment terms?" asked Campbell.

"Cash flow is no problem," said Mason. "We have over twelve million in the bank and we won't go through that for at least a year."

The door opened and Ted Granger walked into the meeting. His shoulders drooped and he was more pale than usual. "Sorry I'm late, Jerry."

"No problem, Ted. We're about to vote on the construction job."

Sloane watched Warrener start to raise his hand and then withdraw it. The guy was a problem and Sloane caught Mason's eye. He tilted his head toward Warrener and nodded.

"Jerry, call the question," said Mason.

"I simply can't support the resolution, Jerry," said Warrener. "You're going to tear down the old lodge, commit to spending money you don't have, and there's a risky EIR report coming."

"What's he talking about?" asked Granger, rubbing his eyes and hunched over.

"Nothing, Ted. Let's take the vote." Sloane raised his hand and said "All in favor of granting the construction contract to Monterey, subject to negotiated payment terms?"

"This still has to be approved on the Lodge floor, correct?" asked Potempa.

"The best way to get it approved on the floor is for a unanimous vote. Now goddamn it, all in favor? Sign of the Stag! And don't give me any crap about swearing, John." Sloane raised his hand.

Sloane glared at Warrener who stared back in defiance. Potempa and Greene raised their hands.

"Opposed?" said Sloane.

"Please record my vote," said Warrener, "as opposed in the minutes."

"Damn it, Harry. I want a unanimous vote," growled Sloane. He threw his folder of documents on the table.

"Well, you're not going to get it. Besides, what difference does it make? The motion carried."

"You're a new Stag," said Sloane. "You don't understand the history here. The Lodge floor is—"

"Why do you people," said Warrener, "always bring up history? Surely, we need to—"

"Forget it, Jerry," said Granger. "There may be some questions but I don't want any more trouble."

"What kind of trouble?" asked Warrener. He looked from Granger to Sloane and raised his hands in an open, questioning manner.

Sloane glared angrily at Granger. "The vote was three-one. Meeting's adjourned," said Sloane, "but I want Mitch and Ted to stick around."

Sloane stared at Greene's rear end as she followed Warrener out of the room. He was so angry he wanted to shoot Warrener. Funny, even bagging Greene wouldn't appease him or relieve the tension. He feared there'd be someone at the next Lodge meeting who would want to know why the motion wasn't unanimous. "We have a week or so to make that prick change his mind," he said. "Any ideas?"

"We'll figure out how to explain it," said Granger. "It's not worth killing someone. I don't want any trouble! Do you understand?"

Sloane watched Granger rub his eyes again. He wanted to rip out the man's eyes. The large kickback were close and this guy would spill the beans to anyone who applied any pressure.

"What was that about the EIR?" asked Granger.

"It's nothing," said Sloane. "There's an old pillbox on the property."

"Really?" asked Granger. "Doesn't that have to be disclosed?"

"Look Ted, it's Hansen's problem. Forget it."

"It better not be a problem, Jerry. This whole deal is turning bad. Maybe we should back out and return the money."

"Are you nuts?" Sloane looked at Mason who shook his head in apparent disgust.

"Let's see if we can apply some pressure," said Mason. "Can we talk to Kelly?"

"Kelly?" blurted Granger. "No one knows where Kelly is, and I just said I don't want any problems."

"We'll do what we need to do," said Sloane. "Talk to Morty, Mitch. If he wants the deal, it's time to belly up to the bar. And don't say anything about that frigging EIR study."

"Me?" said Mason. "Maybe you should talk to him. Isn't that why I'm pay—"

"Mitch!" Sloane wagged his finger at Mason.

Mason nodded.

"What's that about?" asked Granger.

"Nothing!" snarled Sloane. That damn Mason had almost exposed the kickback he'd demanded. Granger had been opposed to him squeezing Mason; it would just be more information Granger couldn't handle.

The three men wandered disconsolately down the long hallway to the parking lot. Large rain drops splattered and lightning flashed on the horizon.

Sloane's heart generated a cluster of PVCs as he climbed behind the wheel. He stared at the ocean and willed himself to fight a rising panic that the deal would unravel and leave him exposed. At least the Indians seemed mollified by his fifty K payment. The current problem was the EIR. He had to know the status of that report. He'd tried to call Pamela McCracken several times but there'd been no answer on her cell phone. He planned to beat down her office door on Monday morning.

SIXTY-SEVEN—MONTEREY

Saturday, March 29th, 2008, 11:30 AM

When the door to his office flew open, Morty Greenspan reached under his desk and turned on the recorders. Mitch Mason stormed into his office with a grave expression. Rain dripped off his jacket and he threw it onto Greenspan's table.

"What's up?" asked Greenspan.

"It's happening again. We have another problem with the trustees. We passed a vote to give you the construction job but it wasn't unanimous. I can't fuckin' believe it."

"What's with this unanimous bullshit? Can't you guys just go with the majority votes?"

"Technically, yes. But it raises questions we don't want. It might even attract the attention of the guys in the district, the next level up."

"For Christ's sake, Mitch. You Stags are unbelievable." Greenspan grabbed Mason's jacket off his table and hung it on an old wooden coat rack. "Slob! Can't you guys make up your minds and stick to a decision? What's wrong now? Who's unhappy with the proposal?"

"We have another new trustee and he says competition is a must. He says we should at least get an independent price assessment. He said he researched your outfit and you do shitty work."

"Who is he?"

"A new Stag. He was friends with Lismore—remember the trustee who died in the Madonna Inn? I ain't sure but I think Sloane encouraged someone, like Kelly, to help that along."

"How about Kelly? Did you call him?"

"Are you kidding? Kelly's MIA. I can't find out dick. Sloane's besides himself over this new trustee and Granger, as usual, is asleep at the switch."

"I'll call Dominic," said Greenspan. "Let's find out what the fuck is going on." He dialed Dominic's number.

After three rings it was answered.

"This is Dominic."

"Morty."

"Yo. What can I do for you?"

"Where's Kelly?" asked Greenspan.

"On a trip."

"Is he coming back?"

"That's an interesting question, Morty. Why wouldn't he?"

"We turned in the construction proposal and now there's a trustee problem."

"We don't care," said Dominic. "You work it out—or not."

"What? When were you going to tell us? You don't want your kick—"

"I don't know what you're talking about," said Dominic.

Greenspan kicked his desk in frustration. Not a good idea, he thought—it might mess up his microphone connections and the recordings. "You guys pulled out? You can kiss your action good-bye."

"You say strange things on the telephone, Morty. It's not smart."

"What do you mean by that?" asked Greenspan. "Are you sure? I've made—"

"Out means out."

Greenspan took a deep breath. He'd almost said something about his recordings. Then again, it meant another million. But, still aggravated, he said, "I'm calling Joey Gee."

"Be my guest." Dominic hung up.

"Shit," said Greenspan. "Those guys are pulling out."

Mason looked up. "Huh? What do you mean, out?"

"I don't know—they ain't part of the deal anymore."

"But why?" asked Mason.

"I don't know," said Greenspan. The more he thought about it the more he liked that extra million. "Who cares?"

"What about Kelly?"

"Fuck Kelly. I still want that contract. We're talking twenty million. This trustee, does he have any pressure points?"

"There's a woman—and a dog."

"All right. Let's put some pressure on her."

"I thought that's not your style. What are you going to do to her?"

Greenspan pulled open the drawer on the side of his desk and looked at the recorder. The red light indicated the recorder still functioned despite the kick. Dominic's comments had unsettled him. He wondered if he should switch it off—then decided to leave it on. There's a book on those recordings, he thought. Next time he went to Chicago he'd take the CDs and play them for Joey Gee. In fact, he remembered, he had to transfer the recent recordings to disks. Then he had a chill. Playing these recordings to Joey Gee would expose the fact he'd been recording him. Not a good idea.

He turned to Mason. "That's *we*, you putz. Let's see how this guy reacts when we squeeze the woman. We'll rough her up and send a message."

"Can you get someone to do it?"

"Maybe, but you're also going to play."

"What? Why me?" Mason looked pale.

"Because it's your idea, shmuck."

Mason paused. Greenspan knew Mason was mad enough—but this was real crime they were talking about, not a little bribe. Still, it meant two hundred grand to the guy. He watched as Mason gritted his teeth.

"Maybe we can sweeten your piece," said Greenspan. "If the mob is out, I can probably find another fifty thousand for you."

Greenspan watched Mason do some internal calculating. His eyes rose. "Okay," said Mason. "Her name is Janet Zimmer and she lives in Los Osos."

"We'll arrange something as soon as possible. I'll let you know when and where."

"What do I have to do?"

"This isn't rocket science. You grab her, tie her up, and threaten the hell out of her. Make sure she tell hers boyfriend. Then you dump her somewhere. You won't be alone. I'll send Andy with you."

"What do you need me for if Andy goes?"

"You take care of the dog if it's necessary."

"Me? You want me to shoot it?" asked Mason.

"Do it any way you like—it's only a dog."

"C'mon, Morty. We're talking about assault and kidnapping."

Greenspan knew it was out of character. He'd spent years working angles, letting the Italians handle the violence, while he tried to stay below the radar. But this deal was worth millions. "Screw it. Did you guys get the rest of your money yet?"

"The deal is pending—we're waiting on an EIR report which is due any day now. Then the Coastal Commission."

"You better get the rest of the money. That twenty million includes your piece of the action. Don't forget that."

"I understand. Right now we only have twelve and a half-million. If the Lodge approves the contract, we'll have to negotiate payment terms with you. The whole deal can't go through until we close the sale."

"I start work—you guys owe me twenty million. I'll wait for the second half, but there's no backing out once we start. That ain't the way it works. Got it?"

"I have to tell Granger and Sloane about the plan."

"Why not? We're all in this together."

"I know Sloane is worried about Granger."

"You guys take care of your own end of this deal and I'll build the building."

Greenspan waved Mason out of his office, reached down, and turned off his recorder. With the mob out of the deal, it meant another million for him and, if Kelly disappeared, he could pay off Mason with part of Kelly's cut—that was another sixty K. He'd even have an additional ten K left over. Even if the trustee doesn't come around he'll still force them to award the contract. A majority vote was all they actually needed and they had it. Who cared if the Stags' officers had a problem?

Greenspan saw Mason stop in the yard next to the fence and pull out his cell-phone. Mason began to wave his arms and shout into the phone. Greenspan smiled. Mason was arguing, he had to be talking to Granger. He knew Mason wouldn't have argued with Sloane.

SIXTY-EIGHT—POCO-POCO

Monday, March 31st, 2008, 9:15 AM

Kelly stepped out of the Tokyo subway train in the Shimbashi Station. Hordes of morning rush passengers swept past him onto the train. He stepped aside for the pushers with white gloves who rammed as many people as possible into the Ginza Line cars. He walked south along the platform dodging the remaining passengers who watched in classic Japanese stoicism, as the train whisked away. After three weeks in Tokyo he'd mastered the subway and train systems. Kelly knew the passengers didn't have long to wait, the next train would arrive in precisely two minutes.

Kelly was on a mission. Sunday he'd felt there were eyes on him as he'd wandered in Hibya Park. There'd been a swarthy, dark haired Caucasian—they called westerners *gaijins* in Japan—who seemed to be dogging him. He'd seen the man several times, even when he wandered through the Matsuzaya Department Store on Ginza Dori, and in the Old Imperial Bar at the Imperial Hotel. Ron had sat at behind the lounge's old brick wall—a relic of the original Imperial Hotel that had survived the massive 1923 Tokyo earthquake—and he'd seen the man wandering through the hotel foyer outside the bar.

Later, Kelly had walked through the Shimbashi neighborhood. Yamanote Line green trains had roared overhead on elevated tracks as he'd wandered from one hostess bar to another until he'd found one he'd liked, up a small stairwell, in a narrow alley, called Poco-Poco. He'd been greeted graciously and seated in a remote corner of the lounge. Drunken Japanese businessmen were singing karaoke and he'd ordered a bottle of Suntory Yamazaki, a Japanese whiskey made in the Scotch whisky tradition. Every twenty minutes the mama-san would rotate a different, attractive, English-speaking girl to his table. He'd begun to relax when the man who'd tailed him earlier had walked in accompanied by two Japanese men in dark suits. Ron had gulped when he realized the Japanese were each missing part of a finger. *Yakuza*, he'd realized. That had convinced him the *gaijin* was a hit-man and he was the target. Kelly threw fifty thousand yen—about five hundred dollars—on the table and moved right past the three men for the exit. They glared at him as he apologized to the mama-san and bolted down the steps. The mama-san had wanted to send a girl to escort him to the taxis but he'd declined.

Despite a cold mist, the streets had been crowded and a long line of taxis had collected outside, on Soto-bori Dori. Kelly, in a panic, had wanted to grab the closest cab but he'd known he had to go to the front of the line. He'd run to the front of the line and jumped in a cab. He'd glimpsed the three men from Poco-Poco on the sidewalk as his cab had made an illegal U-turn and disappeared west bound.

Kelly had spent a restless night, gathered his luggage, and checked out of the Imperial Hotel. His bags had been left with the doorman with instructions that a cab would fetch them. He intended to get lost and then find another hotel. He'd planned a trip on the Tokyo subway and train system intending to lose the tail. His current destination was Ariake on Tokyo Bay. It was an area known for its amusement rides and clusters of European-style restaurants, not far from the Fuji TV headquarters building. One could see a Ferris wheel and the huge sphere that adorned Fuji TV from the Tokyo Bay shoreline. A monorail transported visitors to Ariake from Shimbashi. Kelly had figured a bunch of train-hopping would simplify spotting, and then losing, the tail. He'd already ridden three subway lines and the Yamanote circular elevated train before he'd switched back to the Ginza subway line.

He'd traveled two hours and had begun to feel more secure when he saw the man who'd followed him again, lingering at the opposite end of the Ginza Line subway station. The man seemed alone but *Yakuza*, if they were also there, were impossible to differentiate in the crowd. Kelly walked to the exit and climbed the escalator. The Japanese stood politely to the right and he had no problem accelerating as he ascended. Kelly wondered if Don Cicerone had sent this guy; he hadn't heard from Dominic in days but Kelly had finally realized he'd not been spirited out of Los Angeles on a whim.

On the street, Kelly moved quickly to another escalator that carried passengers to the Yurikamome Monorail Line. The station had glass doors that protected the tracks; he didn't think a threat would materialize until the end of the line, when he'd reached Ariake, at the earliest.

Kelly stationed himself at the glass doors at the end of the platform. He could watch the escalator from that position. Shimbashi was the line's terminus and when the train arrived he entered the closest car. A group of young Japanese students piled in behind him and he was pressed against the opposite door. Out of the corner of his eye he saw the man who'd followed him force his way into the second door of the same car. They were both frozen in position on opposite sides of the car by the passengers. Kelly shivered as the train doors closed and the train accelerated toward Ariake.

The first stop was Shiodome, a relatively new business neighborhood, and Kelly tensed. That station sat in the middle of the tracks and the doors would open on his side. His shadow was trapped by the crowd on the other side of the car. Kelly scanned the platform and saw few new passengers. The doors opened and he lingered, seemingly indifferent. Just as the doors began to close he lurched onto the platform. The train departed and Kelly figured he had about ten minutes to escape before the man could possibly return to Shiodome. He stepped across the platform, Three minutes later an inbound train returned him to Shimbashi. He ran into an NTT phone shop on Soto-bori Dori, purchased an international telephone pre-paid card, and found a KDD phone booth.

Dominic's cell phone voice mail answered on the fourth ring. Kelly hung up in disgust. He dialed his mother's phone.

"Hello?" said a slurred voice. Kelly looked at his watch. It was 11:32 in the morning in Tokyo; the middle of the night in San Francisco.

"Mom? It's me. I need a favor. Can you call the don?" Kelly nervously scanned the crowds around the phone booth. It probably had not been a good idea to return to the neighborhood near Poco-Poco.

Trains thundered overhead on the Yamanote line towards Tokyo Station as Ron waited for his mother to respond.

"Me? You want me to call that asshole? What did Dominic say?"

"He rushed me out of town. Look, Mom, I'm in trouble and I need help."

Kelly could hear his mother stirring in her bed, then he heard a crash.

"Damn," she said. "That was the lamp. All right, what do you want me to do?"

"Ask him if I can come home. I've been here three weeks already and I'm afraid he's mad at me—I need his permission."

"Is all this because of that stupid land deal? I told you not to mess with him."

"Mom, I think they're trying to kill me. I need you to talk to him."

There was a long pause. "Mom? There's still a lot of money involved. You can remind him."

"Okay. You come home. I'll take care of it."

"Are you sure?"

"Yes. I'll talk to him in the morning. Call me when you know your flight. I'll have Dominic meet you."

Kelly hung up. He dialed United Airlines in the U.S. and located their ticket office in downtown Tokyo. First and Business Class were sold out so he booked an economy ticket on the early evening flight to San Francisco. The ticket office was located in the Marunochi business district, a ten minute cab ride away. Kelly took a cab which turned onto Hibya Dori and passed the Imperial Hotel. He had thoughts of retrieving his bags but decided against it. He dashed into the United office, paid cash for a ticket, and grabbed another cab. He had several choices: take a bus to the airport from Tokyo City Air Terminal for about forty dollars, a train from Tokyo Station or other rail stations for about thirty-five dollars, or take the cab directly to Narita Airport for about four hundred dollars. He chose the cab ride to the airport.

At Narita, Kelly called his mother with the estimated time of arrival. Then, United's inbound flight to Narita was an hour late and Kelly roamed the bars at Narita, downing Scotch after Scotch. Airborne at last, he fell into a troubled sleep wondering if his mother had appeased the don.

SIXTY-NINE—GOOD CATHOLICS

A window washers' truck blocked the driveway on Jackson Street when Dominic Franchescini looked out the window of the don's house. He'd received a summons from the don at 8:45 AM ordering him to the study. When he entered the don's study the washers were working on the large plate glass windows facing south.

"Let's take a walk," commanded the don.

They walked down Octavia Street and entered the north side of Lafayette Park. The don looked stressed to Dominic.

"He's coming home, right now. He's airborne, scheduled arrival is around 4:00 PM but it lands at 4:45 PM, late, on a United flight from Tokyo."

It was a bright, sunny day in San Francisco but Dominic felt a chill. "Ron's coming home?"

"Our Chicago friends, whom I asked out of consideration for you, have failed to take care of the problem. I'm afraid I must insist that you get involved."

"What happened? I planted him in Tokyo for his own good. Did Joey Gee—?"

"My sister called me this morning begging me to allow Ron to return. She, of course, is a fool and a drunk. She doesn't understand the threat her son poses to the family."

"But why is Ron returning?"

"He's convinced there's a hit team in Tokyo. He asked her to plead with me for a safe conduct."

"Did you order it?" Dominic wasn't certain whether the don had granted a safe conduct or was still intent upon killing Kelly.

The men had climbed to the top of the hill in the park and had a fine view of the distant Civic Center. The golden dome of City Hall glistened in the morning sunlight and the City sparkled after the evening showers.

"Dominic," said the don, "I want you to fetch Ron at SFO and take him to the cabin at Incline Village in Nevada. You will wait for instructions there. Do not bring him here under any circumstances."

A brisk breeze blew across the top of the hill but Dominic broke out in an instant sweat. He felt a pang in his chest.

"What are your intentions? And what about your sister?"

"Just tell her that the matter is under control. And pray the authorities don't know he's returning to the country—for your sake as well as Ron's."

"I don't know …" muttered Dominic.

"It's quite simple," said the don. "You know what may have to be done. When I give the word you'll take care of business and he will not suffer. If I have to call Joey Gee again, it would be very unfortunate for everyone."

Dominic nodded dismally. "I think Greenspan's been recording everything. When I spoke to him, he was too eager to talk about the deal."

"You haven't sent someone into the warehouse yet?"

Dominic shook his head in misery. "I just haven't had an opportunity. I don't want to ask anyone else to do it; they don't need to know there might be recordings."

"Perhaps I should ask Joey Gee to instruct him to destroy the recordings."

"Do you think he has enough leverage on Greenspan?"

"Dominic, it's been said that the future Antichrist will come from the Jews. They've always been involved with usury and the exploitation of the poor. But they are cowards. I'm quite confident Joey Gee could solve the problem if I ask. Are we not all good Catholics?"

The don turned away and walked briskly back down the hill. Dominic watched the don fade from view and called Alessandra.

"Hello?"

"It's me," said Dominic. "What were you thinking when you told Ron he could come home?"

"It's all right, I talked to my brother. He said it would be okay. Are you going to pick him up?"

"God damn it, Alessandra. We're all at risk now."

"Just get him and put him somewhere safe."

"Yeah, sure!" Dominic hung up. Nowhere, he thought, was safe. Definitely not Incline Village. He wandered back to the mansion.

SEVENTY—APOLLO

Fred Harris chomped on a veal chop in Sam's Café when his cell phone rang. The call was from a telephone in area code 213 and he recognized the number.

"This is Harris. What's happening?"

"Fred, this is Monty, in the task force. There was a hit on the Apollo Reservation System for United Airlines. Ron Kelly is airborne right now, inbound to San Francisco. His ETA is a little delayed, 4:45 PM this afternoon. You can nail him in the customs arrival hall."

Harris pushed his plate aside and rang the call button for service. "That's good news but I still need a warrant."

"I talked to the special agent in charge here and he agreed to ask for one."

"What charge will you use?"

"We'll go in for a RICO charge. You don't want to use murder, do you?"

"No, that'll just get that Deputy Mendoza in SLO involved. Leave it at RICO."

"Okay. We'll have it before the plane lands. I'll fax it up as soon as I get it."

The waiter walked in and Harris ordered a double Scotch and a glass of milk.

He wondered if Kelly would give up information on the don. Harris dialed Sam Bernini and asked him to call the U.S. Customs Office at SFO to alert the customs police that an arrest was planned for an inbound passenger, arriving on the United Airlines flight from Tokyo. Then he called Agent John Lewiston with the news. "Meet me at the United Airlines counter in the international building at SFO at 4:00 PM this afternoon. We're nabbing Kelly."

"What happened?" said Lewiston. "I thought we'd lost him in Asia."

"Just be there."

"What's the charge?"

"We're going in on RICO. But we'll update the charges later, depending on what he gives us."

"Do you really think he'll give up the don?" asked Lewiston. "I can't imagine he's suicidal."

"That's enough questions, John. Just be there."

Harris clicked off as the drinks arrived. He pondered which drink should go first. He elected the milk first, gulped it, and savored the whisky. Lewiston had sounded reticent. He wondered why.

SEVENTY-ONE—ATTACK

Two men lurked behind the edge of the old pillbox on the Stags' property. The sun was still high on the horizon but the beach was deserted. One of the men clutched a driftwood club. The wind was gusty, kicking up swirls of sand. The men's faces were hidden by nylon stockings; they watched as a woman and a dog loped down the beach towards them. The dog led the way. Both men tensed when the dog caught their scent as he passed the pillbox and turned towards them.

"C'mon," yelled Mitch Mason and he and Andy, one of Morty Greenspan's men, plunged down the small embankment. Andy tackled Janet Zimmer.

She yelled, "Thor, help!"

Janet and Andy tumbled to the sand followed by a snarling mass of fur and fangs. Thor planted his fangs on Andy's right bicep and bit deep. Blood spurted into the sand and drenched Janet, who was stunned by the tackle. Mason swung his club at Thor's head. Thor yelped, released Andy's arm, and fell to the sand.

Mason bent down and tied Janet's arms behind her back with plastic ties. He pulled a black bag out of his pocket and threw it over her head. The dog bled from his scalp and his fur was matted with a mix of his and Andy's blood. Mason looked at Andy. "You okay?"

"Goddamn it, my arm's bleeding," said Andy. "Where'd this fuckin' wolf come from? Morty didn't say nothin' about a dog."

"Shut up, you idiot. Don't mention any names. Screw your arm and grab the bitch!" said Mason. "Hurry up, the beach is still deserted."

He reached into another pocket and retrieved a whiskey flask filled with anti-freeze; then poured it into the dazed dog's mouth. He'd checked with a dog fancier and discovered that dogs loved anti-freeze. He watched the dog actually lap at the liquid.

The men carried Janet up to Mason's pick-up truck, on the road behind the lodge.

Janet mumbled "Let me go, you bastards. You better not have hurt that dog."

They threw her twisting, kicking, and protesting onto the back bed of the truck, under the yellow camper shell

"Shut up, you bitch, if you want to live," said Andy. He grabbed a roll of duct tape out of the trunk, ripped the bag off Janet's head, and pasted a piece of tape across her mouth. Then he put the bag back on and slammed the back gate of the truck. Mason and Andy took off their masks and piled into the cab of the truck. It screeched away on the pavement covered with loose blowing sand.

Thor whimpered and lay in the sand. He tried to rise and stumbled. When the old man with a cane found him an hour later, the dog was frothing at the mouth; his head lay in a pool of vomit. Thor tried to thump his tail. The dog acted like he was drunk but the blood on his fur was obvious. The old man fingered the animal's collar and read a phone number on a dog tag. He walked up to the Los Osos Stags lodge and banged on the door.

"There's a sick dog out here. Can I use your phone?"

SEVENTY-TWO—ARREST

Monday, March 31st, 2008, 4:40 PM

Dominic Franchescini stood in the international concourse at SFO and watched the sliding glass doors. Arriving passengers streamed through the doors pushing baggage carts piled high with luggage. He strained to look inside the arrival hall but all he could see was a customs guard checking arrival cards and waving passengers, either through the door, or to a customs clerk around the corner from the door.

The United flight had picked up some time for a change and Dominic was impatient. Ron Kelly had told his mother that he'd abandoned his luggage, Dominic couldn't understand the delay.

He called United Airlines to ask if all the passengers had deplaned from the flight. While he waited for a response, a door marked 'ALARMED— EMERGENCY ONLY' opened and a herd of airport police and two plainclothesmen dragged Ron Kelly, in handcuffs, down the hall. Kelly was swearing and looked haggard.

Dominic followed at a discreet distance as the troupe followed a hallway to an escalator and rode to the parking lot on the roof. He watched them place Kelly in the backseat of a dark four door sedan with government license plates. They must've been waiting. It was possible they'd bugged Alessandra's phone, or, maybe, they'd had a watch list with the airlines. In any event, it was a catastrophe. Dominic had little faith Kelly could stand up to any serious questioning.

He took the parking lot elevator to the ground level, walked to his car, and called Alessandra's cell phone.

"Do you have him?" she asked.

"The cops have him. I never had a chance to talk to him. They must've been in the customs area."

"Dominic, you have to get him out."

"Alessandra, be reasonable. I don't even know who has him or the charges. And I have to tell the don."

"But if you tell him—"

"Look," he said, "he's going to find out. We need the family lawyer, Al Martini."

"Don't you dare tell that asshole brother of mine! You know damn well what will happen."

"Alessandra, I need to go."

Dominic climbed into his Range Rover and leaned his head against the headrest. He could forget Incline Village. Kelly would be lucky to survive a week in prison if he talked, and that was likely. After all, he knew the don had tried to kill him in Tokyo. The Feds would probably offer a witness protection program; if he was lucky it would work, but that would take months, plus a trial.

He reluctantly dialed the don.

"Yes," said Don Cicerone.

"We need to forget Incline Village."

"What happened?"

"They arrested him."

"Do you have any details?"

"I think it's the Feds. That's all I know."

"All right. Check with the informer; find out why he didn't alert us. Then call Al Martini and ask him to work on bail. You come home while I think about it." He clicked off.

SEVENTY-THREE—NEW BALANCE

Harry had prepared to meet Janet and Thor at the Lodge after their run. He'd just picked up his keys when his phone rang.

"Is this that young feller with the dog, Thor?"

"Who's this?" asked Harry.

"We met several weeks ago, remember, when your dog stumbled on that old W-W-II pillbox?"

"Oh, yes. How can I help you?" Harry was concerned. He hadn't exchanged names with the old man when they'd met on the beach.

"I found your phone number on your dog's tags. He's sick, puking, there's some blood on his fur—I think the animal's been poisoned."

"How's that?" Harry was stunned. He'd dropped Thor off to run with Janet several hours ago. "Is there a woman there?"

"Ain't no one but the shep. He's on the beach. I'm using the phone in that Stags lodge."

"I'll be right there." Harry slammed the phone down and raced for his car. Where the hell was Janet? He knew she wouldn't leave Thor unless she was in trouble. The thought, coupled with his concern for the dog, tortured him. He pushed his SUV up to eighty miles per hour when he turned onto Los Osos Valley Road.

When Harry arrived at the lodge the bartender waved him toward the beach. "The old man's on the beach, Harry, down near the water line." Harry barged out the back door and plunged down to the beach.

Thor tried to rise but wobbled and collapsed again.

"I found him like this," said the old soldier. "He's acting drunk but there's blood on his fur and along his neck." The old man raised a hand streaked with blood.

"Thanks," said Harry. "I need to take him to the vet. You're sure there was no sign of a woman?"

"Nope. But there was a lady's New Balance running shoe under the dog."

Harry nodded grimly, picked up Thor and ran for his car. It took twenty minutes to get to the animal hospital on Loomis Street in SLO. On the way he called Deputy Mendoza and asked him to check out the beach and to meet him at the hospital.

It looks like antifreeze toxicity to me," said the veterinarian. "The symptoms are classic to ethylene glycol."

"Someone," said Harry, "must have poured it down his throat."

"Well, he has bruising on his head, a contusion, and matted blood. In any event, this stuff is metabolized by the liver. That can injure the kidneys and they could act up anytime in the next three to five days. We're going to induce more vomiting. I'm going to keep him for two days and treat intravenously with Fomepizole, for at least thirty-six hours. It slows the metabolism. He should be okay but let's take it day by day."

"Okay, thanks." Harry looked at Deputy Mendoza who'd just arrived. Harry nodded glumly and motioned towards the door."

"Deputy, any sign of Janet?" asked Harry.

Mendoza shook his head. There were signs of a scuffle in the sand and we found some blood—"

"That would be Thor—"

"It might. But there was a lot of blood, more than the dog likely lost. He might have ripped into someone. I took a sample of some of the bloody sand but it'll take time to get it tested."

"Who would attack Janet and the dog?" Harry looked anxiously through the window in the door into the examining room where the vet had hooked up an IV to Thor.

"Well, Warrener. I do believe I warned you against messing with the Cicerones. What else has happened lately?"

"I'm having quite a problem with Ted Granger and Jerry Sloane over a trustee vote. We already had an argument. They've been committed from the get-go to give Monterey Construction Company a sole-source no-compete fixed-price contract. You know they had this same problem with Randy. I don't see how that meets a due diligence standard and I can't understand why they're so committed. I'm guessing it's kickbacks."

"Well, we already know that Monterey has ties to the Chicago mob and Cicerone," said Mendoza. "And Ron Kelly, the agent who put the deal together, has been missing for weeks."

"What about Califano? Have they found him?"

"There's no doubt in my mind the Feds know where he is but they have no incentive to pick him up. They're still after Cicerone and, until they're ready to move on him, we won't get anything."

"What if I went to Chicago to hunt him down?"

"Let it be, Warrener. Perhaps, if they locate Kelly, they'll change their minds and pick up Califano to get more pressure on him to give up the don."

Harry frowned. His mind raced with concern for Janet, Thor, and an urge to find Califano. "No promises," he said. "For now, I have to find out what's happened to Janet."

SEVENTY-FOUR—GRANGER

Harry felt murderous when he drove home. Thor was hooked up to an IV and might not survive. Janet had disappeared. He planned to dig Randy's .45 out of the cupboard but he knew it would offer no consolation and was probably a bad idea. His hands gripped the steering wheel, knuckles white, and he realized he was breathing in short gasps. Then he stopped breathing when he saw a blue Hummer in his driveway. He wished he had the gun already.

"What do you want, Ted?" Harry was too surprised to connect Granger to earlier events of the day but he wondered where the other Stag, Sloane was. "Where's your partner?"

"Er, listen, Harry—" Granger rubbed his eyes and leaned against the fender of his car. "I'm afraid someone might try to hurt your friend, Ms. Zimmer."

"What?" Harry grabbed Granger's arm and pulled him through the front door. Inside, he led him to the kitchen and pushed him into a chair. "What do you know?"

Granger's shoulders sagged, his head hung low, and he refused to look at Harry. "I have a confession. I've been taking money in the land deal and—"

"Is Sloane involved?" demanded Harry.

Granger looked up, nodded imperceptibly and appeared to steel himself. "Not only that. I think he was involved in Randy's death."

"Where's Janet?"

"I don't know. I had a call from Mitch Mason that it was decided to put pressure on her to get you to change your vote."

"Well, the message has been delivered. She's been kidnapped and my dog's been poisoned. Who decided?"

"I don't know," said Granger, in a hollow, faltering voice. "I guess Mitch and Morty Greenspan, and—maybe Jerry. Please, let me explain. Jerry and I agreed to take a hundred thousand dollars each in exchange for the land deal. It would've been another half-million, each, if we also awarded Monterey Construction Company the sole-source design and construction jobs."

"Where'd the million come from?"

"We understated the number of permits by four. At two hundred fifty a pop, that provided a slush fund of a million."

Harry nodded. He now understood the confusion over whether one hundred four or eight permits had been issued. "And Randy?"

"Honestly, I wasn't involved in that. I think Jerry asked Ron Kelly to arrange some muscle on him. I don't think they intended to kill him. It was, you know, just like you—to get him to change his position on the trustees. I'm sorry."

"What about Yates and Bateman?"

"Bateman was a real accident. And I regretted talking to Yates. That was a mistake and I have to live with it. I hope Larry recovers."

"So why are you telling me?" Harry looked at his cupboard where he'd stashed the gun. For a moment he considered whipping it out and shooting Granger. Then he decided the man was already in hell.

"I told the district Stags," said Granger. "Jim Thatcher, he was there when we cut the deal with Kelly. He wasn't involved in the kickbacks and thinks it's actually one hundred four units. But when I met him a few weeks ago he said to stop taking money. He said the new building had to be on the front-burner and wanted us to finish the project."

"Does he know that Randy was murdered?"

"I didn't have the courage to tell him my suspicions."

Granger shook his head and raised his hands to his eyes but Harry grabbed them. "Can you help me find Janet?"

"All I know is they were going to rough her up and threaten her. I'm sorry about your dog; no one said anything about that."

"What are you going to do, Ted? You have to go to the police."

"I can't go to prison, Harry. I'm seventy-three and I'm finished. My business is in the dumps. I'm taking my wife on a long trip—I already bought the tickets, and I won't come back. I can't think of any other way to salvage some dignity." He looked knowingly at Harry.

"I better find Janet today, Ted, or I'm coming back tonight, to your house with the cops."

Granger nodded and stood to leave.

"Wait a minute, what was Kelly's cut in the deal?"

Granger shook his head with a smirk. "He gets a million out of our hide—you know that. If Hansen gave him anything, we don't know. Jerry's convinced Hansen is paying a lot more than twenty-six, maybe millions."

"I doubt if you're going to the same place as Randy, Ted, but thanks for telling me."

"I'm so sorry. In retrospect, it was all unnecessary. We never needed a unanimous vote and Randy could still be alive. We were so worried about questions ...."

Harry watched Granger leave and pondered calling Mendoza. He retrieved the handgun and stared at it. When the phone rang he leaped for it.

"Hello."

"Harry?" He recognized Janet's voice.

"Janet! Where are you? Are you okay?"

"I'm at CHP Headquarters on California Boulevard in SLO. How's Thor? Did they hurt him?"

Harry felt some of his tension leave. "He should be all right. I'm coming to get you. Do you need anything?"

"I could use another pair of running shoes. I have a big bruise on my head but I think it's not too bad."

"What happened?

"I'll give you the details when you get here. I told the nice CHP officer who picked me up on Los Osos Valley Road that I'd been roughed up and kidnapped. There's more—but they didn't really hurt me."

"Did you know them?"

"They were wearing masks, but one of them mentioned a name— Morty."

Harry felt his rage explode. He slammed his hand against the side of the refrigerator and took the phone away from his ear. Staring at his feet he counted to five. He was breathing in short, rapid gasps, and took the long deep breath they taught divers, to take occasionally, to manage their air consumption.

"Harry, are you still there?" asked Janet.

"I'm on my way. Thirty minutes."

"Are you going to call Mendoza?"

"Not yet. There's something I need to do before I talk to him. See you soon."

SEVENTY-FIVE—INTERROGATION

Monday, March 31st, 2008, 8:30 PM

The Federal Building in San Francisco occupied a block on Golden Gate Avenue, just east of Post Street. Federal detainees were housed in holding cells in the basement and escorted to interrogation rooms on the eighth floor, just below the U.S. District Courtrooms on the ninth floor.

Ron Kelly, shackled to a metal table, sat in interrogation room B. He was nervous, angry, scared, and tired beyond belief from the time change. He beat his fingers on the table. He gave the finger to the one-way mirror on the wall and considered pissing on the floor when the door opened and the two men who had arrested him marched into the room.

They were no longer wearing suits. The tall one—his name was Harris, Kelly remembered—was dressed casually in slacks and a sport jacket. The other one—Kelly had forgotten his name—wore jeans and a leather jacket over a sweatshirt.

"Mr. Kelly, you remember Agent Lewiston," said Harris. Don't you?"

Lewiston nodded and Kelly grunted.

"We have some questions, Ron—can we call you that?"

"Call me anything you want. I need to take a piss."

"In due time, Ron. Let's talk for a while." Harris smiled and the two agents took chairs at the table.

"You got questions but I ain't got any answers." Kelly stared defiantly at Harris, ignoring Lewiston whom he figured was a minor player.

"We have a recording," said Harris, "of your little chat at Rocky Point last December."

"What chat? I don't know what you're talking about."

"Would you like to hear it?" asked Lewiston.

"It nails you offering bribes to two Stags," said Harris. "It was a criminal conspiracy, Ron, and we have a murder."

"Bullshit. How do you get murder out of a business transaction?"

"So you admit you were there?" Harris smiled.

"What do you want?" asked Kelly. "You jerks always want something. I ain't done nothing. I want a lawyer."

"Are you sure you want that lawyer now? I'm sure your uncle has already contacted him. I suspect he'll show up as soon as he learns where you are—if he can find someone who knows."

"I got to take a piss."

Lewiston stood up. "I'll take you. It'll give you time to think." Lewiston unlocked the handcuffs from the eyebolt in the table.

"How about my hands or are you going to hold it, too?"

"In the john, Ron,"

A few minutes later they returned and Lewiston seated Ron at the table. "I won't shackle you to the table if you're nice."

Kelly nodded. In the toilet Lewiston had said, "Gonna talk, Ron? Either we get you or your uncle does." Kelly had been more than scared but he'd taken pains to hide his fear. The return walk had given him time to think and he'd decided there was no way he'd give up the family. If he hung true, maybe he'd earn some respect and a reprieve from the don. His mother had received assurances he could come home. The Stags and Greenspan were a different matter.

"So what do you want?" he asked.

"We want your uncle," said Harris. "How much money did you give him? Is he involved in the death of a Stag trustee? You give him up and we'll put you in witness protection."

"You guys must be nuts," said Kelly. "You'd have to put me on the moon or Mars. Witness protection, my foot."

"It's a walk, Ron. All you have to do is testify against your uncle. We'll forget the conspiracy charges and continue to squelch the murder charges in SLO."

"Fuck you."

"We're going to let you think about this, Ron," said Harris. "We'll be back tomorrow,"

"Aren't you going to tell me what I'm looking at? Isn't that part of the squeeze?"

"Twenty years to life," said Lewiston with a smile. "Have a good evening."

Harris and Lewiston rose.

Lewiston said, "I'll get a marshal to escort—"

"All right, relax," said Kelly. "You can forget my uncle. You're smoking dope if you think I'll drop a dime on him. I don't know nothing about a murder but I'm willing to give up the Stags. What can you give me for that?"

"We'll be back in ten minutes," said Harris.

"How about some coffee?"

"We'll bring some back with us," said Harris. He and Lewiston left the room.

Ron rubbed his wrists awkwardly and walked around the room. He made the customary stop at the one-way window and gave it the finger again. He was scared of prison but some of his bravado returned. He lay face up on the table when the two agents returned.

Harris carried a paper cup of black coffee. "Here. You worried about your uncle—this coffee might kill you."

Ron sat down again and sipped the coffee. It was blistering hot and tasted terrible but he took a gulp to demonstrate he wasn't intimidated.

"We can't promise anything," said Harris. "It's up to the U.S. Attorney. Reconsider. We're offering protection—"

"I'll give up the Stags. That's the best I can do. My mind's made up. Your turn."

Harris looked at Lewiston who said, "I told you."

Harris nodded. "All right, Ron. I'll talk to the U.S. Attorney. Maybe we can get the charges reduced to conspiracy and a federal prison back east—five years. You point us at the Stags and we'll see what we can get out of them."

Kelly thrust his hands forward. "How about some food? It's a long story."

Harris looked at Lewiston. "John, why don't you get us a bunch of burgers while I talk to Ron?"

I'll call someone. I want to hear what this wannabe has to say," replied Lewiston.

"Just get the food, John. I'm sure I can handle Ron."

Lewiston nodded and left the room.

"What's the matter?" asked Kelly shrewdly. "You don't trust him?"

Harris stared at Kelly. "Why shouldn't I?"

"What do you want to know about the Stags?"

"Rocky Point. Tell me about it."

Kelly smiled. "It all began in a conversation I had with Leonard Hansen—"

"Hansen Property Development," said Harris.

"Yeah. He expressed interest in the land along the shore at Morro Bay. I knew the Stags were desperate to rebuild the old lodge; it was a piece of crap and they didn't have any money. So I called Ted Granger ..."

Kelly rambled on about the meeting. He lied about the cash payments and said he'd received $16.2 million in a check from Hansen.

"So what happened," said Harris, "to the money? I know the Stags have received thirteen million so far."

"I deposited the check for $16.2 million that Hansen gave me in my escrow account and transferred thirteen million to Coastal Title. After that I left the country. I don't know anything."

"C'mon Ron, we're talking three million plus. What happened after it went into your escrow account? Where is it? Was there more in cash? Did you give it to Uncle Alessandro?"

Kelly smiled and stood up. He wandered around the room and pushed his nose into the one-way mirror. He knew Harris wouldn't expect an answer. "I don't know where any money is. If I knew I still wouldn't tell you; you're gonna send me to prison anyway."

Harris continued to pump Kelly. Who'd driven him to Los Angeles? Who was the woman, Pam—did he know she'd died recently? Why'd he owe her money?

Kelly didn't know that Pamela McCracken was dead but he figured someone—probably Dominic—had helped her along. "No comment" was his only answer to the barrage of questions.

Lewiston returned with double cheese burgers from Burger King and the men attended to eating for a while. Kelly found the time change from Japan had spurred an unusual appetite. He wolfed down his food.

"Tell us about the kickbacks," said Harris.

"I gave Granger and Sloane fifty K each," said Kelly. "That's it. I was supposed to give them a hundred each but they were dragging their feet on the design job."

"Where'd you get the cash for the kickbacks?" asked Lewiston.

"I keep a lot in my trunk."

"That was to give the contract to Monterey Construction, right? Why them?" asked Harris.

"I like Morty Greenspan."

"There weren't additional kickbacks from him?" asked Lewiston.

"I was going to get sixty K."

But you told me you offered the Stags' officers a million," said Harris. "That was in exchange for sixty K? Get real."

"No comment."

Lewiston shook his head. "I assume he told you about Rocky Point. This is all we're going to get from him."

"Don't be like that," said Kelly with a snide look. "There's one more Stag and I want to give him up."

Kelly was determined not to talk about his uncle or the consigliore but he was surely going to blow the whistle on Mitch Mason. "Granger and Sloane were supposed to grease the skids, make the construction job a done deal. They appointed this slime ball named Mitch Mason to coordinate between Monterey and Morty. I don't know what Morty was giving him but he was in it up to his ears."

Kelly was afraid to mention that Mason had asked him to put pressure on a trustee. That could open up a Pandora's Box of questions about Randy Lismore and maybe even Pamela McCracken. He stopped talking.

"All right, let's summarize," said Harris. "You've admitted to a criminal conspiracy to bribe three Stags to sell land at a price you set with kickbacks of over a million dollars. You gave two of them, Ted Granger and Jerry Sloane, fifty thousand each. You've acknowledged that Morty Greenspan bribed you to get the Stags' contract. You won't tell us what happened to the money from Hansen—"

"Check the bank account of Kelly Agency. I suspect someone might have stolen my identity while I was out of the country—you know, moved the money to the Caymans."

"That's enough for now. We'll talk to the U.S. Attorney tomorrow. You keep stonewalling us on the money and I don't think he'll be too generous."

Kelly was led back to a different holding cell. It was in a dark corridor off the main holding area. The other cells around it were empty.

SEVENTY-SIX—MESSAGE

Harry barged into CHP headquarters on California Boulevard and found Janet on a bench outside the night watch desk. Her feet were wrapped in a crusted bloody towel but she smiled and stood with a grimace.

"My God, what happened?" he asked.

"I was dumped on the side of the road with my hands and legs tied. There was a bag over my head. The bastards untied my hands, told me not to do anything for five minutes, and then I heard them drive away. I waited about a minute and then ripped off the bag."

"Did they hurt you in any way? What happened to your feet?"

"I lost a shoe in the scuffle—Thor attacked one of the men, hurt him bad. How's the dog?"

"We'll get to that. Your feet?"

"I was in a pretty deserted area so I decide to run towards town. I recognized Los Osos Valley Road—I figured it was about a three mile run to civilization. But I couldn't run with only one shoe so I threw the other one away. The road tore up my soles and I was limping by the time the CHP came along."

Harry reached out and embraced her. He pulled her head down to his shoulder and stroked her hair.

"Harry," she exclaimed, "you're crushing me. I'm okay. Tell me about Thor."

Harry helped Janet to the car while he told her about Thor. "We can see him tomorrow morning," he said. "What did these guys want?"

"There were two of them, masked. One of them mentioned a man named Morty. They told me that this was a message to you, to change your vote or else. I guess it was about the Stags."

Harry grabbed Janet's hand. "I'm sorry I brought you into this. We're lucky the same thing didn't happen that happened—"

"They just wanted to scare me. Maybe Randy fought back."

"We're going home, to clean you up. Then, if you're up to it, I have a mission." Harry told Janet about how he'd followed Mason and the conversations he'd heard in Willy's Smokehouse. "I suspect those recordings contain valuable information. I'm going after them—tonight."

"Why didn't you tell Mendoza what you'd heard?"

"I'm tired of being a follower. If anyone's going to get those recordings, it's going to be me!"

At Harry's house, while Janet took a shower, Harry collected his dive gear and fetched Randy's .45. He piled everything in his SUV, made ham and cheese sandwiches, brewed a pot of coffee, and planned his break-in.

SEVENTY-SEVEN—MACARONI

While Harry and Janet ate their sandwiches, Fred Harris and John Lewiston went to the Macaroni Café on Kearney Street for a drink. Situated next to the Purple Onion, it was a favorite haunt for FBI agents in San Francisco and they found another eight people they recognized in the huge bar in the basement.

They ordered drinks and crawled into a remote booth in the corner. Harris sniffed the popcorn aroma in the air and smiled at the friendly, boisterous nature of the crowd. "This must be what the Stags like about their bars," he said, "a bunch of friendly drunks and no attractive women."

Lewiston grunted. "What do you think, Fred? We have him on the Stags but he ain't rolling over on the don."

Harris sniffed his Scotch. He'd ordered a double Johnny Walker Black but it smelled like Jack Daniels, a common mistake with harried waitresses. He waved to the waitress. "We go after Granger and Sloane immediately and what's his name, Mason—Ron didn't like him, did he? We also take Morty down. But first you pump that deputy in SLO, Mendoza, and find out if he has anything on Monterey Construction in his murder investigation."

"I'll call him," said Lewiston, "but don't expect too much cooperation. I have to give him something. Do I tell him we're coming after the Stags?"

"Why not? You can tell him that the present charges are corruption-related."

"What do you think happened to the money?" asked Lewiston.

"It's apparent; he gave it to the don. The main question is how much did he get? We know there's a check but there had to be more."

"And Hansen?"

"The best we can do is tell the IRS we suspect cash payments were made. They can launch their own investigation."

Harris looked up when the waitress came by and he explained his suspicions about the drink. She picked it up, sniffed snootily, and put it down again. "It's Black, not Jack," she said. "You Fibbies all think you know everything."

Harris frowned and sipped the drink. "Maybe that cheeseburger screwed up my taste buds. Maybe it was Kelly. I'll make another pass at him tomorrow. Meanwhile, you check with Mendoza and get the warrants."

"What about bail? We haven't booked him yet."

"Let's sit on him for a while. I'll ask the U.S. Attorney for protective custody. He's in isolation already."

"You going to tell L.A. about Morty?"

"After we arrest him."

Lewiston gulped the rest of his drink and departed.

Harris sipped some more and wondered if the Stags would give him more pressure on Kelly. They weren't gangsters and were likely to fold under pressure. He pushed the speed button on his cell phone and dialed Sam Bernini. "Sam, we're making some arrests ...."

SEVENTY-EIGHT—WAREHOUSE

Harry and Janet parked in front of the central wharf at Monterey Bay. The parking lot was deserted, just a few cars with trailers for overnight sailors. Harry lifted the rear door of his SUV and assembled his dive gear. He noticed the air tank had about eighteen hundred pounds of air; he'd used twelve hundred pounds in some recreational dives. "There's about forty-five minutes of air under ordinary circumstances," he said. "But I won't be very deep and it's a short dive."

"But how will you get in?" Janet put her hand in the water. The water was cold, about fifty-five degrees. "And the water's freezing."

Harry stretched his black wet suit on and zipped up his dive boots. "I've trained in worse but that's what the suit is for. I just won't be in the water that long, not to worry. Getting in, though, is a theory. I figure the boards under the warehouse are rotted. The rafters I could see from the dock were in terrible condition. The crowbar should be enough to get me into the building."

Janet had a concerned look on her face. "You said they had video cameras. There might be alarms or a security guard."

"I doubt if there're motion detectors. The wharf rats would trigger them all the time. If there's a guard, I'll just have to deal with him."

"Please, Harry, don't hurt anyone—that includes you."

Harry smiled grimly and slipped on a three-mil dive cap. He attached two dive lights to his weight belt, checked his dive computer, and strapped a seven inch SOG Navy SEAL knife to his leg. It reminded him of the knife he'd owed Randy after the shark attack—the debt he'd never paid. It was, he mused, just another nail in the payback coffin.

"Wait in the car. Leave the engine off. There's a blanket on the backseat if you get chilled. Give me an hour—if I'm not back call Deputy Mendoza."

Janet nodded as Harry hugged her awkwardly. He put the crow bar in the waterproof dive bag and slid into the bay. The bag was buoyant and had to be dragged on the surface with a towline. in it. His only weapon was the knife; he'd left the gun in the car. The harbor was quiet except for an occasional bark from a seal. Harry swam about halfway to the dock, to about fifteen feet of water, and submerged. He had a bearing he'd taken from shore and he navigated easily. The bag followed on the surface. Three minutes later he reached the end of the wharf and surfaced.

He stowed his BCD/tank and dive bag on a piling and climbed out of the water. A quick examination with his small light proved his assumption about the planks was true; the wood was shriveled, discolored, and rotten, with gaps offering multiple opportunities for the crowbar.

Harry checked his watch. Twelve minutes had elapsed since he'd left Janet. Plenty of time. A curious seal startled him with a bark. "Shhhhh," he said. He stood on a cross beam and jammed the crowbar into a promising gap and wrenched it up. The wood gave with a mild groan and the plank broke. He pushed the two halves up; the old nails squeaked and gave way. He slipped the crowbar into the next gap. Two minutes later, he returned the crowbar to the dive bag, took off his dive gloves, and heaved himself up into the warehouse. He was in a storeroom. Metal shelving lined the walls and he saw a small bulb hanging on a cord. He ignored it, and switched to his large dive light. Miscellaneous power tools were stacked on one shelf, boxes of tiles and other construction materials were scattered around the room. He tested the door and it seemed to be padlocked on the outside. Jamming his dive knife through the crack he found it gave easily. He winced as the door creaked open.

The main area of the warehouse seemed deserted. He could see a catwalk and a metal stairway to the second floor. Pallets of wallboard and expensive redwood lumber filled most of the first floor. If there was a watchman he'd be upstairs. Sixteen minutes had elapsed. He figured he had about fifteen minutes to locate the recorders which would allow a comfortable margin of time. Harry crept to the stairway and mounted it slowly. His wet boots squished as he climbed. Still no security. At the catwalk he scanned the doors which led to rooms that lined the inside walls of the warehouse. Only one had a glass door. He made his way to it

The door was locked but it offered no more resistance to his knife than the downstairs door. Inside he saw there was a small anteroom and a door to an inner office. The anteroom was probably where Alice worked. It had a secretarial chair, desk, an old PBX-like phone, and a desk lamp. The desk was clean and the wastepaper basket was empty. There was an American Airlines travel poster for Paris and a cheesecake picture of Alice in a bikini on the wall. He padded over to the inner door and found it unlocked.

Inside the inner chamber was a couch, desk, an executive chair, one guest chair, a small round conference table, a beat-up old credenza behind the desk, and an old wooden coat rack. The room stank of old cigars. The desk was messy, cluttered with papers and the wastepaper basket overflowed. Apparently Alice wasn't responsible for cleaning Morty's office. Harry checked the desk. The drawers were locked. Once more he wedged his knife in the locks and the drawers popped open. Elapsed time was twenty-five minutes when he checked the dive computer on his wrist.

Harry pulled open the lower right-hand drawer and found a Dell Latitude 810 laptop and an eighty gigabyte Hotdrive external memory. He followed some wires and found they led to microphones mounted on the lower leading edge of the desk. Bingo, he thought. He didn't have time to examine the machines so he ripped off all the wires and cables and grabbed them. Turning to leave he saw a stack of CDs sitting on the credenza. They had dates written on them with black markers. He stacked them on top of the machines, turned off his light, tucked the load under his arm, and crept back to the catwalk. Elapsed time was thirty-two minutes.

"What the hell is this?" demanded a man with his arm in a bloody sling. He stood on the catwalk in front of the stairway.

Harry gulped. He sensed the smell of Vietnamese jungle. He clenched his teeth, ignored the smell, and charged. Harry slammed into the man's damaged arm. He fell sideways on the catwalk and clutched his arm.

"Son-of-a-bitch," yelled the man. "What are you doing in here?"

Harry put down the CDs and machines and brandished his knife. He put it to the man's throat. "I'm relieving you of some equipment."

The man rubbed his arm and groaned.

"What happened to your arm?" asked Harry. He pushed the knife harder into his throat.

"I was attacked by a dog. What's the big deal?"

"I ought to cut your throat, you jerk. That was my girlfriend and dog you attacked yesterday."

"We didn't hurt her!" pleaded the man.

"Who's the other guy?"

"I don't know. He wore a mask. I was just supposed to be the lookout."

"Sure you were." Harry wanted to interrogate the guy but he didn't have much time. He slammed the butt of the knife into the man's head and his eyes went blank. He ripped the sling off and used it to tie the man's hands and feet. It wasn't much but it would give him another five minutes after the guy came to. He retrieved the machines and disks and fled down the stairs. Downstairs he reached down through the hole in the floor and pulled up the dive bag, stuffed everything into the bag, and jumped down onto the pilings. Elapsed time was forty minutes.

Harry crawled out of the water with ten minutes to spare. Janet stood at the shore, shivering with the blanket in hand. She wrapped him in it. "What happened? I was pretty worried. Did you find the recordings?"

"I had a little problem with a security guard. I clobbered him—he was one of the men who'd attacked you."

"But how—"

"His arm. Thor ripped his arm when they grabbed you. Come on, we need to leave before he raises an alarm."

A few moments later, the dive bag and equipment were stowed, Harry was huddled in the passenger seat under the blanket, the heater set to high, and Janet turned left onto Del Monte Avenue, towards the closest ramp to Highway California 1. "Do you think you can make it back to SLO?" asked Harry. "It's been a very long day for you."

"I don't want to stop. Let's go home. That way we can see Thor first thing in the morning."

"Take 156 to 101, that's the fastest way."

"Okay, Harry, go to sleep."

"We need to hide the CDs and the machines."

"I have a safe in City Hall."

Harry nodded and closed his eyes.

After a surreptitious stop at SLO's City Hall they climbed into bed. It was 5:30 in the morning.

SEVENTY-NINE—CAYMANS

Tuesday, April 1st, 2008, 10:00 AM

Dominic Franchescini sat on a bench in Lafayette Park. It was damp from a morning fog that lingered over the hill. He was uncomfortable and troubled. Kelly was in jail and the lawyer, Al Martini, had been unable to locate him. According to Martini, the marshals in the Federal Building had told him that they'd heard an arrest had been made but didn't know where the prisoner was being held. Martini had called Sam Bernini but he wasn't answering his phone. Dominic was scared for Kelly. Where was he and what was the don going to do?

His phone rang. "Dominic."

A muffled voice said, "Sorry I didn't return your call sooner. I had some real work to do."

"Where's Kelly? We can't find him," said Dominic. "I saw him marched away at SFO."

"You were there?" asked the informer.

"Down the hall. It was swarming with customs cops and two suits."

There was a pause and then the man said, "Well, he's in the Federal Building but the marshals were told to stonewall any inquiries until tonight. He's talking but he didn't dime the don."

Dominic watched a squirrel and two crows battle over some crumbs next to a waste can. A starling flew in and stole the crumbs while the battle raged. Good for the little one, he thought. "Did my name come up?"

"Not yet. They're chasing the money but it seems it went into the ether after the Caymans. The Treasury Department is on it but they're pessimistic. That's three point two million I'm talking about. They think there's more—a lot more, but cash is essentially untraceable."

The sun peeked out of the overcast and warmed Dominic. "So what'd he say?"

"He spilled the beans on the deal with the Stags and Morty Greenspan. They have four names, Ted Granger, Jerry Sloane, Mitch Mason and Greenspan. Arrest warrants are in preparation."

"When do you expect to make the arrests?"

"One's already flown the coop. Granger and his wife left the country today on a Cathay Pacific flight en route to Bali. Turns out he paid cash for the tickets. The other arrests should occur later this week. You don't have much time."

"Thanks. I'll pass this info to the don."

The informer hung up.

He leaned back into the bench and closed his eyes, basking in the weak sunlight. It was time, Dominic decided, to clean up the mess the best he could. Before he told the don, he had to take care of Jerry Sloane. At least Granger was out of the reach of the FBI. He decided to call Morty Greenspan.

"Yeah?" Greenspan sounded aggravated.

"Franchescini."

"I recognized the calling number. What'ya want?"

"You have a problem."

"Great. That's just what I need—another problem." Dominic heard Greenspan yell in the background, "Alice, get that idiot Andy in here now."

"Kelly talked," said Dominic. "The Feds are coming for you, probably tomorrow. He told them about the Stag you're paying off."

"What about—?"

"So far, he's being smart. What's your other problem?"

Greenspan said, "Give me a minute." Dominic could hear him speaking, "If Mason's still here, don't let him leave." The phone was muffled and just a few words came through, "... the guy's girlfriend and dog? ... recordings ... always takes Highway 68 ... brakes ... take ... ram him good ...."

"Morty? You still there?"

"All right," said Greenspan. "Joey Gee is not going to be a happy camper. I'll call my lawyer. What are you guys gonna do?"

"What we must. What's your other problem?"

"Forget it."

"Adios." Dominic readied himself for the trip to Jerry Sloane's home in Pismo Beach. He went into the basement of the mansion and removed a panel below the laundry chute. He retrieved a Smith and Wesson .38 revolver and checked the ammunition. Then he stashed the weapon in his jacket and exited the garage.

EIGHTY—FISH

Jerry Sloane was consumed with rage and anxiety. He'd tried all day to contact Pamela McCracken at the county clerk's office. All they'd told him was that someone would call him back concerning his inquiry.

Sloane's cell-phone rang. "Sloane."

"Mr. Sloane?" said a strange voice. "I'm returning your call about the Stags' land transaction. My name's Philip Anister. I work for the county. There are problems with the sale of your property in Los Osos to Hansen Property Development."

"Problems?" Sloane clenched his stomach. This was just what he needed. "We need to close that transaction as soon as possible. What happened to Pamela? The last time I spoke with her she said it would be just a few more weeks to complete the EIR."

"Oh, I'm sorry. Didn't you hear? She passed. It was a tragic accident—apparently carbon monoxide fumes leaked into her apartment and overcame her."

Sloane mumbled his regrets. A chill passed as he wondered if Ron Kelly, or that prick he'd given the money to in San Francisco, were cleaning up loose ends. "What's the problem with the EIR?"

"The inspectors turned up an enormous hazardous waste on the property. They found an old World War II pillbox on the property. It's filled with old shells, decaying ammunition, PCBs and asbestos, diesel fuel, and kerosene. Further, the beach is littered below the surface with thousands of old .50 caliber rounds—that's lead. I'm afraid the property must be cleaned up before the title can transfer."

"Are you telling me we can't close this deal because of a stupid environmental report? Why isn't it the buyer's problem?"

"Because California law requires complete disclosure by the seller and apparently it's been known for some time that there's a pillbox on the property. In fact, our inspector found someone on the beach that had actually served in the unit stationed there."

Sloane lied. "But we didn't know—"

"In any event, whether you or the buyer—we've already notified Mr. Hansen—performs the cleanup, it must be done. We've determined that it qualifies as a federal Superfund site, an uncontrolled or abandoned place where hazardous waste is located. It could be quite expensive."

Sloane's leg twitched. Visions of his kickbacks dematerialized. "Can we appeal this?"

"You're welcome to see the report," said Anister. "It's in our office. But, even with clean-up, there's another problem—there's a waters contracts fight on the central coast and all contracts must be rewritten because they rely on flawed environmental data regarding the effects of water pumping on threatened fish."

"Fish? Fuck you!" Sloane slammed his phone down. He felt dizzy and nauseous. Five hundred thousand had disappeared; the first hundred was at risk. He tried to call Ted Granger. After ringing interminably, he called Granger's Hummer agency.

"I need to talk to Ted, now!" he commanded.

"Sorry. Mr. Granger has left the country. He left a voice mail that he'd be gone indefinitely. We're going crazy here. No one's in charge."

"Where'd he go?" Sloane couldn't control the twitch in his leg. It shook like a dog scratching its belly.

"Bali. That's all he told us. He was at an airport when he left the message."

Sloane dropped the phone. It bounced and hung by the cord. He put his head between his knees and fought to control the tears. He didn't notice when a Range Rover pulled up in front of his house. The front door burst open and Sloane, startled, pushed back into his seat. It was Joe, or Dominic Franchescini—the mobster who'd given him and Granger their second fifty thousand dollars. Sloane watched him carefully cradle the telephone.

"What are you doing here?" he gasped.

"Well, Jerry, you've been busted and it's time to get lost."

"Busted? What do you mean?"

Franchescini roamed about the room. He looked down the hallway. "Anyone else here?"

Sloane shook his head. "No one can hear us."

"I haven't got time for this bullshit. Kelly talked—the Feds are on the way to arrest you and Granger on a bunch of charges."

"Well, they won't get him. He went to Bali," said Sloane. "Did you hear about the EIR?"

Dominic looked at Sloane. "What about the EIR? Who cares?"

"The county said the land is a major federal Superfund site and needs to be cleaned up before we can close the transaction."

"Well, Jerry, that's yours and Hansen's problem."

"Did Kelly say anything about Lis—?"

"That's what I want to talk to you about." Dominic pulled his .38 out of his jacket. He fired two rounds into Sloane's chest. The force of the slugs pushed Sloane back into his chair and it toppled. He was dead before he hit the floor.

EIGHTY-ONE—HANSEN

Tuesday, April 1st, 2008, 4:50 PM

Dominic peeked outside. It was quiet on the street and he rummaged in Sloane's office. He powered up Sloane's laptop, opened the recycle bin, and discovered the Rocky Point recording was still in the file. He'd been told the FBI agents had left it in place to cover up their surreptitious intrusion. He right-clicked and executed an 'Empty Recycle Bin' command. They didn't need any more copies of this recording. In the closet he found Sloane's briefcase. He opened it and found twelve thousand dollars in one-hundred-dollar bills. He left two thousand dollars; he knew the FBI already knew Sloane had received a kickback. They'd be looking for evidence; leave them some. He pocketed ten thousand and left.

He drove to a payphone at a Pismo Beach gas station and dialed Leonard Hansen. Traffic streamed by on Highway U.S. 101, the Cabrillo Highway, and Dominic wondered when he'd reach the bottom of the cluster fuck. Everything had fallen apart. The murders were piling up, disengagement was impossible, and Kelly, in jail, might lose his resolve to protect the family. Worse, the don hadn't changed his position, and someone like Greenspan, or Joey Gee, might go after Kelly to silence him.

"Hello?"

"Leonard," said Dominic, "I work with Ron Kelly."

"Yes, well, I would call him if I could find him. There's a problem with the Environmental Impact Report."

"That's too bad. I didn't know," said Dominic. He dissembled when he realized it wasn't prudent to admit he'd already learned the fact from Sloane. "However, we pulled out of the transaction some time ago."

"You pulled out? How come no one told me? Listen here. Your agent, Kelly, stiffed me. I want my money back."

"Leonard, do I need to remind you who you're dealing with? According to my understanding you now own the twenty-six acres. No permits mean no additional payments."

"I don't get the damn land. The agreement I executed with Kelly said the thirteen million was absolutely non-refundable and I had to build at least one unit to close the deal. Further, I heard the county clerk died, under strange circumstances, I might add, and it'll cost millions to clean up the land. Even then I might not get the permits. The deal had an arbitration clause but no way am I going to mediate it. This deal stinks and I'm through. I don't expect to recover the thirteen million I gave the Stags, but I want the rest back."

"Forget it. If you don't want to fight over the land, tell the Stags to keep it, or gift it to the city, or whatever. Just hope Kelly doesn't talk about the money."

"What does that mean? Is that a threat?" Hansen sounded nervous.

"What do you think?"

"Where's Kelly?"

"Kelly's been arrested. So far we understand he's standing up but you might have an IRS problem."

"Good-bye. Don't call me anymore."

"Forget the money, Leonard." Dominic returned the phone to the cradle. He drove back to San Francisco in nervous anticipation of the meeting with the don. Disengagement, indeed. The don would be furious. He decided not to tell him that Hansen wanted some of the money back. Dominic knew the don would have Hansen killed before he'd give back a dime of the money.

EIGHTY-TWO—LONE CYPRESS

Tuesday, April 1st, 2008, 7:00 PM

Mitch Mason drove his pick-up south on Highway California 68 from
Monterey, through Pacific Grove to the northwest gate of the Seventeen
Mile Drive. He always drove through the Del Monte Forest. He found
the setting relaxing and his admission to the private roadway was free.
He'd built a retaining wall on one of the forest estates earlier in the year
and still had the grille plaque assigned for the job that permitted access.
Mason needed relaxation today. He'd never seen Greenspan so angry or
Alice so jittery. Apparently, someone had broken into the warehouse, but,
if anything was stolen, no one was talking. Mason had spent thirty minutes
in Greenspan's office making small talk, which was very uncharacteristic
for Greenspan.

Mason drove into the Inn at Spanish Bay resort and parked in the lot
opposite Sticks, a popular restaurant and bar filled with historic Pebble
Beach memorabilia. He quaffed three beers and nibbled at some bar food,
preparing for his long ride down Highway California 1 to SLO. A little
muddled from the beer and still concerned about the unrest at Greenspan's
warehouse, he climbed back in the truck and followed the Seventeen Mile
Drive south. He drove through a wooded area and passed Point Joe, a
landmark originally thought to signal the entrance to Monterey Bay. Two-
thirds of the moon was illuminated and Mason saw whitecaps in the water.
After Seal Rock and Bird Rock, the road climbed about two hundred feet.
He was thinking about Alice when he was slammed forward; he looked in
the rear view mirror and saw a large, black, pickup truck. It had rammed
him and was tailgating him.

He sped up and looked again. He gasped when he realized the driver
was Andy, Greenspan's man. Andy was driving with one arm in a sling and
rammed Mason again. Mason slammed on his brakes. He felt the pedal bite
and then fade to the floor. He pumped the brakes but they were flat. They
must have rigged the brakes! His truck approached a small summit and a
switchback to the left. Andy's truck rammed him again, striking Mason's
right rear bumper. Mason's truck veered left and both trucks roared along
the shoulder on the wrong side of the road.

Mason's truck drifted further left; his front fender glanced off the side
of the hill. He dragged the left side of the truck along the hill hoping friction
would slow the truck. His left side mirror shattered as it hit a rock that

jutted out of the hill. He yanked uselessly on the emergency brake handle and was slammed again. His truck crested the hill and faced downhill. Mason struggled with the wheel and slithered back onto the road. The rocks on the shoulder had bent his front left wheel and it wobbled. He hit the brakes repeatedly but the truck jerked to the right. When Andy struck Mason's truck again, it jumped a small parking curb, and crashed through a wooden slat fence that protected the parking area for another roadside attraction, The Lone Cypress. Mason's truck went airborne, clipped a tree, bounced off rocks in a narrow ravine, and crashed into four feet of flood tide waters. Two hours later the ebb tide slid Mason's truck into the surf and it drifted in three feet of water, shifting with the waves. Private security guards called to investigate the hole in the fence caught a glint of Mason's camper shell roof in the water and alerted the CHP. A trooper worked his way down the hill from a set of stairs for tourists and found Mason's broken body tossing in the surf fifty yards from the mangled truck.

EIGHTY-THREE—*MANO A MANO*

Deputy Mendoza threw his phone into the handset, pulled the phone back out, and slammed it on his desk repeatedly, until it cracked. Agent Lewiston had called to tell him the FBI had warrants for the arrests of Mitch Mason, Jerry Sloane and Ted Granger. But there were problems. Granger had left the country and Mendoza already knew that Mason and Sloane were dead. Mendoza had seen a CHP wire on Mason's accident and the SLO police had reported Sloane had been shot to death. Lewiston would only tell him the warrants were related to extortion and RICO charges; he'd claimed the FBI still didn't know the location of Salvatore Califano. When Mendoza had inquired whether there was any interest in Monterey Construction, Lewiston had hesitated and then said, "You don't have a need to know."

Mendoza stormed into the sheriff's office. "Bullshit," he exclaimed. "The Stags are dying like flies and the FBI is stonewalling all the way. I want the Lismore hit man before they get him. Counting those weird carbon monoxide deaths we could have at least four murders, maybe five, if Mason was killed. I need to go to Chicago."

"All right, relax, Luis," said the sheriff. "I'll call the Cook County Sheriff's office—*mano a mano*—and see what they say."

Mendoza sat angrily in the sheriff's guest chair and watched him explain their interest in Califano to a deputy sheriff in Cook County. "You say you know him?" said the sheriff. The sheriff's eyes widened; he grabbed a pad of paper and began writing. "Thanks," he said and lowered the phone slowly.

"Well?" demanded Mendoza.

"I guess we've been played all the way. The sheriff's office in Cook County notified the FBI weeks ago that they'd recognized Califano. They know where he lives and he's in town now. They gave me his address."

"Who'd they tell in the FBI?" asked Mendoza.

"Lewiston."

"There's something rotten about that guy, sheriff." Mendoza shook his head in fury, grabbed the sheriff's notes and studied the information. "We could have nipped this in the bud if you'd had some balls at that inquest. God only knows how many people are dead because we let the FBI manipulate us." He glared at the sheriff who shifted uncomfortably in his seat.

"What're you going to do?" asked the sheriff. "There's still no money for a trip."

"I'll think of something." Mendoza left the sheriff's office as quickly as he could.

Mendoza drove aimlessly for a while. Then he decided that Harry Warrener was his only ally. When he pulled onto Warrener's driveway Max Cotton was speaking to him,

"I already told him about Mason and Sloane," said Cotton. "We haven't located Granger yet."

"He left the country," said Mendoza. "Ask the FBI where he went. I need to talk to Warrener alone."

Cotton nodded. "How about an exclusive when this is settled?"

"I'll consider it—I'm so mad at the FBI and the sheriff it'd probably win a Pulitzer."

Cotton smiled, shook hands, and left.

Mendoza pushed the notes in front of Harry. "They've known where this guy is all along." The deputy remembered that Harry had offered to go to Chicago; in retrospect it was probably a bad idea giving Harry the perp's address.

Harry seemed more than eager to hear the news. He studied Califano's address with interest but offered no new information. "Janet's okay," he said, "and Thor is doing well. I should get him home tomorrow."

"Did she learn anything when she was grabbed?"

"She said someone mentioned the name, 'Morty.'"

"Could she identify anyone?"

"No, but I figure it's someone from Monterey Construction."

"You're not going to do anything, are you?" asked Mendoza. "Leave this to us."

"Sure. For the moment I just care about Janet and Thor." Harry smiled. Mendoza sensed Harry was detached and the deputy didn't like it.

"I know it's another outrage to those you love, Warrener. But the FBI's probably going after Morty Greenspan on corruption charges so they can put pressure on Don Cicerone. That'll be some solace. Now, pay attention, I don't like to repeat myself, but stay out of Chicago."

Harry nodded.

Mendoza looked at him grimly. "If anything happens to Califano, I'll suspect you."

"Suspicions," said Harry, "don't seem to go far in this town."

"I'll give you that one," said Mendoza. He stormed out of the house.

EIGHTY-FOUR—CHAIRMAN

Thursday, April 3rd, 2008, 2:30 PM

The Los Osos Stags lodge was almost empty when Harry Warrener arrived for a special trustees meeting. Strolling through the bar he heard two Stags talking about Sloane. "… remember Sloane passed out in the bushes during a luau? Stark ass naked …." Harry thought the guy hadn't deserved to die, but he smiled nevertheless. He walked into the lodge conference room and found Lloyd Campbell, Carole Greene, and John Potempa. The esteemed leading knight sat at the head of the table.

"Okay, now that Harry is here," said the knight, "I have some terrible news. Jerry Sloane was murdered two days ago and Ted Granger's disappeared. It seems he flew to Bali and no one knows when he's coming back. That means I'm the acting ER."

Harry stared at John Potempa who looked bewildered. Carole had a grim look on her face, and Lloyd had his face in his hands.

"These guys are my friends," said Lloyd. "This is terrible."

"It is," said the knight. "However, there's more bad news. The developer has pulled out of the deal. It turns out the land we're trying to sell is polluted, a Superfund site. It'll cost millions to clean it up. Hansen can't get permits so the deal's collapsed. We get to keep the money we've already received."

"What about our agent?" asked Potempa.

"Ted," said the knight, "had told me the agent, Kelly, disappeared when we paid the first half of his fee. No one seems to know where he is now."

Harry raised his hand. "What happens to the design with Monterey Construction?"

"We bag it," said the knight.

"I don't want to pay them a dime," said Harry.

"That's up to you trustees. With Jerry Sloane gone, that means you have to elect a new chairman of the board. I'll have to make a temporary appointment to fill his vacancy but that can wait; you have a quorum today."

"What are we going to do with the land?" asked Carole Greene. "And we still have twelve and a half million dollars, right? It's all still there?"

"I checked with Wells Fargo this morning," said the knight. "All the money is still invested through their programs. Jesus, I never thought someone might have ripped off the money."

Potempa blew his nose noisily and reached into his pocket for a bottle of pills. He popped two in his mouth and gulped a glass of water. "What do we do? Who wants to be chairman? I sure don't."

"Not me," said Carole.

Harry looked at Lloyd Campbell who said, "Not me. I guess it needs to be you, Harry,"

Harry thought for a moment while they stared at him. He didn't want the job and he had a special mission that consumed all his energies. Still, he realized, this was one of those moments when it was necessary to step up and accept responsibility. The Stags clearly needed his service. "I'll consider it subject to the board's concurrence first, to give those twenty-seven acres to the city or the Coastal Commission with the proviso that it remain public open land, and second, that after we fill Jerry's vacancy, we consider a different chair. This will be an interim election only."

"But why would the city want polluted land?" asked Carole.

Harry looked at the acting ER. "How'd you learn about the environmental problem? Did you see the EIR?"

"Hansen told me and I called the county clerk's office. The cost estimate to clean up the land's about eight million dollars."

"Okay," said Harry, "you agree to give the land away and I'll see if I can solve the clean-up problem."

"How are—" asked Campbell.

"Let me worry about that." Harry had a plan; those tapes from Morty Greenspan might be useful.

Harry was elected chairman of the board of trustees. The trustees voted unanimously to donate the land to Los Osos, subject to the city accepting the gift, and directed the acting ER to put the deal on the Lodge floor for a membership vote. They suspended payment to Monterey Construction pending a review of a new plan to either raze and rebuild, or refurbish, the present lodge building. They ordered the treasurer to request new bank signature cards and asked the acting ER to try to find Ted Granger.

Harry left to fetch his dog. Thor greeted him with enthusiasm but seemed dopey and somewhat restrained. The vet told Harry that the dog should recover completely but to keep his activity to a minimum for a few more days.

Harry put Thor in the car and drove to Janet's home in Cuesta-by-the-Sea for a reunion.

EIGHTY-FIVE—LOWER LEVEL

On their first day, Tuesday, in Chicago, Harry and Thor had driven to the University of Illinois campus from their Motel 6 in Arlington Heights. Harry had parked on Halsted Street and they'd wandered along the eastern edge of the campus. The Stags' National Memorial Headquarters building stood on Halsted just below the Jane Addams' Hull-House Museum. Harry had wanted to see the memorial to American veterans. The classical Beaux-Arts style reminded him of the Jefferson Memorial in Washington, D.C. It gleamed as they walked around it. The building was originally dedicated, in 1929, to the over five hundred Stags who'd died in World War I.

Harry had researched the building and discovered that the Stags' organization in 1925 had invited four of the country's most distinguished architects to participate in a design contest. In their words, they'd 'conducted an exhaustive search' for a builder, settling on one based in Boston. Harry found it curious that the national organization had enforced strict competitive standards on its own building but the management chose not to enforce the same standards of due diligence on local Lodges. According to Granger, all the district management had wanted was a new lodge—and competition wasn't even required in the statutes.

It *was* a beautiful building. Harry with Thor, tongue hanging out, had shared a wooden bench while Harry reflected on his last conversation with Janet. She'd been sitting in his kitchen when he'd retrieved Randy's gun.

"What's with the gun, Harry?"

"I'm going to Chicago. Mendoza made a mistake; he gave me the address of Califano. I'm going to kill him. It's something I have to do."

Janet had argued against it. "But Harry, it's dangerous, and—wrong. You have to decide what's more important. I love you. You don't have to prove anything to me anymore."

Harry had blanched, his mind in turmoil. He'd been so happy with Janet but thirty-five years of unrest tore at him. "Look," he'd said, "I've spent my life in the shadow of what Randy did for me. It's his turn for payback."

"Even if Mendoza can't arrest Califano—if you kill him that will make you a murderer." Janet had placed her arms around Harry. "I don't know if I can live with a murderer, no matter how much one might think it's justified."

Harry had been adamant he had to go but her words had haunted him the entire trip. "I'll be back in about a week," he'd said, "I hope, no pray, that we can get past this. After this … well, you know what I mean."

Harry and Thor had driven from California so that he could transport Randy's .45 without hassle. If they'd flown, both Thor and the weapon would have been in the hold of the aircraft. Harry had no interest in reporting the gun to the airlines and he'd felt the dog's recovery from the poisoning would be threatened by an uncomfortable caged flight. The drive had taken three days with multiple pit stops, walks, and restless short nights in several Motel 6s.

Harry followed Califano as he roared down Lake Street and turned into the lower level of Wacker Drive. Harry didn't know Chicago, but he grinned when he recognized the roadway and remembered a chase scene that had been filmed there in *The Blues Brothers* movie. After staking out Salvatore Califano's home earlier, he'd followed him from his home on west Lawrence Avenue, in Schiller Park, onto the Kennedy Expressway and then south to downtown Chicago. Califano seemed either indifferent or unaware that he had a tail. Thor had his head out the window, panting.

The lower level was illuminated with orange high-intensity lamps. Pillars separated access lanes to buildings from the main roadway and Harry found it difficult to avoid detection. As they approached the famous Michigan Avenue Bridge, he decided he'd confront Califano on the other side of the Chicago River.

Harry slowed as they crossed the Michigan Avenue Bridge. Then he barreled around a car, passing in the wrong lane. He saw Califano suddenly turn right and park on North Water Avenue, behind one of the pillars that supported Upper Michigan Avenue. They were under the Trump Building, the lower level of the Tribune Tower was just north of them. A large parking lot stretched endlessly in all directions. Califano must have figured it out, thought Harry. After all, Harry hadn't been circumspect and he damn near drove up the guy's tailpipe. He nosed in behind Califano's car, grabbed the weapon, and climbed out of the car with Thor.

Califano watched them in his rear view mirror. He climbed out of his car. "You're following me," challenged Califano. "Why?"

"It's time to pay the piper," said Harry. He brandished the gun.

Califano's eyes narrowed. "You're gonna shoot me? Gimme the gun!" He took a step forward.

Harry pulled the slide back and crouched in a firing position. Thor, sensing malice, snarled.

"Who are you? What's this about?" Califano took another step forward.

"You remember Randy Lismore?" asked Harry. "You killed him in the Madonna Inn."

"That's what this is about? C'mon. His head hit the ledge by accident. I didn't mean for it to happen; I was just supposed to rough him up, apply a little pressure." Califano began to reach behind his back.

"Keep them in front, damn it," said Harry. "Randy was my best friend. I want justice."

"So you're a killer too."

Harry looked at Califano. The man was tough. They'd used him for muscle, and Harry thought he should shoot him without delay. It was strange, he felt no fear but when he began to squeeze the trigger he hesitated. Califano moved more quickly than Harry expected; his leg kicked the gun out of Harry's hand. Califano slipped his buck knife out of his rear waist and lunged at Harry. Harry's SEALS training kicked in—where was the training, he wondered, when he'd had his hand on the trigger—and he threw Califano over his hip. The knife slipped out of Califano's hand and both men watched it—Harry standing and Califano on the ground—slide through a sewer grate. Harry counter-attacked. His first kick landed squarely in Califano's hip; Califano grunted but on Harry's second kick, aimed at the head, Califano grabbed Harry's foot and threw him backwards. Califano sprang up and faced Thor who'd taken a snarling defensive position over the .45.

Harry remembered the panhandler in San Francisco. "Don't go for it," he warned.

"What, you think I'm afraid of your dog?" Califano moved towards the dog and Harry yelled, "Thor, *waffen!*" The dog began barking viciously and crouched down on his front legs, in a stalking position. Harry wasn't certain what the dog would do. But, as Califano lunged for the .45, Thor leapt. He ripped at Califano's throat with his fangs and, suddenly, Califano was on the ground, his hands wrapped around his throat, blood gushing. Thor stood over him growling.

Harry, stunned, looked down on Califano. He twisted and flayed his legs in shock and struggled to stop the bleeding.

"I guess that's also an accident," said Harry grimly.

Blood pooled under Califano's head and shoulders and Harry looked around. They were hidden by pillars from passing traffic. Harry picked up the gun, popped the magazine and placed it in his pocket. He pumped the slide again and emptied the chamber, pocketing the remaining cartridge. Then he wiped down the gun with his jacket and threw the empty weapon on the ground next to Califano.

He waited for Califano's death rattle. When he and Thor returned to the car he washed out the dog's mouth and neck fur with a bottle of water. They climbed in the car and drove off, south again under Michigan Avenue, headed for the freeway connections to O'Hare and westbound back to California.

Mendoza would probably figure it out. The fang marks and the gun were loud signals. But Harry, flushed with adrenalin, didn't care. He knew the deputy had a strong sense of justice. Harry would just have to see how it turned out but he expected the deputy to let it go. Janet, on the other hand …. Harry didn't know how she'd react. Sure, Thor had killed Califano, but the circumstances were clearly murder. Harry was responsible. He dreaded the moment he had to admit it to her. He couldn't lose her. He looked down at Thor, The dog lay on the front seat with his head in his lap. He rubbed Thor's ears and settled in for the long ride.

Hours later, when they crossed the Mississippi River, Harry threw the magazine for the .45 and the extra cartridge into the river. His thoughts turned to Randy and all the good times they'd had. One summer, he remembered, they'd taken a gambling riverboat on the Mississippi and Randy had won sixteen hundred dollars. That money had paid for a long ski weekend at Taos the following winter. He smiled at the memory and noted, for the first time, he didn't feel guilty about Vietnam.

EIGHTY-SIX—MISSISSIPPI

Thursday, April 10th, 2008, 4:30 PM

Yellow police crime-scene tape still fluttered from trees and the mailbox in front of Jerry Sloane's home in Pismo Beach. Deputy Mendoza ripped off the taped seal on the door and walked into the house. The SLO cops had searched for evidence of the shooter, the FBI had searched for evidence of corruption. They'd found a few thousand dollars in one-hundred-dollar bills.

Mendoza searched the house for a connection to Salvatore Califano and the murder of Randy Lismore. He was staring at chalk marks surrounding blood stains in Sloane's office when his cell phone buzzed.

"Mendoza."

"Yo, Cook County Sheriff's office. You guys called us about a Salvatore 'Buck' Califano a little over a week ago?"

"That's us," said Mendoza, interested.

"Well, he's dead. We found his body near the Chicago River yesterday. His throat was ripped. The coroner says it was a dog."

"A dog, huh. Any idea what kind?"

"Dog hairs on the body said German shepherd, so did the bite marks on the throat—what was left of it. You have any idea who would be involved?"

Mendoza had a damn good idea who might be involved. He made a decision, on the fly, not to rat out Warrener. He sensed it was partly because Califano had deserved it, and partly because of his frustration of dealing with the FBI and the sheriff. "No, not really."

"That's strange. We were pretty sure you'd have an idea. We found a gun. It hadn't been fired. It's the same one you checked out on NCIS some time ago. A Colt .45 ACP. It'd been wiped down and the magazine was missing. The pipe was empty. The guy must have known we'd look for prints in the magazine."

"The man who used to own that gun," said Mendoza, "was murdered four months ago here in San Luis Obispo County." But the deputy knew he had to maintain the charade. "I don't know what happened to the weapon after it went into the property cage."

"How come you sound just like the FBI?" asked the Cook County deputy. "They don't know dick-all either."

"What'ya mean? You talked to the FBI?"

"Sure, they're the ones that put Califano's picture on the wire, remember?"

"Who'd you talk to there?" asked Mendoza.

"Some agent named Lewiston in San Francisco."

Mendoza grimaced. "I'll look into the gun."

"Well, don't worry about it. The FBI didn't care. As far as we're concerned, a problem went away so there's no call for action at this end."

"Thanks for calling."

Mendoza re-sealed the front door and returned to his cruiser. He understood why Warrener had been so calm. Son-of-a-bitch, Warrener and his dog, Thor, must have been in Chicago yesterday. He sat in his cruiser and dialed Warrener's cell phone.

"This is Harry."

Mendoza could hear the whistle of wind roaring through an open window and road sounds.

"Mendoza. Where are you?"

"Good morning to you, Deputy. What can I do for you?"

"Cut the bullshit. I know what happened. Where are you?"

"Let's see, I'm in Nebraska—no, strike that, just entered Colorado. What do you mean, you know what happened?"

"You're making good time, aren't you? Did you have a nice time in Chicago?" asked Mendoza.

"Now why—"

"Good trick with the bullets," said Mendoza. "Where's the magazine?"

Mendoza heard the dog growl at something. The sound of wind in the background faded as Warrener apparently closed the window. "The Mississippi is a big river, did you know that?"

"Is that it? Can we both forget this? Or do I have to arrest you?"

"There are still some loose ends but I suspect you'll support them," said Warrener. "Besides, I didn't do anything."

"No, you used a deadly weapon with four legs and a tail."

"Is there anything else?"

"The Feds arrested Greenspan, Harry. What else is there?"

"What about Granger? Did they locate him?"

"I haven't heard anything."

"See you in a few days." Harry hung up.

EIGHTY-SEVEN—HOME

Saturday, April 19th, 2008, 6:30 PM

"Would you have killed him, Harry?" Janet stood in Harry's kitchen with her arms wrapped around her body, distant, aloof, and obviously disconsolate.

Harry had driven all night and day from Salt Lake City. He was exhausted. He'd arrived just an hour earlier. He felt sluggish and hoped it didn't cloud his thinking. He had to save his relationship with Janet.

"I don't know," he said. "I was ready to shoot him but I hesitated. Maybe it was what you said about murder. In any event, he kicked the gun out of my hand. After that it was a free-for-all."

"Was he armed?"

Harry nodded. "A knife. I managed to get it away from him. It went down a sewer. Then he went for Randy's gun."

"Thor did it?"

"I never expected it. I'd trained him to snarl on command—but when Califano reached for the gun he attacked—just like that drunk in the elevator in San Francisco."

"You can't let him do that, Harry. It's wrong." She looked at Thor in the back yard, sleeping on a concrete slab.

"I know," said Harry. "But it's almost all over now and I promise to train him. I'll work with him. Will you accept what happened? I couldn't do it when push came to shove."

Janet seemed to relent a little and sat down. She thought for a while and said, "That's a lot to ask. What did Deputy Mendoza say?"

"I think it's over with him. Is it over with you?"

"What do you mean, 'almost all over'?"

"There's one last task and only I can do it. It's dangerous but the goal is no more killings or deaths."

Tears flowed out of Janet's eyes. "I know what you did was for Randy," she said, "but I can't stand the suspense. I was terrified when you went into the warehouse in Monterey and while you were in Chicago."

"Just one more task. But I need you to make a telephone call."

EIGHTY-EIGHT—KISS

The gates to Don Cicerone's mansion on Jackson Street were open. Harry pulled into the driveway next to a Range Rover. He looked over his shoulder and commanded, "Thor! Stay."

"I hope we're doing the right thing, Harry," said Janet. "We're going into the dragon's lair and all you're armed with are the recordings from Monterey. You haven't even told Deputy Mendoza you have them."

"I can't. He'd want them to apply pressure on the FBI. He's still angry they interfered with the murder investigation and he's convinced there're more murders—Sloane, Pamela, her friend, and maybe Mason. I'm lucky he kept quiet about Califano."

Janet gave Thor a milk bone. "Okay, let's go," she said, "Into the shadow of the valley of—."

"Besides," said Harry, "I don't have Randy's gun anymore."

They climbed out of Harry's SUV and walked to the mansion. Harry looked for the bodyguards but didn't see them. Not that it mattered, he mused; the future depended on how the don reacted to his demands.

Don Cicerone opened the door and welcomed them. "Ah, the two Stags who find Asian art interesting. I'm so glad you called, Ms. Zimmer. The Buddhas await your inspection."

"I'm also looking forward to seeing the Tang Dynasty camel."

"Of course," said the don. He escorted them into the living room. A three-feet high Bactrian Tang camel sat on a Bosendorfer piano. The camel was double-humped with a beautiful sensei glaze; the yellow, blue and green colors splashed on a brown body. Janet paused to admire it.

"Refreshments?"

"Some coffee would be nice," said Harry. He looked around. "I was hoping to see your consigliore. Does he fetch your coffee?"

"Please, Mr. Warrener. That term is more appropriate in the old country. Dominic does many things. Perhaps you have some other business today?"

"Mr. Cicerone," said Janet, "we didn't come—"

"Of course not, Ms. Zimmer. I was just playing along. I assumed Mr. Warrener wished to discuss something with me."

"Actually, I do," said Harry.

Don Cicerone pointed at the two statues that flanked the fireplace.

"These are the Buddhas, Ms. Zimmer. The one on the left is from Tibet—they're both eleventh century. The other is from Cambodia. Why don't you enjoy them while Mr. Warrener and I retire to my study?"

Janet nodded.

"I'll have some coffee sent in. Please, Mr. Warrener, let's go upstairs."

Harry followed the don past a *Ganesha* statue up a flight of stairs to his study. Morning sun poured through the windows facing Jackson Street. Dominic Franchescini sat in a guest chair at the don's massive desk. A silver serving tray with coffee and accoutrements sat on the desk.

"Ah, the consigliore," said Harry.

"So this is the guy that started the shit-storm," said Dominic.

"Please, Dominic, Mr. Warrener is our guest. May we call you Harry?" The don poured coffee and offered Harry a cup. "Cream? Sugar?"

"Just black, thank you. Please, do call me Harry, Alessandro. I've looked forward to this moment."

Don Cicerone smiled. "So what can I do for you today, Harry?"

"I have the recordings," said Harry.

"What recordings?" demanded Dominic.

Harry wondered if they knew Greenspan had recorded every conversation he'd had in Monterey Construction. "It seems your friend, Morty Greenspan, made some recordings. I have them."

The don opened his humidor and offered cigars. Harry shook his head and the don selected a Ghurka Robusto. "I enjoy flavored cigars especially when I sense some unpleasantness. What do these recordings mean to me?"

Harry produced a cassette. "I copied a few samples for you. Morty encrypted the files but, well, he lacked some common sense. I found the encryption key taped to the bottom of his computer."

"That's quite clever," said the don sardonically.

"Uh-huh. This cassette contains a conversation between Morty and Ron Kelly, your nephew. There are other conversations with some gangst … ah, people in Chicago."

"I see," said the don. "I don't think we need to listen to the cassette. You have a point?"

Harry swallowed some coffee. "I have hours of recordings. I understand that Morty and your nephew are out on bail now."

"You've strayed into unchartered waters, Harry," said the don. "It seems their prosecution might be hindered somewhat. The federal charges were based on recordings that have somehow been misplaced by the FBI.

The courts have granted a continuance so that the FBI may scour its files"

Harry didn't know there were other recordings but he knew what he had. "These recordings, then, would be especially damaging to them, presumably they would be troublesome to you. Are you certain that you don't want to hear them?"

"Mr. Warrener, Harry," said the don waving the cassette aside, "you do know whom you're threatening with blackmail, don't you? It seems I should not have to say that."

"It's not blackmail," said Harry. "I don't intend to use these recordings. I just have two simple requests."

"You mean demands, don't you?" snarled Dominic.

The don raised his arm. "Please Dominic, let Harry speak."

"First, I want to be left alone. Enough people have died as a result of your nephew's land deal. This protection applies especially to Ms. Zimmer; she's already had one unpleasant experience with Mr. Greenspan's thugs."

"You killed Califano, didn't you, Warrener?" said Dominic. "Was that your gun they found in Chicago?"

Harry found it curious, and reckless, that the consigliore mentioned Califano and knew about the gun. "Sorry, I don't know what you mean."

"C'mon," said Dominic. "Who else did it?"

Harry shook his head. "Second, I need a charitable contribution; not to me, but to the Los Osos Stags Lodge."

"What figure did you have in mind?" asked the don, puffing on his cigar.

Harry stared through a blue haze at the don. He didn't know how much money the don had siphoned out of the deal but he needed eight million dollars to clean up the land. "Eight million dollars."

"That's an interesting amount, Harry. How did you determine it?" The don smiled but Harry sensed he seethed with anger.

"Think of it as an act of philanthropy. The money will be used to remove hazardous waste from the property. It then will be donated to the city, as a permanent open area with unfettered public access."

The don rose and walked to the window. The cigar trailed smoke; it appeared to be poorly lit and the don pulled an S.T. Dupont lighter out of his pocket and re-lit it. He stood for some time, casting a shadow in the room. Harry forced himself not to squirm.

"And if I refuse your *requests*?" The don continued to look out the window.

"The original and one copy of the recordings have been deposited in two safe locations." Harry decided it wasn't necessary to embellish.

The don turned and looked at Dominic who shrugged. "I think we might find these terms acceptable. The amount is excessive, of course, and the contribution must be anonymous."

"That works for me," said Harry. "Look at it this way—it's an excellent tax deduction for your linen service business. The Stags, after all, are a charity and you're a charitable man."

"I am, indeed, Harry. Is there anything else you'd like to discuss? Perhaps we should rejoin Ms. Zimmer."

Harry stood. "I regret this entire transaction, Don Cicerone. My friend is dead and I'm limited in my recourse. I meant what I said that enough people have died. I hope you'll honor this agreement. And, I'm sure you'll understand if I don't shake hands."

The don laid his cigar in a large Arturo Fuente ashtray. "Perhaps we should kiss, instead," he said, with a menacing smile.

Harry stared at the don.

After a pause, Cicerone said, "No, Mr. Warrener, I understand. We'll arrange for a check to be transmitted to the Stags, with the conditions that the money only be used to deal with the cleanup. I've heard that the Stags are quite fickle and prone to indecision; we wouldn't want them to change their mind and throw a party with the money, would we?"

"It would be quite a party, but the money is intended for the land," said Harry.

"I think that concludes our business. Shall we return to Ms. Zimmer?"

Harry smiled grimly and followed the don and Dominic down the stairs to the living room.

Janet waited with an apprehensive look on her face. "Did you complete your business, Harry?" she asked.

"We had a friendly conversation," said the don. "Have you enjoyed the artifacts?"

"They're magnificent," said Janet.

"Please come again some time," said the don. "Dominic will escort you out."

Thor growled when Dominic opened the passenger door for Janet. "I guess he doesn't like you," said Harry. "Don't try to pet him. He's tasted human blood."

"Good-bye Warrener," said Dominic, giving Thor a second look. "Have a good life. I don't think it's a good idea to come back here." He turned and walked back to the mansion.

Harry took a deep breath and looked at Janet. "It went well, I think. There was an awkward moment, though—it seems the FBI misplaced some recordings they had that led to the arrest of Ron Kelly and Morty Greenspan."

"Oh, no," said Janet. "What does that mean?"

"They're out on bail and the government likely will drop the charges." Harry smiled. "Unless, of course, Morty's recordings surface."

"Did Cicerone agree to fund the clean-up?"

"We'll find out." Harry backed out of the driveway and roared down the hill.

Later, Harry called Deputy Mendoza.

"You just visited Cicerone?" asked Mendoza, with a surprised tone in his voice.

"We had some business to transact. I have something for you which you might find interesting. Franchescini asked about Randy's gun."

"That means they're getting information from someone."

"The FBI lost the recordings they had," said Harry.

"The gun wasn't in the newspapers," said Mendoza. "Lost tapes, huh? I have an idea who the rat is, that pain-in-the-ass, Lewiston. He dragged his ass on the mug-shot and knew about the gun. It's time for some payback. I'm going to call Bernini, the guy who runs the FBI office in San Francisco, and plant a seed."

"Just leave me out of it. I think we're finished."

"Okay, Harry, I hope so too."

"Take care, Luis."

Harry put the cell phone down and laughed.

"What?" asked Janet.

"It took a while, but Mendoza and I are finally on a first name basis." He smiled at Janet, and drove home. If the check actually arrived the Stags would negotiate with Los Osos. It was almost over.

EIGHTY-NINE—SON

Dominic stormed back into the mansion. Don Cicerone waved him into the living room.

"Do you think we can trust him with these recordings?" asked Dominic.

"It's unfortunate that you were unable to find them before Mr. Warrener," said the don. "However, we have little choice. As long as Ron and Morty remain silent, it's a stand-off."

"I thought the problem went away when the informer stole the FBI recordings," said Dominic.

"Ron and Morty are not in jail now, and the trial is unlikely to move forward without the Carmel recording."

"The informer came through when he broke into the FBI safe," said Dominic.

"He did, however his bonus and Ron's bail plus this so-called philanthropic contribution, exhaust the funds we received in the deal. I'd be very unhappy if the costs continue to mount."

"I could try to find Warrener's tapes," said Dominic.

"You could, but those tapes are more a liability to Morty and Joey Gee than to us. Ron's already confessed to the land scam. If the government were to prosecute him with either set of tapes, five years in prison would be good for him."

Dominic nodded. Ron was young, five years was nothing, he'd learn some valuable life lessons, and he might be safer in a distant federal prison than in the Bay Area, "Perhaps we should tell Morty that Warrener has the recordings."

"Let's try to get past this. We should tell Morty and Ron that we have the recordings from Monterey. Ron's safe as long as this goes no further. Otherwise, he'll have to stand up for that dead trustee."

Dominic, relieved, nodded in agreement. "And Morty?"

"You make it clear to Morty that the Chicagoans, who are quite familiar with his old habits of recording, will not be happy to hear they've been taped. That should hold him in check."

"Morty's more than angry at Ron."

"Simply tell Morty we expect him to control his temper."

"Warrener knew we'd made eight million dollars on the deal," said Dominic. "Do you think it was on Morty's recordings?"

"Perhaps, it was a coincidence or, perhaps your son talked too much."

Dominic, astonished, stared at Don Cicerone. "You knew?"

"Of course. My sister told me years ago."

"But then, why did you try to—?"

"God moves in mysterious ways. For now let's say that we've been overtaken by events—as Mr. Warrener said, there've been enough killings."

"Don Cicerone," said Dominic, "Alessandra plays a dangerous game."

"She's a Cicerone."

Paso Robles Weekly Reporter
Monday, April 28, 2008

CHAOS IN LOS OSO STAGS
Lodge Deal Disintegrates in Flurry of Deaths and Suspicious Circumstances
Reporting by Max Cotton

(Los Osos) The $26 million real estate deal for the Los Osos Stags Lodge collapsed this month. Authorities are silent but this reporter has learned that the deal failed to close when a flurry of environmental hazards were discovered on the Stags' property. Decaying artillery shells, PCBs, ammunition, kerosene and other distillates were found in an old World War II pillbox. Thousands of old .50 caliber lead rounds were found below the surface of the beach. A land scam also has been alleged by federal authorities and several arrests have been made. Ron Kelly, the agent who handled the transaction, and Morty Greenspan, President of Monterey Construction Company, were both charged with multiple counts of corruption and bribery. Bail was posted in the amount of $500,000 each.

In addition, a host of deaths of those associated with the deal have been reported including one murder. Jerry Sloane, Chairman of the Los Osos Stags' Board of Trustees was found shot to death in his home. The police report there are no suspects at this time. Perhaps more ominous, three additional Stags, including two trustees, died suspiciously, and the county clerk who issued provisional construction permits, *was found dead of carbon monoxide poisoning. This morning, the* Weekly Reporter *learned that Ted Granger, the Exalted Ruler (President) of the Stags Lodge drowned in a plunge pool at the Four Seasons Resort at Jimbaran Bay in Bali. Details are sketchy but preliminary reports suggest it was suicide; he was found at the bottom of the pool with his arms lashed to a large planter.*

The FBI reported that kickbacks from the agent in the transaction were received by several Stags, but charges were not filed in light of the deaths.

With the collapse of the land deal, the Stags have donated the land to the city of Los Osos. Clean-up will be accomplished with an $8 million grant from an anonymous donor. The land will be preserved for future public use.

The Stags intend to refurbish their existing lodge with the original non-refundable deposit received from the developer. The acting Exalted Ruler for the Lodge issued this statement:

"We regret the circumstances surrounding the land deal. We wish to remind the public that 'Charity is the obligation and goal of every Stag.' Indeed, these words come from our national organization and we pledge to honor them. We're proud that with the aid of our benevolent contributor, we can donate our land to the city of Los Osos. The Stags are confident that working together with the community we will achieve the extraordinary this year."

EPILOGUE

Harry saluted as Randy's funeral flag was raised over the Los Osos Stags lodge in a groundbreaking ceremony. The Lodge had entered into a refurbishment contract for five million dollars. A local general contractor had been selected in a competitive process. Janet, hand over heart in the civilian salute, leaned over and whispered. "Isn't this nice?"

They watched the flag unfurl in the wind to the closing strains of the *Star Spangled Banner,* played on a portable cassette deck. As they dropped their hands, a man detached himself from the crowd and introduced himself. "Mr. Warrener. Harry? I'm Jim Thatcher."

Harry knew Thatcher was the Stags' DDGER and that Granger had confessed to him. Thatcher didn't stick out his hand; Harry suspected the man might feel somewhat guilty for failing to manage the Los Osos Stags. "What can I do for you?"

"Can we talk in private?" Thatcher smiled at Janet who squeezed Harry's hand and said she'd take Thor out of the car and be on the beach.

"Granger was my friend," said Thatcher, after Janet had left. "I knew him for decades. I don't like what happened to him."

"Well, Randy Lismore was my friend and I don't like what happened to him."

"You're a shit-stirrer, Brother Warrener, you rock the boat and you're not a team player. You have an overdeveloped sense of righteousness."

Harry was astonished. He looked at Thatcher and wondered if he smelled alcohol on his breath. But, other than looking angry, Thatcher seemed sober.

"That's what's wrong with the Stags sometimes, Jim," said Harry. "You put team playing and the good-old-boys network above good management and honest leadership. You guys talk about fidelity and justice, you publish books of rules and regulations—"

"We follow the rules!" exclaimed Thatcher.

"Finding someone that follows the rules is an exception," said Harry. "I'd call it selective enforcement when it's convenient."

"I didn't come to argue with you, Warrener."

"So what do you want?"

"There's no room in the Stags for people like you."

Harry took a step forward and pushed his face close to Thatcher's. "You were complicit in this and you know it."

Thatcher stepped backwards. His eyes flashed to the left and right which Harry took as a sign of fear, or guilt, or both.

"Complicit how?"

"This lodge project," said Harry "was on the front-burner as you guys love to call it. Once started, nothing was going to derail it. And, when Granger told you he was involved in a scam, you didn't do anything. Protect the ER at all costs, right? He and Sloane were stealing and you and your 'Taj Mahal of Stag-dom' were more important. Fuck you, Jim."

"Swearing, Warrener, is enough to throw you out. There are many ways to construct a project but your kind of disharmony prevents people from working together. You've embarrassed the order."

"I wasn't taking bribes, Jim."

"Perhaps not but you blackmailed the anonymous donor. We don't do that in the Stags."

"Says who?"

"C'mon, how else could you get the money? I've had enough. There've been needless newspaper articles. I've watched the chaos down here and I believe it's necessary to make adjustments in the leadership. I'm suspending you as a trustee, pursuant to the statutes, and I *will* receive your resignation from the Stags."

Harry, speechless for the moment, stared at Thatcher. The man was serious. Harry turned and looked at Janet and Thor who romped at the water's edge. He'd avenged Randy's death. He no longer had anything to prove. Why should he volunteer? He remembered a French expression he'd read in a novel, *Plus vous leur baisez le cul, plus ils vous chient sur la tête* (the more you kiss their ass, the more they shit on your head). The Lodge was well funded now—it would have millions left over after the refurbishment. Perhaps it could now fulfill the real charitable mission of the Stags.

"You got it." he said.

Harry turned and walked toward Janet and Thor. The new sand sparkled from the recent clean-up. The air smelled fresh and Harry sensed he'd never smell the jungle again. His face broke into a wide smile and he grabbed a stick to play fetch with Thor.

AFTERWORD

Many people helped in the production of this book. Thanks to the gang in Edward's Pipe and Tobacco Shop in Los Altos (the model for the Big Bear Pipe and Tobacco Shop in SLO). This includes Gary Briber who helped me determine the hypothetical weight of $4.4 million hundred-dollar-bills; Debbie Morton, the proprietor of Edward's and a dog breeder, who provided invaluable veterinarian information on dogs; and Gil Oraha, a realtor who helped develop the information about land transactions in California. Thanks to my readers: Mike Conklin, Louis Fried, Denis Losè, David Feldman, Bartholomew Lee, Sid Mak, George Nicholas, Fred Sacks, Kevin Shenk and Rick Wolfrom. Professional kudos to Martha Alderson from *Blockbuster Plots* who consulted in the development of the plot line and characters, the anonymous editorial screeners at iUniverse, and Natalie Wood and Ruth Rabin for their copyedit efforts. My apologies to the city of Monterey, California for my invention of the central wharf (the home of Morty Greenspan's business) in Monterey Bay. The other major locations and restaurants in the novel are real and the Sardine Factory, in Monterey's Cannery Row, does not serve lunch.

For readers who are interested in the charitable activities of real fraternal orders, information can be found on the World Wide Web at the following locations:

http://www.elks.org/
http://www.foe.com/
http://www.mooseintl.org/public/default.asp
http://www.stelling.nl/vrijmetselarij/bpoe_r.html
http://phoenixmasonry.org/masonicmuseum/fraternalism/Stags.html
http://www.lcms.org/graphics/assets/media/CTCR/Stags.pdf
http://www.cephasministry.com/masonry_moose_elks.and_eagles.html

LaVergne, TN USA
02 November 2009
162810LV00004B/7/P